THE FOX WOMAN

TOR®

A TOM DOHERTY ASSOCIATES BOOK
NEW YORK

THE FOX WOMAN

Kij Johnson

THE FOX WOMAN

Copyright © 2000 by Kij Johnson McKitterick

The poems on pages 7, 11, 89, 175, 307, and 377 are from *From the
Country of Eight Islands* by Hiroaki Sato and Burton Watson. Copyright © 1981 by Hiroaki Sato and Burton Watson. Used by permission of Doubleday, a division of Random House, Inc.

This book is printed on acid-free paper.

Book design by Jane Adele Regina

A Tor Book
Published by Tom Doherty Associates, LLC
175 Fifth Avenue
New York, NY 10010

www.tor.com

Tor® is a registered trademark of Tom Doherty Associates, LLC.

Library of Congress Cataloging-in-Publication Data

Johnson, Kij.
    The fox woman / Kij Johnson. — 1st ed.
        p. cm.
    "A Tom Doherty Associates book."
    ISBN 0-312-85429-3 (acid-free paper)
    1. Foxes — Japan — Folklore — Fiction. 2. Nobility — Japan —
Fiction. I. Title.
PS3560.O379716 F69 2000
813'.54 — dc21   99-053591

First Edition: January 2000

Printed in the United States of America

0 9 8 7 6 5 4 3 2 1

For Chris and for Bob. I am a lucky dog.

THE NEW YEAR

This world —
call it an image
caught in a mirror —
Real it is not,
nor unreal, either

—MINAMOTO SANETOMO (1192–1219)
TRANSLATED BY THOMAS RIMER

KITSUNE'S DIARY

Diaries are kept by men: strong brushstrokes on smooth mulberry paper, gathered into sheaves and tied with ribbon and placed in a lacquered box. I know this, because I have seen one such diary.

It is said there are also noble ladies who keep diaries, in the capital or on their journeys in the provinces. These diaries (it is said) are often filled with grief, for a woman's life is filled with sadness and waiting.

Men and women write their various diaries: I shall see if a fox woman cannot also write one.

I saw him and I loved him, my master Kaya no Yoshifuji. I say this and it is short and sharp, without elegance, like a bark; but I have no idea how else to start. I am only a fox: I have no elegancies of language.

I need to start before that, I think.

Book One: Spring

Neither waking nor sleeping
I saw the night out,
and now spend
all day in thought,
staring at these long spring rains

—Ariwara no Narihira (825–880)
Translated by Burton Watson

1. KITSUNE'S DIARY

There were four of us.

Grandfather was an old fox, of perhaps eight or nine years. Gray ran along his narrow jaw and in a broad streak from his black nose to between his black-tipped ears; it frosted his pelt so that he seemed almost outlined in gray light. His joints stiffened on cold wet days, and he liked to doze in the spring sunlight when he could. He was missing a toe on one of his front paws. When I was little and first realized he didn't have the same toes I had, I asked him why, and he told me a *tanuki*-badger bit it off, but I think he was teasing. He was like that.

Mother was simple, even for a fox. My brother and I watched her sometimes catch and lose a mouse a half-dozen times before she remembered to bite it while she still had her paws on it. We were amazed sometimes that she had survived long enough to bear us.

Fortunately, the place where we lived was thick with mice and chipmunks and other small prey. The grasses around our home were too long and dense for hawks, and the few humans who lived nearby chased off anything larger. Our only competition was a family of cats led by a black-and-white spotted female. They lived in a deserted outbuilding near the people, but they hunted in our range, and ignored us rigidly. The cats chased and lost mice, too. I think this was intentional for them, but who can understand cats? Even as a woman I have never understood them.

My brother and I had been born the winter before, down in the still air of the den. At first there were four kits, I think. One died early, before we saw daylight; she smelled sick and then she was gone. Another died when we were barely old enough to suck the juices from meat our grandfather brought us. That kit was the boldest of us; one night when he was still much too young he followed our grandfather out hunting and never came back.

Halfway to adulthood, my remaining brother was a gawky

thing of long legs and oversized ears. His fur had not yet filled into its rusty adult coat, so his brush and neck-ruff were thin and spiky, dun-colored. I suppose I looked the same, but taller at the shoulder, heavier-boned. It was easy for me to pin him, and he usually ended the play by baring his belly to me. He was quiet, my brother.

I did not see all this back then. They were my family: why should I think of them? If anything, I associated them with their smells. Grandfather was bright and dusty, like damp leaves fallen underfoot. Mother was drying mud. Brother was tree bark and woodsmoke.

Words, words, words. There were no words then, just sensation: smell, sight, experience, day and night, as flat and complex as a brocade held too close to the eyes for focus, or a rainstorm full in the face. All details, no pattern. I have words now, maybe too many. I try to describe the fabric to you, but words will not make you wet or shelter you from the rain.

We lived in a tangle of tunnels and rooms hollowed out of packed dirt. Everything was wide—too wide, said Grandfather, who never did anything to change it—and worn smooth, and it smelled of a hundred generations of foxes. Our sleeping chamber was nearly at the bottom, lined with dead leaves and shed hair. We could all sleep together in it, but Grandfather no longer slept well, and he liked to lie nearer the entrance, where he could crawl out and stretch his legs when he needed.

The den was pitch-dark. Surrounded by the smells of my family and burrow, I lay inside on spring days: dozed and waited for the crisp scents of dusk. Filtered through the fur of my brother's haunch, I smelled the air outside, sweet and sharp.

Nights we went out.

Mother and Grandfather hunted, sometimes together but often alone, one leaving the other to watch as we kits played near the den. Mother never had anything to spare, but Grandfather usually returned dragging a soft-boned *kiji*-pheasant or a half-eaten hare, which he threw down for us to bicker over. We caught things on our own, as well: fledglings fallen from their nests, mice, voles. We learned to stamp for worms, and to catch birds, and to cache our kills for leaner days. I played with and ate the blue-black beetles that came my way, felt the smooth knotting of my joints operating, wrestled with my brother for the experience of hunting. I was learning to be a fox.

Our burrow was dug under a structure that was flat and black over our heads, supported by a forest of tree-thick pillars, each resting on a rock. When I was old enough to be curious about this, I jumped up into the structure.

I saw and smelled a cavern supported by pillars and roofed with dead grasses a tree's height over my head. The floor under my toes was of boxwood planks, smooth and cool and flat. Through a crack in the floor I heard my brother barking at my grandfather — impatient little noises. I scratched at the crack. Paws padded below. A nose snuffled upward.

"Sister?"

"I'm *walking* on you?" I couldn't understand this.

"Where are you?"

I didn't know what to say. This floor I stood on was the roof over the burrow, I knew — there was my brother, after all — how could it be else?

A scrambling noise behind me.

"It is a building," Grandfather said, and he stretched and walked across to me. "A house. Humans make them." Brother clambered up after him.

I looked around. There were no walls, just empty screen frames and lattices. Beyond them I saw other buildings, roofed and walled and raised on posts, with covered walkways that led from one to the next. "This is a den," I said, realizing it. "The big buildings are chambers, and the little ones that lead from place to place are like tunnels. Or trails."

Brother sniffed at a pillar's base and lifted his leg against it. "How did they make this place?"

"And *why?*" I demanded. "If it's a burrow, it's open to every-thing. How can it be safe?"

"They were humans, they feared nothing. But it was not like this, back then. It was closed in with walls they could slide away or remove."

"How did they do that?" Brother asked.

"How did they do *any* of this?" I sniffed a lintel rubbed shiny by passing feet. Even now I smelled the shadows of people, ghosts in my nose.

Grandfather made a face, as if he'd eaten something bitter. "Magic."

"Humans don't have magic," I said scornfully. "Magic is spring turning to summer, day and night."

"There are a lot of sorts of magic, little bug-eater. More than you can know."

"What kind is this, then?" Brother asked.

"They have clever paws," he said. "They change things with them."

I inspected my own paws, cinnamon-colored with black-edged toes and ragged claws. Not clever, not magical. "But *how?*"

He bared his teeth: not hostile yet, but tired of the topic. "Give it a rest, Granddaughter."

Brother was marking every pillar, sharp little squirts of urine. I should check his marks, I knew. And Grandfather? He was temperamental at all times and smelled irritable now, like a high wind filled with dust, still a long way away. I should leave Grandfather alone, I knew. But how could I?

"I just want to know how their paws are clever—" I stopped when he took a step toward me. "Well, then, what other magics are there?"

"None that concern you," he said dampingly. "The people will never be back."

"But people live across the garden from us, past the wall—"

Brother came to sit next to us, lolling his tongue. "This is like that, isn't it? Where they live—those are dens, too, aren't they?"

"Mere servants' quarters," Grandfather snorted. "Wretched drafty barns. They bring their stock in to sleep under the same roof."

"I don't understand. Servants?" I said, but he continued without listening.

"This—" he looked around us, at the empty neglected buildings and walkways "—is where the master and mistress lived.

They were sweet-smelling, sweet as flowers out of season. Her hair was black as my feet and fell clear to the ground when she stood. Not a knot or tangle in it. They wore fabrics like spiderwebs. Gossamer. Their lives were a thousand kinds of magic. Poetry, calligraphy, moon-viewing, archery games in the wisteria courtyard—"

Poetry? Moon-viewing? How could I imagine what these things were?

Brother asked: "The fabric was made of spiderweb?"

"No, it was as *if* it were spiderweb."

My brother pressed his ears back against his skull. "That doesn't make any sense."

"Not to *you*. It is as though you see me and smell pine, as though eyes and nose fail to agree. Which is real? Am I your grandfather, or am I a pine?"

My brother whined and backed away.

"You're—" I said, and stopped. Thinking like this made me afraid, made me want to run or bite, to break the tension inside.

"Just because you do not understand a thing does not mean it's not real," Grandfather finally said.

"How do you know all this?" I asked.

"They were *here*," he said irritably. "I saw them. Noise all the time, bustle. We had to watch ourselves, not to be caught, or they would kill us."

"They don't sound so dangerous," I interrupted, bold because of my fright. "Even the humans on the other side of the wall are not dangerous if you stay out of their way, and they are much more active than this 'master' and 'mistress.'"

He grabbed me by the ruff and forced me down. I yelped. "What do you know, little milk-sucker? They are the most dangerous of all—more dangerous than bears."

I abased myself until his grip loosened and I squirmed free.

"If this was their den," Brother asked, "where are they now?"

"Gone," Grandfather said. "There's nothing left here. Come down."

Brother moved to the edge. "Why would they leave this place?"

"Who knows?" he said irritably. "I was not much older than you when they left."

A breeze ruffled my fur. I shivered. "What if they return? Their den is right over ours."

"They will never come back." Grandfather dropped heavily to the ground.

I had this dream, back when I was no more than a fox. In the waking world I never looked at the sky — why would I? There was no prey there — but in this dream I did look. A star hung, dim as marsh gas, in the red-black glow of the sky; in the east, the moon rose over a mountain, and the moon and the star were the same size.

I stood on the mountain I had just watched the moon rise over, and the path was cold under my toes. I stepped forward, but my way was barred by a fox made of moonlight that smelled of nothing.

"Make a wish, little sister," the fox said.

I thought. "To eat well and sleep safe."

He — she? — laughed at me. "Never mind, then."

"Wait!" I said, but the fox turned to a flower and vanished, and I woke, my family's smells in my nostrils. I did not know what it meant — didn't even think, then, that a dream might have a meaning. But I also did not forget it.

Now I wonder: do all foxes dream like this? I only know I did.

The house (and our den) was in a huge space enclosed by tumbledown fences made of bamboo and *hinoki*-cedar latticework. I was careful when I asked questions about the human constructions around us because Grandfather cuffed me down if I showed too much interest; but he took me hunting once, and I managed to learn that the space had been gardens. People had torn up the plants and paths and streams of the place and replaced them with new paths and plants, and rerouted the stream.

"But why?" I asked my grandfather.

"Because they could do it," he snapped, and I knew to let it be.

The sweet-water brook led from the topmost corner of the enclosure, under the raised floor of one of the deserted buildings, and through three little lakes, one after the other. Mandarin ducks nested in the building over the stream, and chased us away when we tried to explore or (more often) to eat their feckless ducklings. A trail strode across the lakes' tops, lifted above the water on structures.

"What is it?" I asked Grandfather, when I saw the first one.

"Bridge."

I stepped onto it, and felt the same cool smoothness under my toes I'd felt in the house. Huge murky shapes moved in the weed-clogged water below me.

"Fish," Grandfather told me. "Eat them if you find them on the shore, but you cannot go in after them—like hunting a shadow."

The rest of the garden was trees and long-dead grasses pushed aside by new growth. An overgrown path led down from the main house past the lakes and to a collapsed gate at the foot of the garden; other small paths trailed off one way and another. They all seemed to go nowhere and then suddenly stop; if it had not been for the large stones the humans laid flat on the ground in ragged lines, I would have thought they were not trails at all.

One dusk it was cold and raining. I woke up before the others and left the den, and sat at the edge of the overhang, looking across the clearing around the house to the rain-heavy grasses beyond. The air smelled cold, like molds and wet dust. I snapped at the puffs of fog my breath made before I got bored.

A female rabbit, wood pigeon–gray, hunched over a clump of grass at the edge of our clearing. They never came this close to our den. I think the rain must have washed down our smell, and the rabbit must have been half-grown (and possibly simple, like Mother), not to know that foxes lived here. Even in the rain, the sweet smell of freshly cropped grass drifted down the slight breeze to me.

It wasn't that I was hungry yet: I had not even thought of food before I dropped to my belly and inched forward. It was the fox-blood. What else could I do? I was so close I could smell the rabbit's sweet-musky fur, and see its whiskers quiver as it nibbled.

Its head came up. It fixed me with a dark eye. I held still, staring back with the fixing-gaze, the gaze that holds an animal to be killed. Killer: prey. And then a rain droplet gathered in the fold of my eyelid, tickling. So I blinked.

And the rabbit was gone. In a single leap it was lengths away from me; a second, and it was lost in the weeds. Water sprayed up from its path. I chased it through thick mats of grass just in time to see it dive under a tall black stone in a clearing. I dug frantically at the hole it had vanished into. I was soaked to the skin and shivering before I gave up.

The rock was riddled with little openings and fissures. Tiny pools had gathered in the pockmarks; mosquito larvae hung on the pools' many surfaces. There were no trees for paces all around, just dirt, white sand and the rock, all alone.

It was full dark by the time I got back to the shelter of the den. My family was awake. Grandfather stood looking out from under the building. Mother sat with a hind leg held rigid to bite at a flea. Brother played with a curved stick, bouncing at one end so that the other popped up and caught him from behind. I told them about the rabbit, the dark stone.

"It is hopeless chasing a rabbit near that," Grandfather said.

"Why?" I licked my paw to warm it.

"They have a safe warren there. Deep, buried under that rock, so you can't dig after them. Your only hope is to catch them away from it."

"It is a moon-rock." It was my mother. I sniffed at her: she never said things to us, nothing that made sense, anyway. "It lived on the moon until it fell off and landed here, but it remembers rabbits. That is why they are safe. Because a rabbit lives on the moon, and it protects them."

"What's she talking about?" my brother asked.

Grandfather hunched a shoulder irritably, as if to say, "Do not ask me."

"God," Mother answered. "The rabbit-god lives on the moon and watches them."

My brother snarled and snapped at the ground, nervous at a thing he could not fight, could not even find. A cold wind ruffled my wet fur. Life was a practical thing to us foxes: what could a god be? I'd never smelled one.

She answered without my speaking. "What do rabbits see when they die? Their god. *Tanuki*-badgers have them. Mice. Oxen. Men. Birds, no. Cats — no one can tell — "

I could not help the hairs rising along my spine, my ears flattened against my skull. "Do foxes?"

"There is no such thing as gods." Grandfather made our mother drop in submission, and that was the end of that. But it took me all night to get warm.

Beyond the fence there was a mountain to one side and behind us, covered with pine trees and ivy-hung cypress. As my brother and I learned to hunt, we followed the deer paths and caught baby rabbits, and once ate part of a dead fawn some other animal had killed. There was a long outcropping of dull red stone and a path of pounded dirt along the ridge that smelled of people, though we never saw any.

Past the ruined gate and fence at the bottom of the gardens were rice fields. People were always fussing over them: making little rows of dirt, and pouring manure mixed with water onto the slick earth. One day they redirected the stream where it exited the garden, so that it flowed through the fields, to make them a mesh of small shallow lakes. Gnats and mosquitoes bred and rose in clouds. I watched *uguisu*-nightingales and enamel-bright dragonflies chase the insects; this made more sense to me than the incomprehensible acts of the humans. Prey: catch. *I* caught a dragonfly once: it was sharp, hot, prickly on my tongue.

On the other side from the mountain, beyond a fence made

of pine strips woven together, was a big pounded-dirt area surrounded by clumps of structures smaller and closer to the ground than those on our side of the fence. This was where the other people, the "servants," lived. I occasionally saw them: more often I smelled them, along with woodsmoke and feces and fowl and big animals, oxen. Human smells. Sometimes at night, greasy-scented yellow light flickered through the lattices of their buildings, inconstant as foxfire, the glow of marsh gas at night. My brother and I crept along the fringe of the open dirt area to hide under a glossy-leafed bush that brushed the house's wall. There was a constant low-pitched babble inside, a rippling noise like water or birds chattering.

"What is that noise?" my brother breathed. "The humans make it?"

"It's like barking."

"No; they're all there, in the room, face-to-face. Why would they need to bark like that?" he asked.

"Maybe they are like dogs and bark for boredom?" Foolish to ask: he knew no more than I. "Let's crawl under the floorboards, maybe we can hear more."

My brother hunched his back and lowered his ears. "Grandfather says they're dangerous."

"We're fast and clever."

"Grandfather says—"

I scoffed: "He's old. Maybe things scare him that we don't need to be afraid of."

"But he's so wise—"

"But he's not here, and I'm stronger and bigger than you, and I say we can do it."

My brother shook his head, as if clearing his face of clinging webs. "No. No." He turned and ran.

I eased into the crawl space, but learned nothing; and when I came back later, Grandfather smelled the house and the humans on me, and cuffed me down. Maybe he was old, but he was still the head of our family.

After that I learned to stay upwind of the house.

This was our lives. My brother and I got better at hunting.

I explored the garden and the woods and fields beyond with the others and alone. I learned many useful smells: rabbit droppings, egg yolk from hatchings, the scent-marks of *tanuki*-badgers and wolves (though we never saw any of *them* — they lived deeper in the forest, and, Grandfather said, only came down when the food was not good there). I killed and ate one of the black-and-white cat's kittens; a gamy mouthful of fur and half-digested mouse, it did not seem worth the effort, so I avoided them after that. My brother was stung by a wasp when he was up in the deserted house over our heads renewing his marks; he was sick for a day and a night.

I watched the humans when I could get away with it, but with less interest than I felt toward the ducks in the stream, or the rabbits that fed near the moon-rock. These were at least edible, relevant to a fox. The houses and verandas, sheds, fences and gardens of the residence — all the things the humans had built — meant little to my brother and me: they were as unchanging as the standing rocks in the woods.

I looked at everything, smelled everything, marked everything. I did not think much, back then. The season warmed, and I grew. I was still a fox. Nothing changed.

2. SHIKUJO'S PILLOW BOOK
The News Year's appointments:

My husband did badly in the New Year's appointments, and when the court was finished with making up its rolls, no position had been found for him — not even the ignominy of a provincial governorship. This was quite surprising, of course: his family is excellent and highly regarded by the retired emperor (if not the current one). One can only imagine that he antagonized some important figure in court. Knowing my husband, such a thing might well happen — not for the political motives so popular these days, but from sheer carelessness. I think it even more likely that his current unhappiness has much to do with it. When two men of equal quality are proposed for the same job, why would it be given to the individual who appears more likely to cast aside the miseries of the world and flee to a life of contemplation in a monastery? And his unhappiness has been obvious enough to his wife and household: my husband has little artifice and I expect it is nearly as obvious to his peers and superiors at court.

Or it might be a random matter. It is not unheard-of for a worthy man to be denied a position due to a simple oversight.

Far more unusual was my husband's response. Other men would have stayed in the capital and campaigned for a good position in the autumn appointments or even next year's; instead he decided to go to the estate his father left him, off in the mountains of Hida province. He did not insist that I (or our son) attend him, though of course it was the proper thing to do. But on that spring night when he told me of this, I said nothing. Our son asleep on the mats between us, I watched the first cherries blooming, their blossoms glowing cold and pale as snow in the moonlight.

"Are you upset?" he asked me.

A good wife is never upset, never unsettled, and I was, in truth, both. And a good husband never corners his wife in this fashion, forcing her to decide between what is correct and what is true. "Of course not," I said.

His unhappiness affects us all.

3. KITSUNE'S DIARY

It was the time when the humans move the rice plants from the seeding beds to the flooded fields. I heard them down past the ruined gate and fence, sloshing through the belly-deep (for me) water and making their barking noises back and forth. The air was cool and heavy with humidity. Everything smelled new, fresh—wet dirt and wild cherry blossoms. My mother and brother were asleep in the den; my grandfather beside me, I lay beside one of the pillars, belly-down to the clammy dirt. A mosquito bit my nose. I snapped at the sharp itch of it.

"Listen!" My grandfather came to his feet, ears pricked forward, toward the fields.

"What?" The humans' barking was suddenly louder and higher-pitched, but that could be anything. It happened every day.

"Horses. Oxen. Carts," my grandfather said.

I had no idea what a horse was. I saw nothing, just the trees and lakes and grasses of the garden stretching to the broken gate. I strained to hear past the white hiss of the mist. An animal, then several, thundered up the dirt path on the other side of the fence. Their hooves hit heavy as oxen, but in the delicate rhythm of trotting deer. Carts rumbled. The sounds settled across from the gate. People barked some more.

"What does it mean?" I asked.

"The worst thing possible," my grandfather said. "Humans."

"But there are already people here."

"Stay here." He vanished in the thick grass.

Behind me, Brother popped his head from the den's entrance. "What —"

"Stay here," I snarled, in the best imitation I had of my grandfather's authority, and followed him. I caught up as we threaded between the lakes. He bared his teeth and flattened his ears at me in disapproval. I was afraid, but I flattened my ears back at him and continued.

Two huge shaggy *hinoki*-cedars, their branches bent to the ground, flanked the tumbled gate. We bellied into one of them, and crawled forward to watch.

The horse turned out to be pretty much what it sounded like: ox and deer. It smelled like sweat and grass, and was the yellow-orange of persimmons. Other horses trotted up, and the men sitting on their backs barked at the peasants in the muddy rice fields. But I could not stop looking at the yellow horse and its rider.

The man was dressed in textures I had never seen before. The people who lived in the cookhouse wore simple clothes in flower-colors of indigo and white. They shed them like skins when they liked, and hung them in the sun and wind. But these robes — pale purple hammered silk that looked like the skin of frost over water, and an oiled cotton cloak colored gray-green,

with a knot of dried grass sewn to the center of its back—these
were utterly new.

"The master of this house." Grandfather smelled old, defeated.
"They have returned. We are lost."

"What?"

He snarled silence.

Two oxen pulling a small closed carriage drew up behind the
horsemen. Walking men chattered. Carts and carriages rumbled
to a stop on the path.

The man—the master, Grandfather'd said—had turned toward us. His narrow eyes gleamed black, dark as a *tsumi*-hawk's.
He was looking at the ruined gate. At us.

I recognized that look; I'd given it myself, to prey. This is
where we would die. There would be shouts and then the feel
of cold metal, arrows dropping us as surely as they dropped the
golden eagle we'd once found dying in the garden.

And then his face turned, and he looked somewhere else.

"What—" I said again, but this time in wonder.

"Come." My grandfather backed out of the pile. He was more
careful, going back to the den.

4. SHIKUJO'S PILLOW BOOK
One wrote this:

One wrote this on first seeing the home she left all those years
ago:

> *Is the garden lost*
>   *or merely hidden by the years' thick grasses?*

And this question only delays the next: which would one prefer?
This should be a simple enough question to answer: I am sure
that civilization must always be preferable to barbarity.

5. THE NOTEBOOK OF KAYA NO YOSHIFUJI

The trip from the capital to the country place has taken two weeks. It is slow traveling with my wife and all her servants (and mine, too, if it comes to that) — we travel only a few miles a day, at a deliberate walking pace, and stop well before dark at a convenient temple or a farmhouse. Some days we do not travel at all, if there is a tabu, or if my wife or one of her more valued attendants feels indisposed.

It is easier for me: I ride my pretty Kiku, Chrysanthemum. Her gait is good for a yellow horse (which are notoriously inconstant), smooth and fluid. Her saddle is built up in such a way that only a sack of rice could fall when she walks, so the fact that I am not a good rider does not matter.

I know I should have taken a carriage. Someone not a misfit would have ridden in an ox-carriage for the endless hours of this trip: as my wife has to, as my son has to. While a gentleman may know how to ride (it comes in handy on occasion), very few "gentlemen" would prefer the jolting, exposed ride they get on a horse's back, given a long journey without urgency like this one.

My son, Tadamaro, who is eight and curious about everything, has pushed aside the bamboo blind that serves as the front of his carriage; now he leans out on the carriage's kite's-tail shafts staring at everything around him, careless of the rain that soaks his robes. He has never been to the country, so all of it — the rutted, muddy road; the half-hidden farmhouses and shrines; the wildness of the world itself — is new to him. Every so often, his nurse's hands appear and pull at his robe. I cannot hear her, but remembering my own nurse when I was small, I can imagine what she says to him.

My wife's carriage is quiet. She undoubtedly sits on a tiny cushion, in a space packed full of ladies-in-waiting. Like salted fish in a barrel, if one can say such a thing of women so delicate and cultured. Air comes in through the weave of the palm fronds that wall the carriage and through a small grille set in the front.

The sights through the grille are all she sees on this trip: the ears and backs of the oxen, the backs of the drivers' heads as they walk alongside with their long switches looped in their hands, the dirt path and the endless reeking rice fields. I imagine all trips look pretty much the same to women.

Still, women are used to sitting in the dark and thinking their thoughts. I do not know if all this bothers her. I do not know if she even tries to look out the grille.

But it would bother me, so I ride Kiku and look around me, and try not to think too much about leaving the capital. What can they do to me, if I am seen riding as if I were a servant or a messenger? I left the capital in disgrace anyway. Well, then: I am unconventional, and now I am self-exiled; here in the country no one of any importance can possibly care about my behavior.

I say this, but it is not true. There was no position for me, but that is more an embarrassment than a disgrace. The situation is fairly common in a government with fewer positions than candidates. Most men failing to receive a position in the New Year's appointments wail and clutch at their artfully disordered robes at the shame of it all, while their friends commiserate and cast doubts on the propriety of the selection process. The failed candidates then redouble their efforts to be appointed next time. And by the next year, the scandal (if such it can be considered, when it is both common and boring) is forgotten, replaced by old Lady Plum-blossom's fling with a guardsman half her age, or the doubts regarding the father of the lovely Lady Cherry's baby.

I could have stayed, but I was miserable anyway. Perhaps I am trying to match my inner misery with my outside circumstances: at any rate, I seem resolved to make things as bad as they can possibly be. I had not expected my wife and son to enter into this self-imposed exile.

We are in the Tani valley, deep in Hida province—which is to say, in the heart of nowhere. Under a heavy silver sky, clouds cling to the slopes around us, shredding like thin silk on the jagged tops of the pines. The mountains that lift to the silver sky are brilliant as lacquer, the greens all bright as snake skins, mingling with foaming banks of pink and white spirea and yellow *yamabuki* and the subtler pink of wild cherries. Smoke ropes upward in the thick tendrils that form in cool humid air. It trails from the local peasants' houses and the nearby shrines: Inari Shrine; Amida Shrine. When my wife and I lived here before, I walked the forested paths and visited all these places. It has been a long time, but I still remember the shapes of the mountains, even half-hidden by mists as they are.

On one side, the road presses against a rocky outcropping; rice fields crowd up on the other, with the narrow river at the valley's far side. The fields are flooded ankle-deep at this time of year, and they smell of manure and young green things. Peasants poke the mud under the water with pointed sticks. Others cluster around the weir that blocks the river; they seem to be removing some mysterious tangle of branch and vine that has clogged it.

These are my fields. Every year rice has come to me from this place. It paid for our house in the capital, for the gifts to the ministers that were to fuel my political career, for my fans and papers and inks and robes, for my wife's needs, for my horse. When I lived here, I did not even know what grew in these fields.

I have not been back to this house in seven? eight? years — since before Tadamaro was born. Shikujo and I moved here when we were first married, even though her father assumed that (like other wives) she'd continue living at home and that I would visit her there. But she insisted we live together in a home of our own. Sometimes it surprises me that she did this: it is the only time she has ever done anything unconventional. The rest of the time she has been perfectly regular in her actions. Like her poems, her life has always been elegant but lacking spark. Still, she has a beauty I will never attain, bareheaded in the rain like a peasant.

The rocks to our left fall away, are replaced by a fence of split bamboo. Even astride Kiku, I cannot see over the small thatched roof that caps the fence, although I can see through the places where the fence has fallen away, into a garden as overgrown as a forest. Where the formal gate to the grounds should stand, there is instead a collapsed jumble of peeled box-wood logs.

My major domo, Hito, shouts at the peasants who stand in the fields chattering, watching us with (one presumes) curiosity (but who can tell what peasants think?). A small man with a dun-colored face as crumpled as dirty hemp shuffles forward and bows. His bare feet and the hem of his short robe are caked with mud and ordure.

Hito yells at the peasant: "How can you have let this place decay like this? Look at this gate. What are we to do? You were charged with its care!" He rattles on and on, high-pitched and angry, more for my benefit than to any purpose — all estates fall into disrepair in their masters' absence; it is the fields that must not be neglected. The peasant's voice rumbles beneath, anxious and placating. My horse shifts under me, as weary of traveling as I am. My thighs ache, and the joints of my hips, and my back. Everything.

"Enough," I say. I take Kiku through the humbled (but still standing) entrance that leads to the stable yard, leaving my servants to scramble after me.

The packed-earth yard is clotted with clumps of last year's leaves rotting into the puddled ground. Disturbed by something I cannot see, a pair of jackdaws flies up, squawking, from the ragged thatch of the buildings fringing the yard. This place has been neglected. It should be brushed smooth; all the thatch needs to be retrimmed to a blunt edge. The yard smells musty, stale. There should be fires set in the buildings to drive the moisture from the dark corners and the vermin from the thatch; but smoke curls from a single building's open eaves. This must be where the servants charged with maintaining my estate live: it looks (slightly) better-kept than the rest.

People swirl past me though the entrance — shouts and chattering, the clattering of tools and wagons, the slapping of feet through water and mud. A groom catches my mare's bridle as I slide gracelessly from her back. My back aches as I bend over to remove the leg-coverings that have protected my silks. I walk back the way I came, past my wife's and my son's carriages; past the gold-colored ox we have brought with us for luck; past the carts loaded with our chests and baskets and boxes; past the chattering servants and through the stable yard gate—back to the ruined formal gate. The peasants in the fields still watch. Under my eye they resettle their huge straw hats over their eyes and turn back to their fields.

Nothing is left of the gate, just this pile of logs grown mossy on their north faces. The logs, the moss, the grasses around— everything shines with moisture that reflects the gray sky. The air of this place seems to watch me in a silence that the shouts from the stable yard only accentuate.

I cannot walk *through* the gate; I can only step over it. Holding the folds of my hunting robes close, I step onto the nearest log. A burst of red-brown at my feet tips me back on my heels. By the time I've caught my balance, the whatever-it-was has gone. Only the rustling of the tall grass settling back into place proves it ever existed.

It seems that more than the air watched me.

The fence enclosing the formal gardens is almost invisible in places, but whether it is covered with uncontrolled growth or missing altogether, I cannot tell. Up the hill I see the house, huddled under its dull tile roofs. Many of the walls of the wings are missing; the covered walkways leading from wing to house look sound, but everywhere there are fallen tiles, moss, weeds springing from floors and roofs.

This is my gate, my fence, my home: its disorder is my fault. My wife in her cramped dark carriage, my son's impatient boredom, the loneliness of this uncivilized place, my inability or unwillingness to embrace the delicate life that would have given me a future in the capital. My fault.

If I had known I would have to return, I would have tended things better.

6. SHIKUJO'S PILLOW BOOK
The exigencies of moving:

In the scramble of packing, one loses the black enameled writing desk with the Michinoka paper and one's favorite writing-brush. It may not turn up, even at the new place.

Being boxed up in a small carriage for days is exhausting and annoying. Even when the carriage is well sprung and the oxen are smooth-gaited, you are jostled around until not even the carriage's padding and all your robes can protect your knees from bruises.

Nights sometimes there is nowhere to stay but an abandoned hut. One's women try to make it comfortable, but the air smells of mold. It is worse still if bad weather or some directional tabu makes it impossible to go on, and one has to stay all day in an inhospitable place.

It seems so silent in the country, away from the shouts of the vendors and the rattling of carriages passing by on the street. One would not think it possible to miss a thing like that, and yet one does.

To move to an unfamiliar place is hard enough, but it seems worse to return to an old home. It has changed so much in the years since one was there last. Ducks have built their nests in one's rooms, which are dusty and have a neglected air. All one's favorite things to view in the garden are in disorder or even lost altogether. The memories of what was before make the experience doubly painful.

One's family is suddenly far away. Even a husband and a son close at hand cannot make up for being so far from one's parents. It is hard not to be lonely.

And the fear, of course. Of the wildness, so far from the security of the city. Anything might happen out here.

I mention this fear to Onaga, and she snorts. "Anything? When the capital is crammed with ruffians and thieves, merchants who overcharge? The city is filled with villainy, lady!"

She is right, of course, but I find this cold comfort. Any problems there (except for fleas in our robes, and animals stealing from our storehouses) were human in nature. I do not even know what powers rule this lonely place.

7. THE NOTEBOOK OF KAYA NO YOSHIFUJI

I am drenched when at last I go inside. Though I stayed on what used to be, what should have been, the path, there were places where the stones were impossible to find even when I remembered where they should be. The bridge over one of the lakes was missing planks, and I chose to go around instead of across, and stepped into a knee-deep bay hidden by reeds. The mist in the air has done the rest.

"My lord!" Hito lays down the screen he holds against an opening for a carpenter's measurements, and bustles over to me, clucking. "You are soaking, get right out of those things."

"I'm fine." I kick off my wooden clogs and step up onto the veranda of my building, the main house. "Really, Hito, you sound just like my old nurse when I was Tadamaro's age. She had that exact tone to her voice."

"Your *sendan*-lilac silks, too! They are stained green everywhere."

I shrug. "The washers will get them clean again."

"Grass stains?" he says dubiously. Not wanting the lecture, I gesture him back to his work. But I change, obedient to the dim memory of an old woman from childhood.

My house is full of light and noise. All three rooms of my wing are lit by oil lamps. A man scrubs the veranda's floor with rushes and *muku* leaves. Charcoal glows in black iron braziers and smells of sandalwood incense. Air ripples over the glowing coals; thin smoke lifts toward the dark wood rafters and seeps out the triangular openings under the eaves. The torn and missing screens and panels I saw from a distance are now replaced — by gutting some of the outlying wings for intact materials, I imagine: no one can produce a good *shoji*-screen in an hour, let alone wall a room.

The only difference between this room and my rooms back at the capital, and every other room I've ever lived in, is not that I've added a clothes chest or two, or replaced my writing desk recently: it is a certain smell to the place I cannot place, very slightly sour and peppery and wild.

I am alone, although a dozen men (and women, too, I suppose) will run in if I shout. Except for that elusive smell, the order of a properly run house settles over me as surely here as back at the capital. I grieved half a month ago, when we left it behind. Then why does this order irritate me?

"My lord?" A maid stands on the threshold of a paper door slid open to the corridor.

"Yes?"

"May I please—" In one hand she holds a long stick with a piece of cotton rag tied to one end. The long sleeve behind which she hides her face for propriety is rimed with dust and spider-webs. "I was not able to reach all the cobwebs, so I made this to . . ." She gestures up with the stick.

Over my head, a huge web that spans the vault of the roof reflects silver from the eave-gap above, gold from the lamps below. Silver and gold laid like crackling over the darkness of the rafters. I have a lacquer comb-box that looks a little like this, only not so delicate. The spider that fashioned the web must be very large.

"Let it stay."

"*Sir?*" She forgets to hide her face: she is young, plain, her hair neatly cut to just below her shoulders. "But the spider—"

"She has been here longer than I have. Do I have any right to cast her out?"

"What about the *young?*" she says.

I feel a pang, thinking of my own son, here in this spiderweb of circumstance. "I see none. It is just her. And me."

She looks at me unhappily. I am sure she wants to argue; mercifully it is not possible. As much to change the subject as anything, I say, "Why does it smell so odd in here?"

"I am so sorry, my lord. We think a wild animal must have been in here in our absence."

The smell suddenly makes sense. "And it *urinated* in my rooms?"

"I am so sorry, but yes. It is all quite clean now. Really, the smell is not nearly as strong as it was. We should have it scrubbed completely away by tomorrow. Would you rather sleep in one of the other wings?"

I have to laugh.

8. SHIKUJO'S PILLOW BOOK
The first night at our new home:

*T*he *first night* at our new home, I received a note from my husband, written on one of the thick colored slips of paper he keeps in his sleeve, and twisted around a wet twig.

> *Too sour and damp to stay alone in my empty rooms —*
> *perhaps you will allow me to share your sweeter air?*

I could not find my writing chest, so I had to use one of my women's. At last I found a long thin slip of pale silver paper. Attaching a duck feather with a bit of black cord, I wrote:

> *The ducks say, You did not need to ask.*
> *Thank you for letting us sleep in this stolen nest,*
> *but it is, after all, your house.*

9. THE NOTEBOOK OF KAYA NO YOSHIFUJI

What does she think, when she writes these poems? The erotic connotation of the soft paper I used, the hints of tissues wiping away passion's wetness—this cannot have escaped her; and yet she sends back this poem, on a paper as hard and ungentle as mica.

Is she saying she does not belong here? Or that she gives up her privacy as reluctantly as the ducks undoubtedly did? She surprises me sometimes, this usually predictable wife of mine.

It is still raining, softly and easily as a poet's crying. The air is cool, humid; my breath curls like smoke. Although the walkway's roof protects me from the rain, the cold seeps in through my layered robes and the soles of my *tabi*-socks.

The wings people live in—my wife's, my son's, the attendants', mine—have paper windows cut through the walls, which now glow dimly with the lights inside. Beyond these lights lies the uniform black of the rainy night. I know what lies out there—where the lakes are, where the trees stand, where the moon-rock is, the viewing pavilion, the thousand-year oak—but all I can think is that it was never this dark in the capital.

We were never this alone, not even when we were here last.

10. SHIKUJO'S PILLOW BOOK
Ordering one's rooms:

Arranging the trunks along one wall. Hanging blinds from all the crossbeams overhead; most are rolled up to a standing man's eye height even though no men are likely to see us; but if the blinds were not there, one would of course need them. Arranging the little freestanding chest-high or waist-high curtain-stands around the room; each has a low table or armrest beside it. Hanging the spring *kichō*-curtains—some seem as fragile as grasshopper wings or spiders' webs, and yet they are surprisingly sturdy when we accidentally snag one with a trunk's corner. Setting up the curtained bed enclosure with sleeping robes and ceramic pillows. Placing the paulownia-wood brazier near one's favorite sitting place.

Keeping the outside *fusume*-panels and grilles closed, of course. All this careful arranging and rearranging would not seem very important, faced with the immensity of the night.

11. THE NOTEBOOK OF KAYA NO YOSHIFUJI

My wife's wing, the north house, is shuttered close against the crisp air. The women inside move about, and cast shadows that blur and sharpen in a crazy dance.

The house looks secure; but I stand half a dozen paces away, and I hear as if I shared the room. A poker scrapes against the bottom of a brazier; silk robes brush the hardwood floor. Women's voices ripple like water, clear but meaningless to my ears, until I hear my wife's among them.

There are conventions for those of us who live in paper-walled houses: we do not hear what is not spoken to us. Courtesy demands that we be deaf to the goings-on on the other side of the screen. We are not, of course: we listen avidly and gossip (if there are people nearby with whom we can gossip) and think about what they mean, the things we hear. As I do now, a spy in my wife's house.

"Your first night here, and already he visits you?" The voice of Onaga, my wife's leading maid. "You should have claimed a tabu, a sickness—you are not feeling well, lady. You said so—"

"Then his presence will ease me." My wife, her voice low, as sweet-pitched as a flute. I flush up, completely embarrassed, not willing to hear more. Praise of oneself is harder to hear than certain criticisms. If she means it.

Waiting a discreet moment, I tap on a screen cut with a pattern of interlocking waves, or perhaps crescent moons. "Wife?"

"My lord?" Onaga says.

I roll my eyes. Who else? Unfortunately, Onaga slides the door open just then and catches my expression. Onaga's narrow face sours before she turns away. I step through after her.

Shikujo's rooms are like mine, perhaps a little smaller. There are the same lattices and screens, the same stacks of oversized chests, the same high dark vault overhead, swallowing the lamp-light and the brazier's smoke.

Where my hall is spare, empty, hers seems filled with color and clutter. Her handful of women are shapeless piles of layered robes in spring pinks and whites and plums and greens. Every woman has black hair falling straight to waist or knee or floor; every face is hidden, by screen or fan or sleeve or averted head. As if they were not all my wife's women, and I could see them by merely speaking. As if I could see anything in this fitful light, filled with shadows as it is.

One of the women sets down a thick rush pad and gestures for me to be seated if I wish. "Wife?" I say again, squinting around me. I've been married for nine years, and still I cannot pick my wife out from her attendants if her face is concealed, unless she gives me some sign.

"Husband?" Shikujo's voice, low and curious. Of course I could not find her: it comes from behind a moss-patterned curtain hung from a waist-high frame. As elegantly placed as any court lady's, my wife's sleeve peeks beneath it, white brocade with a magenta-colored lining—all the correct seasonal tints. I cannot see her face.

I sit on the pad beside the curtain. "What are you doing behind a screen like that?"

"I am sorry. I have always—"

"We are no longer in the capital."

Onaga clears her throat. "I did not think that the ordinary conventions of life were dependent on living in the capital, my lord. I thought they were universal."

"What is the point of them here, Onaga?"

My wife answers for her. "Because when we are in the wild,

it is that much more important to behave like men and women. To separate us from the animals."

Even remembering the absolute darkness around us, I have to laugh in this cluttered formal space. "*This* is the 'wild,' wife?"

"It is wild enough. We are beyond the control of the eight million gods."

"We are never out of the Buddha's control, or Kannon's, or Inari's. Or any of the others, I suppose. Why are there shrines here, if not because the gods are strongly present?"

I cannot see her behind the screen. Without the clues given by her face, her words are expressionless. "Because we are afraid they are not. There are so few people here: we are as isolated as the survivors of a shipwreck."

"Really, wife," I laugh.

"It is quite true. Months will pass here, and we might never see a face other than our own and those of our servants."

"And the peasants," I add absently, but we both know that their presence does not change anything. "And we are somehow saved from this isolation because we exchange poetry and hide behind screens?"

She hesitates, as if choosing her words. "We are saved from living like castaways, at any rate. We are saved from the wilds."

"The 'wilds' exist beyond this place, whether we admit it or not." We are back where this conversation began.

"My screen bothers you, husband. Let us remove it."

"That is not the point," I begin, but one of her women slides the curtain stand to one side.

Shikujo kneels on a straw mat. Her robes fall in crisp cherry-shadowed white folds around her, like the irregular slopes of a mountain frosted with snow or blossoms. Her hair flows in a slow black river to the mat, and it hides her face from me. One slim hand holds an undecorated white fan the shape of the moon against her robes. Back in the capital, she is known for her skill at scent-making: now she smells spicy and sweet, like wisteria and young pine.

"My lord, you are tired after the long journey. You will feel better after you've eaten something."

"I have eaten," I say, but her women bring me food anyway — slices of pickled white radish and rice, and hot wine in a carved jasper jug.

She is right, of course: I do feel better after food. Shikujo is always right, my flawless wife, which I find unaccountably annoying. I would feel better if she showed some cracks in her perfection. Certainly I would feel less inadequate as a husband and a man.

I remember the guarded poem she wrote. "Thank you for allowing me to share your 'stolen nest' tonight."

She spreads out her hand, a dispelling gesture. "It is nothing. We had ducks here. They made their nest in the corner over the stream, but it was simple enough to clean up after them."

"Everything is so orderly here."

She does not realize this is not a good thing. "Are your rooms still disordered? I am so sorry, I should have sent my women over to help."

I shake my head. "No. In fact, I told the girl to leave my spiderwebs."

"Perhaps you would feel more at home if you had them removed . . . ?"

"No." My voice sounds abrupt, harsher than I intended. I say, to soften it: "Her web is as much home to the spider as the room is home to me. More, really: she has raised her children there, and I took mine away to raise him."

"How enlightened of you," Onaga interjects, "to spare the spider's life. No doubt you will earn a lot of good karma for it." Is she being ironic? She is bent over the brazier so that I cannot see her face.

"How is the boy settling into the west wing?" I say finally. Even now, I cannot help but smile when I think of him. He is a charmer, my son.

Shikujo sees this and smiles in her turn, and for the first time in this conversation our eyes meet. "Onaga has talked to his nurse. She says, very well. He has managed to tear a *shoji*-screen already." I sigh. He averaged two screens a month, back at the capital. I can see nothing will change here. "Can we call him to visit us? I'd like to see the boy."

"His nurse would suggest that we not do so. It is late. He is either asleep or so overwrought it would be no good for him or us."

"Perhaps I can stop by and see how he fares."

"Perhaps," she says. After a moment, she continues, "There was another thing, husband. His nurse said that he slipped out into the garden."

I laugh. "I wonder I did not see him, then."

"Please!" she says. "This is no laughing matter. He was out there alone!"

"Why keep him out? It is fenced around, and I did not see anything to worry about. He can't get lost and he'll enjoy it."

"There might be animals, husband. He might be bitten." Her voice is tense now.

I remember the flash of red-brown, down by the gate. "He'll be bitten by a squirrel?"

"Or a fox, or a snake, or a *tanuki*-badger. We have not lived here in years. The servants have not maintained the garden. If we have raised a boy in that time, who knows what families of vermin have grown up here?"

"Animals are not so dangerous, wife. If he makes enough noise—and you know he does that—they'll slink away. He'll never even see them. You worry yourself unnecessarily."

She chewed her lower lip, a graceless gesture for a woman otherwise so aware of her elegance. "He might fall into the lakes, then."

"He never fell in the lakes at our house back in the capital. What are you really afraid of, wife?"

She fidgeted with the fan. "It is all so new to him. You and I—we've been here, in the wilds, before, but he—has no idea of the risks."

"There is nothing so very dangerous here. He is surrounded by servants, and soon the gardens will be civilized again. He'll learn how to get on here."

She has been writing: her ink stick rests against her slate ink stone, with its puddle of drying ink. Slips of paper of every color rest in untidy heaps at one end of a dark wood writing desk. Every *spring* color, I should say: absent are winter's dark greens and browns; autumn olives and rusts; summer's crimson and cornflower-blue.

"What is this?" I reach for a piece of paper shaped like a blade of grass as long as my hand. Her sharp-edged calligraphy skitters across the bright green surface.

"No —" She tries to take it from me, but I have beaten her.

> *Afraid of the dark hollows,*
>   *still, I followed you here —*
> *but are those eyes I see*
>   *beneath the ruined gate?*

"What did you see?" I ask.

"Nothing, my lord. It is of no account. Please return my poem."

"What animal?"

"Truly, it was nothing."

Her hands pluck at mine until I give back the slip of paper. Her skin is soft and cool. I can just feel the pulse in the pale blue veins of her wrist as I stroke it. For the second time in the night, she meets my eyes.

I suddenly want her, this woman who is my wife. I forget sometimes that she is a real person, not some pretty artifact in my life. I do not know what she thinks of me from day to day, but I suspect it is something similar. I am like a colored thread worked into a brocade: one part of the pattern of her life, generally noticed only as a part of the whole. But sometimes she notices, or I notice, the single thread again, and wonder at the color or the fineness, the *uniqueness* of it. We meet each other's eyes and remember: *There is a soul on the other side of those eyes.*

After a moment, she waves her free hand. Her women move away with the rustling of robes and paper screens pulled to.

Like cicadas on a summer night, or a single man's footsteps pacing a street at dawn, these sounds are as deep as true silence.

Like the silence that such a noise defines, it is her company that defines a woman's solitude. No woman is ever truly alone; there are always others within earshot. Shikujo's attendants are behind screens at the opposite end of the room, or a bare pace away, in the room across the corridor. Onaga herself is only half-hidden, behind a screen painted with red-crowned cranes, as she warms her hands over a porcelain brazier.

But we are alone, my wife and I.

I raise her to her feet, lead her to the bed enclosure. It is raised a step high, curtained with night-blue hangings brocaded with silver clouds. I lay her down on a heap of padded robes.

I want more than the cool elegance of her body shaping to me, more than the feel of her skin, the sight of her flushed face and disordered hair, the sliding silk robes pushed out of the way. I want her mind, her soul. I want the place in her she has never given me.

Not even that. I want the place in *myself* she has never given me. Because no one can.

But I can try. Touch has often replaced talk between us. At its worst (for it is never bad), it offers a moment when *talk* and *self* and *souls* are meaningless.

I remove the moon-shaped fan from her slackened grasp, and push her silk robes back from her shoulders to hang from her elbows, baring her throat and the inner curves of her small rich breasts. I stroke these places until she makes a tiny noise, like a breath that snags in her throat.

Her crimson silk *hakama*-trousers envelop her waist in swollen, rounded folds. I untie the elaborate knot that holds them, and they fall past her hipbones and puddle at her feet.

Over the perfume, I smell *her*, musky and animal. I touch her nether lips, hidden in the short soft hairs, and they are already wet and swollen. She parts her legs and moans, barely a breath in my ear. I release myself from my own clothing and sit upright. I feel my pulse, throbbing through me, a connection between throat and belly and sex. The cold air defines the boundaries of my body. I wrap her small hand around me. She touches — gently at first, then more vigorously — moves flesh against flesh. The tension in me is sweet and sharp and suddenly unbearable. I sit back on my heels, and pull her around, until her back is to me, raise her hips and pull her down.

Hot wet folds part for me. She takes my full length until she is seated in my lap, her back pressed against my chest, her face twisted to my neck. I feel her gasp against my throat, feel her breast heave under my hand as she raises and lowers onto me. I pull her nipple between my fingers until it is impossibly distended and hard, the texture of its skin as defined as the surface of a stone.

She moves on me, slides the length of me. Her inner muscles knot and loosen with her movements, until I am numb to sensation, feeling only pressure and heat and friction. Her belly muscles snake under my hand. I am seeping, a tantalizing taste of the full release. Our juices mix, and are pushed down by her movement.

She releases first, as she should; but at her sudden liquefying and the shudders that wrack her, I match her. The pressure churns out; my bones soften and run.

We are still for a long time before she lifts free.

I pull a pad of soft papers from my sleeve — the same sort of paper I wrote my poem to her on. (Perhaps she understood my meaning after all.) Together we use them to wipe first myself, and then her, clean. Her floor-length hair was pinned between us, and is knotted and dull with our sweat. The smell of us combined with the wet earth outside reminds me of the animal-smell of my rooms.

Later Onaga and the others will bathe her and perfume her, and brush out her hair until it is smooth again. For now, I fiddle with a snarl until it separates into individual strands, fanned across my fingers.

"I'm sorry." I blurt the words out, surprising myself as much as her.

"Really, husband, it was most pleasant. You have —"

I raise my hand to silence her. "It is a bad thing that I did so poorly at the appointments. I disappointed you. Life looked so promising, but now —"

She wrinkles her brow at me. "You never disappoint me, husband," she says, but she is hidden again, and I do not know what this means. "My place is with you."

"But you do not want to be here."

"I would never —"

I shrug impatiently. "You know it. I know it. When we were here the first time, you did not dislike the country as you do now. But it has been years since you went as far from the capital as the shrines of Nara, and that is a bare day's journey."

"No — my lord, I am so sorry. That foolish poem! I never meant — It is just the country. The strange noises, the wild things. The garden — in such disarray. It is all so frightening. Please, I meant none of that. Forgive me."

"What did you mean, then?"

She picks at the glue that holds her fan together. "When we were here before, this place was so pretty. I knew it was better to be in the capital, better for you, better for me. But you wanted me here, I thought."

"I did, and I did not." There is no politeness in me. I speak the painful, rude truth. She is too well bred to flinch, but I feel it in her stillness: *What is the correct response to this?* There is no correct response, I want to snap, but instead I find myself excusing things, glossing them over. "I inconvenience you here. I'm glad you came with me, but it was not necessary. Your parents wanted you to stay with them in the city. You might have been able to salvage something out of this, for the boy at least, if you had stayed in the center of things." An influential mother is often of more importance to a boy's furtherance than his father: just as well, in this case. Shikujo has never been anything but perfect. Her only mistake in judgment has been that she did not divorce me when I turned out to be so useless.

"My place is beside you," she says again. Is she impatient? Hurt? I cannot tell.

"Why?" I ask baldly, but there is no answer she can give me.

Passion? We have shared that before this, but lovers offer that as well. Love? Husbands and wives do not "love" each other. Duty? I feel responsible enough. I want to stop my mind's monotonous circling, so I pull her to me, and kiss her, harder than before.

The second time we have sex is as fierce as the animals she fears. She does not moan softly: we both cry aloud, uncaring of the women in the room.

She falls asleep afterward, or perhaps she only pretends. Her fan lies beside her head, a dim moon in the darkness. I touch its papery surface; then, on impulse, pick it up. I suppose this is a piece of her, of this night, that I can keep with me.

Restless, I pull my robes to and slip from the curtained enclosure. The lamps are extinguished, and the lattices are all closed and covered. The only light comes from the brazier's dying coals. Onaga kneels by the brazier, rubbing her hands together for warmth. The dull red light deepens her wrinkles and tints her face the color of a winter sunset. We exchange a look, but I cannot read what lies within the black wells of her eyes.

My wife's other women sleep behind a cluster of curtain-stands in the back of the room; I hear one of them sigh, and fabric shift and settle as she moves.

This room full of people is as empty as the dark spring garden. The spiderwebs in my wing at least fill space.

12. SHIKUJO'S PILLOW BOOK
In gaps in the rain:

In gaps in the rain, I met the moon's eyes —
Welcome as it is, I wonder that it hides behind tears.

And why is it in any way surprised that we do not race outside to greet it, when we are likely to see only more rain.

13. THE NOTEBOOK OF KAYA NO YOSHIFUJI

I slide a panel aside and step into the dark corridor of my son's
rooms. The *shoji*-screens between the corridor and the main
room glow very dimly, as if a single shuttered lantern were on
the other side. I can see where my son ripped the paper of one
of the screens, because the gash has already been neatly mended
with a patch shaped like a moth, right down to the feathered
antennae.

A *shoji* whispers against its frame when I push it aside and
step into the main room.

It could be an adult's room, except for the scale of certain
furnishings. There is a Chinese-style chair tucked in a corner of
the room, its seat scarcely ankle-high to me. My son has a shrine
in his room (as he should: it is never too early to begin one's
spiritual path), smaller than I would expect, and simpler than
my or my wife's shrine. There are many trunks and chests lined
up against one wall. A few are too small to conveniently carry
anything larger than a child's possessions. The room has a scattering of lumps strewn across the room's flat surfaces. The large
ones are sleeping servants, the small ones probably toys. I nearly
twist my ankle on a wooden Korean-style chariot no longer than
a child's forearm. A toy cat (or perhaps it is a dog; sometimes
these things are hard to tell) watches me, its silver bell gleaming
in the light from the brazier.

The hangings of the bed enclosure rustle aside and the boy's
nurse slips out. Dressed in undyed sleeping robes, her gray and
black hair loose to her shoulders, she sees me and bows in greet-
ing, picking her way through the room.

"I came to see my son," I whisper when she is close enough
to hear me.

Her lips tighten. "I had trouble enough getting him to sleep,
my lord. The child is exhausted. Must he be awakened?"

"No. I just want to see him." Of course this makes no sense,
but she understands and leads me back to the bed enclosure,

mouthing *Do not wake him up* before stepping away to leave us alone.

I push the curtain aside and look at my son.

I can see immediately that there is no need to worry about waking Tadamaro up: he is sound asleep, and nothing short of a typhoon will awaken him before morning. His sleeping robes were obviously just rearranged by his nurse, for they are unnaturally smooth. He is holding something in one hand: I bend over to look at it, and see it is a colorful thread-wound ball with tassels. His face is slack, mouth half-open. For sleep, his long black hair was pulled back into a little tail at the nape of his neck, but hairs have strayed. One hangs in front of his nose and quivers with each slow breath.

My chest aches when I look at him. He is such a precious thing, this son of mine. I love the fact that his spirit sends him careering off into an unfamiliar garden. I cannot take my wife's fears seriously. We always let him run about the garden at the house in the capital, and he knows better than to approach lakes, there or here. *He is a child*, I think rebelliously. *He should be allowed to run around, to have fun, to live*. To live, as opposed to what? To not live, to merely survive, lost in the despair of adulthood.

I stand on the veranda, to look at the neglected gardens that lead to the gate. The sky has cleared; the moon wets everything down with cold light. A shadow slips from a tree limb and falls to the ground. Something, perhaps a mouse, screams, and the shadow-owl returns to its perch with a ragged clump of darkness caught in its claws. Down by the farthest lake, a stag dips its head to the water.

There were foxes in the garden when we were first married and lived here. I wonder if there are still any.

14. KITSUNE'S DIARY

Grandfather and I hid all the day the humans came, deep in the lake rushes, where we could watch and not be seen. I suppose, thinking now about it, that there were not so many people — fifteen? twenty? — but they seemed to be everywhere, more than I'd ever seen before, more than I had imagined could exist. Men in servants' clothes scrambled around the garden, on the roofs, and along the walkways. They carried chests and bundles into the wings.

And the noise! Now I have been a woman, and discovered that people are always moving around in a cloud of noise; but then it was all new. Feet thudded across the floorboards like padded sticks striking a wooden drum. Mallets pounded pegs in place; wood splintered as broken screens were ripped free. A twig broom made a sharp scratching noise as someone swept the floors. The humans themselves barked back and forth continually. I startled every time the humans dropped something or made a sudden loud sound. I could only imagine how it must sound to my brother and mother, trapped in the den beneath the buildings.

"How will we live," I whispered to my grandfather after one of these crashes, "if it is to be like this from now on?"

"This is their moving day," he said grimly. "The servants will organize everything for their master and mistress, and they'll all go back to the stableyard, and things will be quieter, safer, then. But it will never be as we remember, no. Be still, now."

It was dusk when my grandfather finally touched his nose to mine. "Home," he told me as I blinked and stretched. He vanished into the reeds.

I followed the tip of my grandfather's tail glowing dim violet in the twilight, flickering like marsh gas just in front of my nose. We moved in a great arc through the weeds and ran silently across the narrow clearing that surrounded the house, into the darkness under the veranda.

We had always rested outside the den, in the slice of world between earth and floor, and went underground only to sleep; but now no one was out. Grandfather crawled into the burrow immediately, like a coward or a mouse, I thought. I paused first to scent the air and smelled hot pottery and charcoal and sandalwood incense before following him.

They were pressed against the back wall of the bottommost chamber. During the day Mother had urinated in the den from fear; even now old terror rose from her like a musk. Dried froth was on her jaws. Brother smelled nervous but without the tang of panic.

We pressed in close until we four all lay together like the pieces of a wood puzzle nested in its box. The air was close and warm. It was like when we were young, pressed against our mother's belly. I do not think much about that time — nothing happened, after all, except eating and sleep — but now I felt reassured.

We crouched in the den for a long time. I listened to my family breathing. Noises sifted into the den from above.

Foxes are not like men, who choose their words with less care than starlings. We wait until our thoughts take a shape, and then we say what shape that is. We do not use words, exactly, but we say what we need to.

"When we were hiding," I said at last, "he saw us, that man. When he was on the horse."

"He *saw* nothing. Tsst," my grandfather said, "they are as blind as oxen. Always have been."

"He looked right at us!"

"They have eyes in their heads, but they have no idea how to use them. They see what is outside through whatever is happening inside."

"Then why did he come back to the logs?"

"To examine them — who knows?"

"But why?" I demanded again. "He can't eat them."

"Who can tell with humans?"

"Grandfather," my brother said suddenly. "If the humans had seen us, what would they have done?"

"They would kill us," Grandfather said.

"Hah," I said. "If they're this blind, we're safe."

"We will never be safe, now that they're here."

"Well," I said, "even if they do want to kill us, we have so many escapes: we have our bolt-holes, our safe places, our trails and paths."

"They do not seem to care enough about anything but themselves to be dangerous," Brother said.

"You are milk-suckers," Grandfather spat. "You have no idea."

"If it is bad, why do we stay?" my mother asked. "Why not run to the woods and live with the *tanuki*-badgers and wolves and killing animals? We are small, we will be just a mouthful to the big ones. Perhaps they will ignore us."

"No," Grandfather said finally. "The kits are still too young —"

"They would be gone already, if you were not who you were," Mother said.

" —and you are too simple," he continued. "And I am too old. And you know this already: a killing animal never ignores. At least the humans won't eat us."

"There is more to this than that." Mother's tail lashed once. "You remember the humans from before, and it confuses you. My mother was alive then, and she said —"

"Leave it," Grandfather barked. She had made sense for once, at least to my grandfather. "There is nothing."

I was not convinced.

They found our den the next day.

15. SHIKUJO'S PILLOW BOOK
The ducks left more:

*T*he *ducks left more* than we thought. The first morning at the estate, Tadamaro's nurse brought the child in to greet me. While we discussed his settling-in, he explored my rooms. Behind a large trunk that had been brought in early, he found a coiled clot of dirty marsh-grass and, nestled in the clump, an unhatched egg. We removed it from him as soon as possible — what bad luck must be associated with a duck that could not even free itself from its egg?

It is also disturbing to think that Tadamaro was more delighted by this discovery than all the toys and gifts my parents gave him when we left the capital.

The weeds and the animals have had their way with our home. What else will we find?

16. THE NOTEBOOK OF KAYA NO YOSHIFUJI

On the first morning, the sky is glorious. Even though the sun is bright, the sky is covered with a pale green mist. As I watch the mist shred, a crane flaps off the water to settle in the thousand-year oak, like a blossom returning to its tree.

Hito brings me breakfast: rice soaked in vinegar with *ayu*-trout, served on a lacquered red tray painted with a trail of black ants so realistic that I can see their antennae if I look closely. I eat automatically as I answer questions about the things that have been neglected in our absence — yes, rebuild and rethatch the fence; yes, rebuild the gate, retile the roofs, clean the stableyard, dredge out the irrigation systems for the garden. Yes, yes, yes. If we are to live here, at least I can make it habitable.

The servants are still full of their cleaning. I could tell them to be silent, and they would leave me and my spiderweb in peace; but knowing I have this power in some way compels me not to use it, so I retire to the grounds.

No one knows when exactly the garden was started, and how much of it was natural and how much man-made. When I first brought Shikujo here, I thought that my gardeners worked only on the potted trees and shrubs of the graveled courtyards, and swept the bridges and sanded walks throughout the garden. The plants and stones and streams of the grounds seemed wild, nearly untouched by their hands.

But I have learned it was more complex than that, this making of a beautiful garden. All the moss-grown paths and ragged bamboo copses were carefully trained to look untended. In pre-dawn spring cold, I have watched the gardeners pull the water-logged petals from my cherry trees after an overnight rain ruined the flowers. In the summer they brushed the pine trees to shake free the dead needles. Preparing for winter snow, they tied up the pine branches so they would not break, and they insulated the thick moss beds with a carpet of pine needles and straw.

And now, after all these years of neglect—! The garden is not much different from the land around it, anymore. The stones of the path are slippery with wet moss. Covered with clumps of dead leaves the color of old blood, a snapped branch hangs in my face, held to a scarlet maple by a strip of bark. A slug feels along the branch, looking for a way back to the tree.

How am I to fill my time, here in the country? I filled it but poorly before this.

Hito flutters by the ruined formal gate, his robes bright as an iris's flag in the sun and shade that chase one another across my gardens. Half-naked laborers—peasants taken from the fields for the day—cluster around the tumbled logs, still wet with dew. Laborers seem the same anywhere: they spend much of their day looking idle, seeming to enjoy the day's air in their faces, before they burst into action that completes their task in an impossibly short time.

My son, Tadamaro, crouches in a patch of grass, digging with a peeled stick half his height. I suppose his nurse is ill, or he has escaped her; certainly she would never allow him to come so close to the dirt and danger of building, or to wear pale silks if he did so. Knowing my wife's fears, I suppose I ought to have someone escort him back to the house, but it seems a shame. He is so absorbed in what he is doing, whatever it is.

"My lord." Hito stands over me, looking solemn.

"What is it?" I say resignedly.

"I am afraid it will be quite impossible to repair the gate at the moment, my lord," Hito says. "This peasant has convinced me that circumstances will not permit it." He sounds sorry that he cannot blame the man for shirking.

"Really," I say.

"Even so, my lord. He claims it is quite impossible. See the ground here?" He steps neatly around Tadamaro as if the boy were no more than a rock in his way.

I look at the patch. It is overgrown with weeds of some sort and looks no different from any other patch I've seen in recent months. Except that water weeps from the sides of my son's excavation and reflects the sky.

"Well?" I say impatiently to Hito. I would rather watch Tadamaro.

"The ground has been quite waterlogged. We cannot possibly get the posts set until we can drain off the area."

"Well. Then drain it."

"If you insist, my lord. Only—"

I glare at him, and he starts speaking again, as if compelled. "—because we would need to drain off the lowermost lake as well."

I look at the lake. It is a pretty thing, the largest of the three, fringed with rushes and reeds and rabbit-cropped grasses. Or is it cropped by rabbits? For all I know, gardeners creep down here while I sleep and trim it back with little jeweled knives. Trees and blue sky and white cloud reflect perfectly in the still water, except where a merganser trails growing circles as she swims. If we drain the lake, we will have three acres of stinking, baking mud.

"If not now, when?"

Hito looks relieved. "In the winter, before the rains, but after the rice crop is in, and we can divert the stream. We can empty out the lake altogether, reconstruct its clay bottom where necessary, and refill it before winter."

"The lake has a clay floor?"

"Of course, my lord; they all do. We need to seal them, to prevent leakage. They are not natural lakes, after all."

I choose not to ask about the cropped grass.

"It is just as well," Hito adds. "It is never possible to make repairs on one's gates in the summertime."

"A tabu," I sigh.

"Doku is not a *major* deity, but he is quite insistent in this matter."

"Father!" Tadamaro's voice: excited, he has forgotten everything he has ever learned about respecting his elders, about being silent and polite in our company. Hopping from foot to foot, he points toward a blur of gray fur that just resolves itself into a rabbit, running for the deep grasses along the lake's edge.

Hito looks for a moment as if he wants to reprimand the boy, but he cannot; he is a servant, and the boy will someday take my place, for what little that place may be worth. And Tadamaro is long gone, himself dashing like a young hare after the fleeing rabbit.

I follow him, at a more reasoned pace. It is a relief to leave behind the unsolved problem of the gate, and it is good for an adult to keep an eye on him, but I know my real reason for following him is neither of these. It is wistfulness.

A rabbit and a boy leave an easy path to follow. A notch has been carved through the grasses pushed away from their passing. The nurse will be relieved to hear that Tadamaro's clog-prints skirt the lake at a safe distance.

The boy is completely out of sight, and the grasses are starting to straighten. Now that I am safely out of sight of any servants or peasants who might find amusing the sight of their master jogging in green-and-yellow silks, I force myself to a trot.

The trail ends at the moon-rock. I have not actually been here since I was myself a child and this house belonged to my mother. She had no daughters to pass it on through, and it fell to me when she died, before I married Shikujo. Coming here is a little like returning to Tadamaro's age.

The rock reaches my chest, gray and slick-looking with rain. Some of its pockmarks are filled with days-old rainwater and reflect the silver sky. The white sand that surrounds the rock shines in the light. I would have thought the sand got dirty in the years we were gone. Perhaps it did, and has been replaced, but it only reinforces my sense of strangeness.

The silver reflections on the rock look almost as if the pale sand behind were showing through holes in it. The silver patches shift as I move, making the rock seem somehow insubstantial. I feel light-headed — I assume, from the unaccustomed labor of running here.

Tadamaro crouches at the moon-rock's base, a bright little shadow against silver and gray. He pokes a pine stick in a gap beneath the rock and the sand. His serria-gold clothes are dimmed with a haze of greenish pollen and grass-dust. His long hair is tangled. A clump has pulled a little loose of the thong that holds it at his neck; now it loops upward, making a tangled black cockerel's crest that bobs as he moves. I feel a certain sympathy for my own nurse so many years before, who used to loudly bemoan the impossibility of cutting a child's hair before he attained manhood or its semblance; I would look like a servant child, she used to say, but at least I would look like a *neat* servant child.

My head is spinning. My son, caught up in this moment, notices only the rabbit, the stone, the stick in his hand. The *now.* I lean against a tree for support.

Life was like that once for me. When I was Tadamaro's age, everything I saw (or heard, or tasted, or thought) was new. Even though I had seen springtime come before, each one was special, the first time I had seen *this* spring, *these* new leaves, *this* family of squirrels. Even the horrible things — my first taste of *sake,* the abscessed tooth I had when I was fourteen — were intensely experienced. The future promised a string of equally interesting sights and tastes and thoughts.

I still felt this way when I married Shikujo. The time we spent together was like discovering new sutras every day, each written in silver characters on indigo paper, beautiful and precious, but even more so because of their contents, the words that added meaning to our lives.

When did this change? I only know it did. At some point I realized that life was not as sweet as it had been. Nothing tasted as good as it did the first time—or as it might taste again, in the undetermined future. No: I am trapped in *now*, a drab "now" completely unlike my son's *now*, a *now* that is not as good as "then" or "soon." Worse, experience has taught me that when I get to tomorrow, it will turn into yet another drab *now*. How can I fight such a despair?

I watch my son. Things are still new to him, still absorbing. Perhaps I am hoping that he will somehow miss this dying inside, that he will never have to reach my *now*.

Still unaware of me, Tadamaro talks as he pokes. He seems to talk at the rabbit, warning it that he will dig it free and have it made into supper for his nurse.

"The rabbit is gone," I say. He barely turns his head; keeps poking. "He is hidden, under the rock. You won't get him, son." *Life is like that,* I want to say, but I only touch his shoulder, and he turns to look at me.

"Where did he go?"

"I do not know," I say honestly. He is disappointed for a moment, but loses interest and walks away, gouging a furrow in the sand with the stick. He is already on his way to his next discovery, his next wonder.

We do not spend much time together. Why should we? He has nurses for that. My responsibility to the child is to father him, to acknowledge him as my own when his mother announces her pregnancy, and to make sure he marries properly. In the interim I keep him fed, get him educated. When he is the proper age, I make sure a relative of suitable distinction presents him with his first pair of *hakama*-trousers. It has never been a necessity of being a father, knowing one's child.

A necessity? I suppose not. But it should be one of its delights. And I have chosen not to spend more time with the boy, because it was so painful to watch him and realize that someday he would lose what made life worth living and would be as lost and sad as his father.

·   ·   ·

As it grows darker, I stand on my veranda, and watch the gold light filter through my wife's screens. I hear women's voices across the still air, like *biwa*-lutes from a distance, as muted in their way as the light. What are they talking about?

A woman is reading in a light, pleasant voice, not like my wife's accents, a ghost story from some old *monogatari*, some century-dead collection of tales.

"She was too gentle," Onaga's harsh voice interrupts. "She should have —" Silence, but there must have been a gesture, for the women all laugh. I do not hear my wife's voice among them. Perhaps she is in the outhouses, or in another room.

This is what they talk about now, but it will never be more than a tenth, a hundredth of their time spent talking. What do they find to talk about? Perhaps their light shines less brightly somehow. This despite my wife's often witty (if always proper) poems and letters, despite the tales she loves to read—all of which seem to be written by women. I have to assume that they are not less brightly lit, but more so, that they can draw on a place I as a man cannot even imagine.

And my wife? I have sometimes envied her the company of her women, Now, when she is silent, I wonder if she is not as alone as I.

17. SHIKUJO'S PILLOW BOOK
The poem with which he invited me:

*T*he poem with which he invited me to his wing was written in elegantly gradated ink on dusty pink paper and attached to a twig covered with cherry blossoms, and said:

> *A sight worth seeing —*
> *the moon's face is always welcome in my rooms.*

PERHAPS WE WILL SEE IT AS CLEARLY AS LAST NIGHT. . . .

18. THE NOTEBOOK OF KAYA NO YOSHIFUJI

The house has two pavilions attached to the house's wings by
long roofed walkways that thrust into the formal garden.
The sunset-viewing pavilion is the easternmost. There is a gap
between two mountains, where a stream has carved out a path;
just at dusk on certain days in the winter, the sun drops into
the fold of land and shoots a heatless red shaft onto the faces
of viewers in the pavilion. This is spring, of course. The view is
still beautiful.

The lake-viewing pavilion is smaller and (currently, until we
replace the panels) open to the air, built out into the closest
lake in such a way that the water gurgles around the support
pillars in a south wind. An ornamental stone lamp stands unlit
on a rock in the lake's center. I wonder what my servants
would do if I ordered them to light it. Wade into the water, undoubtedly.

It is late afternoon. The sun eases toward the fringe of pine
on the ridge's crest. Its light mellows and pours across the garden, and fades. Mosquitoes thicken until the air seethes black
and hums. Swallows move sharply among them; an early bat
startles me by darting an arm's length from my face. I should
be grateful, as the mosquitoes are eating me alive despite my
waving them away with my wife's white fan, which I have unaccountably retained. If I slap them, they leave bloody traces on
my hands.

I could go back inside, away from the insects; but even after
a day outside, I am not ready for that. The pounding and scrub-
bing will be over. The smell should be gone. The spiderweb, I
hope, remains. I asked Shikujo (which means Shikujo and her
women) to attend me in my rooms tonight, ostensibly to watch
the moon rise, perhaps to have sex again, mostly to break the
stillness there, but also out of a small malicious delight in confronting her with the web. I am hoping one of these four reasons
will satisfy me.

A man's shocked scream from the house: raised voices. It

would be silly, I think, to wait until they come out to me and realize I am sitting out here being eaten by insects simply for pique. I wipe my face clean and stand, and then laugh. Anything short of a murder among the household staff should be manageable by Hito.

I walk back anyway.

My men surround one of the lesser servants, a small stout man wearing no more than a dusty loincloth. He pants and clutches his chest.

"What is all this?" I raise my voice over the babbling.

"My lord!" Hito looks so horrified I nearly laugh. "Have we disturbed you? I am so sorry your enjoyment of the evening was interrupted by this fool's—" he kicks at the servant, who jumps back "—completely disproportionate reaction to a minor discovery. He—"

I rub my eyes. "What did he find, and where?"

"It is only that Maki here was in the crawl space under your rooms, making sure that there was nothing, ah, inappropriate in the dust there to justify the, ah, unusual smell of your chambers, and he found some sort of a deserted animal hole—"

"It was not deserted, my lord," the peasant interrupts, and then bows placatingly to me, then to Hito. "I am so sorry, but it was a foxhole, I *know* it—" he glares at Hito "—and there was a *fox* there."

"Nonsense!" my major domo begins. "Some small rodent—"

"How did you know?" I ask.

"I had to crawl, it is so low, but I had a little lamp—*this* lamp, my lord—and there were footprints—*fox* footprints— everywhere, so I followed where they seemed to be pointing, and there was a hole, bigger than a mouse or ground squirrel, whatever *some* people might say, and I saw eyes glowing at me from the den's mouth, and then they blinked away. They were horrible, like—"

"His imagination," Hito gets in at last, "or a stone reflecting. My lord, it is *nothing.*"

He sounds nearly panicked. Why? Does he think I'll have him beaten because some animal has a hole under my house?

Not *some* animal, I suddenly realize. Foxes are bad luck to peasants.

"Give me the lamp," I say.

"My lord?" Hito stares at me blankly.

I smile blandly at him. "Hito, please tie up my sleeves."

He swallows heavily. "As you wish." He ties my big sleeves close to my arms with some black silk tape he pulls from a secret recess of his costume.

"My lord?" says a woman's voice from the shadows of my curtained-off veranda. Shikujo has already come to my rooms, though of course it is not she who speaks: she would never speak in front of all these commoners.

"Yes, Onaga?" Using more of the tape, I lace my loose trousers tight against my legs.

"My mistress your wife wonders what exactly you are going to do." The acid tone is clear.

I drop to my knees and reach up to take the little metal lamp from the peasant's slack hands.

"You cannot go in there! —my mistress says," adds Shikujo's woman.

"It is almost dark!" Hito chimes in. "If anyone, let the servants —"

"My lady is concerned that you might be hurt. The beasts might still be there."

"Tomorrow," my man says. "You could check tomorrow, if you insist; or better yet, *I*—"

"They are savage! They are animals; they'll bite —"

My wife speaks aloud. Her low voice cuts through the babble: "Be careful, husband."

19. SHIKUJO'S PILLOW BOOK
Waiting in one's husband's rooms:

The spiderweb is a beautiful thing,
unless you're a fly.

Waiting in one's husband's rooms, one watches the spider's web, but cannot see the spider anywhere. This is somehow much more worrisome than seeing her, however large or horrible she might be.

Leaving would be a relief. But one is summoned. So: wait, and watch the web, and worry.

20. THE NOTEBOOK OF KAYA NO YOSHIFUJI

Of course I go, in the darkness. Why am I so mad? Foxes are savage little creatures; I saw a vole shredded like paper by one, back when we first lived here. It was so many years ago; they must all be dead by now, their children scattered. This will be an empty hole, and the eyes the servants saw just a peasant's fancy. Why do I wish to—no, need to—see this place? What am I proving and to whom?

The servants' clucking is muffled as soon as I crab-walk under the veranda. The house is a flat dark roof just above my head, supported by a maze of heavy black crossbars and waist-thick pillars balanced on rocks—for stability during earthquakes, I am told, though there have been no earthquakes here. There should be small river-stones laid under the house to keep the dust down in the dry season, but time has buried them in a powdery layer of earth, soft to my hands and knees.

The lamp throws swinging shadows. Pillars of darkness rise and fall around me as I move past the posts. An unexpected shape startles me. It is only a strangely shaped foundation stone, but I am surprised again at the shadow of the next. When someone crosses a room, the wood overhead resonates like sullen thunder.

The ground under me rises until I am nearly on my belly. Ground into the dust by layer on layer of small four-toed prints are coarse red hairs. The air smells faintly of fur, sour and musky.

Nothing in my life has prepared me for this. I have always

been the center of things in my life: *my* wife, *my* servants, *my* world. But there are other worlds, completely alien to me, and here, caught between *my* floor and the earth, in air clogged with another presence, I am not even irrelevant: I am *other*.

There is a hole an arm's length ahead, perhaps as large as my fists joined, round as a coin but utterly black, without shine or reflections. I move the lantern to get a better view. Almost hidden inside, two chips of light flash at me.

My heart pauses a long moment: a sudden ache in my chest leaves me breathless. Pale against the soil, kinked undercoat hairs float in the lamplight.

I watch without breathing for a long moment before the shining flecks sort themselves into the irregular faces of a stone. I am alone.

I pull the stone out and hold it: gray pearl-colored quartz, left over from the gravel of the old days, to shine like eyes. And now it is no more than a stone, cold and dusty in my palm.

They lived here, but we frightened them off. And when I saw the glow I thought was eyes, it was not fear that stopped my heart. It was longing.

21. SHIKUJO'S PILLOW BOOK
Continuing to wait:

*W*ait, and watch, and worry. Mercifully, one is rather good at these things.

22. THE NOTEBOOK OF KAYA NO YOSHIFUJI

On my return, the men are still waiting. "Nothing there, after all. Really, you might have saved me the trouble by not panicking." I hold out the stone nestled like a *sake* cup in my hand. I am relieved that my disappointment does not show in my voice.

The servant flushes, bows. "My lord, I swear—"

"That is quite enough," Hito says. "You have somewhere to go?—" His glare encompasses the crowd, which dissolves like a mist: then he turns to me.

"Your Korean brocades!" Hito brushes at the shoulders of my robes, matted with cobwebs and dirt.

"All this country living is hard on my wardrobe. Maybe I should get some nice peasant-garb?"

He clucks, unamused. "It was totally unnecessary, my lord, for you to—"

"I wanted to see."

"And were they there?"

"Didn't I say they were gone?"

"I only thought—"

"You think too much, Hito, about all the wrong things."

He stiffens and takes refuge in formality. "My lady your wife awaits you in your rooms."

I stretch: "Yes." My wife, unlike the foxes, is at all times where she is supposed to be.

I clean myself up and change, and come in to find my wife angry. She never shows it directly, but we've been married too long for me not to recognize the signs.

"I hope you had an interesting day, husband."

"Yes," I say simply. "Thank you for your concern over me, but it was really unnecessary."

"Going under the house could have been very dangerous, if they'd still been there."

"Then why didn't you try to stop me?"

"Could I have?" She speaks with faint bitterness.

I say nothing. The answer is "no," but to admit this would be impolite.

She says suddenly, "They are evil, foxes. They steal babies' breath, and possess people like demons, and lure men off the roads to die in the marshes—"

Even knowing she hates to be mocked, I have to laugh. "How do you learn these superstitions? They are suitable for a farmer's wife, but for *you*?"

Unaccountably, she blushes. "*Everyone* knows it. The tales are written down. When have you ever read a story where the foxes in it were not vengeful and evil in their dealings with people?"

"You read too much fiction, wife. They are no more vengeful spirits than you or I are."

"They can destroy everything! Our house, our lives together, our child."

I stare at her in amazement. "Foxes? They don't care at all about us, certainly not to hurt us."

"Don't they?" she says bitterly.

"How could they? What matters to them is life, and their kin, and survival, and—" *Hope,* I do not add. *Joy. Dreams.*

She fiddles with the tasseled fan in her hand, her face averted. "Nevertheless," she says finally.

"I suppose they might bite us all and give us some disease, or we might catch fleas—"

"Do not *mock* me, husband. What have I done to deserve derision?"

She is right, of course. I touch her hand in apology. "Maybe they were never there, wife—the servant panicked over a chip of stone and a long-deserted den."

"They were—here—before. When we were first married and lived here. Remember? We saw them in the woods one night."

"Yes." I'd forgotten, but it comes back to me. "Their wary gold eyes when they saw us . . . but they were charming, until they saw us and fled, so beautiful and quick-moving."

"They were animals," she says flatly.

"It has been years since then. They're gone." I think of the floating hairs and am silent.

She sighs almost inaudibly: "Of course you are right, husband. I am just nervous, here in the country. Forgive me."

She is not convinced, of course: nothing has changed. She only wants it over, and she says what is necessary to end the discussion. I send her away without pointing out the spiderweb as I had planned, too annoyed with her company and myself to watch the moon rise.

23. SHIKUJO'S PILLOW BOOK
Foxes:

I've heard the servant-girl from Uji tell this one to her friend:
A man who shot a fox in its hind leg followed the wounded
animal 'til it led him to his home. Out of reach of his arrow, it
turned into a man with blood running down his leg and a torch
in his hand. The fox man touched the torch to the thatch of the
house, and, becoming a fox again, fled. The house burned down.
The story does not say if anyone was killed, but surely someone
was injured.

This was in a collection of old stories Lady Shōnagon lent me
before we left the capital: a man and his servant went out hunting for a lost horse. Caught by the darkness of a moonless night,
they saw a huge tree, bigger than it could possibly be, and for
some reason feared it might be an evil spirit seeking to lose them
forever in the woods. They shot arrows and hit it, and the tree
vanished. When they returned the next morning, they found a
balding old fox with a tree branch gripped in his jaws and their
arrows sunk in his side.

Even the smallest child knows about foxfire, the dull flames
that rest on foxes' noses and lure people from the marsh-paths
to their deaths on dark nights. My husband has said that this is
an old wives' tale; but my father has seen the flickers over the
marshes of Ichi.

Another: a man weds a woman and does not discover she is
a fox until he sees her tail peeping from under their bedclothes.

And all the tales of foxes overrunning an estate, and making
the lives of the residents miserable — They end well sometimes,
with the master of the house striking a bargain with the foxes,
but only after he has threatened to destroy them utterly.

I do not think we could make deals with *these* foxes.

And one has a tale of her own. When we lived here last, I
had a frightening dream about foxes.

We were recently married. There were no positions available
for a man of his rank and youth, so there was no reason to stay

in the capital. We did not care, then, about living in the wilds, and we loved this house and its gardens, and the mist that lifted from the forest at dawn. There were a thousand things, beautiful and exciting.

My husband was gone on a trip of some sort, and life seemed very difficult. It was summer, and the air was so thick with scents that they gave me headaches. Beyond that, I was not well. I shook with chills or fever, and gasped for breath, and not even curative fires could assuage my ills.

Onaga was afraid for my health. She ordered sutras at the monastery. She wished to call in a priest for an exorcism in case the disease could be removed that way, but when I was a girl I had seen my grandmother's exorcism and it was a horrible thing.

Then, the priest had brought a peasant girl, too young for monthly courses, to my grandmother's sickbed. He chanted and struck at my grandmother with his hands and a peeled-wood stick. The girl began screaming and clawing at her own face, jerking her body as if it were pulled with strings. It was the demon of the disease possessing her. The priest asked the demon which it was, and how he could cure it, but the demon laughed hideously and said the problem was in my grandmother's liver, and that she would die. Which she did, half a month later. The priest dispelled the demon from the medium, but the girl could only lie there, her face dull gray. The demon had dislocated her shoulder, and I watched them push it back into place. I was perhaps six, but this terrified me; even now the smell of burning poppy seeds (for they burned these during the exorcism) makes my heart beat faster.

And so I refused to have a medium for my illness in the country.

The third night of the sickness was the worst. My women were around me, but they were all asleep, which is how I knew it must be a dream since they would never have left me to lie awake in my pain.

I heard a man's voice outside the *kichō*-curtains around my bed. He was singing some peasant's song. To my fevered mind, it sounded a little like animals, yipping in the hills.

"Go away, I am not well," I said, annoyed that my women had let this man in.

"When I have come so far?" he said, from the other side of my screens.

"Who are you," I said crossly, "and what are you doing here?" This was not the capital, where personable young men were thick on the ground; no doubt he was visiting some neighboring estate. There are not any estates close enough for such visits, but it was a dream, after all.

"Let me come behind your curtains," he said. "I mean no harm. I know you are unwell, so I will leave you strictly alone."

I protested, but he pushed a panel aside and slid into the bed enclosure.

It should have been dark, so far in the building as we were, and at night as it was; but we were both clearly visible in what looked like moonlight, cold and clear. I knew I looked terrible: my face flushed, and my hair a mass of tangles. This was, I was sure, not what he had come to call on. I hid my face, but he caught my hands in his. For a second I felt claws against my skin, but when I looked his hands were normal.

"I've watched you and thought of you constantly. I cannot live without you. Please take pity on me."

I had not looked at his face yet: how could I? I was newly married, and shy besides, and puffy with the fever. But now I looked up and saw a fox.

It was a dream, of course; it did not have to make any sense. He was dressed like a gentleman of the fifth rank at court (and here we were in the wilds). His face was a fox's mask: black shiny eyes and a narrow muzzle and broad ears, all shades of cream and rust. And at the same time I saw a man: handsome face round and pale in the shining moonlight, with a noble's black lacquered cap.

He leaned forward (he moved like a man) until his muzzle — his face, I mean, it kept changing in my fever, fox to man and back — was a breath away from my face. I felt warmth on my lips, and he recited a poem.

It was a dream; it does not make sense after that. I remember every other word the fox man spoke, but I cannot remember the poem he said to me then. If it *was* a poem: the images were not the usual ones, being too strong for poetry (or most prose, either). Silk robes pushed aside . . . red *hakama*-trousers and a russet sash thrown over my gold-covered screen . . . a peach-colored paper fan with broken sticks in a tangle by someone's head . . . the feel of skin against fur (or fur against skin? which stroked which?), like patting an animal, or stroking a man . . . warmth, and wet, and a shivering inside. I remember bits, but the poem makes no sense to me.

And then the dream was gone. My husband returned several days later, when I was better, and visited me. But I could not forget the dream.

After I had recovered, I went to a dream-diviner, a tiny wrinkled man who wore skins and lived under a pile of pine branches a day's travel from our home. My women set up a portable screen for my privacy, but I peeked through. His teeth were as black as if he painted them for court. When he cackled—which he did when I offered him a set of undyed silk robes—his mouth looked like a hole. I suppose it was funny: silk to a man wearing skins even a hairy North Island savage would shun.

"Well?" he barked.

I told the bits I recalled. "Can you explain this?" I begged him.

"Only that you are too pretty to be alone in the country."

I had been so careful that he not see me! "What does that mean?"

"Longings cause dreams like these."

"I *caused* this dream?" I asked. "But my husband and I are very well suited! Indeed, we—" I stopped in confusion.

He laughed at me. "Did you think that satisfaction with one's life stops one from wanting other things?"

"I do not!" I exclaimed. "I could not have caused this! I am very well pleased."

"I didn't say *your* longings, did I?"

"But—" I said, through lips suddenly gone numb.

"Forget that. I tease you, is all."

I shrugged impatiently. The man spoke nonsense. "What do I do to stop these dreams?"

"Move back to the city."

Of course, I suggested no such thing; but thereafter I was nervous in our home, and that autumn, before the leaves on the *nikko* maple had fallen and been trampled, Yoshifuji and I returned to the capital.

My husband *must* be careful. He does not understand how dangerous foxes can be.

24. KITSUNE'S DIARY

Safe under an outlying wing, we foxes watched the men mill around the building where our den had been, heard them bark, smelled the excitement on their sweat. When their master vanished underneath, the men remained, scribing little circles of aimless activity, like ants outside a hill.

Energy crackled through me. I wanted to run away; I wanted to snap and snarl and hurt them; mostly I crouched, paralyzed between the two desires, knowing in my bones both were dangerous. Mother whined softly and bellied backwards until Grandfather breathed a snarl at her: dead serious, prepared to draw blood. Crouched next to him, Brother shifted anxiously.

The master reappeared to more barking, more milling; but even over all the other smells, there was something unidentifiable in his scent. I was so tired from the fear and the not knowing what would be next that despite the babbling, I fell into a tight-muscled doze.

"Wake up, Granddaughter. They're all gone inside." It was dark beyond our shelter.

"They would have found us," Brother said wonderingly as he stretched. "You made us leave before they came. You knew they would."

"I suspected," he said.

"Why did they crawl under," I asked, "the one after the other?"

"The master could have lost something," Grandfather said, "dropped some small thing through a crack in the floor. Or he was looking for us."

"But—" I said.

"He would be crazy," Brother said. "It would be like walking into a *tanuki*-badger hole, not knowing if it were there or not."

"Nevertheless," Grandfather said.

Mother spoke: "He smelled strange. Sad. As if a mouse had gotten away. He did lose something, and he wanted to find it in our den."

Nothing made sense. I think the fear turned sour in my blood and made me light-headed, made everything like a dream of a chase.

"We can never go back to our den," Mother said suddenly. "The humans will devour us."

"We're just foxes," Brother said. "We're not edible, unless they're starving, and they're not—I've smelled all their food."

Grandfather barked impatiently. "We're more than food to him. He means no harm to us, but he hunts us just the same."

"That does not make sense," Brother said. "Why?"

"If we wanted to find out, we could ask, I suppose," I said.

Grandfather's ears flattened. "No."

"But if he is harmless—"

"I never said he was harmless. I said he meant no harm."

We scraped out a shallow dig under a gatehouse set into the side wall around the estate. We could watch the gardens and the main house from there, and we could slip out to hunt in the woods behind without being seen. The scrape was cold and rough-sided and smelled of raw dirt. I missed our big old den.

25. SHIKUJO'S PILLOW BOOK
Things that are lonely or frightening:

A doe standing at the forest's edge at dusk, calling for her fawn. She will not find him: we saw him, dead and half-eaten by animals back on the path we traveled to get here. Now she will be alone through the summer and winter, until mating season next year. This seems a long time to wait.

At night in a new place, I listen to the first crickets of the year chirruping all around the house. They fall suddenly silent: what did they hear? What stands outside?

An exorcism. It is frightening enough when it succeeds, but even more horrible when it does not.

Sometimes one wakes up from a terrifying dream. There were mists and voices, two pale mocking foxes, and a snake made of smoke, a man with a stick—too many things to easily recall when at last one sits up in bed, trembling. But one's women are all asleep, and there is no one to listen, to help explain away the dream. That is a very lonely time.

The howlings of wolves, high in the mountains. The roar of a bear. The sight of a fox or a *tanuki*-badger.

Illness. Despair. The loss of hope.

The sudden death-scream of some small animal in the garden. A bowl left overnight on the veranda outside suddenly clatters to the ground. The sounds of breathing outside the *shoji*-screens.

—Really, I do not know why I write this list. In such a place, everything is frightening. I fear the night noises, the solitude, the sense that there are no rules out here to hold us safe. No one here is telling us what is real. How will we know?

26. KITSUNE'S DIARY

I learned more of humans in those first few days than I had ever thought I might want to know.

Of course my brother and I were curious. I have since learned that this is universal among young animals and children. They are like mosquitoes: they have to get their noses into everything, even if they get slapped for it. Even if they die.

We were curious but afraid. My brother and I played in the wilder bits of the garden, away from the sprawled wings of the house. We hunted in the woods, and ate the mice that moved into the kitchen storehouse when the food was placed there. We cached meat when we could, burying it for leaner days. In this we were good.

But we were also *bold* and curious, and we (I especially) could not stay away from the humans. We stayed awake days to hide in the thick bushes and under the walkways, watching them, stalking them when they left the house and stableyard.

It was all fascinating to us. We could not ask Grandfather because then he would know what we did, but we discussed with each other the strange actions we saw, and made wild guesses as to their meanings.

The servants went everywhere. They watered and fed the horses. They yoked the oxen and used them to pull things to and fro. They worked in the kitchen gardens and the rice fields.

There were always a handful of them in the formal grounds chopping at things with axes and saws. "Why are they doing all this?" I asked my brother, but he only snorted.

"Why should I know? Grandfather said they would."

"They have to have a reason for doing things, though, don't they? This doesn't feed anyone, and it doesn't look like play."

There were other things that *did* look like play. Some were obvious: they barked and wrestled and tussled like kits, and chased monkeys and crows when they could; but there were other things that only their excited smell told us were play. Slapping small stones on a low table was play. Drinking *sake* and urinating into the bushes seemed to be play. Mating was play, for them: we found a man and a woman in the bushes one night, and everything smelled and sounded and looked just as we would have imagined, except that it seemed to be fun, as well.

We saw men throw knives at a circle drawn in the dirt. When they did it correctly, the knife-tip bit into the ground.

"Play? Why would they do this?" my brother asked. "It seems completely useless."

"After they all throw, everyone praises a single man," I said. "Maybe this is how they decide who is the dominant person."

"But Yoshifuji never does this, and no one doubts he is the master of the house."

"That is completely different," I exclaimed. "These are mere servants!" I had only an imperfect notion of servant and master, but my brother and I pretended to knowledge, aping old guesses back and forth as if we knew what we were talking about.

"Perhaps it is the same thing as us using claws when we play," my brother whispered.

"Their teeth are such useless things, maybe they make these magic ones of metal."

"And their lips never hide them, so their teeth are always bared," he said, and we watched on.

I never saw the mistress, Shikujo, outdoors: her female attendants almost never. On warm days the screens of her rooms were all pushed back. If I crept under the wisteria, I could see a little way in, but it was all shadows (and dull), and the wisteria was thin cover, at best.

I watched the master, Yoshifuji, much more, because there were so few people around his rooms and I could hide in the lake reeds. He often sat or knelt on one of the main house's broad verandas or just inside an opened screen. Mainly he painted.

This was a more complicated activity than it sounds, a matter of many small wood boxes and their contents. He laid out these things and fiddled for a bit with them and then was still. I would have thought him dozing if it had not been for his smell: taut, like a cat watching a bird, only there was no bird, no prey. Sometimes nothing happened, and he eventually went inside.

Other times, he caught whatever it was he hunted. He uncoiled suddenly, not in a leap, but with a flurry of markings on slips of colored paper. Afterward, he leaned back and eyed his kill.

• • •

I saw Grandfather sometimes, watching the house from a low hill halfway down the garden. I never dared ask him about this.

27. SHIKUJO'S PILLOW BOOK
Lately I have had difficulty:

Lately I have had difficulty sleeping. My women rest as easily as always, so I know it is not merely the weather, which has seemed unseasonably warm at night. I find myself alone in my rooms, listening to their slow even breaths, and to the words the youngest maid slurs out in her sleep. Often I lie in the darkness staring up at the black space under the eaves and I try not to think of the children of my husband's spider.

Other times I design costumes in my mind to wear for imperial holidays, should I ever return to the capital and my responsibilities as a lady-in-waiting to the old princess. If a baby is born to her daughter (recently married to a Fujiwara), I will wear white, of course — everyone wears white on such occasions — but I recall from other such occasions that the attendants end up looking very much the same, despite all their attempts to present a unique and intriguing appearance. And in white, my skill at dying will be irrelevant. So (I ponder as I stare into the blackness overhead), perhaps embroidery? White-on-white brocade? Silver threads stitched into the seams? Multiple cuffs on the Chinese jacket, or a single cuff?

Other times I cannot lie still, and I step carefully over my ladies' sleeping bodies until I reach a screen that can be pushed aside. I look out at the garden, silver in moonlight or dusty with starlight or dim under clouds. For once it is not the wisteria courtyard I watch, but the larger garden, the place of trees and shadows and lakes. The building containing my husband's rooms is to one side. There are times I see the warmth of lamplight through paper windows, and I wish he would visit me, to stop my mind's circuits; but he does not.

I feel strangely free at such times. To behave properly is to be always courteous, always clever and subtle and elegant. But now, when I am so alone, I do not have to be any of these things. For this moment, I am wholly myself, unshaped by the needs of others, by their dreams or expectations or sensibilities.

But I am also lonely. With no one to shape me, who stands here, watching the moon, or the stars, or the clouds? I feel insubstantial, as if the wind might suddenly dissolve me, like a weak mist.

Perhaps my husband feels this all the time. I do not know how he could stand such misery. My proper life at least insulates me from such pain.

28. THE NOTEBOOK OF KAYA NO YOSHIFUJI

My son has been playing in the garden today. The sands around the moon-rock did not look dirty to me, but they have failed to pass some judgment or other, and they have been painstakingly scraped into trays and laid out by the lake. Buckets of clear water were poured over them until the sand showed silver and the water ran out clear. My son sees these tiny fields of wet sand as an opportunity not to be missed, and builds a series of miniature mountains, each terraced with rice paddies. Now he plants cooked rice, one grain to each paddy, with gardeners waiting patiently for the young master's fun to be over so that they can respread the sand where it belongs.

This attempt to make order of disorder, layer on layer, moves me strangely.

I have always been a man of words. Aren't we all? Words are what earn official positions or court lovers. We learn to shape attractive characters as soon as we are old enough to hold a child's brush. We learn the informal *kana*-script of love notes, and the ancient Chinese formal language of philosophical debate and examinations. We learn how to use these two styles together in elaborate puns. Words define us; they will define this moment: my son, the rice.

I look through my writing desk until I find a single sheet of translucent paper spangled with threads of milkweed. I pull an ink stick from my writing box, drip water into the little hollow on my ink stone, and rub the stick back and forth against the stone until it grinds down and the water turns as black and thick as oil. I dip the wolf's-hair brush into the pool of ink and hold it over the paper, waiting for the words, the image, to come. This poem will be about my son, but will make sense, somehow, of this restlessness, of our being here, of the hole under the house that held no more than a stone.

But writing is like trying to smooth ripples from water with one's hand—the more I try, the more disturbed things get.

And the ink dries there, on the brush above the unwritten poem, until in frustration I wash it clean and leave my table.

29. KITSUNE'S DIARY

One night Yoshifuji left his sheets of paper out on the veranda. Mother was already gone; having caught a squirrel early, Grandfather was napping in our scrape.

"Come on," I said to my brother. "Let's go see."

"What?" he said warily. "The master—"

"Inside," I said scornfully. "It's late. There's nothing to be afraid of. Don't you want to see what he does up there?"

"Yes, but—"

I growled at him and he subsided. I forced him up onto the broad wood planks. The screens were all closed, but I heard Yoshifuji's even breathing. He was asleep.

We eased forward until we stood beside the low table. Smelling faintly of dried mud, a cake of ink lay in a shallow dish. A small red pot held brushes made of hair bound to bamboo sticks with waxed thread. A few sheets of paper had slipped to the floorboards, but most lay heaped on a corner of the table, silver and shiny white and bright red paper splashed with black ink like the markings on a moth's back. They were nonsense.

"There has to be more to this," I breathed.

Brother sniffed a page. "It smells like him. Is this some form of scent-marking?"

"It would be like taking all day to mark a leaf, and it's not urine, so the smell won't last, anyway. And what's he marking here that doesn't already smell of him?"

"And why would he spend so much time at it?"

I pushed at the pages on the table with my nose, and they cascaded to the floor. Squiggles and squiggles. Sometimes the squiggles made shapes that looked somehow familiar.

"Look at this." Brother pawed at a sheet of paper so white it almost glowed, and the ink looked like holes in its shining surface. And then the image shifted inside my eye. The brushstrokes were not flat, after all: they outlined light and shadow and gave depth to the page.

This happens often enough to humans that they give it a name: *satori,* a sudden reseeing of things. But this was my first experience with it. I looked *past* the paper, into the shadows. I saw a picture.

Two half-grown foxes nearly hidden in a clump of ornamental grass beside a great stone: one lay on his side, panting in the day's heat; the other sat upright, her ears pricked forward, watching something.

"There are foxes in the paper," I breathed. The fur on the female's side was rucked up where she had just scratched. The male had a ragged white blaze running down his face. A breeze ruffled their fur to show the white undercoat. I sniffed the paper and smelled ink and, dimly, Yoshifuji's hand. All this was really just strokes of a brush.

Brother said with awe: "That was us, this afternoon."

"No," I said, not sure it was not. What if it was? The female's—my—eyes gleamed half-lidded. When I bent close, I saw the dried black lake of brushstrokes that made a pupil, and a tiny island of uninked paper in the middle, the gleam.

What did that mean, if we were there on the page and here, in ourselves, at the same time? If ink and paper were somehow also us? Black spangles hovered around the ink-foxes' heads: the flies had been thick, this afternoon.

I said, "How did he know what we looked like?"

"He must have seen us," Brother said. We looked at each other and bolted.

Later, in the security of the gatehouse scrape, while my mother hunted, I lied to my grandfather.

"We found a page of paper loose in the garden."

Grandfather was gnawing at a flea bite, but he looked sharply at me. "And . . ."

"It was a picture."

"And you saw it."

"Not at first," Brother began, but I interrupted.

"You know about pictures."

"Yes." Grandfather eased the leg down stiffly, and stretched.

"How can he do that?" Brother asked. "There is not anything really in the paper, is there?"

"No. Yes. Art is itself, but also the thing it appears to be." We looked at him, confused, and he sighed. "Like the moon and its reflection in a puddle. The puddle does not have the real moon. If you bite it, it shatters, it is just water in the dirt. But every detail of the moon is there, so, yes, it is the moon. What was it of, this reflection?"

"Of us, Grandfather," Brother said.

There was silence for a long breath. "That *is* bad."

"Why did he draw us, Grandfather?" I said, desperately. "We were careless to let him see us, which was a mistake; but what good does it do him, to draw us? What can he want?"

"The least of it is that you were seen. They have a place in themselves we lack: a soul. This is what makes him watch."

I did not understand. What was a soul? And I wondered how this was different from my grandfather on a hill, watching the humans.

30. THE NOTEBOOK OF KAYA NO YOSHIFUJI

I watch my son, and I watch the foxes. The foxes and the boy share certain things. Life is new. They eat with delight, sleep with abandon, play when they can. They laugh, or rather, my son laughs, and I imagine that the foxes laugh: they seem capable of it, anyway. They have the same sorts of adventures, the adventures of novelty.

I watched the two young foxes today, as they rested by the lake before sunset. When dusk came, they stretched and shook themselves, for all the world like Tadamaro awakening from a nap. One snapped at an insect of some sort and caught it in its (his? her?) mouth. I think it stung him (or her, but let us say "him") then, for he jumped straight into the air, and bolted toward the side gate, tongue hanging out. The other fox loped after.

This is very much the sort of thing Tadamaro would do if he were a fox. And when he climbs into the roof over my rooms, hunting for baby mice in the thatch, I can only imagine the foxes would do something similar if they could.

The difference is that my son will learn painful lessons, and at some point one spring will feel very like every other spring. And the foxes will learn nothing, but they will at least enjoy themselves.

31. SHIKUJO'S PILLOW BOOK
On the first day of the fourth month:

This is the day the season officially changes. My women are shaking out my bright summer silks, and folding my heavier robes away in the newly emptied trunks. Now, even if it rains — even if it *snows*, unlikely though that would be — I will wear these clothes.

I've been watching spring shift into summer. The rains have

finally stopped, and the sun shines late enough into the night that I can read an entire *monogatari*-tale in a day. The trees' leaves have shifted from their young translucent greens to darker, more permanent shades. The air itself seems to grow heavy with heat, humidity, pollens, scents.

The darkness of my rooms is welcome when the outside world is so bright. With the walls pushed back, breezes pull the rich scented air through — how I wish I could mix a perfume that has this taste of young summer in it! Our diet is certainly getting better, as the new cabbages and other garden things come in.

But none of these things is as sudden as the calendar's change, spring to summer in a day. It is incontestably summer today, but it was not incontestably spring yesterday.

Where is the true line between the seasons? Things become easier as it becomes summer, as food becomes better and it stays light into the evenings and the weather turns gentler. Perhaps we will be fine here, and things will improve. Happiness is not a thing of absolutes, either.

32. KITSUNE'S DIARY

It turned out to be a harder life than we had thought.

Our new scrape under the side gatehouse was small and raw: only two small holes and a single tunnel, dug in a day from rocky dirt that sifted down on us whenever we moved. The side gatehouse had been abandoned by the humans for many years, and now was no more than a ruin: a single tiny structure, roofed in shingles, walled in wattle, gated in pine. Its raised floor was close enough to the ground that I lowered my head when I stood beneath it, and even so, my eyebrow whiskers brushed the rough boards. Sometimes Mother mourned for our old den: once she woke me up as she stepped across me in her sleep, trying to return to the burrow in full daylight. We held her down until she woke up whimpering. Sometimes I wanted to go home, too, even knowing it was no longer home.

The advantage the side gatehouse had was that it was ignored by the humans, built into the fence bordering the formal grounds. People had to walk along a long and narrow (and treacherous, from a human's perspective) walkway with no railings and a broken roof to get to it. Mostly they did not. The major domo, Hito, brought a carpenter to look at the side gate and the walkway roof. They seemed to decide against repairs. After that, it was ours alone.

We could escape to either side of the fence. Outside the garden was a narrow track no wider than a pawprint. Overgrown with tendrils of ivy, the path skirted the plaited cypress fence, leading down to the road or up to the ridge path. Edged by forest, we walked there often, but hunting in the woods was no more than adequate, and we ate up our caches almost as soon as we buried them. I think we were not very good at hunting; the garden had spoiled us.

If we slipped out on the garden side, we were hidden in a patch of rhododendron growing through leaf-strewn sand. From there, it was simple enough to creep unseen into the formal garden or along the back of the enclosure, to the stableyard or the kitchen garden.

It did us little good. The servants cut back the growth in the formal garden, and there were fewer mice and rabbits to eat. Those that remained and bred were warier and more clever. The tempting foods the humans brought were locked away in a storehouse that stood in the center of the kitchen garden. The servants did throw food leavings into the midden heap in the kitchen garden's corner, but we got sick more than once from eating rotting fish entrails.

Still, it was easiest to steal food. It was dangerous, but we were young, my brother and I, and never thought of death. We crouched in the shadow of the storehouse, nostrils filled with the strange, rich scents over our heads, and watched everything that went on in the garden, waiting.

The cook, a huge man with eyes lost in rolls of fat, came out some days and pulled roots from the dirt. Sometimes he would drop one, and I would wait until his back was turned, and run

out, exposed to the world, and snatch it. This was mostly un-
satisfactory. Roots are poor fare; even as a woman I have
thought so.

Often the cook came to the storehouse. In our hiding place
beneath we eased farther back, listened to the latch lift, the door
slide open, and the man's heavy footsteps over our heads, one
board creaking; and then the sounds of his leaving, the latch
being secured and sounds of his footsteps scuffing up the walk
to the house.

One day we listened, and there were the noises, just as there
should be, but—the latch was not closed. I looked at my
brother, who crouched beside me. There was no reason to speak.
We knew what we wanted. No one was in the garden. We
crawled out, and ducked in the open storehouse door.

There were the foods, just as we had smelled them: a hanging
yamadori-pheasant and dried fish, pickled radishes, *sake* and vinegar. We knocked over jars and chewed open boxes and ate and
ate.

The shout at the door took us completely by surprise. The
cook was back: he cursed at us, at the damage we'd done. I
spun around, but there was nowhere to hide; I backed into a
corner and bared my teeth. The cook slammed the door shut,
and this time we heard the latch.

A fox always has an escape route. We hid in small places,
and slept every day in a hole in the ground, but there was always
a bolt-hole, someplace to run. Except here, in this storehouse. I
had never been closed in like this. Panicked, I tore at the boxes,
at the walls, at the tiny cracks in the floor. I cracked my claw
and left threads of blood where I scrabbled. I smelled the
copper-dirt smell of the blood, and beyond that, the air outside,
clean and sunbaked, crisp with azalea and pine.

"Out! Out!" my brother was keening. Far out of reach, a tiny
pale patch of sky showed in the triangular screened eave-
opening. He jumped from the barrel toward the light again and
again. Each time, he fell hard to the floor. He fell on me once,
and I ripped blindly at him.

Voices. The door was suddenly thrown wide. Waving a knife

and barking with rage, the cook stood too close to the door to
slip past him. Several male servants off to the side held poles
and barked to one another.

A huddle of brightly dressed women stood behind the cook,
a child clinging to the robe of one. They gravitated around a
single woman in rich robes, with a huge red fan concealing her
face. I knew she was the mistress of the house, Shikujo, though
I had never seen her or her women in full daylight before.

Shikujo tilted her fan slightly to stare in at us. Light through
the fan colored her skin crimson, but I could see she was very
beautiful. Her face was round as the moon. Her mouth was fine-
lipped and small, open over tiny even teeth. Her eyes were deep
black, and met mine. A killer meets the eyes of its prey: a superior among foxes stares at lower-level members, who avert
their faces. She was not killer or prey or fox, and still she sought
my eyes.

A jolt ran through my body, as if I had run full-speed into a
chest-high wall. Terrified, I growled. She screamed and jumped
back.

"Foxes!"

I understood her. For the first time, I heard the humans'
barking as speech, as communication. And I could understand
the others, as well. The men shouted for assistance and spears.
One woman, older than the others, held Shikujo's sleeve and
insisted she go back inside. Shikujo only watched with her black
eyes.

"Yoshifuji," she said. "Where is my husband?" She smelled
of, she sounded filled with, fear.

This broke me out of my panic. *She* was afraid of *us*? She
had all the advantages—servants and weapons and all the incomprehensible powers of humans—and we were only half-
grown foxes trapped without escape in a storeroom.

"He's coming!" There was a flurry of noise from the crowd,
and the master walked to stand beside Shikujo.

This was Kaya no Yoshifuji: the master of this house. He was
in hunting dress, blue and gray, with dull silver medallions woven into the pattern of his outer robe. In one hand he held a

short bow; arrows stuck over one shoulder from a quiver on his back. His hair was oiled and arranged in a loop over his head. His eyes were deepest black; his voice when he spoke was low and humorous.

"Shut up, all of you! You are making it worse."

"Husband!" Shikujo cried. She was shaking. "Destroy them!"

"They are only animals—foxes, young foxes. Quiet, you are frightening them."

"Frightening *them?*" Shikujo's voice cut across the babble. Later I realized that many of the humans would never have seen her or even heard her voice before, and this is why the crowd fell silent. "No! Foxes are evil—*everyone* knows this. Kill them, please!" Her voice broke. There was water on her face.

"Go." Yoshifuji made a gesture at the cook and other men-servants staring openmouthed at Shikujo. They ran away, up the path and into the house. The women hovered protectively around Shikujo until he waved them away, too, leaving a mere handful of attendants around her.

My lord turned to Shikujo. "Wife, what is this? You've always been a lady, and I find you barefaced and screeching like a *sake* seller. What are you thinking, to forget yourself so?"

"Well, *you* went under the house like a servant—"

"Is that what this is about?"

She looked at the fan in her hand. "No. I am so sorry, husband, you are quite right, I've behaved like a peasant, but—foxes, they are so dangerous. I had to know—for Tadamaro's sake. Please kill it now."

"If it were a squirrel doing this, would you want it killed?"

"Yes," she said, but then added, "Foxes are evil spirits. All the tales say so."

"Evil? What harm have they done? Knocked over a few boxes? They're simple animals. If we give them a chance, they'll run off on their own; undoubtedly, after this exhibition they will never be back, and you can be comfortable again." Yoshifuji touched her fingers where they twisted on the fan's sticks, and stopped them. "Go inside."

Her head was down, but she looked in at us with a slantwise

gaze. I felt my ears flatten again, my back prickle with lifting hairs. "Your foxes. *Anyone* would kill them — but they possess you, husband, just as surely as if their spirits possessed your body."

"Go," he said again, angry this time, and Shikujo left us.

Yoshifuji knelt in the dirt by the doorway for a long moment with his hand over his eyes. "Ah, well, little foxes, so it goes, eh? —

> *If you are simply a fox,*
> *then I must be the complicated one."*

I recognize now that what he said was a poem, even though I did not know then what a poem was. It is a human thing; I do not know how well a fox will ever understand it, even a fox woman.

He stood and brushed at his knees. "I will be back in a bit. It would be wise to be gone before then." He paused. "Run, little foxes. Be free while you can."

I could not stop watching him as he walked up to the house. It was not until my brother bit me on the shoulder that I followed him through the door.

33. THE NOTEBOOK OF KAYA NO YOSHIFUJI

> *Foxes half-seen in the darkness;*
> *I courted knowing less of my lady.*

*A*m I obsessed with the foxes? I had not thought so. I drew them, yes, and I wrote poetry about them; I thought about what a fox's life might be like; on my long walks, I have sometimes hoped I might come near a fox. I certainly crawled under the house hoping to see one. I had not thought of this as an obsession. If this is, I have been obsessed with every woman (or man) I've slept with, with my son, with poetry, with every *go* game I've played, with the twisted little maple that grew in the central courtyard of the house in the capital, with the herb balls my wife hangs from the eaves for New Year's. The foxes are filled with life, immortality of a sort, and this draws me to them: one fox is replaced by another as they die and are born; foxness, the state of being foxes, remains.

But Shikujo fears the foxes with all her heart.

34. KITSUNE'S DIARY

We bolted out of the storehouse, ran the shortest distance toward the woods, north across hillocks of beans to the back wall of the property. We squirmed on our bellies under a tied-bamboo gate and ran and ran, and we did not stop until Brother dropped to the ground, heaving with exhaustion.

We hid shivering under a collapsed and rotting cedar tree.

"How did we get free?" Brother asked, when he could breathe easily again, but I was still off-balance. I did not know what had happened to me, in the time I had looked at Yoshifuji's eyes. All I knew was that I felt dizzy and confused, and the feeling did not go away when my heart and breath returned to normal.

At dusk, Grandfather came into the woods, and we ran to him and Brother told him our story: the humans' speaking, and Yoshifuji's leaving us alone. Brother besieged him with questions: why did he let us live? Why did he make his wife go back inside? At the end, the extraordinary words he spoke to us: what were they? Question, question, question. Grandfather did not say much, just led us back towards our scrape.

I spoke at last. "The woman. Her face was wet. There was — a look —"

"Tears, child. You understand them or you do not. There is no explaining."

I learned to cry that night. Crouched together in the scrape, my family listened in silence. After a time, Grandfather laid his muzzle against mine.

"Is this sadness?" I said. "How can I live through it?"

"You have magic in you. That is how you can cry, and how you will survive."

"All foxes have magic, Grandfather," I said. "They don't all cry."

"Not this magic," he said. "This magic is love."

BOOK TWO: SUMMER

Now summer's come,
smoky torches at every house
drive away mosquitoes —
and I — how long will I go on
smoldering with love?

—ANONYMOUS, FROM THE KOKINSHŪ
TRANSLATED BY BURTON WATSON

1. KITSUNE'S DIARY

It was summer, and I was in my first heat.

I was young for this, but I had been born out of season and now I burned out of season, my mother's daughter. I fought constantly with my family. The smell of my mother made me berserk; one night I attacked her fiercely enough that she ran from the scrape and hid in the woods. My brother had vanished as well; I suppose he and Grandfather had also fought. Even being near my grandfather annoyed me. I snapped at him any chance I got.

I knew this fever that ran under my skin for what it was, my heat; but knowing this did not make any difference to my restlessness or my hostility. I lay nearly unconscious from the feel of my own now-unfamiliar blood throbbing through me. I shivered sometimes, as if itchy, hot and cold all at once. It was the same feeling I've felt before a thunderstorm when the air almost crackles; but heavy, blood-filled.

Grandfather kept following me and nuzzling my flanks. It was affectionate, but drove me to madness. The only place he would not follow me was under the house.

Human words and mannerisms seemed a waste of time just then, when I was throbbing and irrational; but to be free of the world, with Kaya no Yoshifuji's scent in my nose — this was the closest to ease I found. Too restless to lie still, I hid beneath his rooms and paced with the footsteps overhead.

One night it was raining and so I paced in utter darkness. My master and his wife sat in her rooms. Her women were all asleep or silent; only the creak of a floorboard when one shifted her weight told me they were there at all. Yoshifuji and Shikujo talked and talked, as unending as the stream to the lake. I was too absorbed in my own discomfort to pay much attention until I heard Shikujo moan softly and realized they had stopped talking some time before that. Then I stood alert, ears and nostrils focused upward.

This was human sex. I heard the sounds. I know now, learned

soon enough, that this was kissing: mouth tasting mouth, lips
and tongues and teeth. Then it seemed incomprehensible, as if
each partner were tasting some dainty food.

Silk brushed away from skin, and flesh stroked flesh. How
could I tell who touched whom? It did not matter. His breathing
was ragged; hers was languorous, but it caught in her throat
sometimes. I smelled her musk, his sweat.

It was not like my heat, an uncomfortable irritable experience.
There was a delicacy to the humans' sex, an elegance. The only
word she spoke was his name, once, on an unsteady sigh. I
whined softly and arched my hips.

"Sister." I whirled when I heard my brother's breath in my
ear. He had returned from wherever he was hiding. He smelled
hot, restless.

"Are you sick?" I breathed back; but we must both have been
sick: me to hunger in so exposed a place, Brother to sneak back
into grandfather's territory and follow me here and make noise
so close beneath the humans. His ears flattened, but he snaked
against me. I felt the heat of his flank and could not help pressing against him.

"Your smell —" He rubbed his muzzle along my neck ruff.
His own scent was thick and musky.

"Leave me alone," I snapped, but I kneaded at the dirt and
twisted my face to his shoulder.

"Why, Sister? I can smell the itch on you. I have it, too. Why
are we flat in the dirt here, instead of running in the moonlight,
hot with this?" He never dared, my quiet brother, but now he
leaned his paws over my shoulder, hind legs shifting behind me.
He bit my neck hard enough to hurt.

I writhed away. "Animal!" A new word, an unfamiliar one,
meaning somehow base. It must have come from the humans'
words: I had never used it, or thought it before. He seemed as
surprised as I.

"What?"

"Listen. *That's* what I want. That — elegance. Beauty."

Brother snarled, as if tired of my mood. "Do you? We're *foxes*.
It's not that way for us, it's hot and strong and — can't you *smell*

what it's supposed to be like? It's *rut*, Sister. Who smells right, he or I—who will you crouch for?"

He nipped at me and nipped at me. I whirled to bite him, kill him, anything to stop his harassment and my anger and wanting; he grabbed my neck, pressed me chest-down in the dirt, and mounted me. I snarled and fought when he jabbed into me; but he had me between his forelegs, under his teeth.

This is the way of fox-sex, hard and panting and fast. He entered me suddenly with his hot unsheathed penis, thrust quickly, and spent. A quiver ran through my entire body, a knotting and release as sudden and sweet as the flash of blood across my tongue when I bit a rabbit's throat.

Afterward was uncomfortable. He stayed inflated in my vulva (also the way of fox-sex; I knew this in my blood, as surely as if I'd experienced it before) so we could not separate; but he moved off me, and we shifted until we stood tail to tail, linked by his penis. I hung my head and shivered from the dissolving hunger, sides heaving, blood drying on the bite marks in my flanks.

The spear came from nowhere and stabbed at us. Brother screamed and tore free of me; and *I* screamed from the pain in my vulva, ripped raw.

Later, when I had time to think, I knew Yoshifuji and his wife must have heard us mating and sent a servant to chase us away. I must have noticed the noises and the dim light of his approach and, exhausted, ignored them. People make noise as constantly as a river; their lights are everywhere, as senseless as fireflies. How could any particular noise in such a flood be important? This is a human trick. I have used it myself as a woman, to conceal a true or hard word in an ocean of noise.

Then, all I knew was pain; the smell of the spear's metal head; someone shouting "Fox!"; torches and flight; and, finally, the moon-rock. I lay in its shadow, pressed against its cool pockmarks, until I stopped shivering and could limp home.

2. THE NOTEBOOK OF KAYA NO YOSHIFUJI

My wife stands behind me, watching the torches hare off into the rain. They bob around like marsh gas in the garden for a while and eventually straggle back through the gate to the stableyard. "They got away," I say finally. "Whatever they were."

"Foxes. You know they are foxes. And they are not gone."

Her voice trembles. The light is dim, but when I turn I see her face, wet with tears. She holds her night robes loosely around her as a child bundles in quilted sleeping robes. Shocked, I touch her arm. "Come inside, wife."

"Do not touch me. Please. My lord." She averts her face and hurries in to sit on a mat behind a curtain. I am her husband, so I follow her and sit beside her. Her women cluck around us, arranging Shikujo's hair and robes, until Onaga waves them away like an impatient farmwife shooing hens.

"Cannot you see she does not want you all? Go, go, go. Mistress, you are not well. You've been terrified, kept outside like a peasant—" She glares at me, gestures to one of the women. "Go, get her something warm to drink. Give her *room*, if you please, my lord."

"I did nothing," I say mildly, but she ignores me. The warm broth in a little dish and all Onaga's fussing fail to stop my wife's crying, which has the steady hopelessness of autumn rain. At last Shikujo says, "Go away." It is a moment before I realize she means Onaga, and not me.

We sit in silence. Her tangled hair hangs between us, a curtain more impenetrable for being less formal than the silk of the curtain beside us. The humid air feels cold and wet against my skin.

There should be something I can say to stop the hopeless crying. "I am sorry," I breathe at last, knowing this is not it. But I am: sorry for her tears, for her feeling this way; sorry for the foxes and for my interest; sorry for the summer that settles around us here, which is nowhere. For my existence. My chest hurts, a clenching pang. Numbly I watch her weep.

Her voice when she speaks is low and flat. "This house is cursed."

"It is just a house." Even I hear the foolishness of my words. It is not just a house; for me it is a punishment — or a place to escape to, a place to remember bright *nows*. "We liked being here before, you and I."

"The foxes did not haunt us then. You did not paint them, or write poems to them, or talk about them in your sleep."

"I do that?" I say, startled.

"You have." She rocks so slightly I think she is not aware of it, like a hurt child cuddling itself when no gentle adult is near.

"I suppose I dream of them; I dream of a lot of things."

If she were not my wife, I'd swear the sound she makes is a disbelieving snort.

"Is that what this is about?" I say. "You're jealous? There were *always* other things in my life. My duties and my friends and the ten thousand things — " Mistresses, of course: poems and sex; flirtations with other noblewomen. A gentleman can do no less. She knows this; I know this. She has never been jealous of the other women, my perfect wife. I thought.

"No. There is more to this than foxes," I say, knowing it is true. "What really bothers you?"

She smoothes a fold in her sleeve so that it curves in a perfect arc from wrist to floor: creating order, even as the tears still shine almost forgotten on her cheeks. "What do you see, when you see them?"

"When I see what?" I ask, then continue without waiting for her answer, suddenly tired of playing this nasty little game with my wife, too tired to speak anything but the truth. "They seem so — free. Alive. Joy-filled. More than anyone, anything else we know."

"Joy? They are *animals*, and you place this 'joy' on them. They feel nothing — not as we do anyway; I am sure they feel pain and — " she hesitated " — lust, passion: the mating instinct anyway. But that is all it is, all any of it is: instinct. They eat and mate, and are as hemmed in by these needs as we are by our fates."

"Are they?" I know that *we* are, but I do not want to think that there is no freedom anywhere. "Perhaps their karma permits them dreams."

She shivers, perhaps from the memory of the foxes' mating screams under the building. "Perhaps. But there are so many stories, about men offering a pretty woman a ride, and she is a fox; or the men who saw vast mansions all lit up in the marshes, and there was nothing there when they came to them—"

"You say I'm obsessed, but it seems to me that you've thought about them at least as much as I."

"How could I not," she says sharply, "when I see your thoughts full of this fantasy?"

"Fantasy? You said yourself. They eat. They mate—under our house, sometimes, but they mate. They play. I expect they sleep and defecate and fight, too. They are nothing *but* reality, wife, more real than this life of ours."

"What do you mean by that?"

I wave my hand at the civilized room, at the jagged shapes hurled by the iron lamp that hangs near us. The ironwork is formed to look like grass bent in the wind around the flame. This lamp is two hundred years old, pounded out by a blind smith—an heirloom of my wife's family. "We look at this instead of the true grass, and this is art. The foxes lie in real grass. They get their light filtered through real reeds. There is no illusion at all in their lives. No art, no artifice. Sometimes it seems as if we were the ghosts, and they flesh."

"They will destroy us." Caught in her private misery, she has heard nothing I've said.

"They did not before, when we first lived here—why would they now?"

She stands. "I must return to my wing. I do not feel well."

"You're just going to walk away from this," I say, "as if this conversation were of less account than a poetry exchange. You can do that? Not stay and see this discussion to its resolution?"

"This seems like an intellectual exercise to you; but to me it is very real. Forgive me; I will not irritate you with my opinion about this again. Please excuse me."

She raises her hands to her forehead in a very proper gesture of respect, then walks out before I gather my thoughts enough to speak. This slick courtesy of hers is the strongest weapon she has. She may forget her place (a subjective thing, a woman's place. I know women at court who can say any outrageous thing with impunity: a man, as I've learned, does not have these options); I could go after her, force the argument if I wanted, but what would be the point? She has given up already. If she will not fight, there will be only me ranting at her.

But I know she left upset, because she forgot to take back her moon-shaped fan, which still lies beside my bed. I run my finger along its pale surface. I look at the foxes and see freedom and joy. She looks at them, and sees — something. Who can tell what? She will not say. Perhaps she sees the joy, the freedom, too, and that is what she fears. This annoys me: all her energy spent pushing away the very thing I crave. But at the same time, she has been more interesting in her anger about this thing than she has ever been in her correctness.

Was I right to press her so hard? Would I have been so defensive if I did not think I was in the wrong? Not in thinking these things, no — how can I help that? — but in insisting she think them as well? She has a right to her own thoughts, I suppose.

Bamboo ribs show between the fan's layers of thin paper. Are freedom and joy in these creatures an illusion? Maybe I stain their actions with my own longings. The law of karma says their freedom is an illusion, as it is in all of us. As it is in me.

I lean back against my pillow. Its cool maple saddle cradles my neck. The rain has stopped, but the eaves still drip. Overhead, the spiderweb glistens in the moonlight that filters through the eave openings. The gossamer lines are almost too fine to see as anything but a lightening of the darkness. I've seen the spider whose web it is, a gray lady as broad as my son's hand. Knowing what she looks like makes it easy to find her, even in the gloom.

She hangs in an especially dark corner, near a furred gray shape that clings to a beam. A mouse she has somehow amazingly caught and hauled up? I squint a long time before I realize: it is an egg sac. She is breeding.

She exists, and soon (no doubt to my regret) her children will exist. Her life is no fancy. Surely *she* has freedom. Her very absence of mind must make it impossible for her to doubt as she treads out the measure of her fate. Can the foxes be any different?

Freedom? When I can brush away her entire web and all her children with a single broom stroke? Or less: when I can wave my hand, and another does the work?

She has no freedom; the foxes have none; my wife and I have none.

When the oil in the lantern burns low, I make ink and wet my boldest brush. The surface of the fan is so white, so blank. I write on it.

> *The spider's web can catch the moonlight,*
> *but cannot keep it.*

3. SHIKUJO'S PILLOW BOOK
How a man should act after a disagreement:

How sweet it would be if he were to send a poem apologizing for having disturbed one's serenity! It would be nice to be sure he even thought of one after one left. A poem, after all, requires but a moment's thought, another moment's act, if it comes at all.

Certainly he should be gentler, until all is forgotten. He should understand that one says these things not from a sense of contrariety, but from fear and love. You would not want him hurt, and they pull at him, the foxes.

Best of all would be never to disagree. You were so afraid for him, and so you spoke more abruptly than you would have otherwise. Why can he not see that it is concern that drives you?

Conflict is never welcome. It is better avoided, even at the cost of honesty.

4. KITSUNE'S DIARY

I limped back to the scrape. Brother was nowhere to be seen. Mother was back, lying under the rhododendrons. She ignored me, all her attention caught up by a mayfly that hung just in front of her nose. I think she thought that if she did not see me, I would naturally not see her. But this was my mother: perhaps she had forgotten my heat. Perhaps she truly saw only the insect.

Grandfather walked across and sniffed at my hindquarters. I flinched when his nose touched the torn flesh.

"This is not what I wanted," I sobbed. "I want — "

"Kisses. Soft words. Love. Human things." He nosed along my flank. "I know."

"But — "

"Do you think you're the first fox to have fallen in love with men?" he said shortly. "It is common as ditchwater. Their tales are full of it. We see them; some of us learn to hope for things we cannot have. You are not the first. You will not be the last, either. We are susceptible: wise enough to see something, foolish enough to think that's what it is like."

"They were so beautiful — "

"Beautiful," he snorted. "Not even for humans is it that. We see the surface, not into their hearts. There is pain, inside and out, and there is loneliness, and, even for them, heat is heat and needs to be satisfied."

And he mounted me. We were animals and this is what animals do. He was the head of my family; my grandfather probably; my father possibly; but mostly he was a male, and, sore as I was, I was still in heat and hungering.

My heat, my matings, did not take. I had no kits then.

5. SHIKUJO'S PILLOW BOOK
It seems it will never stop raining:

It seems it will never stop raining. It poured rain all through the Sweet-flag Festival, which restricted our celebrations to what could be done inside: hanging medicine balls, decorating our hair with iris, hanging special mottled green-and-white blinds. I know iris leaves were stuffed into the roof-thatch of the building, but only by hearsay, as I have not actually left my rooms in several days. Still, whenever the rain eases a bit I see purple, yellow and white blurs by the lakes. I am sure these are irises, and I expect they are quite lovely.

I sat with Onaga in my rooms, poring over a letter from my mother. Her calligraphy is always difficult to interpret, since she tends to write quickly and with a nearly dry brush, which makes her characters fade into the paper at times. I often require Onaga's assistance in reading my mother's writing. So far as we could tell, after some time spent in perusal, my father is well, my brothers are well, my old nurse and the kitchen cat and everyone are, in fact, well. The household (minus the cat) leaves for the house on Lake Biwa in a few days—those days now long past in the time it took this letter to arrive from the capital.

Unable to get outdoors, Tadamaro was practicing his characters. He knelt over a small desk on the veranda just outside the room, nose nearly touching his work, a smear of ink on one sleeve. Beside him, Tadamaro's nurse basted together the pieces of a new robe, in an attractive but sturdy silk patterned with kites. Her stitches are grown large. He grows so fast and is so active that he constantly rips the seams of his clothing; perhaps she has given up on making anything that will last more than a handful or two of days.

Tadamaro's brush slipped from his hand and rolled out of reach, leaving a thick black mark across the planks. He sighed heavily and cleared his throat. His nurse raised her eyebrow at the sound, but made no attempt to retrieve the brush, continuing

her large even stitches as if nothing had happened. "Nurse?"
Tadamaro said. "Pick up my brush."

Silence: stitching. Ordinarily I would not permit a servant
(even a relatively elevated servant) to disobey my son, but I said
nothing, trusting that this was a lesson she was teaching him. It
seemed to be so, for after a time he sighed again and untangled
himself from his writing desk so that he could retrieve the brush.

"My lady?" Onaga frowned at the letter in her hand. "I cannot figure out what the lady your mother writes here. Can she
really be saying that the *fish* are thriving?"

She might indeed. My father has a new hobby, having to do
with carp bred for exotic characteristics. By the time this was
explained, Tadamaro had vanished.

> *Perhaps I called your name so loudly*
> *trying to outshout my panicked pulse.*

He returned some time later, soaked to the skin from the
interminable rain, carefully carrying something small in one corner of his now mud-brown robe. "I found this," he told me, and
showed it to me. "Beneath Father's rooms."

I ignored Onaga's horrified cry when I took my son's finding
in my hand. It was a slip of soft mouse-gray paper, with startling
black characters drawn as fine as whiskers or toenails. I bent
closer to read whatever poem might be there, and my son said,
"Someone has eaten it, see?"

And he pointed to its ripped-out throat, and I realized that
in some unfathomable way I had mistaken things. The slip was
not paper, but in truth a killed mouse. I screamed and dropped
it and ran to the darkness of my innermost room. And even
there, I could not forget that for the instant I held it, the object
truly seemed both paper and mouse.

I am afraid. What is wrong with me? With all of us?

6. KITSUNE'S DIARY

The moon returned to full before I crept again onto the veranda of Yoshifuji's wing. The weather had been dry for
several days, and he had taken to sitting outside again. He left
his writing things out (he did this a lot: I did not realize until I
was myself a woman how strange such carelessness was), but
there were no drawings this time, only sheet after sheet covered
with tracings of ink.

Smudged with black markings, a round white fan lay half-
hidden in a drift of papers. I pressed my nose to it. It had the
slight sourness of the paper and glue, and the mud-scent of ink;
and faintly, like a reflection on water, his own smell, musk and
tiger lilies somehow mixed together.

It was easy to pick up by the handle, but surprisingly awkward. I carried a *uguisu*-nightingale in my mouth once, and one
wing kept flopping free and dragging on the ground. This was
like that. I lifted my head high and took hesitant steps, trying
not to drag the fan or trip on it.

I knew it made me dangerously visible, this huge moon-shape
glowing dim white in the night, but I carried it anyway, and felt
sick with relief when I got it into the shadows of the rhododendrons outside the scrape. Holding it between my paws, I tried
to snuffle free the smell of him.

"Sister?" After my heat had passed, my brother had returned,
and, strangely, my grandfather had allowed him to do so. It was
as if we were kits again.

"Leave me alone," I said, a sort of refrain I found myself using
again and again with him.

My brother would have run away at my anger a month before. He was growing stronger. "Why did you take that?" he
said, and sniffed the fan.

"It's his. He painted it."

"That's a reason?" he scoffed. "He's painted a lot of things,
none of which you bothered to take before this."

"It smells right. Like him."

He craned over my shoulder at the ink marks. "But there's nothing here. Hunger is a reason for doing something. Heat. Fatigue. Fear. Fun. *Those* are reasons."

"Humanity does things." Grandfather came up behind us. "They make no sense to milk-suckers like you, but they have their reasons. Your sister is learning things. Bitter things. They make her sad."

"Why must she?"

"Try and stop her, why don't you?" he snorted. "She does not have to. She chooses to."

"I do not!" I exclaimed, hurt by the thought that this misery might be voluntary. They ignored me.

"She's crazy then," Brother said bitterly. I snarled and reached to cuff him.

"As are we all," Grandfather said.

7. SHIKUJO'S PILLOW BOOK
Mixing scent:

It was the height of summer, and everything was perfectly all right in one's life. The rains had stopped, replaced by a lovely sequence of perfect days and starry nights. There were no bad dreams, no unwanted memories. The heat gathered under the dark eaves of the house, so one spent as much time as decently possible on the veranda rimming the wisteria courtyard. With all the screens modesty requires, it was not perhaps so much cooler. But it was different, and welcome for that.

A friend from the capital wrote, gossiping about the doings at Lake Biwa, where everyone is summering. She sent as a gift a length of pale-blue fabric light as a cricket's breath; and she begs for a special perfume blend one had made for her before. So pleasant to hear from an old friend! — one perhaps remembers her with more affection than the friendship deserved because she has written at all, even to ask for something.

One's scent-mixing boxes sit on an unvarnished table, surrounded by all the little bottles and jars and packets and mortars and pestles of the task. One pot broke traveling here; now the slips of paper tied to the necks of all the others are saturated with attar, almost unreadable. White gardenia–scent is so thick that it is difficult to mix anything at all.

Each vial and pot contains something precious. Together they seem to make a poem with great beauty but no sense: aloes, cinnamon, conch shell, sweet pine gum, tulip and clove, gum resin and honey and *murasaki*-lavender. Scents are filled with memories; this collection would be as reminiscent as a diary — if one could smell anything but white gardenia.

One's husband comes. It must be one's husband: no one else would walk so directly up, such a hasty straight line across the floors of one's rooms. Others would be more circumspect.

He brings bad news, which destroys the possibility of mixing anything at all.

8. THE NOTEBOOK OF KAYA NO YOSHIFUJI

I find her on the veranda, closer to barefaced under the sun than I have seen her since that strange day she screamed at the fox in the kitchen garden. I do not know that I want to see her face, so I kneel discreetly outside the maze of screens her women have constructed for her.

"Wife."

"Husband! I was just preparing a perfume."

"So I perceive. What is that smell? Not something you're mixing, surely?"

"I would never mix anything so heavy or characterless." She sounds offended: an artist's pride wounded, perhaps. I am no artist, I would not know. "No, I am so sorry. A bottle broke in traveling here."

"I'm leaving for a bit," I blurt.

"What?" she says gracelessly; then, recovering herself, adds, "I hope your trip will be a pleasant one. Only I thought we were settled for the summer."

"*We* are. But I must go."

"Is it restlessness? My lord, I know you have not been altogether content since we arrived here." I grimace, bitterly
amused; this is one way to put it. "Perhaps you would feel better
with a concubine, to take your mind off things? Even living out
here, we should not have trouble finding a woman of grace from
the capital who would be willing to share our time."

"A woman is the least of it. You know this." I am unusual, I
know, in having only a single wife and no concubines at all; but
I have never wanted another permanent woman. A lover, someone held once or several times without responsibility—that is
mine anyway. I sleep with court ladies and prostitutes and
neighboring girls when they are pretty; boys once in a while. It
is not new love I long for: it is a new self.

"Well, then, is it an adventure you seek?"

"Yes. No." This is a strange question, coming from her. What
does she know of seeking new things? Once, when we were
young together, I remember her laughing at the antics of someone from court. *Adventures are what happens when an event is flawed,
a mark of imperfection*, she'd said then.

I am certainly imperfect, but I am unwilling to mention it at
this moment, so I grope for a reason she will accept. "I had a
dream last night. I need to visit the Kannon's shrine by the sea."

"But that is days—no, weeks!—away!"

"Not if I travel fast."

"Why not talk to the old man who lives in the forest? If he
is still alive. We used to consult him for dreams, when we were
here last—remember?—and he was quite competent." Her face
drops, as if recalling something.

"No, I must go to the shrine."

"What was the dream? Perhaps I might . . ."

"Uh," I say; because, of course, there is no dream. I lie about
a goddess out of simple restlessness. "Well. Kannon stood in a
field of rice and offered me a jewel shaped like the moon. When
I took it from her hand, she said: "Wear red and the wish will
come true.""

"What wish is that?" she says softly.

"Peace of mind," I whisper. My lie has trapped me into this

honesty. All our times together: I have never been so honest with her as I am now, in this moment.

Time stretches. She snaps it closed. "Do you have anything red to wear?"

"What?"

"For Kannon. She said in the dream that you must wear red. What about the layered crimson brocade with the lotus medallions? It is from the princess's own hands: most appropriate for the Kannon. And—"

"Are you hurt by my leaving?"

She pauses, all correct surprise. "Hurt? You've dreamt of a bodhisattva. She summons you. How can I be hurt?—and you could take the seven-robe set that shades from red to white, to leave as your gift to the goddess."

"Whatever you suggest," I say numbly. Honesty is dangerous. Rejected or unperceived, it leaves me more alone than I've ever been before.

9. SHIKUJO'S PILLOW BOOK
What is a wife's duty:

What is a wife's duty to her husband? To accommodate his needs, and to bear him a son. To be patient, generous, correct in all things. To ease her husband's heart when he is distressed by life—if such a thing is possible.

Not to cause pain. To suffer her own hurts as meekly as she can.

I say all this to Onaga, who snorts. "What is a husband's duty to his wife, then?"

I do not know. I do not know if I am being failed or not. Or if I am failing him.

Or myself, I suppose. Even this is possible. For whatever reason, the scent was not blended that day.

10. THE NOTEBOOK OF KAYA NO YOSHIFUJI

The morning I leave, I hear a soft scratching on my closed screens. "My lord?" A cultured voice: one of my wife's women, though not Onaga, who leaves the north wing as little as does Shikujo.

I gesture for Hito to admit the woman and an attendant. (Even maids have maids.) She enters with her face averted: dressed in pale yellow robes under a silk Chinese jacket dyed irregularly in gold and rose, and spotted with raindrops (for it is raining again). She could be anyone, this pretty artifact of a woman, shifting nervously so that her black hair hangs between us. I send my men from the room.

"Well?" Nothing I can say or do will make her more comfortable in my evidently dangerous male presence: best to get it over with.

"My mistress sends you a small thing, of no account; you might consider carrying it with you on your trip, but it is hardly necessary—"

Shikujo is capable of gifts even when hurt. Sometimes I resent this in her. Marriage to an apparently perfect person is frequently more difficult than others might imagine.

I nod. The maid kneels swiftly and leaves a small parcel on the floor before slipping through the open screen.

Hito magically reappears. "My lord, how generous of my lady! Sending one of her own women, too, instead of a mere servant, or asking you to attend her. Shall I—"

"Yes," I say. "Bring it over." I do not mean to sound ungrateful, but I suppose I must, for Hito frowns (shades of my old nurse again: really, will I never be free of the woman?) and brings me the package in silence.

It fits easily into one hand. Special paper—red on one side, bright yellow on the other—has been so cunningly folded that the package is secure without ties, its folded edges showing both colors. I pull one edge, and it unfolds as easily as a *hirugao* bloom on a summer's day.

Inside is an amulet case. A lot of women wear these tiny drums of brocade hung from a twisted cord, charms for fertility or some other equally feminine thing. Presumably there is something inside for it to be called an amulet case: I've never taken one apart to find out. This one is about the size of my thumb, of jade-green silk, heavy with silver thread turned the purple-gray of new tarnish. A medallion the size of my fingernail is sewn to one side: two cranes flying in opposite directions across a Chinese cloud-shape.

She has written on the inside, the red side, of the paper a correct little poem about cranes symbolizing eternal (married) love. And beneath:

Leave this for me, as an offering and a prayer for marital happiness, when you visit your shrine. That you find what you seek is a desire we both share.

Prayers for marital happiness are nothing: all women do this. But the little cranes flying eternally in opposite directions—I cannot decide what the message in this is, so I write a forgettable poem in response, saying nothing about the cranes.

11. KITSUNE'S DIARY

One day there was all this activity, packing and saddling and such. Servants ran pell-mell across the stableyard, tight little bundles held tight against their bodies, away from the rain. It was not until I saw the flower-yellow horse saddled that I went in search of Grandfather. I found him in the back garden under a special storehouse where the people kept silks and flammable treasures.

"What does this mean?"

He sighed, if a fox can be said to sigh. He no longer tried to stop my watching, seemed somehow resigned to my questions. Perhaps he'd given up. "He is traveling, child."

"Why? Where would he go?"

"Who knows? It could be a trip back to the capital. It could be a pilgrimage. Maybe he heard of an antique bowl in some backwoods estate somewhere, and he is off to buy it. Maybe he is restless."

"How can he leave his home?" I said. "I can't even imagine it."

"No? But when the humans came, you moved quickly enough."

"That was different. It was not so far, and we had to, to survive."

"So. Maybe he needs to do this to survive. For men survival is more than shelter and food."

"What else could it be?"

"Do I know?" he snapped. "Men: it is their nature to go, as it is women's to wait. But they come back. Usually."

"How long will he be gone?"

"Weeks probably. Months perhaps."

"He can't!"

"Can't he? How will you stop him? You're a fox — maybe you can bite him and make him sick?"

"But —"

He cut me off with a snarl. I bit at the muddy dirt in frustration, and then ran off to watch.

A pair of spotted oxen dozed in rigid wooden yokes, hitched to an oak-wood wagon piled with bundles and trunks. The horses stamped through puddles in the stableyard. Despite the rain, flies and servants clustered at the heads of the animals, who bore with the people as they took the flies: the oxen calmly, the horses by tossing their heads and rolling their eyes.

The servants who were traveling were gathered in the stableyard, dressed in serviceable traveling clothes of indigo and white and gray cotton and hemp, broad straw hats protecting their faces. When he came, Yoshifuji's starched silk made him look like an egret among common marsh birds; when he mounted, his yellow horse glowed among the steadier browns and roans

and bays. He exchanged a few words with Hito before he turned
his horse and splashed through the stableyard gate. The swarm
of servants followed, buzzing.

He was leaving. I did not know when he would be back. I
did not even question my only possible action.

I crawled through an unrepaired break in the fence and followed.

12. SHIKUJO'S PILLOW BOOK
Rain does not stop for partings:

*T*hough *the rain has not stopped*, a woman stands outside her
rooms and watches her husband leave. When will he come
back? Not even he would be able to tell her this; and they fought
before his going, so that he left with no more than the standard
formalities.

She writes this poem:

> *Which are harder? —*
> *the nights I watch your windows glow*
> *but you do not come,*
> *or the nights your rooms are dark*
> *and you cannot.*

She does not look forward to the time to come.

13. KITSUNE'S DIARY

I followed Yoshifuji and his men at a distance. They moved
slowly, at the oxen's pace, so it was not hard to keep up,
although I could not be as quiet as I would have wanted: my
feet splashed through water, and rustled in the matted ivy and
weeds, and hissed as I moved through the long grasses. But the
people and their animals set up such a barking and creaking and

clopping—I do not suppose they would have heard me if I had fallen from a man's height into standing water.

I'd never wandered far from the garden before, certainly not along the roads, so it was soon new to me. I still smelled pine and *hinoki*-cedar, but somehow they were not the right pine and cedar, spicier or less spicy. How can I explain what I mean? Words are inadequate for so many things. Smells are one of them.

The road wound through the hills—always a slope leading up from one side, always stream or rice field or meadow on the other.

As Yoshifuji and his attendants approached, people moved off the path to let them pass, waiting knee-deep in wet weeds or brush. I'd hide then, too. Some of the peasants had chickens or ducks tied by the feet and hung from sticks across their necks. A few led oxen or goats. One small man carrying a stick as tall as he was had a bitch on a bit of plaited straw rope.

No one can live near people and not have seen a dog. A farmer down the valley had several, and sometimes (before Yoshifuji came) the largest one, a stocky black male, came up the road and urinated on the ruined gate. Grandfather said this was far outside the male's range; but he went over the marks with his own, anyway. I could smell that we somehow shared blood with this male, but we ignored him as we did the cats. And he ignored us—except for the scent-marks.

But this bitch was different. I watched her from the heart of a rotted log: about my size, about my age, short coarse gold hair, tail coiled tight over her back. She shifted restlessly, sniffing the air. If she'd been moving, or if I had, she might have ignored me; but idle and bored, she smelled me.

"Fox!" She threw her weight against the rope, which parted. "Fox!" she barked as she ran up the hill toward me. "Fox, I will kill you, and rip your hot heart out and eat it, fox; I will tear out your throat—"

I did not have time to run and there was nowhere safe to run to. I backed down inside the log and bared my teeth, my hackles tingling. She slammed against the opening, barking.

"I will pull your intestines from your body; I will rip your skull free and eat your brains—"

"Leave me alone," I said. It was barely a breath in my throat, but my chest throbbed with the sound I held in. "Go back to your rope and your master, you belly-up cringing licker of hands. Or I will kill you, you not-fox, you cur—"

She dived at me, broad jaw snapping. "You are not fit to be tamed! They cannot eat you, you are no companion—"

I did not care who killed whom. I knew in my bones that I needed to destroy her, and the thought of her blood in my mouth made me crazy, I think. I did not bark—whom would I call?—but I bared my teeth and lunged.

The log boomed around me. "Dog!" a human voice shouted over the barking. "Get *out!*" Another boom, and then a solid thumping noise: stick against flesh. The bitch yelped and backed. I saw her grovel in front of the man who had hit her, but she still quivered with hate for me. He swung his stick at her again and she rolled out of the way. The man grabbed the rope around her neck, jerked her to her feet, and dragged her down the hill. "A marten," he shouted to the other humans.

I waited until I could not hear the trudging footsteps of the oxen before I crawled out of the log. There was no one in sight. Yoshifuji and his attendants had rounded a curve.

I could follow my own trail home, or I could go forward, until nothing at all was familiar except Yoshifuji. I continued on, but I trembled as I walked.

They stopped just as it was growing dark, in a little clearing beside a cold stream that crossed under the path. Yoshifuji swung off his horse and shouted orders to the men. They pulled thick bamboo poles and bundles of cloth from the ox cart. I watched, fascinated, forgetting even Yoshifuji for a bit, but I did not see how their clever hands took these things and made a little building roofed and walled in dark oiled hemp. They un-folded more bundles, and made a fire (there had been no rain here, and the ground was dry) and cooked rice with dried fish and roots.

I caught a lame half-grown squirrel to eat: hardly a mouthful. I was still hungry, but I was afraid to stray too far. They were all I had, Yoshifuji and his men. I watched them until it grew dark and their fire faded into embers. Two men spoke softly together. Others snored.

I was alone, surrounded by unfamiliar things, separated from my family, cold and hungry and lonely and terrified. And mad: I'm sure of it now.

I crawled under the wall of Yoshifuji's traveling tent.

The little cloth room was empty except for him, and he was asleep: I heard his heavy, even breathing. I took a step closer. He lay on a thick reed mat, under a pile of padded robes. His pillow was his sash, wrapped around a pad of pulled grasses. He was dressed in what he had worn all day. I smelled perfume, without knowing what it was, and beneath that his own and his horse's sweat.

I'd never been so close to Yoshifuji, not even when I was trapped in the storehouse. I stepped forward until I stood with my front paws on the reed mat. I bent down and touched his face with my own and tasted his breath by pressing my muzzle against his lips. He did not move, only sighed.

I must have fallen asleep, curled up under his chin.

I do not know how much later it was that I awakened. I heard a scream, and opened my eyes. I did not remember where I was or why; only blinked. Yoshifuji moved beside me, and even that made no sense.

"My lord!" It was one of the servants, holding a small lamp. "Hold still—" He pulled a knife from his belt and lunged at me.

Just as Yoshifuji shouted, the man cut me. It did not hurt, exactly, when the knife sliced open my shoulder. Mostly it surprised me. The pain started later. More men, more lights, poured in.

I do not remember getting free of the tent. I just remember running blindly through the woods, bleeding.

14. THE NOTEBOOK OF KAYA NO YOSHIFUJI

The fox sleeping against my heart —
if not for the blood she left
I would have thought she was a dream.

15. SHIKUJO'S PILLOW BOOK
I would have given much:

I would have given much
to sleep against your heart last night,
instead of lying awake listening to deer complain.

16. KITSUNE'S DIARY

I ran until I was too exhausted to go on and stopped at last in an open glade where the moonlight lay in strips between the trees. I was lost, far from anywhere familiar, panting too loudly to hear anything, leaving a trail of panic and blood any killer could follow. I was alone and about to die, and there was no one to help me.

Help? I did not know what this was, then. I "helped" myself; if others helped me, it was because the family's survival was aided by my survival. But I asked anyway, my first prayer. "Help me."

The air was thick, misty. Lights flared, soft unclear blurs of color and brilliance. A gong sounded a long way away. It faded slowly, forever in its decay. I was dizzy, the way I had been when I was young, and had eaten the dried head of a China-poppy I found in the abandoned garden. My ears cupped, listening for enemies. Unsure, I twitched—run or fight? What is appropriate when all I can see is a matter of blurred lights?

"There is no enemy," a voice said in my skull. "The foe is inside you."

Steady light shone ahead, different from the smears of fire around me. I padded toward it and it widened, clarified, into a small dark shrine, closed on three sides, an oil lamp hanging from iron chains fixed to the lowest branch of an overhanging cypress. I passed under a dozen red *torii*-arches, each smaller than the last, to reach the shrine. The last arch was just tall enough for me to pass beneath if I bowed my head.

Inside the shrine was a block of white wood carved into a shape. Image: reality. Like ink on paper that was also foxes, this was wood and also a little woman, no taller than I was. A statue. The smooth wood was stained black on her hands and belly and face from the oil of humans touching it. Her eyes were at exactly my height. In front of her clustered little dishes of brass and dark wood. I smelled cooked rice and fresh water. I dipped my head and drank.

Two foxes coalesced from the moonlight. Their fur glowed; their eyes were dark. Flames flickered on the tips of their noses, gold to their silver. They smelled of nothing at all.

"What is it you want, who drink our offerings?" I could not tell which one of them spoke. The voice was like the echo of the gong: every note, no note in it. I hung my head, exhausted from blood loss, drained of anything but the exhaustion-poisons I felt in my muscles.

I did not think to be afraid. Why would I?—there was no smell to threaten me; they were like the moonlight itself. "I don't know where I am. I want—" What did I want? Kaya no Yoshifuji. Help. Home.

"A fox can smell home, and find her own way. Why can't you? Is your nose clotted with another perfume?"

"I do not understand."

"Why should you?"

"Who are you? You have no smell."

"Whereas you smell of blood and weakness. We serve Inari, the rice-god the humans worship." The statue flared with light from within for a heartbeat's length.

I sniffed at the statue's base. "This is a god?" I asked. "It smells of wood, and men."

"What did you expect a god to be? Inari is this piece of wood and a goddess and a god. And the people who believe in Inari and the rice in front of the statue. Also other things you do not understand."

I shook my head, to clear away the strangeness. "My mother spoke of gods."

"Your mother knows both more and less than any fox should."

"How does a fox serve a human god?"

They seemed amused. "We are not really foxes. And Inari is not necessarily a human god. We only said that humans worship Inari."

"Well, what are you then?" I said a little crossly. "You have not said."

"Perhaps we are a dream a god once had of foxes."

"Do foxes have gods?"

They laughed without noise. "You are a fox. Tell us."

"I do not understand," I said again.

Painted marks appeared before my eyes, shining like black ink. "Can you read this?"

The black marks were the same as the barkings of humans, I realized. They were *words:* they meant things, just as other brushstrokes meant two foxes in the reeds. These marks were pictures that were also sounds and also words themselves. I spoke them.

> *The spider's web can catch the moonlight*
> *but will not keep it.*

"They are the words painted on the fan I stole," I said, knowing it. "But they do not make sense. What spider? And what moonlight?"

"Any spider. No spider. There are a lot of things you do not understand, aren't there? Poetry is perhaps the least of them."

"This is poetry?"

"You are lost between two worlds. Hard to balance on the edge of the fence, little fox." And they dissolved back into the moonlight.

I licked the cut in my shoulder until it smelled clean, and slept that night under the *torii*-arches. In the morning, the way back seemed clear, but it took until the middle of the afternoon to limp home.

17. SHIKUJO'S PILLOW BOOK
Things one does in one's husband's absence:

*C*alligraphy and painting in the Chinese or the modern style. Playing on the thirteen-string *koto* or the *biwa*-lute. Playing the *shō* pipes, the *hichiriki* or in fact any sort of flute makes one look ludicrous, and more important, feel like a fool. There is no point to performing on the seven-string *koto*, unless one is very good, since its difficulty throws the performer's imperfections into unpleasant relief.

Poetry. We memorize famous poetry and use it in various games, matching the correct ending to a beginning offered at random, or even writing a new ending.

I write my own poems, when it is possible, or there is a reason. I also rewrite the poems of others, practicing my brush-work.

Go. Sugoroku-backgammon. Dice games. *Rango. Tagi.* Children's games like shell-matching.

Contests of various sorts. We dig roots and judge them for shape and character. Or we attempt to mix the sweetest scent, or the spiciest, or the gentlest. Or we race to gather the most duck feathers or some such small thing. These were more amusing in the capital, when it was possible to match the women against the men, but even here, I and my women contrive.

Temple visits, and consultations with dream interpreters, and asking questions of visiting monks and nuns, if they are not too unkempt for polite society.

Writing sutras out in one's best hand. This is useful for salvation, to lessen the number of lives we must suffer through; and also good for one's calligraphy.

When there are no date tabus, bathing and washing one's hair. Also cutting one's nails.

Onaga likes binding notebooks, though this seems tedious to me. What is the purpose of an empty book?

Layering robes, according to the season and our preferences.

Making flowers of colored papers.

Tending one's gardens.

Reading *monogatari*-tales. Sometimes one wishes she were one of the characters in the old stories.

Truly, in a list like this, my life does not seem very exciting. And perhaps that is the comfort of such an exercise, in this circumstance at least. One's women watch one through all of this, of course, but I feel at times that another watches, as well. Perhaps if my life seems dull, that one will choose another direction.

18. KITSUNE'S DIARY

I slept the rest of the day I returned and all the next. I ate nothing, even when Brother brought me half a rabbit; barely staggered from the scrape to defecate and drink water from the nearest lake.

The second night, Brother followed me when I walked across the *susuki* grass, in clear sight of the main house. It was dusk and raining lightly. With Yoshifuji gone, there was no reason for anyone to be in the wing that overlooked the lakes most clearly, but mostly I did not care who saw me, did not care about anything but the most immediate need: thirst.

He hunched beside me as I lapped green-tinted water. "Are you sick?"

"Perhaps," I said.

"Grandfather says yes, but that it is not a disease we can catch from you, the rest of us."

I drank.

"What happened? Were you hurt?"

"No."

"You have a cut on your shoulder," he said mildly.

I shut my eyes and felt the water-scum dry on my lips.

"Sister! Tell me what is happening! How am I supposed to feel when you're lost like this?" Brother said other things, ignorable things. Eventually he went away: I felt the grasses brush back in place against my muzzle. It got dark and surprisingly cold. The air thickened and settled into a band of fog no higher than the tops of the pampas grass clumped around the lake. The mist around me was too dense to see through, but overhead I saw the sky, dark as mourning, and the ill-fed sliver of the moon. I shivered uncontrollably, hardly aware of it.

I could die. I did not understand the how or the why, but I felt it like a pulse under my skin. I had smelled death before. I had killed often enough; and then there were my other two siblings: there and gone, as easily as that. I had never truly thought of it as something that might happen to me, but how hard could it be? I tried not to think of the moon-foxes' mocking, tried not to think at all.

An animal skirted the nearest clump of pampas grass and hushed through the shorter grasses toward me. It flopped with a grunt beside me.

"So." Grandfather said. "You followed him, and something bad happened."

"There was—a knife—" I halted out; and then the story tumbled from me: the dog and Kaya no Yoshifuji's smell when I slept under his chin and the knife and the running. I was crying again; it seemed to be all I did anymore.

"This is the cut." He touched his nose to the wound on my shoulder, sealed over and nearly lost in my fur. "It is not serious. So."

"It is not that. He let them hurt me, and he did nothing."

"Well?"

"But I love him!"

"You're a fox. An animal."

"What does that mean?" I asked.

"You have nothing in common. Why should he love you?"

"If we're so different, how can *I* love *him?*"

"Love is curiosity sometimes. Concentrated wondering about the other one."

"He draws us," I said slowly. "Perhaps he does love us?" My chest hurt at the thought.

He snorted. "If humans *can* love. We're foxes, we know what this is. But him? We're just something else to wonder about."

"There was more," I said slowly. "When I was running? I came to a human place, a shrine. And there were foxes. They were made out of moonlight, and they had no smell, and they said strange things to me."

"You've seen them." Grandfather seemed sad.

"You have too?"

"When I was young, hardly older than you, yes. They're Inari's foxes."

"The foxes told me Inari is a god."

"A humans' god. Maybe a goddess. Not even the humans seem to know. Humans love their rice. He oversees it all — plants, fields, season, harvest. She."

"Why did they come to me?"

"Who knows," he snapped. "Ask them, why don't you?"

What could I say? There was no answer here.

19. THE NOTEBOOK OF KAYA NO YOSHIFUJI

There are mornings it is almost impossible to awaken. My life will be what it was when I fell asleep the night before. Why arise? Why dress, break my fast, make polite conversation, write artificial poetry? Nothing will have changed in the night.

When I feel like this my dreams seem infinitely preferable and I cling to sleep. Asleep, I hold a dream in my hands. It is like an exquisite fish that I've found in a dark pool, so beautiful that I cry at the shimmer of its scales, or the translucent fans that are its fins. Someone speaks on the other side of a screen or a loon calls; I half-wake and the fish drops with a splash back into the pool in which I found it. I reach after it, willing myself back to unconsciousness.

Often I find the same dream waiting; I touch it again and swear that this time I will remember all. Waking, I recall only fragments—a smell; or a voice, rich as a temple bell; or the skin of a woman's inner thighs, softer and sweeter than cherry petals; or a certain quality of light falling like snow around me.

This trip I made to the shrine of Kannon was like such an unremembered dream. I remember fragments: a field so filled with blue cornflowers that its grasses seemed drowned in a lake. A young rice field (further along than my own, which are higher in the mountains and thus slower growing) shimmered like drying silk hung in a breeze, giving forms to the wind's dance.

My first night traveling, a fox crawled under the wall of the tent. I think she must have fallen asleep next to me, although my servants ran in and frightened her off before anything dangerous could happen. I know that this was true, because Hito fretted for days afterward about what might have happened; but it all seems so unlikely that I feel I must somehow have dreamed it, and Hito and the rest with me.

Kannon's temple seems somehow less real than the fox at my heart.

A few years back certain monks of the capital carved a statue of Kannon from half a cypress tree and threw it into the ocean, swearing to build a shrine where it washed ashore. A strange way to worship: casting her to the seas, as if she were driftwood or a fisherman's boat. She might have landed on the North Island, or been dashed to pieces on some rock out at sea. Or even floated to Korea, I suppose. The monks seem to have had a touching faith that she would restrict her interest to the civilized world.

Which she did not fail: the statue washed ashore on an abandoned beach a not inconvenient distance from the capital. The priests built a shrine there on the shore. Here.

I suppose the temple and its outbuildings would not seem so impressive in the capital, where the main palace's roof-peak stands taller than a cedar tree. Here, with steep hills and uncontrolled forest to one side and the shell- and seaweed-clotted beach on the other, they are miraculous.

I greet the appropriate officials and mention the offerings I intend to make — the scarlet-to-white robes, and my wife's amulet case, and a number of gold coins, and a commission for the Lotus Sutra to be copied in silver ink on midnight-blue paper and illustrated with silver and gold paintings from the Buddha's life. All this is evidently acceptable.

Dressed in red (having claimed the goddess spoke to me, how can I not?), I enter the central courtyard. The day hangs heavy and humid around me.

The shrine stands on posts in the center of a large square of white gravel. The gravel is perfectly clean. Not even a leaf disturbs its blankness. The shrine is built of cypress and cedar, its posts dyed black, its deep eaves edged with gilded carved disks. The low grille of a dog-barrier circles the shrine.

A broad flight of stairs leads up to the entrance. Trees stand in chest-high earthenware pots on either side, cherry and bamboo, neither at its best at this time of year. The trees seem filled with mulberry-paper butterflies: prayer slips tied to the branches as high as a man can reach.

The air inside is even hotter, and cloyingly sweet from the heavy clove and anise incense. I squint against the darkness after the hard summer light. The temple is large, but the initial impression is of a rich madman's treasure house, a chaotic jumble of artwork and silks and scrolls.

Kannon stands at the opposite end of the high-vaulted chamber, her silvered cypress wood stained with soot from the oil lamps that give the room its dim light. Kannon is both male and female; in this manifestation, she is female and stands three times a man's height, a soft woman with an expression that might be merciful forbearance. Carved in the Chinese style, her robes probably cling to her limbs, showing the shape of her legs; but in fact she is quite modest, nearly lost in the layers of robes and scarves pilgrims have draped over her. Her feet are lost in a jumble of offerings and silver lamp-stands.

The rest of the shrine is cluttered with the statues and offerings of healing Buddhas, bodhisattvas, spirit generals and miscellaneous esoteric deities and demons. (The gods seem to love company as much as men do: you never see one in a temple without a cluster of others to keep him or her company.) It all seems fussy and graceless.

I gesture and one of my servants brings the robes and the amulet forward. I kneel on a gold-embroidered cushion, bend forward until my forehead rests against the cool floor. A conch horn sounds. Words are said.

I close my eyes, trying not to be ill. I am dizzy from heat and incense and sadness, disappointed hopes I had not even realized I'd had. Kannon is the goddess of mercy. I lied about the dream, but I had hoped that somehow this silvered statue would have the power, the magic, to cure my sorrows, and allow me to return at peace.

And nothing has happened. Nothing has changed. There is no mercy, no magic. I am still Kaya no Yoshifuji.

Evidently the priests saw me thus—kneeling, eyes closed, fighting nausea and tears—and assumed I was praying. Perhaps I was.

20. KITSUNE'S DIARY

When I started to feel better, I began to watch Shikujo. She was human; she loved Yoshifuji. She must understand.

It was the end of the fifth month, but surprisingly hot for the time of year (my grandfather said—how would I know? It was my first summer). Most afternoons the sky clouded over and it thundered and rained, but the air never seemed to clear. It stayed humid.

Mostly she moved in the innermost shadows of her wing. Because of the heat, the outer walls were pushed aside or removed altogether. Often her curtains and blinds were all tied up to allow the slight breezes to cool the rooms. Only fox-eyes could have seen her there, in the heavy gloom.

Shikujo was very beautiful: elegant and graceful. Her voice was low-pitched and sweet (especially compared to her main servant, who cawed like a crow). Wrapped in unlined silk robes of blue and yellow, she lay beside an armrest and a writing desk, and fanned herself with a painted fan. Her servants brought her things to drink and little trays with bits of food on them, but mostly she did not eat. Even in the heat, she and her women wore so many robes that sometimes I could not tell which heaps of silk were women and which just cloth.

They played children's games with tops and hoops; they wrote and painted; they talked endlessly; they sewed still more robes; they called out the plaited-palm carriages and went to the monastery one valley away and listened to the sutras being read. Occasionally they played with one of the black-and-white cat's seemingly limitless kittens, or with what I took to be a servant's child.

It seemed clear to me that all these things were merely to fill her time until Yoshifuji came to her. Her life seemed full of twilight and waiting, and unacknowledged (and disappointed) hopes. What else would she do? I knew that her only reason to live must be Yoshifuji, as he was mine.

In his absence, she sat often on her veranda overlooking the wisteria courtyard, where no one could see her, at a little table and wrote on hard pale gray paper stitched with red tape into a notebook.

Yoshifuji had done this, too; but when Shikujo left her things strewn about the veranda, her women followed her and picked them up, like young animals catching the scraps that fall from the adults' mouths. Even they forgot, one night.

There was more danger here. Yoshifuji's main veranda looked out on the formal garden, but the wisteria courtyard was comparatively small, paved with light-colored gravel, and enclosed on all sides by walkways. Except for the porcelain tubs holding the wisteria, there was nothing to hide behind, leaving only the walkways or the house itself under which to hide.

But I had learned this much from the things that Yoshifuji left on his veranda: that the risk brought the reward. When she went inside in the evening, she seldom came out again, and never without such a rustling and chattering on the part of her women as would scare away even a crow in good time. I could not resist.

She had left her notebooks out, flipped open, on a low mahogany writing desk with legs shaped like cats' paws. She had written with a narrow brush in characters that seemed skittery, complex as the patterns of birds' footprints in mud.

"I watched the last of the small robins leave its nest in the scarlet maple today. How transitory youth is!"

I nosed the page over. "How terrible to be left alone by a man! Worse still, if he does not say good-bye before leaving."

The next page: "I remember . . ." The writing trailed off, as if she had forgotten to write.

There was a noise inside. A woman sighed heavily, as if awake. I crept off the veranda, and ran back to the scrape.

21. SHIKUJO'S PILLOW BOOK
One hot night I did not sleep:

One hot night I did not sleep well, and had a frightening dream. Somehow I found myself in the main garden standing by one of the bridges. The fox man I had the unsettling dream about so long ago stood near me. He was much older and grayer but still straight-backed and elegant, wearing a robe leached of color by the moonless sky. He bowed wordlessly. Because it was a dream, I bowed back, barefaced but unembarrassed and equally wordless.

He held a half-eaten mouse in one long hand. *This is a memory from my son the other day,* I thought. I reached out and took the mouse in my fingers — and instead of flesh I felt a scrap of furred pale gray paper. The calligraphy was sharp as whiskers. I do not think it was a poem.

A woman struggles against the shape of her life, as do we all.
I am sorry for the pain this causes.

"I do not understand," I said at last, though I do not recall my lips moving.

"I expect not," he said. "Nevertheless."

"What do you want?" I asked, thinking of *hakama*-trousers thrown over a curtain-frame, and a poem/not poem whispered.

He snorted, which seemed very unlike a dream to me. "What do you think?"

Robes pushed aside, flesh against flesh. "No," I whispered, meaning: *I understand,* and *Please do not ask me this.*

"I thought not," he said, sighing slightly. "Your son is well?"

"Yes," I said, not thinking until later what a strange question this was. "He is grown tall for his age, and clever. But then you have watched him in the garden."

"I have. Why have you tried to hide him? Did you fear I would want him?"

"No," I said, and knew I meant it. He had his life now — a mate presumably: children, certainly.

"Why are you here in my dream, then? To give me this?" I held the mouse/poem out.

"Perhaps." He coughed. "And perhaps to ask you: do you remember that time years ago? When last we met?"

"I remember, yes." Then, because it was a dream, and could not actually matter, I asked, "The poem you spoke then, so long ago. I've never been able to remember it."

He smiled slightly. "I have never forgotten it. But it would take all night to repeat properly. Shall I recite it to you?"

I shivered without knowing why, and shivering I awoke. I had walked in my sleep into the garden.

22. KITSUNE'S DIARY

She's so sad all the time," I said to my brother later that night. We tore at a merganser I'd caught, underfeathers making sticky clouds around our heads. "What must it be like, to feel things like that?"

"*I'm* sad, I'm lonely."

I snorted. "Not like her—you're just a fox."

"What are *you,* sister?"

I ripped the duck's head free in silence.

"Do you think we're so different, foxes, from humans?" he continued. "I want company, I sleep alone, I'm bored, waiting for you to run with me. I hate how all you do is hide in the shadows and brood. Your fur falls out in clumps, and you eat too little, even when we catch things. You smell sick. Come play. Hunt. Anything. Be my sister again, be a fox."

"Don't you see? It's not that simple anymore. I love him. I've learned to *cry.* Everything has changed."

"How? If I cried and loved him, would this make me as good as you? Would you play with me *then?*"

I growled, warning him to leave it alone.

He only shook his head irritably. "I'm healthy, I'm young, it's summer, and there's enough to eat. Life is good. And you whimper in your sleep and agonize over nothing. It's like watching your reflection in a pond and waiting for it to rise out of the water and touch noses with you. What good is there in this?"

I lunged for him. I have noticed since becoming a woman that this is more common than I would like to think, that we hate the ones who tell us the truth. I hope that this is not universal. Even though our dominance fights were long past, and I had won, at that moment I wanted to pin him and prove with the strength in my body that he was wrong.

It is rare for adult foxes to fight, but we did. Even when we were kits, fights lasted a few heartbeats, no longer; as I've learned, only between humans do they drag on. I won, but he ran away before I could pin him, and I was too tired to chase him.

I despised him then. *I* was the strong one, the clever one. *I* had fallen in love. He had not.

After this, I stopped watching even Shikujo. Why should I? Yoshifuji was not there.

23. THE NOTEBOOK OF KAYA NO YOSHIFUJI

The trip home from the shrines: there are trees, mountains, lakes, a pair of waterfalls. Willows and reeds, vivid green from the rain. A clacker in a rice field: it falls with a sudden noise, and a flock of crows and starlings whirl up from the wet stalks, to return moments later. A man walks through a field of grass so tall that his broad straw hat seems to float across the wet grass tassels, gold against silver-gray. All these things I should have exclaimed at and written nice little poems about; but I rode through them all, uncaring.

The trip was one dream; I return to another, grimly hoping that all the things I ran away from have somehow changed; that life with Shikujo in the wilds will now satisfy me. I am numb, halfway between two dreams, waiting to be happy again.

24. SHIKUJO'S PILLOW BOOK
On reading the Manyōshū:

> *Poems in a notebook, stones in a bowl—*
> *they fall through my fingers*
> *and speak to each other, if not to me.*

25. KITSUNE'S DIARY

Yoshifuji returned on a hot, wet afternoon, when the air alternated between the silver haze of rain and the golden haze of rising steam. I dozed in the cool silence beneath the side gatehouse, dreaming restless scraps that slid away whenever I woke enough to shift my weight.

I felt his return before I heard anything: a horse's hooves making the ground thrum. I jerked awake. There had been no horses since he left. I bolted through the garden, not caring who saw, down to the ruined gate. I heard my brother's startled yelp behind me as I ran. Perhaps I'd stepped on him.

He came up as I huddled in the logs. "Sister—"

"Shut up!" I snapped. "He's coming!"

He backed away, ears pressed against his head.

The servants Yoshifuji had left behind had heard the noises of his arrival almost as soon as I had—I could hear their shouts—but my brother was gone, and I was hidden before they made their way to the road.

I stayed out of sight in the bushes, but his horse shied when he passed too close to me.

"Easy, easy, Kiku," he said, and patted the horse's neck. "We've been through the forest; what here at home can frighten you?" He looked into the brush, where I was hiding, but I knew he did not see me: I would have sensed somehow if he had. When the horse was calm again, they passed into the stableyard.

I followed and watched him dismount and walk through the gate between the yard and the formal grounds. I ducked under the fence, and paced him along the covered walkway. He went straight to his wife's wing without stopping by his own rooms, even to straighten his robes.

I stole under the house. Women's voices slipped through the floorboards. Light, rapid footsteps thrummed overhead. His footsteps were heavier, and made the floorboards shiver slightly, so that dust sifted onto my upturned muzzle. As he moved, the footsteps and talk died away in a circle around him, ripples of silence in a pond of noise. I wonder if he realized that they stilled themselves for him, or that the other, the chattering and running, went on at all.

He stopped walking. "Wife." His voice was low compared to the women's light tones of a moment before.

"My lord?" The crow-voiced woman, Onaga, spoke. "This is all quite unexpected. We had imagined — "

"My wife. Is she here?"

"But of course. She will be so pleased to hear of your visit. Alas, she is quite — "

"Where is she?"

"In seclusion, my lord."

I could imagine his impatient gesture, from having watched so much before. "Will I be made unclean by seeing her?"

"No, it is not *that* sort of tabu, but a dream told her to — "

"Wife?" he called, stumping from corner to corner of the house. The women overhead scurried like mice away from his tread, squeaking among themselves. More dust fell on me. I stifled a sneeze.

"My lord — " Onaga sounded frustrated. "If you insist on disturbing her reflections — "

"Here, husband." Shikujo's voice was lower than her women's, weary. She must have had screens pulled around her, making a tiny paper-walled room, because I heard one slide back in its runner. I padded over to stand beneath her. There was a long crack between two floorboards, as if they had warped after being placed. Cool gray light slivered down on me, and a scent, cedar and aloes.

"Wife. I am back."

"So I perceive." Humans. They talked so much, and so unnecessarily, stating obvious facts to one another. I did not know then about the polite nothings humans seemed to need, or about irony. Yoshifuji seemed to understand both: he faltered.

"I am sorry. I know you were in seclusion, but I needed to . . . I did not realize you were reading your sutra."

"It does not matter," she said. "So, husband. Welcome back. Was your trip a pleasant one?"

"It was a longer trip than I had expected. Please forgive my absence."

I heard a noise, a scroll being rolled and slipped into its case.

"So silent, wife?" he said finally.

She said: " 'The rabbit said nothing, but not from having nothing to say.' "

I did not understand at all, but Yoshifuji said, "What stops the rabbit? Are you angry?"

"Of course not. I am grateful you are back."

"Are you? Please send the women away. I'd like to be alone with you." Shikujo said nothing, but I heard many light footsteps crossing overhead. "Now. What is wrong with you?"

There was a long pause. "I am sorry, husband. It has been difficult of late. But you've returned safely. This is all I prayed for. Did you receive what *you* prayed for?"

"Oh, yes," he said flatly. "It was wonderfully enlightening."

Even I could hear the lie in his voice, so it surprised me that Shikujo could miss it as she seemed to.

"Tell me about your trip then."

He sighed. "I went; I am back."

"That seems rather brief."

"It seems that way, now. I missed you, wife."

"Ah," she said, but her voice seemed softer, more forgiving. I did not understand this exchange: anger? sorrow? Perhaps humans used their words so poorly that they used other signs to truly communicate, signs I did not understand.

"Please come here, wife."

They embraced, soft noises of skin and silk. After a time I smelled their desire like a thin herbal smoke. I was past my heat, but my body hurt from the tension in my muscles, the *wanting*.

It did not seem strange to me then, that she might want him even as she fought with him. In my experience desire was independent of anything but the need of flesh for flesh. Now that I have been human, I wonder: how could they have reached through the miscommunications and loneliness to expose their throats to each other in this fashion? Perhaps they hoped that sex could reconnect them. Perhaps it did. Perhaps it was yet another weapon between the two of them, as words and silences had become.

For me then, what did I want from him? All I knew of closeness was how mating felt with my brother and grandfather; the warmth of my family crushed against me as we curled up in the scrape; the brief instant I lay against Yoshifuji's heart. I wanted his breath, his body, as close as that again: any space between us was too much.

I jumped onto the veranda. The outside walls of the rooms were all pushed aside or lifted; but inside was a maze of screens and curtains placed at all angles. Most of the women had moved across the corridor. I could see none of them, but I smelled their perfume and sweat, and heard their soft voices.

I moved without breathing through the weird little chambers and halls the screens and curtains made, toward where Shikujo and my master were.

Silk moved; then Yoshifuji laughed throatily, and said:

> *"Hot rainy days —*
> *Is it heat or lust that soaks your robes?"*

"Tears, perhaps," she said. Poetry again, but she had known what he meant.

And then it hit me like a blow, so hard it dropped me to my belly: I will always be on the outside. Poetry was the least of it. Everything I did, all my work to understand his world, was useless. I was still a fox.

I remember running through the darkening air. Mother and Brother were there, but I wanted Grandfather, who was scratching fleas behind his ear with a hind leg. I snarled and tumbled him onto his back, biting whatever I could reach but hoping for his throat. I meant to kill him.

"How could you do this?" I screamed. "You knew it was hopeless. You *knew*."

"Shut up," my mother snarled at me, and bit my leg in the soft web where it joined my body. "You'll kill us all!"

Grandfather rolled me over, until he and my mother had me pinned, spine to the dirt and belly bare. My face was crushed against my mother's rib cage, so I could not scream, could only grab mouthfuls of dirty hair that caught in my throat and nose.

"Kill me if you must, or drive me away," Grandfather panted; "but not now, not for this. Listen to me."

I held myself still, quivering. Mother rolled off me, and began licking her plucked side.

"He is a man," Grandfather said. "You are a fox. What did you expect? You smell of musk and carry vermin and you shit where you please."

"You knew I had no hopes!"

"I hoped you'd learn."

"I cannot live like this!" I said. "I will die."

"There is one thing we can do," Mother said.

Grandfather snarled at her, "Crazy fox!" She ducked her head between her shoulders.

"What?" I asked her, ignoring Grandfather's anger.

"Magic," she said. I still trembled, but I stopped trying to hurt them.

"What do you mean?"

"She means you can take a human shape," my grandfather said wearily.

"It's possible?" my brother asked. "It's not just stories?"

"I've done it, once."

I burst out, "Why didn't you tell me this before?"

"*I* would not have told you at all," he snapped. "You're a fox, child. What else could you be? You can change your shape, but you will still be a fox."

"Change me," I hissed, "or I will kill you, and then I will die."

"I suppose you will have to learn for yourself. We will become human."

"Wait!" Brother's ears flattened. "Why should I have to become human?"

"We all will," Grandfather said.

"I can leave," Brother said. "I am an adult now; I should go find my range, a mate."

"You should," Grandfather said. "But you have not. Your destiny is as tangled as hers. And ours. No. We will all become human."

Mother interrupted. "We must. Because humans are so alone. We will need each other not to die of loneliness."

"Why should I follow her into this?" Brother asked Grandfather.

"Because this will be my pack someday," I snarled.

"It's still mine, little milk-sucker."

"Why not mine?" Brother asked. "She's too rash!"

"And you are not rash enough," Grandfather said. "Her curiosity and courage will keep her alive when all your caution will not."

"And if I were bolder?"

"Then you would not be truly yourself."

"You say this, then you tell me to become a man? *That* is 'myself'?"

"Peace," Grandfather growled.

"I know myself: I'm a fox. I have my sister—or had her, before this madness—I have a whole wood full of things to eat, and smells, and adventures: why would I trade this for humanity?"

"Humanity offers things we cannot even imagine," Grandfather said. "That is their magic—that they can always see beyond what *is*. Which is what your sister does, when she dreams of Yoshifuji."

I shivered miserably, despite the hot night.

26. THE NOTEBOOK OF KAYA NO YOSHIFUJI

After sex, my wife and I walk to my wing, where I change from my (now twice-stained) traveling clothes, and then we walk down to the lake-viewing pavilion. The evening sky over the mountains is the color of certain day lilies, gold and peach shading together, with dark smudges of cloud overlaid.

Great *ayu*-trout as long as my forearm hang motionless in the water, their shapes looking like mossy stones. Dragonflies hover over the water's green-rimmed surface. The water dimples when one lands. A fish flicks upward. Its mouth sucks water; the dragonfly vanishes. It happens as fast as a man can draw a breath. There are predators everywhere; I am not overfond of trout.

Servants have placed incense pots in the pavilion, to keep the mosquitoes away. Thin smoke hangs around us, making our eyes water; mosquitoes still bite us, but no doubt there are fewer of them.

"Look!" Shikujo suddenly cries.

"What?" If she were anyone but herself, I would think her cry a scream.

"At the other end of the lake. See it?"

I squint through the darkening insect-thick air. "I see some weeds, a bit of the thousand-year oak, and the half-moon bridge over the stream. What am I supposed to see?"

"An . . . animal." She is white-lipped and looks about to faint. "A . . . fox."

The fragile peace we forged with our bodies shivers. "A fox, again? They'd never come so close to people — " I stopped, remembering the fox under my chin.

"But they do!" She looks as if she watches the fading sky, her head tilted back, except for a single streak of tears that runs across her cheekbone and into her black hair. And her words, which pour from her in torrents: "I am so sorry, but they've been watching us. Me, while you've been gone. I have stood in my rooms, back in the shadows, and I've seen them. Their ears and throats glow white in the moonlight, it is simple enough to see them. I found muddy pawprints on the veranda by my writing materials one morning. Why would they watch, if they did not crave our souls?"

"Well," I say blankly.

"And you, my lord! I looked through your writing box and I —"

"You read my letters?"

" — I found sketches and poems. About the foxes. What karma are you working out, that we are haunted by them?"

"And *your* karma? What makes you behave so strangely? You talk as if *I* were the center of everything here."

Unexpectedly, she flushes. "Please. If I have been at all satisfactory, find the foxhole and dig it out."

"I'm sorry for the dream, but I will not kill them," I say. How can I kill them, when I do not understand yet what draws me to them? I am sorry for her, but I am also angry, hurt by her pain, by her unwillingness to pretend everything is all right.

Shikujo stands.

> *"Howl all you like at the moon;*
> *yelling brings it no closer."*

I sit alone until darkness settles, but I see no foxes.

27. KITSUNE'S DIARY

My brother and mother lay outside our scrape, on the forest side of the collapsing fence. I was going to be human and Yoshifuji would love me; for the moment I could lie beside them without the constant frustration that had haunted me so.

It was late, but the sky overhead was the color of cherry blossoms, fading to dark blue in the east, where a peach-gold moon rose. I say this, "the sky," as if it were a thing, when "sky" is no more than space. When had I learned to notice such nothings? What did I see, when I saw "sky"? I tried to explain my puzzlement to my family, but only Mother understood, putting down her much-gnawed deer leg, scavenged from a mountain wolf's leavings.

"Yes," she said. "Seeing the sky is like seeing a hole."

"Anyone can see a hole. The sky? There's nothing to see," Brother said irritably. He'd been impatient a lot lately.

She pointed with her long muzzle. The bamboo fencing had a gap large enough for a fox to jump through. "What do you see?"

"The hole."

Mother yawned. "No. You see the fence. You see the garden on the other side. But that is *through* the hole: not the same."

"Are we seeing through the sky? What's on the other side?" I asked, but Mother was already chewing the leg again.

Brother snorted and jumped to his feet. "I see a crazy old fox, is what *I* see. And a crazy young one."

Grandfather appeared suddenly from the forest. "It is time, Granddaughter."

28. SHIKUJO'S PILLOW BOOK
Little comforts in difficult times:

eat chipped ice with liana syrup. For a moment it is possible to forget how hot it is.

A dragonfly settles on the end of my brush. There are no words for how beautiful I find it, like a jewel owned by a goddess. I lift the brush, to see it more closely. I think: *here it is,* but it is already gone, flown away in an eye-blink.

Rereading a letter from my mother.

A bee walks slowly across a *shoji*-screen, leaving a trail of tiny gold-pollen footprints.

Onaga combs my hair.

I cannot bear to cut dew-wet flowers, but sometimes my

women bring them in for me. I love the green smell of the broken stems, the delicate scent of the dew.

The waxing moon. I look for the rabbit there: surely life cannot be all bad, when a rabbit lives in so unlikely a place?

29. KITSUNE'S DIARY

It is hard work becoming human," Grandfather said. "The magic is complex."

"Is it the clever paws magic?" Brother asked.

"A different one." Grandfather flattened his ears. "A painful one. Do you really think it is worth it, Granddaughter?"

"Yes," I said. What did I know? All I knew about pain was from thorns and pulled muscles, the knife cut on my shoulder and the ache of my interrupted breeding with my brother. Thorns worked themselves out; muscles healed; the cut's scab had flaked off, leaving healthy pink flesh and new hairs. Pains were not permanent. Any of these things seemed a small price when I saw Yoshifuji sit alone drinking *sake* and watching the night.

"Well. Find a human skull and bring it to me."

"What?" I asked.

"Why does she need a skull?" Brother tipped his head, eyeing Grandfather from the corner of one eye.

"Your sister wants to be human: she needs human eyes, a human mind. Where else is she going to get them?"

"If it is anything like an animal skull, there won't *be* any eyes left," Brother said with gloomy satisfaction.

"If that's how it works, won't we all need skulls?" I asked.

"No," Grandfather said. "You're the center of this. Do you want it or not?"

"Yes, but why do we need skulls? Can't you just, um, do something? Something magical?"

"Magic does not happen by itself. You want to be human? Find a skull." He settled on his haunches and closed his eyes: the end of the discussion.

So I left, trotting along the humans' path up the ridge.

A near-full moon moved through a sky filled with clouds that shredded across its face and glowed from behind. The path flickered dark to light under my toes as I walked through the tree shadows. The moon paced me, soared from cloud to cloud, like a crow following a killing animal.

Where would I find a human skull? I had never seen one, although I'd torn flesh off bones often enough to imagine what it should look like. I could not kill a human for its skull: not even a wolf alone could do such a thing, unless the human was small or weak. Somehow I'd have to find an existing skull.

Back in the spring, before Yoshifuji had come to the house, one of the peasants had died in his sleep. I smelled his death the night I killed the kitten. Its taste had still been sharp in my throat when I'd crouched in the bushes behind the big kitchen house.

It had been late. For a change there were no fires, no chattering coming through the crack in the wall beside me. The wind changed and blew through the house and drifted out the crack, and then I smelled death: the sourness of loosed bowels, and a human's last breath — not a sudden squealing, as I was used to (the kitten had squealed), but a long, soft exhalation without a following in-breath. The human must have lain just on the other side.

The next morning the others carried him up into the mountains and I followed them. They laid his body in a box covered with an orange cloth and laid that on a stack of wood in a clearing in the woods. A man touched the stack's bottom with a torch in several places. It caught fire quickly enough that I think they must have done something to make it burn more easily.

The smoke was incredibly thick. It smelled greasy, like an oil lamp, and burned my eyes; but I did not leave, even frightening as the flames and the people's howling were. In the morning they put out the fire with *sake*, and dug the bones from the ashes and placed them in a pot. There had been a skull, but it was in pieces, shattered by the heat.

Now I walked up to where the man had been burned, hoping. There was nothing left, not even the taste of ash in the dew on the grass. A path led from the clearing higher into the mountains. It smelled of a single man's sweaty feet, so I followed it. Perhaps, I thought hopefully, another man would die in the night, and this time I would be there to steal his skull. I was young; I knew nothing then.

The path led to a small hut without a raised floor and thatch falling from its roof in clumps like diseased fur. The lintel over the door was snapped in two, and the entire hut buckled around the angle caused by the break. There was no light and no brazier inside, but I heard someone singing.

It was a man: he smelled of stale urine and grime, age and sickness. Seeing only darkness past the collapsed lintel, I crept closer to the dark doorway.

The singing stopped. I froze, one paw off the ground. Now I saw the eyes gleaming out at me, and a glint that might be a knife raised by an invisible hand.

"Really, fox," he wheezed. "You might wait until these old bones are at least a little cold."

I watched, knowing I was going to die.

"I'm not going to hurt you," he said, as if he knew. "Not that you don't deserve it, trotting up like someone's pet dog. I suppose I could, to keep you from stealing my rice; but this late in the game, I just can't force myself to care. Even a fox has karma; maybe yours is to harass me, hey—or a chance at rebirth. Have you heard the words of Buddha, fox?" The gleam resolved itself to a metal begging-bowl. "Speak up, speak up."

I put my paw down carefully. No human had ever talked to me. Even Yoshifuji, when we were trapped in the storehouse, spoke more to himself than me. "What is karma?"

More laughter; more coughing. "So you *can* speak. My whole life, no animal has ever talked back when I spoke to her."

"Why did you talk to me, then?"

"It couldn't hurt."

"Tell me what karma is. Also Buddha."

"Right to the point, little fox? You must *crave* enlightenment.

Fifty years I've been a monk — that's more generations of foxes than you have toes, I expect — and I still don't know." He did not seem dangerous. I sat down, cocked my head. "I suppose you deserve a better answer than that. I wish I had one. Well. Buddha — who was a man, a long time ago; now he's a god. This happens — his lessons taught me to listen inside until I heard nothing, and then I would be there. In Paradise, which is also nothing. Karma is the way we get there."

This made no sense. "Is that poetry?" I asked.

"It's a contradiction, is what it is. So I've searched for the silence my entire life, and all I found were more questions. Whereas I expect you've had nothing but silence your whole life, eh? Except that you're talking to me now. How silent can your life be?"

I shook my head, confused, trying to dislodge his rambling conversation, which buzzed like a fly in my ear.

"Well, I'll find silence soon enough, I expect," he said. "Too soon, maybe, except that it's never supposed to be too soon for the next stage of enlightenment. So. An old man wants silence; but what does a fox want? I've never been able to ask before. I guess I'm dying, hey."

"I want to be a human."

"You do?" He started laughing and coughing again. At last he hacked out a gob of mucus and spat it on the dirt between us. "Well, well. So I suppose you're out hunting for a skull. You can't have mine, you know," he said sharply. "I'll fight if I have to."

"I would not — "

The old man relaxed. "I shouldn't encourage you, anyway; you should go through the cycles of rebirth, not try to jump straight to human without learning the lessons; but I don't care. Either you have a soul or you don't; I'm no bodhisattva, to teach you."

"I saw them burn a man once," I said, "when he was dead. There was nothing left afterward except scraps. And the smell."

"And you're wondering what the soul is, if there's nothing left but smell, hey?"

"Yes," I said slowly, confused. "I suppose so."

"It's gone. Hah. What you should worry about is where will you find a skull, if they all get burned up."

I had not even thought of this, not yet. His mind made leaps I could not follow, so that talking to him was like talking to my mother. Only he was human, so he must *know* things; and my mother was half-witted.

"Well," he said. "Sometimes they're buried, dead people. There's a cemetery, up by the shrine for the mountain *Kami*. But don't tell the ghosts I told you, or they'll never let me rest in peace. Now go away. I can't imagine what I'm doing, talking to a fox. Shoo!" He threw the metal bowl at me. I had not expected it; it caught me on the chest and I rolled over backwards and then bolted.

I ran, and then (a safe distance away from the old man and his fly-bite conversation) I walked the direction he told me to go, up to a ridge and into the next valley. When morning came, I had not found it yet, so I slept out the day with the smell of mint so strong in my nostrils that I knew I'd never be found.

I found the temple early that evening, following the thick incense that threaded through the woods. It was nothing like the little shrine where the moon-foxes spoke to me: it was a real building of dark-stained timbers and shingled roof. The incense came from inside the temple. A dozen men's voices sang words on a single note so fast that I could not understand. Near the temple were smaller buildings: a kitchen building (it smelled like food), a dormitory (sweat), a stable (oxen), a guest house (disuse). And overlaying all these scents, light as dawn fog as it burns away, was the smell of cleaned bones and rotting flesh. It led me a few steps down yet another path, into a small clearing clustered with wooden tablets hung with prayer flags.

The scent of the nearest grave was muted by the earth it seeped through, but I could smell the single rotting body. I tracked the scent to a hillock of dirt hidden in the shadows of a tree at the edge of the cemetery. I checked carefully: no one was there. So I dug.

Foxes can dig and do. But this was harder than digging the scrape under the side gatehouse had been: harder than anything

I'd ever done, anything I'd even heard of any fox doing. The dirt was hard-packed, heavy, with clay in it. When my toes got caked with dirt, I bit the soil out from between them, and dug. After a time my paw pads were raw, and the dirt I bit free tasted of blood. The smell of the corpse got stronger.

Why would humans do this? It had not made sense to me, that they would burn their dead, but this was worse. They had to somehow *make* this happen, go out of their way to cause it.

My claw caught on fabric. I pulled free, and brought a bit of snagged cotton with my paw.

"Hey!"

I jumped backward, out of the hole, and whirled around, and saw a woman made of mist. Like the moon-foxes, she had no smell (though the corpse certainly did); but they were strange and perfect, and she was a warty, decaying old lady without teeth.

"What are you?"

"A ghost."

"Can you hurt me?"

"Yes," she said. Her hair whipped around her head, like lake weeds in a storm. She bared her toothless gums.

"I don't believe you," I said. How could she? She was made of mist, of nothing. She had no teeth. I went back to digging.

"Stop it! I was a rich woman. I was the primary wife to Taira no Sadafun, when I was alive."

"You're dead now. Why are you still here?" The corpse's rotting robes fell apart when my claws touched them. The skin of the face sloughed from its cheekbones. The eyes were gone: gummy dirt-crusted sockets. The mouth opened and spoke.

"Where else would I go? This is my body."

I paused. "I've seen bodies before. Mice and things. They rot away, and then there's just bones."

"They tell me I'll be reborn, and I believed it when I was alive, but now—how can I believe them? I didn't think I'd die, and look what happened."

"Reborn? Everything dies," I said.

"What do you know? You're a fox. They say you do not have

a soul, but I do not believe that, either. Why should I? I have one, and I'm afraid of the darkness and of rebirth, forgetting everything I am."

Even as a ghost, this woman chattered the way all humans did. I scraped more dirt free.

"Leave me alone, this is all I have." No longer supported by soil, the head lolled on its decaying neck.

"Go away." I said.

"Why?" the dirt-clogged jaws said. "What makes you so important that you dig me up?"

"I need your skull to become human."

"Hah. You'll never be human. A fox and a ghost—we're neither of us human, but at least it was *my* skull once. Leave it alone!"

"No. At least you've *been* human."

"You're alive and I'm dead and *you* envy *me*? I'd rather be a fox running alive in the woods than a dead Buddha. What can you want?"

"Love." I mouthed the neck and tasted grainy sweetness.

Something moved against my lip as the ghost laughed bitterly. "There is more to life than love. Mercifully. Humanness will not assure that he loves you."

"But it gives me a chance. A fox and a man? I have no other hope."

"It is better to live as a fox than love and suffer as a woman. I know: I waited for my husband's step out on the veranda, and his touch at night. But now that I'm dead, I've learned some secrets, and one of them is this: that a woman's lot is shadows and waiting. I'd have traded it all for the chance to stand barefaced in the summer sun. You're a fool, fox," the ghost said, and spat dirt at me.

I had her neck between my teeth. I was furious; I jerked my head, and her rotting spine snapped. The head spiraled through the air. The ghost-woman lunged for it, but her hands passed through it. She shrieked and shivered into blades of light, like light through a tree, and was gone.

30. THE NOTEBOOK OF KAYA NO YOSHIFUJI

The valley is too hot, too relentlessly fertile for my present tastes. The rice plants seem a finger's width taller every morning. Even the trees —larch and birch and witch hazel— look uncomfortably hot, their leaves restless and too pale. The only options for hunting just now seem to be frogs in the fields and the thousand birds that seem to live on frogs: gulls, herons, crows.

Above all this, I stride restlessly in the thick cover that forests the slopes. It is slightly cooler than the valley; mostly it is shaded. The forest is really too thick just here to use a bow effectively, but I do not enjoy spear-hunting. The killing is too direct, too immediate, for my civilized tastes. Instead I kill my prey at a decent distance, and servants (of course there are servants; there are *always* servants) collect the kill and discreetly make it vanish into the kitchen building at the end of the day.

Before I left, Hito asked what I was hunting and I had to admit that I had no idea. I am here because it is a hazy hot afternoon in the valley, a day suitable for sleeping or drinking or making love, and not much else, and I am too restless for these. I am here because I think (in some unenlightened corner of my soul) that it will feel good to kill something.

After the first night of my return from Kannon's shrine, my wife has been unavailable. She went into seclusion for her monthly courses the day after I returned. Then she was observing a fast date; then she was preparing to pray at the local monastery. Lately she has not even had excuses. She is just tragically, apologetically, unavailable.

I would be annoyed, but I realize this withdrawal is just a logical extension of an already existing state between us. She has been unavailable to me for much longer than a few weeks, but the fact we still had sex concealed it somewhat.

It might be better this way. I am not happy, but I have not

been for a long time. Now at least I realize that I cannot and should not expect my wife or son to miraculously make sense of my life, to make me happy.

I have seen nothing of the foxes, not even out here where I stalk, longing to kill.

31. KITSUNE'S DIARY

It took a full day to return. The ghost cried for a while. Her sobs resonated through her skull into my jaw, sound without noise. I found the skull harder to carry than the fan had been; too heavy and round to hold firmly in my teeth, it often slipped free and rolled along the ground.

I was halfway home, teetering down the bank of a little stream, when it fell and bounced down to land half in the water. I slid after it; it was not going anywhere, so I stood paw-deep in mountain-cold water and drank. The water was chill and sweet, and cleared my mouth of the sticky gaminess of the skull's flesh. My neck and jaw ached. I stretched and yawned hugely.

The cover downwind quaked. A lot of scavengers had smelled my skull and come to see what it was, but they'd all been birds or rats. Whatever disturbed the bushes was my size. I braced my legs over my skull and growled.

A fox stepped through.

She was a female somewhat older than I, with a mask that outlined her mouth and elongated eyes in black. I'd never seen her before. She belonged to a different family.

I was in unfamiliar territory, alone, and I needed the skull. She had family; this was where she belonged. I did the only thing I could: abased myself to the strange fox. "I am passing through, back to my home," I breathed at her, watching warily from my averted face. "I am sorry I am here. I will leave now, immediately."

She picked her way down the side of the stream and stood a bare lunge away. Silent.

Keeping my head turned, I grabbed the bit of spine at the base of the skull and dragged it through the water, away from her. She made no move to follow me and made no noise.

I've never understood this, even as a woman. It was as if we were different breeds and could not speak, or as if she were unthinking, a mere animal. But she cannot have been that. She was a fox, as was I. Where was the difference?

32. SHIKUJO'S PILLOW BOOK
In the seventh month:

In the seventh month, one felt safe again. One's husband had returned from a trip. The air hummed with the sound of a cicada close to the ruined gate at the bottom of the garden. On its way to the first new moon of autumn, the moon was plump in cloud-free skies, and the world outside seemed brilliantly lit. The garden was tamed now, and few creatures would step across the shining stones and sands between the grasses and the house. Nothing could happen to us, even if we left the blinds open.

My women were asleep, but I often found it too hot. Onaga would have stayed up with me, but I craved solitude. I ordered her to sleep, and a few times she even did so, dozing in spite of her intention of only pretending unconsciousness.

There was one such night, when the moon was still nearly full and the air hung hot and still. I sat reading a *monogatari*-tale sent from the capital, until the moths found the flame of my lantern and hurried to their next life, dropping their shed bodies as delicate ashes onto my opened scroll. After that, I snuffed the lantern, and sat in darkness, watching the silver light of the moon ease across the wisteria courtyard, shadows shifting imperceptibly until they seemed to suddenly leap across a railing or stone. I had a white fan once, as bright and round as the moon—no ornament, no ink staining its surface. Where did it go? I wondered.

As silently as the gliding shadows, someone seated himself beside me, smelling of spices. "Lady," he said, and the voice was as familiar as a remembered dream. The fox man.

"Why are you here again?" I turned my face away, and my hair fell between us. "I have told you I will hear no poems from you."

"But this is a new one," he said, and his voice was half-amused. But only half-amused: the rest held sadness and a surprising shyness. "Do you wonder why your husband watches foxes?"

I stiffened. "I have no idea what you are talking about." This was a stranger, after all, even if I was only dreaming him. It seemed inappropriate to speak of such things to him.

"No doubt. Nevertheless. He watches them because he is lonely for something you cannot give him."

I said nothing.

"He is wild; you are civilized. Too much so, I expect. I am civilized, too—more so than your husband, even being what I am. My granddaughter? Who can say? She is still young."

There was nothing to say; I had no idea what he was talking about.

"So, lady. He longs for you to be as wild as he is."

"Indeed, we are quite—wild, as you say. There are times—" I stopped, my face unbecomingly warm. I was telling him things I would not have said to my husband. A memory of the poem of shed *hakama*-trousers and soft touches returned with startling clarity.

"I expect so," he said. "Wild enough, at least in sex. But your heart? Soft and easily startled—a rabbit's heart."

The moonlight had shifted again, and a fragment of light glittered on the porcelain of one of the wisteria pots, picking out a pair of painted indigo *kaodori* birds. I had seen the pot so often before, in sunlight and rain: how had I never noticed before this that the birds danced together? "I am no rabbit," I said slowly. An extraordinary conversation, even for a dream.

"Oh, they are fierce enough, rabbits. But he does not understand a rabbit's heart, does he? — And he keeps hoping your heart will be something so grand that it transforms him. Not *you*. In the end he is too selfish for that."

"I do not understand. I need to change?"

"No. There are those who prize your heart as it is."

"You?" I said sadly.

It was a very short poem he told me then. A poem in which a long-fingered hand touched my face. I stopped him before the poem went on, to subsequent lines or the *envoi*.

33. KITSUNE'S DIARY

The wait for the full moon was a long one. Grandfather was often gone those nights, and said nothing of where he had gone.

"Tonight," Grandfather said. Grabbing the skull in my teeth, I followed him out through the ruined gate, past the reeking humid rice fields, into the marshes. He led me in silence through brambles into a clear space saturated with icy light, and floored with short grasses and water glittering between their stalks. A *torii*-arch like the one I'd seen at the moon-foxes' shrine stood to one side: packets of food lay beside it.

My teeth chattered. "Is this a shrine to Inari?"

"Inari is one of a thousand gods," he said. "Ten thousand. Who knows why people worship here?"

"When I am human, I'll know," I said.

"Poor little bug-eater," he said. "You think everything will be solved if you take a woman's shape. Are you so sure this is what you want? There is no way to unlearn these lessons."

"It's too late," I whispered. "I know what I want."

"Very well. Place it on your head," he ordered.

"How do you know how to do this?"

"Do you think you're the only one who has done this? Now."

I had no hands, no clever fingers to lift and balance the skull. I pushed my nose under, as if pushing aside a heavy bough.

My grandfather's eyes were hidden in the shadows cast by his own ears. He seemed terrible and remote, and somehow unbearably sad.

"Bow to the seven stars of the Great Bear."

Afraid it might slip, I tipped my head carefully, but it clung as if held there by sap, a heavy rotting weight on my head, the upper jaw an arc across my brow. I felt each tooth like a heavy bead.

He told me: "You will say this." And then he said words, in the language of the humans.

I'd spoken with others: my family all my life, the old man in the woods, a strange vixen and a dust-colored bitch-dog, a ghost. But I had never spoken aloud, not this awkward writhing of lips and tongue. My grandfather's voice was harsh and unfamiliar: a bark and a sob together.

I tried to repeat the sounds he made, but all that came out was a whimper. "I can't do this. Show me another way, Grandfather."

"There is none. Speaking is part of becoming a woman."

I tried again, but my throat knotted and silenced itself. "I can't."

"Then you'll never be a woman."

I tilted my face up to the moon, the skull clinging like a cap. I barked once, then again: anger and grief and frustration. A fox noise.

The moonlight hissed like mist falling around me. Washed silver, my grandfather seemed to shimmer. Like a reflection on water, one of Inari's moon-foxes overlaid itself and spoke: "Choose."

And the words came. My jaw clenched from the effort, but they came out in halting breaks, strange sounds forced through a throat and mouth never meant to speak.

I stood in the hissing silver space. Nothing happened. There was no magic, no changes.

I shook the skull free and screamed at my grandfather. "This was *nothing!* You *lied!*"

He jumped out of my way easily, as if he were in fact the moon-fox I'd so foolishly mistaken him for.

"Wait!" he called after me, but I was already gone, racing toward the garden, insane with anger and disappointment.

The valley spread before me: rice fields and marshes, over-hung with trees that tore the strange silver light to shreds.

I ran faster than I ever had before, my spine curling and extending too tightly: a cat's run. Pain shot up my spine, along my bones. My flesh clenched and caught, cramping and stretch-ing. Low branches slashed at my eyes and face. My pulse thrummed through me like the throbbing of gongs. I splashed through warm water, sticky with summer's green slime. It felt like blood, smelled like rotting things, and burst into pale cold fire as I stepped through it: marsh gas. Foxfire.

I smelled blood from a hundred scratches, and then realized I was bleeding everywhere, from the nine openings of my body—eyes and ears, nostrils and mouth, vulva and anus—from every hair's root. I was dying for no reason, for the folly of placing a dead woman's skull on my head and wishing.

This was magic like the moon-foxes. But that had been eerie, like a dream after eating poppies. This was *now*, this was real. I screamed with pain and fear and anger and ran on. There was no reason to stop. Magic could kill me as surely running as standing.

The little stream that ran between two of the lakes lay just ahead. I gathered myself and leapt across. In the reflection I glimpsed my outline against the sky: a woman's shadow cast against a *shoji*-screen.

I stumbled when I landed. I was a woman. I had hands; breasts; narrow feet; hips. When I touched my face with my fingers, I felt a nose and cheekbones and eyebrows. There was no blood anywhere on me. Perhaps the copper-smell had been a dream, part of the magic.

I tilted my head back and laughed, my first sound as a woman.

Someone rustled. I froze. I had ended here, beside the lake

closest to my master's wing. When I looked up, Yoshifuji stood
on the veranda, almost lost in shadows my fox-eyes would have
seen through instantly. I squinted; he squinted back. I was a
woman now. What would I fear? Carefully (my body was unfamiliar to me, a huge gawky thing held together by balance and
sinew) I stood. The moon fell full on me. I was naked. I waited
for him to see me, to come out into the dew and moonlight and
mate with me.

And he laughed: "Bright nights, little fox, make men and
beasts restless." He had seen me, but not as a woman. I sobbed:
my second sound.

My grandfather appeared beside me, nuzzled at my fox's face.
"You thought that was all there was? That you were human
now?" His tone mocked at me, but I wept on. "You're naked,
you have no arts. You cannot speak to him, cannot match robes
or write poetry or do anything civilized. He has a wife who is
beautiful and gentle and clever. And you, you're still a fox. No:
you saw a glimpse of a woman in the moonlight, of the woman
you might become. This is just the beginning of the magic."

And we began.

34. SHIKUJO'S PILLOW BOOK
This journal of mine:

This journal of mine is like gossamer, no more than a shimmering in the summer sky, or the thread of a spiderweb
that gleams across a doorway.

I write about the things that interest me, that might perhaps
interest friends in the capital. I make lists, write about visiting
the monastery, or the smell of the ornamental grasses gone to
seed outside my rooms, or the taste of cold green noodles and
vinegar when my women bring food to me. But these things are
illusion, my pillow book an illusion of an illusion—like a painting of spiderwebs, not even the spiderweb itself. And even the
spiderweb can be stepped through. My thoughts—abstract and

uncertain as they are — are the true reality, because they shape all the illusions.

A spider spins her web in my husband's house. He does not care, but I do. I cannot watch him collapse in on himself, like a beggar's hut. More: I cannot allow my son to watch his father dissolve like this. My thoughts are not the only reality I can control.

35. THE NOTEBOOK OF KAYA NO YOSHIFUJI

I am writing, or trying to. At last I saw one of the foxes again, last night. I was pacing along my veranda, and caught her watching me. Her? I guess her gender. How could I tell, half a garden away? I am not at all sure of my ability to tell. Even the fox that slept under my chin: I imagine her to be a female because this in some way fits what I imagine of foxes, or of myself.

Unable to forget, today I grind ink and select a furred paper with a cast of orange so slight as to be almost invisible.

Three lines have come to me:

> *While I watched the moon,*
> *the moon watched the fox,*
> *and the fox watched me —*

"Where is the rest of the poem?" Shikujo, standing behind me. How surprising: she has walked across to my rooms in the clear daylight. Onaga and the inevitable others stand a few paces away. She must have told them to keep their distance. "There are still two lines missing to make a *waka*."

I look up at her and smile. "I do not know," I say honestly. "I'm still waiting for them to come to me."

"The poem and your life." She sighs slightly and kneels beside me with a single fluid movement, like a cat. "I know better now than to ask you to give up the foxes, to destroy them."

I look down guiltily at my poem. "I—"

"I am so sorry, husband. I've tried to be a good wife, but I find myself failing, again and again."

This must be irony. She is exemplary; she must know this as surely as I. "I do not think—"

"Let me end your poem." She tips her head to one side, and that incredible hair of hers conceals her face. One hand reaches up to brush it back, but she stops there, hand in the air, like a statue of a dancer in the formal court dances.

She speaks:

> *"While I watched the moon,*
> *the moon watched the fox,*
> *and the fox watched me—*
> *Trapped outside this circle of three,*
> *others moved unnoticed."*

My throat closes. I clear it, but my words sound hoarse in my ears. "What are you saying, wife?"

"Please forgive me. I am returning to the capital." Her voice is calm, but the pale hand still hovers as if she has forgotten where she left it.

"There is no point to returning until the new season. It's too hot to travel comfortably. Can't we—"

"I am sorry, no. It must be now." She touches my hand. I feel her trembling and realize this serenity she shows me is like a paper boat on a river: the tiniest wave will swamp it and it will dissolve.

"Why?" I ask baldly. "I know you fear this place, but—"

"Fear it?" She laughs once, such a harsh sound that I do not immediately recognize it, coming from her. "I suppose I do. I must leave, husband."

I have been here for several months, drunk on a sort of bitter wine of sadness and self-pity. She wishes us to leave, my wife; well then, we could leave, and be back in the capital before the first leaves fall there. Perhaps there, we would again share more than courtesy and sex. Perhaps. My heart twists within me, a pang of anguish. It is as if she were holding out happiness to me again, and I —

I cannot take it. As trapped as a drunkard, the bitter wine will not let me go until I have finished it. "I must stay," I say finally. My face feels numb. I can scarcely force sound past my rigid throat.

"I did not expect you to leave." A single frown line creases the perfect skin between her eyes. "Your karma is here, now. But not mine. And not our son's."

She does not even want me to accompany her. She was not offering happiness — not to me. The world is spinning; my vision is dim and narrow, as if I were squinting at distant green fields on a blinding summer day. My voice sounds like a stranger's to me. "You will return to your family?"

"Yes." She does not realize how hurt I am. "My old rooms are still available. Now that he has retired from his position at court, my father has more time to see his grandson. He — "

"Do you want a divorce?" The words fall gracelessly between us.

"No!" She covers her mouth for a moment, as if to conceal its quivering. "It is only here and now I want away from. Visit me as husband in the capital. When this is over, this craziness of yours, we'll talk."

"Not later. We must talk now."

"We talk now and nothing happens. You brood over your unhappiness as if you were the only one to know grief or longings. You nurse your self-pity like a crippling wound. Until you are through this, nothing changes in you, and nothing changes between us."

"And you are so capable of change?" I snap. "This is my fault? You run from 'here' and 'now' and 'us' like a rabbit."

"Rabbits run to survive." Her lips are white.

"I brood, but at least you know my feelings. What are *you* feeling, wife? When will you let me know?" I snap, wanting to swamp her paper boat, see her awash in the emotions that threaten to drown me.

"Feel — ?" She averts her face, pushes the word away with a

little gesture. "I will miss you so much. Every night my sleeves will be soaked with tears. But I have no choice in this. The foxes—they will destroy me and the boy. Or you will, not caring for us."

"And Tadamaro?"

"He returns with me. I may be able to do our son some good in the capital; I do none here."

"He is eight—nearly a man. I'd like to see him grow."

"Then come to the capital, live with us at my father's house. Nothing changes between you and me that you do not wish to change."

This catches me by surprise. I stall for time: "I am sorry I've hurt you."

"Please, husband." She stands. "Farewell, Kaya no Yoshifuji. I will pray that our fates allow us to be together again soon."

Tearstains on the dark blue silk of her sleeves.

36. SHIKUJO'S PILLOW BOOK
Preparing to travel:

> *I will travel praying for rain —*
> *an excuse for my wet sleeves.*

37. THE NOTEBOOK OF KAYA NO YOSHIFUJI

I caused this.
I sit in the lake-viewing pavilion watching the ornamental grasses bob. The sky is the strange cherry red of cheap ink. The lake is thick with chickweed, a mottled brocade over its surface.

The noises have died down, as the servants have finished removing my wife's trunks. She will be gone before dawn; apparently no unfortunate tabu mars her speedy removal.

I sent her a farewell gift, a pair of silver hair ornaments I laid aside as a gift some time ago. They are carved with grass patterns, and each has a fine silver chain, from which hangs a tiny enameled day lily. I think they are Chinese: I only know that when I saw them, back in the capital, I thought of Shikujo's hair and I wanted her to wear them. I do not know why I never gave them to her before this. She sent back a poem:

> *Today is summer.*
> *Like certain dreams, the wild lilies thrive.*
> *Soon, autumn.*
> *Their season will be past —*
> *Will they then die?*

I should accompany her on her trip, for at least the first mile, a common courtesy to a traveler leaving one's home. But I do not think she would welcome my company.

Hito comes to me from the main house. When he is close enough, he bows, waiting for me to acknowledge him before he interrupts my reverie. But before a word is exchanged, a shout floats across the lake. "Father!"

Tadamaro stands beside his nurse on the veranda of my house. I expect Hito told them to wait until he could inform me of their presence, but my son has a different idea. The boy bounces across the walkway toward us, his nurse trailing behind. She grabs for his sleeve, hissing something under her breath; he slips free and bolts forward. He pauses for a moment to bob a bow at me—"Sir-I-trust-I-find-you-well"—and he throws himself at my waist and reaches as far around as possible. He is quite old enough to behave properly, but this is so charming that I lift him and hold him close. He is getting heavy, Kaya no Tadamaro.

His nurse, caught up at last, clears her throat in a way Hito, my son and I all recognize as significant. The boy, cued, says, "Father, I am to say good-bye, since we leave tomorrow."

My eyes burn. "So you do. Will you be good?"

"Of course!" he exclaims with the indignation of childhood. "I will behave properly. Only —"

"What?" He smells good, like sun and heat and grass.

"I would rather stay."

I hold him closer. "Why would that be?"

He squirms a little. "It's bigger here. There's more to see. And you'll be here."

"But your mother will be with you. And your nurse. And your Grandfather. And—"

"Hah," he says. "I want to watch the foxes!"

I put him down abruptly and turn him to face me. "What did you say?"

"The foxes! They are very fine. One of them is old. He is very nice, I think."

Almost accidentally, I meet his nurse's eyes. She looks anguished, as if he suddenly speaks the language of demons. I talk as much to reassure her as myself. "That's a game, isn't it? You make believe."

"I suppose," he says, his attention already straying. "Look!" He points at the darkening sky. "A bat. It's eating. Please, can I stay?"

I might have wished it before, but now I think my wife is perhaps wise to take my son away from here. I like to watch him, hoping his joy will remind me of when I felt similarly. But I do not wish my son to catch the sickness my wife sees in me, and I do not wish foxes to speak to him: he is too young for such madness. "No," I say gently, and turn him to face me. "There are bats in the capital, and birds, and fireflies, and foxes and everything else. And your grandfather has strange fish for you to see."

"He does," Tadamaro says, still not totally convinced. "But the foxes will not be the *same* foxes, will they? None of it will be the same."

"It will not." I straighten. "It is your duty to go. Do not worry your mother overmuch."

Tadamaro sighs heavily, but he is a (more or less) good child, and does not argue. "Very well, Father. I have not seen the old fox. Please say farewell for me."

We embrace again, his cheek pressed close to mine. "Watch

over your mother," I whisper. "Be careful." Meaning: *do not dream of foxes.*

We separate. He bows, a small boy carefully executing a lesson. "Farewell, sir," he says. "I will do as you instruct." Meaning I do not know what.

They leave me, Tadamaro trailed by his nurse and Hito, a small entourage for his dignified recess. The sky overhead burns with a cold lurid fire. The sky, the child, the attendants, are blurs of color through my tears.

The sun sets. The evening cools until I am grateful for the hot *sake* one of my people brings me. There is not much moon, and what light there is has been softened by the air's humidity, but it is bright enough to touch my house with silver. Servants have set torches beside the verandas; in the still air, their smoke makes straight black columns that rise to a certain height before flattening and floating east. Gold light flickers behind the *shoji*-screens of my wife's rooms, but there is no noise.

I drink *sake*. I will miss them—I will be alone here, more alone than I have ever been. But for better or worse, something has been set in motion. Start over, with fresh paper and a new poem.

38. SHIKUJO'S PILLOW BOOK
Leaving:

rasses drooping by a stone well. An abandoned hermitage: pillows of grass for my women and me. A bat whirs by, squeaky-silent.

The evenings cool more quickly now. I am glad of this; the days themselves are brutally, searingly hot, the carriages we travel in more so.

Any gentler air is welcome.

39. KITSUNE'S DIARY

I was so deep in my learning that I hardly noticed Shikujo's leaving. I do not think I considered it part of the magic, exactly, that my rival would be removed; it just seemed inexorable, like the purple clouds that piled high each afternoon and collapsed into showers. Of course she left. What else would she do?

Where I used to watch when I could get away from my grandfather, now I watched constantly, day and night. With Shikujo's women gone, there were fewer people in the wings and walkways, although just as many out in the stableyard where the servants worked. The plants in the garden and courtyards were thick with their late-summer growth, so it was simple enough to approach the house: even, at night, to crawl into the rooms and watch Yoshifuji or his men asleep.

With Shikujo gone, Yoshifuji spoke less, wrote more. He talked to Hito and a few other servants, ate, mated with a serving girl, slept under a mosquito net. I watched.

The servants were more lively. They interacted in groups, in pairs, and *did* without stopping. They cooked and gardened and tended the animals. They played, all the ways my brother and I had seen before. They twined ropes, tied thatch, built chests, washed laundry—and always they talked. They gossiped about the neighboring estates, and about their master and mistress. They were never alone, and never still.

No one seemed to think it strange, that a woman would just *leave* as Shikujo had. I've since learned a little of what might drive a woman to abandon someone she still loves; then I felt superior to this strange silent woman. *I* would *never* leave Yoshifuji as she had. *I* was a fox; I understood family loyalty, and conveniently forgot the trip that ended with Yoshifuji's breath in my fur and the moon-foxes' words.

I watched, and practiced. It was hard to concentrate: I had never done so before, except for the short time it took to track and catch prey, or to find my grandfather and ask a question.

My head throbbed sometimes, so that I rubbed my muzzle against the bare ground in a frenzy trying to ease it.

I do not know exactly how the magic worked. As I said, I concentrated. Sometimes my family and I talked about something, and there it was; later, after we had made the servants, I would see *them* making a screen or a fire we had discussed, just as human servants would have done. Our shapes shifted between human and fox.

We made the scrape beneath the side gatehouse a many-roomed house, with floors and beams worn to a glow from servants' constant rubbing; and trunks and lacquered boxes filled with silk robes and tortoiseshell combs, porcelain bowls and silver chopsticks, Michinoka paper and bamboo-handled brushes and cakes of ink, a ceremonial tea set glazed to look like pebbles seen underwater. No, we did not *make* these things, exactly: it was still just bare dirt and a dry little hole. But we made it seem *as if* it were so. I can't explain.

The house was scraped together out of bits of Yoshifuji's house, only bigger, more elegant. Things came to us as we paced the bare halls, things we'd never seen but somehow *knew* should be there. That was how some of the inner sliding walls came to be covered in squares of gold leaf; and the source of the Chinese-red brocade curtains that hung around Yoshifuji's bed.

I looked around what would be his rooms and spoke: "There, in the corner by the scroll-chest. I think there should be an ornamental screen," and there it was: ponies dancing through a splashing stream.

We made a garden around the place filled with stones and ponds and thick bushes. It would have been a fox's dream, had I still been a fox; even so, it tempted me to set aside the shape I was learning to use. We placed a sun, a moon, stars, just like the real ones; once set, they arranged themselves into an orderly procession of day and night, new and full moons. The peonies in the fox-garden bloomed.

We made many servants, all quick and quiet and clever. We sat one day in a room (it would be my room, I knew) and they each walked in and bowed, and this is how they came to be. The last was my primary woman, Josei: slim as a reed, dressed in double-indigo robes—a calm, efficient woman.

"If you will forgive me, my lady?" she said in a voice like a flute, and bowed herself out as gracefully as she had entered the room. When I (woman-shape) followed her a moment later, she was in a neighboring room, already organizing my women (there seemed to be a hundred of them, more than Shikujo had ever had; although I don't suppose the room could have held more than a handful) to laying out lengths of autumn-colored silk she had unearthed from a trunk and sewing the pieces together into robes. They talked among themselves quietly as women will who have known one another for a long time, and have no news to chew over. Unsettled, I backed out of the room (fox-shape) and searched out my grandfather.

He sat in front of a desk stacked with papers of every size, forepaws neatly together, ears forward, absorbed. A male servant in neat dark robes read to him.

"Grandfather!"

Man-shaped now, he straightened and frowned, gesturing with a hand; the servant rose and bowed and slipped through a half-opened *shoji*-screen. "You shouldn't be running around like a fox anymore. The servants—"

"Where did the silk come from?" I interrupted. "How can they know what the pieces of a robe look like? How can they know how to *sew*? I've never seen how the fabric holds together; where did they learn it?"

He held up a hand to silence me. "They're shadows—not real. A shadow doesn't know what it does."

"What do they mimic, then?"

"Magic sometimes does more than we can do, sees more than we can. Because it is not real, it can afford to be perfect, you see."

I did not, but I was too lost in the wonder of what we did to pursue this stray thought. We created a world. Yoshifuji would be mine here.

40. SHIKUJO'S PILLOW BOOK
Returning to the capital:

The mile markers pass —
no way to prove they are not the same few repeating —
it is my heart that says they are not

41. KITSUNE'S DIARY

The human shapes settled more comfortably around us as time passed. My brother became small and exquisite, with narrow poet's hands. His hair was shaved, except for a tail at the back that he wore in an elaborate knot, as we had seen Yoshifuji wear his. He dressed in green and red like a young courtier.

He hated the changes, and fought them until Grandfather (or I, when he was gone) forced him to remember his position in the family.

I asked Brother once about this. We walked in the garden, looking at sweet flags (which were improbably in bloom, though it was the end of summer: the sun and stars and moon had not yet settled down). "Are you jealous?"

"How can I not be? You were my sister, partner, mate. Now you change everything. Where do I fit?"

"I need you."

"Do you? You have this man you love. You have this *shape* —" He jabbed at my chest. "You have everything you want, Sister."

"But we're so similar." I lied, of course — smug in my humanness. "There's a place in this for you, as surely as there is for me."

"As what? I'm a fox. I want nothing else. You and our grandfather are the ones maddened with this — disease."

"Please. You'll find things to love about it: you'll have a human form, and perhaps a profession —"

"Don't confuse my wants with yours," he hissed, and (suddenly fox-shape) his ears flattened. "Your madness makes you and Grandfather unfit to run this family. Why should I listen to either of you?"

It was growing harder for me to maintain my dominance; I cared less and less about heading the family, and fought more to save the magic. But here both were united: my body flickered to fox-shape and I bit him.

"Embrace it," I snarled.

As I said, he hated these changes.

Not that it mattered. Grandfather would still have been the head of our family, and he shaped the magic as much as I did. I remembered Grandfather's anger about the humans before they had returned, and wondered sometimes that he permitted these changes. But truly? — I did not really care. I would have Yoshifuji. This was all that mattered.

Grandfather was very handsome as a man. He wore russet robes with small medallions on each sleeve; when I bent close to see what they represented, he snorted and pulled away. *"Kamisori,"* he said: fox-lily. He had always seemed sad as a fox; this was stronger now that he was a man.

My mother became a slender woman with tiny wrinkles at the corners of her eyes and a single streak of silver in the black hair that fell to her knees. She adapted very poorly to her human life, and, despite the magic, she was always untidy, and she wore unattractive color combinations. She was never intelligent: even in her human shape she was barely more than a fox in her nature. She slipped shape back and forth more easily than any of us. Sometimes one or another of us would have to follow her into the woods and remind her of the shape she needed to return in. She was simple, my mother.

And me! I lived in my new shape, so I could not see it as I saw the others; but I felt the new knitting of my muscles, the strange connections my joints made. I had fingers that parted and picked things up. My hair fell past my robe's hem when I stood, and coiled on the floor like a pool at the base of a black waterfall. I had a Chinese mirror made of silvered bronze, with swallows twining on its back; when I looked at my reflection, my face was as round and pale as the moon.

I loved my new form. "How could you give this up?" I marveled as I stroked the silky hairless skin of my belly, lifted one breast to peer at its round pink nipple.

"Close your robe, Granddaughter. You are a maiden now."

I wrapped it absently. "How could you not stay forever in this magic?"

"The price is high," Grandfather said slowly: "You lose your sharp eyes, and your sense of smell, and you are cumbered by this—" He held out the sleeve of his robe.

"I do not care about that," I said. I would not miss these things: the eyesight, the speed, the stability of four feet on the ground as I ran. Losing them was just a minor inconvenience, I knew.

"Don't you? Humanness is more than robes. Or tiled roofs, or poetry."

"Then what?"

"Expectations. Separation from things. Loneliness. Sadness. Truthfully, I was glad to give it up, to run again. Not even love can make it worthwhile."

"You don't know that," I said hotly. "I'd die if it weren't for this."

"So I thought when I was your age. But I nevertheless lived." Grandfather snorted. "The wisdom of defeat. Some lessons are too hard to complete. I walked away from *my* examination."

"I never would!" I said, shocked.

"Perhaps you are stronger than I was." But he did not sound convinced.

"Here, Granddaughter," my grandfather said one day. "You will need this."

"What?" I asked. I looked up from my ink stone, where I had been trying to grind my ink stick evenly, and had only made a mess.

He gave me a small ball the color of the moon. I say, "the color of the moon"; I mean it glowed in my hand like the full moon on a clear night. "What is this?" I asked, turning it over.

"A ball. All fox maidens carry one. You will find it useful."

"What do I need a ball for?"

He shrugged. "It is something a fox maiden has. You are giving up a lot of things; some you do not even know about yet. This will help fill the time."

"*Fill* time?" I repeated. There was so much to do: lessons and learning and practice. How could I ever need this?

"It seems unlikely, I know; but there will come a time when this will serve its purpose."

42. THE NOTEBOOK OF KAYA NO YOSHIFUJI

Last night I was restless, I suppose: certainly drunk. It was a dark night. I groped my way to the place where a giant *hinoki*-cedar had fallen when this house belonged to my grandparents.

A jagged section of the cedar's trunk still sits there, broader across than a man's height and covered with furred weeds. Now a tree-tall hedge of matched trees marks a perfectly round space. No doubt other, smaller trees have made their stands here and been cut back by my ruthless gardeners. Instead, the clearing is filled with dry broad-bladed grass. I silenced the crickets as I walked: I heard the grass rasp against the ankles of my *hakama*-trousers.

I do not know why I did this. I've done strange things since my wife left: drinking too much *sake* and stumbling around my own garden in pitch darkness may be the least of them. I had a bottle in one hand, and my portable writing set tucked into my sash: perhaps I meant to write poetry.

At any rate, I climbed up onto the trunk section and looked upward. Humidity blurred the stars. There was no moon.

And then I saw a flash of light and a long brushstroke of fire that ended in a tiny ball of light, an explosion like a Chinese fire-work. The thick air itself seemed to pause and then breathe again.

This morning it seems like a dream. If it is one, I would rather live in the world where I dream of shooting stars than exist in reality.

43. KITSUNE'S DIARY

We were finished.

I sat in a billow of skirts and sleeves behind a red-and-green *kichō*-curtain hung from a black-lacquer frame. I had a folding fan painted with cranes in one hand; I kept staring with wonder at the way the fan snapped! open, and then shut, and at the quick gestures of my human fingers that made this happen. My family was arranged around me: my mother behind the curtain with me, Brother and Grandfather decently on the other side. Mother had a flea; I saw fox-her lift a hind leg and scratch behind one ear, and, like a reflection on water over a passing fish, I saw woman-her raise one long hand and discreetly ease herself.

"Mother," I said, shocked. "What if he sees both?"

She looked ashamed, and Grandfather asked what was going on. I explained and he laughed. "He will not. He is a man; he will see what he wants to see. Are you happy, Granddaughter?"

"It is all beautiful, I think. But Yoshifuji does not love me."

"Yet," Grandfather said. "I'm enjoying this despite myself. It has been too long since I got into mischief—not since I was a kit, and my brothers and I used to lure travelers into the marshes with foxfire in our tails."

Brother made a derisive noise. I longed to see his expression, but the curtain separated us. Grandfather said: "Be respectful, Grandson. Be as human as you can, for your sister's sake."

Brother's voice sounded sad when he replied. "Why can't she be happy as a fox? We played and ran and ate and slept. It was good."

"Because she loves a man," Mother said. "We are doing this for her."

"I know," Brother said. "I will try to be a good brother to her—and a good son and grandson to yourselves—but this makes no sense."

"This man will help us all," Grandfather said. "He will be a good provider, and perhaps he will find you a good position in the government somewhere."

"I will try to be dutiful and satisfy all your expectations," my brother said. He did not sound dutiful, only melancholy and angry.

"Well," said Grandfather. "Granddaughter, are you ready for the next step?"

"Grandfather, I will do anything."

"Then go tonight. Walk in the woods, and when Yoshifuji comes out, let things happen as they may."

I left the beautiful house—which meant I crawled out of our dusty little hole—in the company of several ladies-in-waiting. There was a fox-path that appeared to lead through gardens and over a stream to the forest path, but it was really just passage through some thick weeds behind the side gatehouse. We moved down to the path and walked there in the twilight.

He came; though duller than they had been as fox-eyes, my human-eyes saw him before he saw me. He was in house-dress, simple silk robes without elaborate dyed patterns, and not even sewn up in the back. He wore no hat, but his queue was arranged just as it should be. His face was sad—missing his wife, I imagined, as well as he might, she was so pretty and gentle. What was I doing, stealing him like this? Now she would wait in her dark halls forever, with no one to break the dim monotony of her life. I wondered if I should just shed this maiden's body and ease back into the ferns that fringed the path.

But I was a fox: I steeled myself easily, and said aloud, "I would rather she were alone than me."

Perhaps he heard me, or saw the ladies-in-waiting, who were dressed in bright colors that glowed even in the gathering dark. At any rate, he walked toward us. My women squeaked and averted their faces, hiding behind their fans. They were magical, so of course they did just as they ought; I, who was only mortal (and a fox), stared barefaced, with no maidenly reticence. He met my eyes. I have given that hunting stare; I know it well. I responded as the animal I am. I turned to run.

He was beside me before I could gather my skirts, and laid his hand on my sleeve. "Wait!"

I felt trapped like a mouse in his killing gaze. My women fluttered up, making meaningless noises of concern. "Please let me go," I said.

"No. A pretty thing like you?" I remembered my fan, and brought it up to hide my face: he caught my wrist to prevent me. The touch of his skin against mine made me dizzy. "Who are you?"

"Nobody," I stammered. Of all the things we had remembered, all the unfamiliar things we had been so clever about — the tea set, the stones in the gardens — we had given ourselves no names! But he seemed to accept this.

"I am Kaya no Yoshifuji. Why are you here, walking in my woods, with no men to protect you?"

I groped, thinking desperately. "It is a contest. We write poems to the dusk, my women and I." The ladies chirruped in agreement.

"Do you live near here?" he asked.

"Oh, yes. Just on the other side of the woods, my lord."

He nodded; fox magic made him accept this, even though the woods are a day's hard travel deep, and he has made this journey himself. "Still, it is very unsafe, and it is really too dark for you to walk home. Would you and your ladies honor me by coming as guests to my house, to wait there until your relatives can be sent for?"

I thought of those rooms, and thought suddenly of Shikujo, drifting aimlessly, waiting as she so often did for Yoshifuji. Even in her absence she would be a ghost there. I shrank back. "No, I could not possibly!"

He looked relieved; perhaps he felt her, as well. "Then where do you live? I will escort you."

"That would be very nice," I said with relief. "I live over there."

Maybe he would have seen the falseness that first time when he stepped from the true path onto the fox-path; but he was looking at me, his head bent to try to see past the fan I had managed to raise. It was hard walking in my many robes, but he mistook my inexperience for night-blindness, and he was very solicitous.

The fox-path was long and wandering. We walked along it until we saw lights. "Home," I said, and took his hand and led him the last few steps. He was lost in the magic then, and did not notice that he had to enter my beautiful house by lying belly-down in the dirt and wriggling under the side gatehouse. I stood on the veranda and servants clustered around, shielding me from his gaze and exclaiming.

"You are the daughter of this house?" Yoshifuji asked.

"I am," I said.

He looked around, at the many torches and stone lanterns that lit the garden, and the quality of the bamboo blinds edged with braid and tied up with red and black ribbons. "Your family must be a fine one."

He followed me into my reception room, where servants had set up a curtain-stand; they would preserve my womanly modesty here, even after I had committed the solecism of allowing a man to see me walk, and to see my face unshielded. I sank to the mat behind the panels of red-gold gauze.

My lord still stood. "Perhaps I should go, having seen you home," he said.

"Oh, please wait! My family will wish to thank you for your kindness. Please sit." I heard servants bring a mat for him.

A door slid open with a snap, by which I knew it must be one of us foxes, as the servants were all perfectly silent when they moved around the house. My brother spoke. He sounded awkward, reciting what we had practiced earlier. "I have only just heard of your presence in our house. Forgive me that my sister was your only welcome."

I think Yoshifuji gestured, but I could not see this. After a moment, my brother went on, "I am the grandson of Miyoshi no Kiyoyuki, and in his name I welcome you." (I sighed with relief. Someone had remembered!) "Please accept our hospitality for the night."

"Thank you. I am Kaya no Yoshifuji."

"There will be food brought to you. Let me inform my grandfather; he is in seclusion tonight, but he will be deeply honored by your presence when his tabu has been lifted and he can socialize again. Please excuse me, so that I can arrange to have a message sent to him." The screen snapped shut, and I heard my brother's narrow fox feet pad away from us.

He did not come back that night. Nor did my mother or my grandfather appear. Our only company was my women, silent and efficient. We talked and Yoshifuji teased a little. After a bit, I dropped my fan in such a way that one of the panels of the *kichō*-curtain was pushed aside, and I could watch his face in the dim light of a single oil lamp.

My women brought my lord a little lacquered tray with dried fish and seaweed and lotus seeds arranged on it, and a heaping pot of white rice, and a little cracked-glaze pot with herbs brewing in it. There were also carved ivory chopsticks and a small shallow bowl for the rice and then the tea. I sniffed the air, and I smelled perfume and these delicate little foods; and at the same time I smelled the single dead mouse my brother had been able to catch and save. My lord lifted bits of the mouse with scraps of straw held between his fingers, and drank rainwater from a dead leaf, and thought nothing of it.

We talked and talked. He said:

> *"A mountain seen through shredding clouds;*
> *a pretty woman glimpsed through a gap of the curtains.*

"I would be glad of a clearer view."

I knew the appropriate response was another poem, but I had no idea what to say. The silence was stretching; if I said nothing, he would know something was strange, and he would look around and see that he was not in this house, but crouched in the dirt, hung with cobwebs — "Please sit beside me," I said.

This was forward of me, but I could think of no other way to distract him; at any rate, it worked, for he barely blinked, just stood and moved behind the curtains with me.

My ladies-in-waiting were of course present; but they slept, discreet little heaps in the darkness. One even snored, a tiny undignified sound. I was grateful for that snore; it would make the women seem real, and our privacy seem absolutely convincing to my lord.

I hid my face with my fan, which he took away from me; with my sleeve, which he gently brushed aside; with my hands, which he captured in his own and kissed. His soft lips made me dizzy.

"Please," I whispered: my second prayer. I had asked the moon-foxes for help, and they had mocked me. Now I prayed, and Kaya no Yoshifuji kissed me.

I had never expected anything like this. His mouth was warm, and his lips firm but soft over mine. He pulled at my lower lip with his teeth until I opened my mouth, and his tongue entered me.

Kissing is not a universal thing, I have since learned: then, all was new to me, kissing no more or less than the rest. His mouth moved down across my throat. I tilted my head back. Flat even teeth bit at the joint of neck to shoulder. My blood throbbed in my arteries past his lips.

Clever hands fiddled with the little knot that fastened my Chinese jacket, and opened my robes, baring my breasts and belly. He pulled back and looked at me for a moment.

I stared back, unable to breathe.

"No one has even told you to be modest? To struggle and weep?" His voice was hoarse.

"Am I supposed to?" I gasped.

"No. Oh, no." One hand reached forward and traced a path from the hollow of my throat under the curve of my left breast. When his nails flicked across my nipple, I shivered. Nothing in my life as a fox had prepared me for this sharp sweetness over my heart, my breast feeling the way certain berries tasted, tart and sweet. The nails flicked again. I almost cried out loud.

"What is this you're doing?" I said.

"Making love," he said, and bent forward. The hand he had touched me with cupped my breast, my nipple pressed between his fingers. His mouth took my other nipple, tongue circling and lapping, and then the feel of teeth and suction and warmth.

His hands moved along me. The magic had given me this woman's body; but his hands defined it and made it real. I wanted him desperately, as crazed with longing as I had been during my heat; but when I tried to move onto my belly, he only pressed me back into the bed robes.

His hands cupped my knees and separated them. He touched me between the legs with his finger, and I sobbed aloud. He released himself and took me.

Even now, with experience behind me, familiar with his love-making, I can't describe this first time successfully. I had mated before, felt maleness before. I had watched, and I had listened to, and I had smelled human sex. But now! He was large and hot, and thrust a thousand times into me. My inner places wept clear fluids as sweet and agonizing as tears of joy.

Afterwards I cried.

He brushed at my tears with a fingertip, and I sobbed more helplessly, and hid my face in my hair.

"What's wrong, my love?" he whispered.

"How she will mourn," I said to myself.

"Who?" he asked.

"Your wife," I said.

He shrugged. "It is you I love."

And that is how I knew that the fox magic had taken him.

Book Three: Autumn

A time comes when
leaves yellow in the blustering wind
pile up before you know it
like heaps of gloomy words —
is it that time now?

— Ono no Komachi (mid-ninth century)
translated by Burton Watson

1. SHIKUJO'S PILLOW BOOK
Traveling to the capital:

Alone, I retraced my path —
this pillow of grass was softer when we shared it.

I have never traveled alone before: seldom traveled at all, in fact.
And in truth, I do not travel alone now. I have with me my
son, my women, and a large number of male attendants. We are
not unprotected in this world, and yet my women cling together
in terror, fearing bandits, wild animals, *tengu*-spirits and demons
of every sort. Knowing things are difficult between his father
and myself, Tadamaro is subdued, just in tune with my own
thoughts.

The season is bad for traveling. Though autumn has begun,
and the mornings are refreshingly cool, it is still too hot to travel
comfortably, especially in closed carts. The days are still long,
but the moon is new; once the long twilight ends, we are stuck
wherever we may be, trapped in almost total darkness.

Diviners have told me that this is a dangerous year for me.
Usually one fears death in such a year — childbirth is worrisome;
journeys seem fraught with risks of every sort. I comfort myself
(if so it can be called) with the thought that danger comes in
many forms: the dissolution of a marriage may be one of them.

But no, I am not prepared to think that. This is not a dissolution. It is a pause, no more — a moment when my husband and
I can draw breath and think, our minds uncluttered with immediate annoyances.

The journey would have been a pleasant one, if not for the
weather and my racing mind, unwilling to leave things be. We
threaded our way down the narrow roads that bordered the
river of the Tani valley. I have never traveled to the river's
beginnings, so I cannot say what it is like, but where it runs
beside my husband's *shōen*-estate, it is young, like a flighty young
woman dressed in random brocades made of water-current and
stone and whirlpool. But the river matures quickly as we de-

scend toward the ocean. Several days later, the river is a matron, slow-moving and gracious, dressed in the plain silks that only great personal elegance can make seem rich. The trees on either bank are stately attendants. Leaves are no longer the fresh brilliant greens of summer, but are muted, duller, with a matte look to them. Here and there a tree has already turned to its autumn colors: here is the startling red of *urushi*-lacquer trees; there the glowing gold of gingko.

And a day or two later, the river has changed again, to the dim grays of mourning, or a nun's garb. Girl to woman to crone: the river pours at last into the tidal basin of Narumi Bay: dark waters lost like the smoke of a funeral, into the ocean.

The tidal basin is a strange half-place: neither land nor sea, neither sand nor soil, neither sweet water nor salt. Perhaps this is exaggerated in my mind, for I also am suspended between *then* and *now* (or *now* and *to-come*, or past and future). The pale sand of this broad half-beach is dirty, mixed with soil blown down from the fields and forests above. The dirt and sand have layered themselves into patterns like watermarks or wood grains—overlaid with rocks, driftwood and shattered trees. In one place, a field of ragged pinks ram through the pounded sand, like embroidery over dye-work.

I think much of dyeing as we travel. It is natural: after all, coloring fabrics is something I do well and gladly, and it is (at least technically) autumn, the proper season for such things.

A day or two later, we travel through a field of tall *obana* grass. Its feathery seed heads tower far over the heads of the oxen, and shake down onto the carriage as we pass. The grass has the shimmering gold silkiness of certain well-made fringes, and I ignore Onaga's warnings about spying bandits with rape on their minds, to push the orange blinds aside and touch the soft grasses.

Except they are not as soft as they appear. The tassels may be soft, but the leaves are sharp, with serrated edges that cut my fingers. I snatch back my hand, hot with sudden ragged pain.

When we pass the next shrine, we pause to offer prayers against the bad luck of shedding blood on a journey.

The shrine is small and old, just a rock with a plaque explaining why the rock is worthy of our worship. An unraveling straw rope drapes across the rock's unprepossessing shape, strung with mulberry-paper prayer strips dissolving in the sun and wind and rain. Careful packages of unknown foodstuffs have been laid before the rock — unknown because wild animals have broken into them all, leaving only the husks and cloths that served as wrappers. Onaga watches me worriedly, afraid that the intimations of animal presences will prove difficult for me.

The last few days of the journey are quickly past. The more closely we approach the capital, the more traffic we encounter — messengers, or rows of carts bearing goods to the city, or finer carriages arranged in great convoys, off to visit shrines or country estates or provincial governors. The weather is colder, which compensates somewhat for the increase in dust that works its way into the carriages. I look out the grille from time to time, and see the first black-headed gull of this journey, welcoming me back to the capital.

We come to the Osaka Barrier in the middle afternoon of a cool windy day. A guardsman tries to shove his head into one of the carriages, but Onaga deals with him easily enough, and we pass through quickly.

The last few miles of the road are broad and crowded. We parallel the city wall, now scarcely more than a collapsing mound covered in serria and *kuzu*-vines, its moats glittering with standing water half-concealed by reeds. The gate; the shopmen's district, noisy and reeking of cheap torches; the broad avenues of the west side, separating abandoned plots and forgotten homes decaying into wilderness; Nijō Avenue; and just as the last dim purple of evening fades with the rising moon, the house I have shared with my husband for these many years: noise and lights, and outside the garden's walls, shouts and wagons and running horses.

Strange to feel alone surrounded by so many. Did I move too

hastily in leaving my husband? No, because it was not my husband I left to escape from. It was an unfortunate obsession.

But was this obsession his or mine? Or did it belong to someone else altogether?

2. KITSUNE'S DIARY

*Y*oshifuji and I did not sleep: his smell and the feel of his skin against my own made me tireless. The things he did and showed me to do were strange, but left me shivering. In the end, all I could do was hold him with my new fingers and shake.

Gray dawn's light sifted like powder from the eaves when he at last pulled free of me and stood. Chilled air filled the man-shaped place he left in the quilted robes of my bed: the rude embrace of air after the warmth of flesh. We had not noticed, but the night must have become cold.

I sat up to watch. Yoshifuji's unbleached robes hung like ghosts about him. He stared at the grille over a window shaped like the opening petals of a lotus, his hands tying the knot of his trousers automatically, the way men dress when their minds are elsewhere.

"My lord?"

He looked down at me; even in the darkness I saw his teeth glow suddenly as he smiled at me. "Dear little lover," he said. "I did not mean to wake you when I left."

"I was not asleep. Do not leave." I reached out for him. He took my hands in his and pressed my wrists against his cheeks and lips. I burned for him again, a sharp pang between my legs.

> *"The springs were deep,*
> *and the water sweet —*
> *Too much for a single drink.*

"Perhaps I may visit again?"

Poetry, I presumed. "You even wonder?" My throat tightened. "But why leave at all? You could stay here —"

He knelt and pressed his face against my bare breast. "You *are* new to all of this, aren't you? I can't stay. It would be completely improper and might ruin you. What if someone saw us?"

"Saw us?" I exclaimed. "They've certainly heard us."

He looked amused and embarrassed. "That is, of course, different." He laid his fingers against my mouth, already asking the next question. "No. You must know that this is the way things are."

"Well, wherever you're going, may I go with you?" I asked wistfully.

But he only laughed again and stood. "Thank you for sharing your robes with me, pretty one." He slid a *fusuma*-panel aside and stepped out into the veranda. Gone.

I waited a moment, then: "Grandfather," I hissed. *"Grandfather.* Where *are* you?" My voice sounded panicky in my ears.

"Yes, I'm here." Where else could he be? The illusion shimmered; he lay curled up nearby, under the gatehouse with me. And then my rooms were rooms again, and his voice came through the panels leading to a corridor. "What?"

"He left!"

"So." Grandfather entered and came to stand beside me, a pine-straight man in blue and sage-green robes. He looked older, more tired, in the gray light.

" 'So'? He's *gone!*"

"Of course. He is a gentleman. And you are now, despite rutting all night like a monkey in heat, a woman. He leaves at dawn, before your family and friends discover you." He clapped his hands. My woman, Josei, her hair tied back and her robes disordered from sleeping, brought him a fat reed mat without speaking. His face twisted with pain as he lowered himself onto it. "It is turning to autumn, Granddaughter. The night frosts will kill me."

I did not care about his pains, or the cool heavy air that dimpled my skin. "But he will slip back to his other world and he will be gone!"

"Are you so unsure of your charms, little bug-eater?"

"No. Yes. Grandfather, I can't lose him now!"

"So this wasn't enough."

I looked at him curiously. "Did you think it would be? No."

He sighed heavily. "I hoped. Very well, then, we will not allow him to step free of the web, even for a day. Grandson!" he called.

"Yes." There were rapid footsteps, and then my brother slid a screen open and came to us. He shifted sometimes in his sleep and forgot to change back; but this time he was altogether human, a slender man with heavy eyes, his topknot tousled and his clothes in disarray, as if he had slept in them. Which he had, I suppose.

"Do not just walk in here!" Grandfather snapped. "Her women will offer you entrance and direct you to sit beside a screen."

"I did not think it mattered," Brother said mulishly. "Yoshifuji is not here to see. She is my sister, and *you* just walked in."

Grandfather rubbed his eyes. "I am the head of this family, an old man, and the least likely of any of us to forget that under this shape—" he gestured at me as I sat naked among my bed robes "—we are still foxes."

"I'm not—" I began hotly, but he interrupted:

"Grandson, go. Find him."

"Now? Why?"

"Because I tell you that you must do this." Grandfather and Brother locked eyes.

Brother turned his face away and ducked his head. "I'm so sorry. I do not mean to be disobedient. I'll keep him in the fox magic." Brother bowed and left. I heard him shouting for his servants as he ran to his wing: fresh robes and hunting gear. He was better at humanity than he thought, my brother.

"Granddaughter." Grandfather's voice surprised me; I had forgotten he remained on the other side of the curtain. "You were pleased?"

"It was—" What? There were no words. Humans assign words to things and pretend the words are adequate, but I knew the truth even then, that the sentence that truly described the night would be exactly as long as the night itself, and could only be spoken with touch and taste and the feel of skin sliding. Any words could only be a robe over the truth. "Yes. I was pleased."

"Mmm." He nodded once. "Just so. And now you want to keep him."

"I love him," I said with what I hoped was dignity. "I can't live without him."

"Hah. You barely know him, even now. You do not even know what *you* are. Who. You've formed yourself into what you think he wants. This is not love, not yet."

"What is love, then, if you know so much?"

"Letting go, sometimes. Fighting to keep someone, others. But you do not care about that now, do you?"

I raised my chin. "I want him for my husband. Why did you show me the magic, if you thought this?"

"Because you *would* have died and I'm a sentimental old fool. Why should I care? You have a brother. But we're alike, Granddaughter. And you would have gone to him anyway, even without me, and there are ways that would have killed you."

I was silent, remembering the tent and the knife, and before that the smell of the metal spearhead under Yoshifuji's house, thrusting at my brother and me.

"You'll have him, I don't argue with you. But know this: you've no idea who he is. Or yourself, trapped between woman and fox. Very well, we will continue. Arrange yourself."

I realized suddenly that I was sitting upright in a bed that smelled of sex, bare-breasted before my grandfather; and I flushed. Such details were often hard to remember.

3. THE NOTEBOOK OF KAYA NO YOSHIFUJI

How can I never have met her before? Her family is obviously prosperous, so much so that I can't imagine the court is unaware of them. How can I never have met *them* before: if not in the capital, then locally at least, hunting or at the temples nearby? I've never even heard of these people, and I should at least have met the hierarch of the family when Shikujo and I were first here.

And the daughter! I would not have seen or even heard of her then: she looks perhaps sixteen, so she would have been scarcely old enough for her first pair of *hakama*-trousers when we were here last, eight years ago. Such a beauty she is: even in the darkness that seems inevitable in women's rooms, this was clear to me last night.

All the Chinese poets I've read who rave about their lovers offer a catalogue of virtues; when I was younger and first learning the language, I read these avidly and wondered what such women might be like. And she surpasses them all, her beauty a fortunate mix of the expected and the unusual. She would not be out of place as an emperor's bride.

Her eyes are a surprise: enormous, a luminous gold instead of black in a face otherwise flawlessly conventional, with skin like crystal white jade (as the more clichéd poets — and evidently I — would say), and eyebrows like willow leaves. Her hands are longer than expected, and she tends to use them as if her fingers were new to her, so that they cut through the air as a single graceful shape. Her feet are narrow and long, and white as a fox's paws.

Her breasts are small and finely shaped. She coils like a cat and moans when I touch them, as if she has never been touched before. Perhaps she never has, despite her age — buried as she is, with no one to appreciate her beauty in this forgotten place.

Her hips curve sweetly around a warm liquid sex that last night parted for me at first hesitantly, then joyously. Exhausted as I am, I am hard again, even thinking of the feel of her, inside.

I've stayed all night with women, even made love through the night instead of lying quietly and talking or exchanging poetry or even dozing, my head against their breasts. In the mornings I've been tired, and looked forward to writing the morning poem and then going to sleep; but nothing has prepared me for this absolute enervation I feel. My body seems too light for itself, as if any stray breeze might lift it like a kite. Everything is misted over, as if I see through a curtain as transparent as silk gauze.

The sun rises, hot cherry-red, flooding the sky. It seems too large, snagged as it is by the outlined branches of a great *katsura* tree. The heavy dew over the garden flares with the new light; my breath (it is cold enough for my breath to have a shape; thus autumn begins) is tinted red.

I am in Miyoshi no Kiyoyuki's garden. It has to be, though the garden's layout is similar to my own, with three lakes and two pavilions built out onto their surfaces. Mist hides the pillars that must support the pavilions; they float, as if celestial.

Even the placement of certain objects is similar to my own home. A stone lantern stands in the lake nearest the house, although here it is shaped of black stone threaded with the color of peonies. The slate-dark stepping-stones across the middle lake make a similar pattern to my own. But it is all different, better in some indescribable way. The lakes are bigger; their surfaces through the dissolving mist are a purer blue; the pretty little pagodas half-hidden in the maples are somehow more poignant.

Off to one side, I glimpse a clearing approximately where my own moon-rock clearing would be, but nothing stands in its center. For a moment I wonder if they are waiting for the rock to fall and have prepared its resting place in advance. A fancy of my fatigue, I know: last night was sweet, but I am nearly thirty now. It must be this that leaves me so tired.

The path from the house leads down the hill before me, down to a huge Chinese-style gate let into the horse-high bamboo fence. Like mine, the gate is of peeled boxwood logs; unlike mine, it is intact. Its roof is covered with blue tile so bright it might have been cut from midsummer sky.

I look back (I must have walked a long path to get here; but all I remember are the rockless clearing and the stepping-stones, a frog the color of jade lying comatose on one); the house is a jumble of buildings and walkways half-hidden by the trees between us, the gentle curve of the hill hiding its (no doubt) thousand cypress support pillars.

The house shares the gateway's tiles. The roofs cluster together, showing a thousand — ten thousand — angles, that same blinding blue tile edged with black along each roofline's arc. Bleached-wood medallions edge one such eave: the main entrance to the main house. I can't see what is carved into them: no doubt it is the same unfamiliar (to me, anyway) lily brocaded into the grandson of Miyoshi no Kiyoyuki's sleeves. The effect of all the bright blue roofs, the black and near-white, should be gaudy. Instead it looks rich.

How can they possibly afford this? No, this is not the question: rich men abound, even rich eccentrics who for incomprehensible reasons prefer their rustic estates to the capital. (Not that this is rustic in anything but location: princes in the capital live under plainer tiles.)

The question is: who are they? And why do they live here? "Because they can" is not answer enough for me. She said little enough about her family last night. Now I am curious.

More than even the questions of why and who is how? How did all this get here? The roads (I know) are bad, certainly not capable of bearing the weight of the many carts that would have been needed. Did they somehow carry all these tiles (impossible to produce locally) from the capital? They might even have come from China itself: surely that would have been no less impossible.

I pause to squint, imagining my own gate, completed and roofed in this brilliant parrot blue. Perhaps I can persuade my newly discovered neighbor to part with some of his spare tiles.

"Sir!" A light male voice behind me. "Wait!"

I turn to see my pretty lover's brother loping down the path. He moves easily, as if more accustomed to this easy ground-eating trot than a more respectable walk, and when he stops an arm's length from me, I see he is not even breathing heavily.

In the pearly dawn, he looks more like his sister than I noticed last night: a slender young man of about her age, sharing her flawless features and candid gold eyes, dressed today in fawn and orange-red hunting robes, a wood-block quiver at his waist and a bow case thrown over his shoulder. A single peacock feather has been tucked into his narrow sash. I cannot imagine where it came from. I have not seen peacocks since leaving the capital, not even here, in this amazing garden.

He bows as awkwardly as a boy half his age. "Good morning, sir. How fortunate that I chanced to see you! I hope you slept well?"

"Good morning. I did not expect you to be awake so early, or I would have taken my leave formally—" A polite lie, of course.

"No, you would not have." The youth, incredibly, snorts. "You had sex with my sister. You'd leave quietly, no matter what. Grandfather says so."

"You realize," I say mildly, because I can't think of what else to do and I am afraid I might start laughing, "that that is a completely shocking comment." He seems to share his sister's ability to say anything at all, regardless of the proprieties.

He shrugs. "You mated with her. We all know that. You were very noisy."

I've been walking beside him toward the gate, but at this I stop. I find I am blushing, which makes me laugh out loud.

"My lord?" he says. "Did I say something?"

"No," I say, and touch his sleeve. "I'll go home now. I need to—"

"Oh, *no*," he says, his face gone suddenly pale. "You can't. No, stay with me and perhaps we can go hunting."

"That would be pleasant. But I am quite tired, and . . ." I trail off. No one would fail to see this for what it is, a polite refusal. No one but my lover's brother.

"The hunt will make you feel better. I always find it so. Please." Perhaps he has no friends, I realize suddenly. If his grandfather keeps him as sequestered as his sister, this seems very possible. I feel a little sorry for him.

"That would be nice, but I'd only hold you back, unarmed as I am."

"Oh, I have a spare. I hoped you might agree to hunt with me." He swings his bow case around to show that he has brought *two* cases, and I somehow missed the second. "Here's

yours. And your quiver." Somehow, the quiver I saw strapped
to his waist was in fact two quivers; he hands one to me. I *must*
be tired, but now there seems no gracious way to back out.

The bow case is of finely quilted felt with a brass amulet of
some esoteric demon or other sewn onto each side. The bow
inside is made of horn bound and strung with sinew; light glim-
mers through its pale mottlings when I hold it up to the bright
sky. The quiver is a block of paulownia-wood polished with
bee's wax (I smell the sweetness) until it glitters. The perfect
arrows are dark-fletched: raven or crow feathers, I suppose.
This is a kit for an emperor. I am effectively silenced by his
casual presentation of these things.

"Shall we go?" This odd young man leads me beneath the
gate's shadow. I shiver for a moment, chilled.

The Miyoshi estate is pressed against the side of a valley I've
never seen before. Still, all valleys (and all estates, too, I suppose) look somewhat the same: I see the usual peasants and
fields, the rutted dirt path that passes the front gate, the steep
slopes that loft up and up to lose themselves in the light clouds
at the mountains' height. I look around trying to locate the path
to my own home: I should not be so exhausted that I can't
remember the path, though I seem to be.

My companion views the valley with something approaching
wonder, as if he has never seen this place before. I watch him
curiously until he notices. He flushes and ducks his head. "It is
very beautiful today," he mumbles.

"Look." I gesture across the valley at a copse of trees around
a little shrine. Their green is touched by the faintest brush-touch
of red and gold: remnants of the cold night. "Autumn is starting
already."

"I know, I smell it. Let's go this way; perhaps we'll find some
kiji-pheasant." His voice is high and happy, excited, the first
thing he has said to me that he seems to feel really comfortable
with.

"Wait." I catch his sleeve and bring him to a stop. "The morning poem! I'm so sorry, but I *must* go home."

THE FOX WOMAN 189

"You can't!" he says. "Not now, not when you've promised."

"I have to write the morning poem, or I'll offend your sister utterly and she'll never consent to my visiting her again."

"About *poetry?*" He barks a laugh. "I think she won't mind."

"Yes, she will. Any woman would." I glance at him. "You *have* been with a woman before this?"

"Oh, well, the servants, to see what it would be like—" He stops.

"You've never slept with a woman of any gentility?" He really *has* been kept sequestered.

He shifts his weight from foot to foot. "If you want to write this 'morning poem,' perhaps you could do so somewhere besides your home?"

"I suppose so," I say dubiously. "But—"

"The shrine," he says with sudden decision.

"Well—" Even though it didn't seem so last night, it looks as if it must be a long walk back home (even supposing I remember where the pass back to my valley is: I feel like a child, getting lost in my own mountains); the shrine shimmers in the morning's new warmth, seeming a mere step away. "Very well."

I am very tired, which gives the path a sense of impermanence, as if I might turn suddenly and see a different path than the one we've just walked down. The youth seems nervous; but he is such an unaccountable creature, it could be anything, even fretting about the *kiji*-pheasants he is missing.

The shrine is a pretty little building of dark red wood in the copse of *urushi*-lacquer and gingko trees that showed the flicker of autumn from the gate. A single priest uses a twig broom to scrape together the first few fallen leaves, all colored the bright gold of sunlight. He turns his face toward us for a second, showing eyes the moon-white with blindness. "Hah! Welcome, lad, my lord. You'll find a little flask of something on the table in my quarters. Writing materials are there, too. Don't forget to leave a little gift for the shrine when you go, hey." He shuffles around the side of the building.

"How did he know what we needed?" I ask as we step into a smaller, low building beside the shrine.

"He's a priest; he's supposed to know everything, isn't he?" My lover's brother is right; I suddenly feel that all priests I've met previously have been in some way defective for *not* knowing everything.

The single room is dark and smells strange, as if the priest has been kenneling some creature in here with him; but there is a low table in the center cluttered with plain wood boxes. A small blue jug and two carved wood cups stand on a corner. One of the boxes contains mulberry paper, much too elegant for this grubby room; another an untouched ink stone and ink stick and several writing brushes. I sit down on a cushion made of rushes and prepare the materials.

"*Sake?*" my lover's brother asks.

"Mmm," I say. I drink from the cup when it is handed to me, and I cough: this wine is strong as any I have ever tasted, pungent and warming. My companion sips carefully, with a wariness, as if not knowing what to expect.

I am already thinking about my morning poem. Being with her was extraordinary: it would be nice if my poem could in some way break through all the standard imagery to give her an intimation of my feelings.

"You can just do that?" My lover's brother interrupts my thoughts. "Just sit down and write a poem? How do you know what to write?"

"If I'm not disturbed, I can." He blushes and I laugh: "You and your sister. Neither of you really understand poetry, do you?"

4. KITSUNE'S DIARY

Josei brought me new robes of off-white and a dull green: autumn colors, she told me. Robes! I was expected to care about such things now. I shrugged into them and resumed my restless pacing.

"My lady. Now your hair." She bowed and gestured for me to kneel.

"No." I wanted to jump, to run, to doze in the sunlight, to follow Yoshifuji. Anything but wait in the gloom of my rooms, getting my hair combed.

She shook her head. "My lady, I have to get the tangles out and comb it smooth, or you will look like a madwoman when my lord returns."

"Well, make it smooth, then."

She sighed. "If you let me comb it out, I will."

"No," I said. "I mean *make* it happen. Magic."

"My lady?"

"She doesn't know." Grandfather stood in a doorway.

"My lord!" Josei exclaimed. "You are not supposed to see her!" She pulled me down behind the nearest *kichō*-curtain, amber-colored crape hanging from a chest-high frame; at once (maybe this was what she wanted all along) she began separating my snarled strands with her clever fingers. Magic of a sort, after all, her fingers.

Grandfather said nothing, only eased himself down onto a cushion on the other side of the screen. "Josei, is it? Will you leave your mistress and me for a moment?"

She looked at me: I nodded and she bowed and moved silently away to where the rest of my women sat at the other end of the huge room. They were surrounded by clutter, as if they had pulled all my chests open and strewn their contents around: paper and brushes, scrolls of poetry and *monogatari*-tales, fans and fabric and armrests and little boxes and ornaments and colored papers to make flowers from. I was surprised by how many *things* people seemed to need around them; the only things we had as foxes were a few bones left over from our kills, brought home to gnaw free of marrow. While I occasionally fought my brother for possession of one or another of them, these bones were generally interchangeable.

"You cannot ask her to use magic, Granddaughter. Any of them."

"Why not?" Josei had left a comb behind, of tortoiseshell

carved into a cloud so that its teeth were the streaks of rain. I
picked it up and started worrying at a snarl.

"Your maid, all the servants, even the peasants outside—not
that you will have much to do with them—don't know about
the magic. They imagine they're real. And here, now, they *are*
real."

"But they're *not.*"

"And what are you, Granddaughter, in your borrowed shape?
A real—what? Fox? You don't look one. A woman? Hardly."

"But—"

"Not yet, Granddaughter; perhaps not ever. But we made the
illusion. Now we live by its rules."

"We made it all up!"

"Josei and the other servants don't know that."

"They must!"

"Why would they? Are *you* going to tell them, little milk-
sucker? They wouldn't believe you if you did."

"No," I said slowly. "But—"

"Good," he said. "Good servants are hard to find, out here
away from the city. Even magic ones."

I stopped combing for a moment. "Could Josei do something
I don't want?"

"She is meant to be quiet and correct. Like any good servant.
She will always be that. So, no. But she has her own life, and
she will try to be a good servant whether you want it or not.
So, yes."

I looked at her. She knelt across a small cleared space from
another woman, playing a board game of some sort. A strand
of hair had fallen forward from her forehead; it brushed the floor
as she leaned forward to lay a little marker down.

"What does she do when I'm not with her?" Perhaps she felt
my eyes on her; she leaned back on her heels and watched me.

"The same things you do when you're not with her—except
that you're the mistress. Did you think she ceased to exist when
she left the room? Perhaps. But you will never know, will you?
She might as well wonder if you were real when she sits around
a brazier exchanging gossip with the other women. Neither of

you can be sure. But for your peace of mind, I suggest you assume that in your absence they talk about you, and run your errands, and flirt with the male servants, and eat and defecate and sleep. Assume they remember childhoods and lost loves and old holidays. Assume they dream."

I shivered. Josei took this as a permission of sort and left her game. "Do they?"

He laughed. "Who knows? Perhaps she thinks she does."

"What would she dream of?" I asked.

"Ask her."

I shivered again. "No. I don't want to know what a dream dreams."

"She is only slightly more illusory than you, bug-eater."

"I am so sorry to interrupt you, my lady, my lord; but my lady looked cold." Josei tucked a lined robe around my shoulders and removed the comb from my loose grasp.

There was shouting outside, and the thudding of feet running along a walkway. We were supposed to leave our clogs on great stepping-stones between the dirt garden-path and the veranda, not stomp around like oxen on a bridge. The servants would never —

"It's Brother," I gasped.

"He left Yoshifuji," Grandfather said grimly.

"He can't have. He'll ruin everything!" I threw the curtain aside despite Josei's exclamation and met his eyes.

A lattice leading to the veranda slammed aside. Brother stopped abruptly in the doorway, squinting. Of course: it was dark here, compared to the outside light pouring in, outlining him. "Sister?"

"I'm here, we're here." I ran across to him, ignoring the heavy thudding of my heart. "You *left* him?"

"It's all right. He's in the garden, watching a red-crowned crane go after frogs in the middle lake. We're going after *kiji-*pheasants. But he made me bring this back first." He pulled something from his sash and handed it to me.

I turned it over wonderingly: a branching maple twig with a single yellow leaf clinging to it. In the crotch of the twig was a neat little arc of silver: spiderweb. A soft scrap of rope was tied loosely around the twig. "What is this?"

"It's paper, see?" Misunderstanding, Brother loosened the little rope with his fingers. "He didn't even think about what he wanted to do or how to do it. He just knew what he wanted, a rope from paper, and he made this." He fiddled with it, and the rope unrolled into a finger-long slip of paper with furred edges and tiny writing.

> *Last night was cold enough*
>   *to startle the spiders into sleep;*
> *Awake together, we were not cold at all.*

> *We are bound together forever, my love.*

Grandfather nodded. "A very proper morning poem."

"What is this?" I asked again. Meaning: the poem, the twig, the little rope he made.

"This means that he loves you," Grandfather said. "Or thinks he does. Or says he does. At least you didn't give him a total disgust of us all. What are you going to write back?"

"Write?"

He snorted. "Of course, bug-eater. You have to respond. Or did you think the magic would write your poems for you?"

"Quickly," Brother said. "I don't want him wandering off."

"I thought you didn't like him, hey?"

Brother ducked his head. "He's nice enough."

I plucked Grandfather's sleeve. "He couldn't think that I don't want him, could he? After last night?"

"He can think a lot of things. He can even be hurt if you don't write back."

"Can't she just tell him she loves him and leave it at that?" Brother touched the tip on the twig. The spiderweb vibrated slightly. "That's what this is all about, isn't it—love?"

"And the proper way to do things." Grandfather's breath puffed out: a laugh. "You think what *we've* created is illusion? It's nothing compared to the illusions people make for themselves. They *all* live in a world as false as ours. If you don't offer him the illusions he is used to, you'll disappoint him."

"And he might leave," I said through numb lips, and handed the twig to Grandfather. "You understand. You write the response."

"No. This is your illusion, your magic," he said firmly, and handed it back.

"Now," my brother said.

Somehow I scrambled and made up the words, and Grandfather and Brother watched over my shoulder and made comments that might have been useful if I hadn't been too afraid of failing at this to listen to them. Even I could tell it was a halting, graceless thing. But we were still more fox than human; it was the best we could do.

5. THE NOTEBOOK OF KAYA NO YOSHIFUJI

I am watching dragonflies. The crane I was watching flew away, off to warmer waters, I think. The fish here are beautiful, glimmering carp, but a fish is not an absorbing sight. The weather is getting cooler (last night it became actually cold; this morning I can see a ghost of mist as I exhale) and the dragonflies will be gone tomorrow, the next day: soon, anyway.

But they survived the cold night, and now that the sun has warmed the lake, they hang over its surface, iridescent blue. I am so tired that I forget sometimes that they aren't part of the sky, diffracted in my eyes. I'd give everything I own to go back to the blue-roofed house and the darkness of her rooms, to sleep in her arms until dark and then do it all over again. But I cannot with any propriety (not until dusk, at the earliest), so I watch the sky shiver into splinters that move over the dark water.

Her brother startles me when he returns: again that silent effortless lope. He brings back her reply written in brushstrokes as sharp as the marks of claws in mud, black ink on blood-colored paper of a strange amorphous shape, unlike anything I have seen before.

> *Sweet to see autumn —*
> *Sweet to see you.*

MY LOVE...

The strokes trail off as if she has run out of words, but even these few make my heart pound and my sex stir.

"Well? Is this all right?" Her brother interrupts my thoughts.

I try not to laugh. He is so young, so puppylike in his desire to please—as charming as his sister in some ways. "Very properly expressed," I say, thinking of the poem. The *envoi*—that is mine alone.

We hunt all day, killing two *kiji*-pheasants and a young rabbit, and return at evening.

6. SHIKUJO'S PILLOW BOOK
With my parents in the capital:

> *Each autumn day is short,*
> *but not so short as the summer days*
> *when we were close.*

The capital is very much what it was—crowded, dangerous, filled with noise and smells. The season of epidemics is past, but the smells are never gone, though I am sure the cooler air has improved them somewhat.

The first night in the capital we went to the house my husband and I shared. We left less than six months ago and already it seems abandoned! Sharp-scented weeds have overgrown parts of the garden, and sage and mint crowd against the walkways. My women and I stayed there that first night, but I wept and couldn't sleep.

Mercifully, my parents were not still at the summer estate on the Toko bay at Lake Biwa. (Why did I not think of this, when I left so intemperately! I had no time to send ahead; we might have arrived to find my family gone, the house deserted.) My household moved in with them, into the wing that had been mine when I was a child. Everyone has been very kind, and asks no questions at all.

7. KITSUNE'S DIARY

Women never see anything directly. Our — this word has always fit uncomfortably, even now: can a fox woman be counted as a woman? — our worlds are dim-lit and fragmented, seen in snatches through a gap in a curtain, or over a fan, or through our hair, or around a sleeve. Obliquely, from the corners of our eyes. No doubt this is how men see women, as well: as muted color and form in the dark recesses of a room.

My first experience of this was our first night, when I never clearly saw his face. Of course, I'd seen it often enough as a fox, watching — my eyesight then was not so sharp as a woman's, but I saw more clearly into darkness, and I watched constantly, so that I knew the shape of it, his expressions.

But as a woman? He came to me at dusk. The walk home, and our time talking — there was always something between us. The braziers were all the light there was in my room, and we lay behind curtains anyway, so that my memory of our mating was limited to smell and taste and touch and the sound of his voice. Limited! When I was a mere fox, my vision had been the least of it; now my other senses were dulled, so that sight was important. And denied to me.

When he left, the dawn-gray light lay like dust on him, dim highlights that hid more than they revealed.

I spent the day in my rooms. I wasn't familiar with waiting; even now I don't altogether understand it. It is mostly a human thing, though I've known a dog to wait with more patience than I ever could for his master's return. Waiting seems absurd: time is not like coins, that you can put in a box and take out later to use. It is like water in a river, already past before you have even seen it. Then, it seemed even more foolish: as a fox I ran when I wished, hunted when I wished, slept and played and ate when I wished. Not to do so was to lose the time I might have been running or hunting or sleeping or playing. Nothing seemed worth that.

Waiting required a future to wait for: a falsehood. I know now that there is only *now*. I remember things that happened months (or was it years?) ago: old worn-out *nows*. The future happens, but it is always shaped from a series of *nows*. *Now*—the now of this moment, not the memory of the now when I first met Yoshifuji—*now* I stand in frozen darkness, waiting to hear clogs in the snow; *then* matters only in how it shapes why I stand here.

I waited for Yoshifuji. I felt a connection, a line between us, like a spiderweb that had torn free when we'd stepped through it the night before, and now clung to us both. I felt his movements through the web. I don't think he felt mine.

They returned at dusk and came to my rooms, where Mother and I were sitting together. I heard Yoshifuji's steps falter as he walked into the room and saw my grandfather on his side of the screen, visiting us.

"Sir," he said, and waited.

"You're the lad," Grandfather said. "I'm Miyoshi no Kiyo-yuki."

Yoshifuji bowed. "I am—"

"I know who you are; my grandson came to tell me about you last night, but I was in seclusion. Please forgive me for there being no one but my granddaughter to entertain you."

My lord bowed again. "Your granddaughter is a woman of rare beauty and charm."

"Yes, well," Grandfather said. "I hope you mean that."

"I do," said Yoshifuji. "And your home, so elegant—"

"Well. You were always meant to come here. Now you must stay."

"It will be the delight and honor of my life," my lord said.

"Come drink with me," my grandfather said. "We have a lot to arrange."

Light-headed with happiness, I watched Yoshifuji and my grandfather leave the room. When they returned, it was settled: we were to be married.

8. SHIKUJO'S PILLOW BOOK
Settling in:

It has been pleasant, if odd, settling into my old rooms. My mother and father have both visited to welcome me, speaking not at all of life's difficulties, treating me a little as they had when I was young and easily frightened by things. I grew up in this house, and there are times — when I walk down certain corridors or walkways, or when I am half-asleep — when I feel I might be ten again, knowing no more of life than might be winnowed from the *monogatari*-tales of my old nurse.

Tadamaro has adapted immediately to the house, which is, after all, not unfamiliar to him, since we've visited my family many times, and stayed for months on end when it was appropriate; but I know he thinks the grounds sadly small, compared to certain others.

The fish in the small lake are as long as my son's arm. Breeding carp for exceptional characteristics is an eccentric hobby of my father's; thus certain of the fish are the color of moonlight, and others are spotted black, white and orange, like a lucky tricolored cat. My son tells me that there is also a huge basin of blue-and-white China porcelain containing a single fish, my father's pride: a gold fish the size of a rabbit, with eyes that nearly pop from their sockets. There is a mesh that goes over the water's surface, to keep the cook's cats out. The cook, evidently, feeds any stray with bits of leftover food, and by now has what must be eight hundred myriad visiting cats. Well, perhaps not so many; but they sun on certain large rocks in the garden, and the gardeners clean up after them constantly. I've seen none of this, or no more than glimpses: it is all outside, and I stay indoors, of course.

He tells me that there are foxes, as well, that live in the gardens of the estate next door, and have dug a hole beneath the plastered fence. I watch his face closely when he tells me this, but to the boy it is merely something to see, of no more importance than the fish or the cats. He seems not to have inherited the obsession. Onaga (who remembers when I first had the dream, so long ago) watches with me, and says he is safe.

I think he is, because it is not the same here. These are just foxes.

9. KITSUNE'S DIARY

My time with Yoshifuji in the days before the wedding was a blur. Each night he came to me and we had sex again and each night I fell even more thoroughly in love with him.

As my grandfather explained it to me, part of what would make this a true marriage is that my lord, instead of leaving in the dawn (which he would ordinarily do, were I a mere lover), would remain with me in the mornings, allowing anyone to know he had stayed the night.

This seemed unaccountable: we'd been together all night, in spaces cluttered with people and walled with paper: of course everyone knew we'd been together. But humans seem to love pretending that every encounter is shrouded in secret.

He stayed with me and played with my hair and clothes until I slapped his hands away when my women tried to make order. We made love often, and lay in each other's arms watching dawn start, its sudden red warmth driving back the night's chill.

Even so, I spent many hours alone, when my lord met with my brother or with Grandfather to discuss the marriage arrangements. A ceremonial sash came to me at one of those times, an indicator of the marriage to come, but it seemed the merest formality. Of course we were getting married: this was the final goal of all my family's cleverness. It was only once in a while, when my time without him seemed as clear and piti-less as ice forming a skin on the water in a bowl, that I won-dered what would happen after the goal was attained and he was mine.

We could not know if we were doing things properly, or in the proper order. There was so much to human marriage, an-other example of their mania for complexity and mystery. We did our best, sending formal letters back and forth, pretending to knowledge or ignorance as ritual demanded. But it was all guesswork: nerve-wracking.

The day before the largest part of the wedding ritual, Grand-father took Yoshifuji off to his wing of the house to discuss something about the marriage. There was nothing to do. I waited.

Brother burst in, slamming the screen against its runner so hard that the frame cracked. "You," he said, and pointed at my women, all too surprised to conceal themselves. "All of you: go."

"My lady?" one of the women asked.

I waved them out without looking to see them go, my atten-tion all for my brother. He paced restlessly, his brown-and-green robes rustling, until they were gone. His gold eyes were anguished.

"What is it?" I asked at last.

"I can't stand this!" He dropped to his knees beside me. "Sis-ter. Please mate with me."

"*What?*"

He jumped up, back to his pacing. "I need you. I know it's not your season. But you and he—I hear you, and smell you—"

"I'm getting married!"

He stopped and looked down at me, his face contorted. "You and he smell thick and hot, like a rabbit's lifeblood between my teeth, like mating. Like musk. I *need* this, Sister."

"No." I was shaking my head. "You're my brother. I can't—"

"What does that have to do with anything? You could be-fore."

"That was different. We were foxes then."

"And now we aren't? Does this shape change who we are?"

"It must," I said, hoping.

"Please." He knelt, his hands over his face. "I've taken this shape even though I didn't want to. Because you and our grandfather told me to. Give me this, at least."

"I can't, don't you see? I'm a woman now; I have to behave as one. I'm promised to Yoshifuji now!"

He raised his face. "And me? What are my options, Sister? The unreal servants? I've tried that. They're perfect, a dream a man might have in the night. Mother? She's still half-fox."

I remembered the vixen I had seen, the day I carried the skull. "There are other foxes, other packs."

He slammed his fist against the floor. For a moment his image shivered: we knelt beneath the gatehouse, his fist in the dust. "You know I can't do that, any more than you. Sister, what am I supposed to *do?*"

"I don't know. I cannot sleep with you," I said softly.

He tilted his head back; tears glistened on his face. "You were my companion and my mate. And now there's him. I've lost you."

What could I say? It was true. He left me and didn't return until the wedding.

10. SHIKUJO'S PILLOW BOOK
It wasn't always so:

I was sixteen when we wed; you were scarcely older. My coming-of-age ceremony had been two years before. My women put up my hair in the Chinese style, and my father's uncle tied on the pleated *mo* skirt that meant I was a woman. One month later, I put on a court train and entered the ninefold enclosure of the palace, in service with the old princess. I was shy, but she charmed me into relaxing. I soon grew used to life there.

The women of court are considered loose, willing to untie their sashes for any personable man; but there are as many attitudes towards such encounters as there are women. I was one whose "gate was closely guarded," as they say: I was not interested in the glib nobles I met, knowing that my parents had plans for me.

When our parents arranged this marriage, you were no more than a character based on you, in a story my mother told on my occasional visits home from my responsibilities at the princess's court. Not even that: you were a character based on a character based on a man, because my mother had never seen you, either, only heard of you through the matchmakers. Your family was good, she told me, and you were clever and correct. You would go far politically. I didn't care: despite my service to the princess, my dreams have always been more immediate than success at court.

Before I came of age, I had a nurse who smuggled in *monogatari*-tales, to cry over in her private moments. I read them, as well: my price for not telling my mother about their existence. After a time, we were both implicated and I couldn't have turned her in without exposing myself.

With my cousin (who was a year younger and quite adventurous; she had crept out one full-mooned night to exchange poems through the fence with a boy her age: "playing at love," I called it, superior in my upcoming marriage), I pored over the much-thumbed scrolls, reading again and again the descriptions of Genji and Kaoru, and of the tragic, perfect women they courted. These women all seemed to die, but I envied them the romance of their brief lives. I learned two things from these: the importance of refinement, of elegance (as if I were not told this daily by my nurse, who sometimes expressed doubts that this was, in my case, possible). And love.

I met you the night we first slept together, after the marriage had been arranged. You were so solemn! — a slim blade of a man dressed in scarlet, high cheekbones in a narrow face, a proud nose. The tales all told me to admire a man with a face as round and pale as the moon, but to me you were as beautiful as any prince in a story. I thought all the stars of heaven had dropped into my rice bowl.

I loved you instantly: how could I not? The only men I had even met were my father and brothers and uncles and various priests and diviners (all by definition uninteresting); at court men had visited, but I had always hidden myself away in the back corners of rooms, behind screens and panels. Even the pain of first sex seemed sweet and right. I was with you: blood was a small price to pay.

It wasn't until after the wedding that we learned to talk. Your sober propriety began to slip and show a man-boy who observed everything and laughed unaccountably at things I couldn't understand. I interested myself in your duties at the court, your friendships, your hobbies — striving to be the perfect woman a *monogatari* prince might wed.

I had my own interests. I made perfumes and dyed silks and answered my occasional summons to the princess's suite. None of these things seemed somehow appropriate to discuss. The perfect women of the tales did not bore their partners with their small doings.

I tried to be the perfect wife, to give you reasons to love me as I loved you. I never let my serenity slip. A man might be lighthearted, but a woman had to be calm, to stay a worthy wife and mother.

How did the talking stop? I only know that it did.

Were you trying to talk to me, back at the estate? I didn't hear it: heard only foxes and obsession, and ran.

11. KITSUNE'S DIARY

Kaya no Yoshifuji brought fire to our house and lit the torches here. My grandfather led him to my rooms (as if he did not know where I slept by now!). My mother laid the sleeping robes. Yoshifuji and I ate the third-night cakes, and the next morning knelt in front of a priest to drink *sake* together. I somehow expected there to be more of an event related to our actual wedding; even fox mating games were more complicated. But this was it: a three-times-three exchange of wine cups carved of glowing jade: nine swallows of cold sour wine. My family was not supposed to witness this ritual (such as it was), but my mother and grandfather and brother watched anyway. My husband was too far gone into the magic to be surprised at their presence.

I saw the wedding as my lord saw it: our bright robes and the priest's long hands gesturing at us, my family watching, an aster twisted forgotten in my mother's hands; but when I cried, the wedding blurred into patches of color over the truth of the thing: four foxes and a dirty madman crouched in filth and dust and darkness.

I loved Yoshifuji: didn't I want the best for him? Could this be better than his lovely house and his beautiful waiting wife?

No. I didn't care what was best for him. I wanted what I wanted. I was only a fox, after all.

12. THE NOTEBOOK OF KAYA NO YOSHIFUJI

She is mine now: we are married. Or I am hers.

The wedding reminded me of my wedding to Shikujo. While that one took longer to work out (marriage brokers being what they are), certain things were the same: the rice cakes and wine we tasted together; the banquets over the next few days; the sense of beginnings; my delight in discovering her thoughts and her lovely body. I recall when Shikujo and I first wed, and I explore the memory like the hole where a tooth once was. Strangely, I feel nothing.

I know (abstractly, as if I read it in a story once) that there are things wrong with how my life has moved from marriage to Shikujo to marrying my new gold-eyed wife. I know there should be grief and divorce and time elapsed and new settlements. And there is none of this. And somehow this has not mattered to me.

Why should it matter? I sit here on this perfect rush mat looking out on this perfect garden. My ink is as velvety black as a raven's underfeathers; this paper gleams like a winter pelt.

Soon I will put down this slim brush and walk to my wife's rooms, and she will be waiting for me, warm and welcoming, dressed in dark red lined with shades of green, her perfumed hair coiled like a skein of silk at her feet.

Nothing in memory is as real as *now*, or as entrancing as the possible what-will-bes.

13. SHIKUJO'S PILLOW BOOK
Cataloguing the autumn leaves:

The urushi-lacquer tree was once glossy green, its long ranks of leaves a neat procession. Now it turns brilliantly red, as red as my husband's finest robes. I long to reproduce that hot bright color in silk, but it is expensive and a secret I have not yet learned. Even the silk with which I made his robes for his visit to Kannon came to us as a gift from the princess at court.

The *katsura* trees are much subtler: turning a gold tempered with green. The birch, now yellow; the maple; the *basho*; the gold slashes of narrow-leafed bamboo—

Why do I write this list? Things shift even with my eyes on them; the world itself is changing color, as inconstant as love or mist. Perhaps in categorizing these trees I try to stop the shifting.

I was bored and lonely in the country (and afraid); I am bored and lonely and afraid here, in the city. The only thing that has changed is what I fear. Perhaps it wasn't the wilds that were the problem.

Not wanting to think about this, one found a slip of pale gray paper, and wrote this poem for the princess she once served, rolling the paper around the handle of one's favorite writing brush, and securing it with an iridescent red gauze ribbon:

> *The brush wept black tears*
>   *thinking of you.*

> *This one has returned from the hinterlands.*

14. KITSUNE'S DIARY

*M*arriage was good.
　　He lay beside me, his head in my lap. On the other side of a movable lattice, Josei read aloud from a scroll about the Buddha's life, but I ignored her (the Buddha, or Buddhas, seem very complicated and give me headaches if I think too much about them). Instead I played with a moon-shaped fan I had found at the bottom of a black-lacquer dressing-case patterned with sly-faced animals in court garb.

The fan looked familiar, but I thought nothing of it until I flipped it in my hand and noticed writing.

His hand caught my wrist. "I was reading it!"

"No!" I snatched hand and fan away and pressed both to my chest. My lord rocked upright to face me, amused.

"Why so reluctant, hmmm? Is it from an admirer?"

"I—that fan is getting ragged. It's just a leftover of the sum-mer. I meant to discard it."

"Well, let me discard it for you, then." He held out his hand as if I would just drop it into his palm.

"Truly, it's nothing," I said desperately. "Just an old—nothing."

"Then I'll read it, if it's nothing." Moving more quickly than I could follow, he caught my hand and effortlessly twisted the fan free. If we had been foxes, I would have been as strong and fast as he; I could have wrestled him for it.

He held the fan up to the light and frowned. I closed my eyes, not wanting to see.

　　　" 'The *spider's web may catch the moonlight*
　　　　but may not keep it.'

"This is what you wanted to keep from me?"

I opened my eyes and caught him smiling at me. He had not recognized it as his human wife's fan.

The poem had changed, or it meant different things, and what

I thought it meant was different from what he saw. How did this happen?

Marriage was good, but it was also hard. We were always on edge, those first days. There was so much we didn't know, or knew imperfectly. Anything might break the illusion and allow Yoshifuji to see the truth.

Mother was often a problem; she seemed to slip between fox-shape and woman-shape as if there were no difference to her. Luckily she spent much of her time away, unhappy with the restrictions she didn't understand.

I was relieved when she was gone. Only now do I realize why this was: she was the flaw that made it impossible for me to believe the illusion myself. If it hadn't been for her, I might have forgotten that after all, I was still a fox, and he was still a man, and we were sharing an impossible dream.

After a time, Yoshifuji began to leave me alone more. The fox magic was such that my lord had responsibilities as he had in his other life. I never understood what exactly his duties were — does any wife? — but there was a constant stream of people in our house, with messages and problems; there were even envoys from the capital. He had many contacts, and traveled a lot. He found a position in the neighborhood for my brother as a secretary for an official of some sort; sometimes my brother traveled with him.

This sounds so strange, even to me: we were foxes; what kind of work could we do? And there really was no job for Brother, and no messengers, no reports to be sent to the capital. The cloth he gathered for taxes was cobwebs and dirt, his papers were dead leaves that crackled underfoot beneath the gatehouse; the precious gifts that passed through his hands were pebbles and bones. It was all just dreams. But our family felt benefits from this influential life Yoshifuji lived, as if it had been real and we had been human: hunting was better than it had been, and the autumn weather held, as water-clear days and cool brilliant nights.

Even at home he spent more time with Grandfather or

Brother. I heard them some nights in one of the other wings, laughing and exchanging tales. I sighed then and fidgeted with whatever thing I was supposed to be practicing, but I knew this was the nature of things, that men will seek out the company of men.

He still came to me often and with joy. It was only when he left that I walked aimlessly through my useless rooms. I didn't wish I were still a mere fox, but I wished being a woman were less of a burden.

15. THE NOTEBOOK OF KAYA NO YOSHIFUJI

My pretty wife stares through an opened screen at a red squirrel and a gray squirrel. They bicker over nuts from the beech tree outside her rooms; on hands and knees, she is as absorbed as a stalking cat. I imagine that if she had a tail, she would flick it.

Her robes are red and gold with irregular white patches and neat clusters of crimson dots like berries, and trails like tiny black animal tracks or abstract calligraphy. Accustomed as I am to the robes of court, hers are of so unusual a pattern I would think she was guessing.

Her women kneel or lie behind screens, as ladies should. Their (much more standard) robes peep demurely from beneath their screens. It is only my wife who wears the brightest shades of autumn and laughs aloud at the squirrels.

Will I recall this tomorrow? I seem to be having a bit of trouble recalling things lately. Perhaps it is a condition of age.

I had a dream the other night, in which I saw my wife catch a warbler and eat it raw, tearing the flesh with her slim long hands.

An uncomfortable dream.

16. KITSUNE'S DIARY

I practiced my calligraphy. I was good at mixing my ink so that it was just the right thickness to leave a black shiny mark. I loved this. Foxes always love to mark with urine the borders of our land; but no fox ever left a mark so strong.

I loved the blackness of the ink and the smell of it, like wet dirt in the spring. I practiced on papers, on bolts of plain silk, on the paper walls of my rooms. Sometimes the fussy little characters humans use got too constricting, and I would swash ink without any intention, just to see the shapes it formed.

This is how it seemed as a fox, but as a human, I knew I was supposed to notice the meanings of the shapes I made as much as the shapes themselves. It was only much later that I realized I was perhaps as close to understanding poetry in those joyous ink-splashing moments as I will ever be.

In one other thing was this similar to urine marking: that in the mornings, when I awakened, the magic had somehow washed my walls and verandas clean, and I would begin again.

17. THE NOTEBOOK OF KAYA NO YOSHIFUJI

My wife's robes are covered with a pattern of ribbons and chrysanthemums on a creamy field. Under it she wears a red robe, and five shades of white, and a dark mossy green robe with a geometric pattern. Her hair has been flipped into a knot at the small of her back, to keep the ends from trailing on the floor. She plays with a small ball that looks a little like a pearl, except that it is palm-sized. It catches the light around it so that it seems to glow, though this is of course impossible. She is not very good with it, and it falls from her hands and rolls across the floor. When it does, a single crease appears on her forehead, and she claps and a woman brings it back to her. I have to laugh: sitting as she does, with the robes obscuring her limbs, she is like a dog throwing a ball for a person.

It is strange how perfect her house always is—no spiderwebs here. The weather, too, has been fine, an endless sequence of crisp glowing days and hazed nights. Peasants seem always to be working in the rice fields here, filling tightly woven baskets with gathered grain, racking green-gold hay on endless frames. Musicians play as they work, bright charming country tunes I can never remember even a moment later. At night, the lakes in the garden are filled with floating lamps shaped like waterfowl. It is the same everywhere: perfection.

My new wife, her family, this house—even the valley itself—seem to me fragmented, slightly distorted. Sometimes a room or a path in the garden seems to shift in the corner of my eye; when I turn to look, the place is just as I remembered it. Or is it my memory that shifts?

I have felt no great drive to write—why would I engage in painting words and images, experiences given secondhand, when I have the option of breathing, walking, touching, making love? Reality is always more compelling than fiction.

18. KITSUNE'S DIARY

We mated often: most often when he quoted poetry to me. What else was I to do? When we were not pillowed together, he lounged in my rooms, and read things to me, and occasionally fiddled with my soft-bristled brushes and ink. He sat sometimes writing quickly on a lacquered lap-desk, black, shiny ink on white paper: wet slate in the snow. I looked over his shoulder. Written in large, strong characters:

> *The bowl's dark glaze reflects the sky:*
> *Which color is the bowl? Blue or black?*

"What does that mean?" I asked, and then I realized: poetry again. He looked at me strangely, and I blushed and blurted, "What do you write, when you sit there?"

"I keep a diary," he said. "I always have, though not so much lately. My wife . . ." His voice trailed off. I held my breath, for I knew he didn't mean me. After a moment, he shook his head and laughed. "I had a thought, but it escaped me. Perhaps it will come again."

"Come to bed," I whispered, and he left that thought, and did not return to it.

When he was gone (as he was more often these days), I obsessed about poetry. The house seemed to come equipped with a number of poetry collections; I fluttered through the scrolls restlessly, looking for something that made sense, that showed the difference between poetry and mere observation.

It was dangerous to keep, but I couldn't discard the moon-shaped fan, scrawled with the poem that Yoshifuji had written.

> *The spider's web is soaked with moonlight*
> *How can I keep it?*

I came back again and again to this, trying to make sense of the writing there as more than a string of words that shifted meanings confusingly with each reading. It had taken me time to recognize Yoshifuji's ink strokes on paper as a drawing of foxes; I kept hoping for a similar shift in understanding about this: *I see! This is what poetry is.* But it did not happen.

One day Josei came to me. "My lady?"

"Um, yes." It was hard to remember sometimes that I was "my lady."

She bowed. "The master, your grandfather, is asking if you'd have the time to speak with him?"

"He is always welcome."

"I hoped so," Grandfather said from over her shoulder. "I hope I'm not taking you from anything."

This had to be irony, a recent discovery for us. What would

I be doing? "No," I said. "I've been trying to understand poetry, that's all."

Josei moved back to a cluster of women seated around a paulownia-wood brazier shaped like a fat eight-petaled lotus bloom. They were exchanging scrolls. I wondered what they might be reading, or if the scrolls would be blank until they were read by me. Did they write poetry, these women of mine? Was it better than my own stumbling attempts?

"Yes. Well." Grandfather settled himself painfully. Josei, who knew his aches, brought him a little metal brazier that hung from a frame and set it beside him. "Thank you, girl. This isn't why I'm here."

"You don't need a reason to visit me," I said. "I always love company. It gets a little quiet."

"You miss being able to run around, hey?"

"No." I remembered the feel of needles under my toes, the intense smells of the forest and garden, the bright vivid taste of freshly killed meat. "Well, yes. Sometimes."

"I would imagine. Well, Granddaughter, I have news for you," he said with a certain satisfaction. "Your husband will do well in the next set of appointments."

"How will that work? Will he have to return to the capital?"

"You should know better than to ask too many questions about any of this, pretty bug-eater," Grandfather said. "It just is."

"I suppose," I said, flipping the fan between my hands.

The silk curtain between us was slightly transparent. Through it I saw him lean forward and squint. "What do you have there?"

I slid the fan under the curtain to him. His dark shape picked it up, and tilted it this way and that. "It's not seasonal and it's getting a little scruffy," he grunted, "but the calligraphy seems attractive enough. Why are you playing with a summer fan at this time of year?"

"I am not 'playing,' " I said. "I am curious. The writing, the poem—I still do not understand these things."

"I expect you won't," he said.

"I have to understand this," I said to my grandfather, "or

he'll never love me. He'd spend more time with me if I understood it."

"His wife understood poetry, one assumes; I do not recall he spent much time with her. If he loves you, it will be for the fox-heart of you, for the animal he tastes when he kisses you. Poetry is not for foxes."

"No," I said hotly. "The foxes at the shrine spoke the same words to me, so *they* must have understood poetry."

He snorted. "Those were not foxes, those were *Inari's* foxes. Totally different from mere flesh-and-blood you-and-me foxes."

I tipped my head to one side, distracted by a thought. "Grandfather? I have always wondered. Why did the foxes speak the same words as those on the fan?" If they *were* the same words.

"I imagine you are part of a larger plan, girl."

"Karma?" I asked.

"No, karma is human."

"But the old man, the priest in the woods, told me I had karma, that karma is what makes me wish to change from fox to human."

"What does he know?" Grandfather snapped. "I am an old fox, and many things have happened in my life. But I have no destiny, no karma—just longing and satisfaction, cause and effect. We foxes know better than to hope for second chances. Except foolish kits, of course."

"Then how can I be part of a plan?" I said.

"You have no karma, but the humans around us do. Perhaps you are part of Yoshifuji's fate, or his wife's."

"That can't be true! There must be more to my life than satisfying another's destiny."

"Why?" he said irritably.

There was no answer to that. He returned my fan to me, and left.

Yoshifuji came to me one afternoon. I was wrist-deep in a silver basin of maple leaves. My women and I were having a contest to select the brightest, largest and most perfect leaves. The smell was good, like dirt and autumn.

"Are you well, wife?"

"Hmm?" Why was he asking? I was always well; that was one of the gifts of being human in the fox magic: no human illnesses, no coughs or runny noses or stiff necks from sleeping badly.

"I hadn't thought of it before this," he said, "but you have never retired for your monthly courses, and it's been months? years?"

This was another thing my family hadn't thought of, though there seemed to be no harm in it, when he had been with us for so long before noticing. "Yes." I thought quickly. "They are different than you are used to, I suppose. They don't come so often as usual for women."

"Does this mean you cannot bear children?"

I turned him off with a light answer, but I was confused. Children? Later, after Yoshifuji had gone off to finish a document on local rice production for the ministers in the capital, I spoke with my grandfather.

"He asked about children."

"Ah. He's thought of that, has he?"

"He wants to know whether I—whether we—can have children. What do I tell him?"

"Have you ever had any kits?"

"You know that! Of course not."

"So: maybe no. But you're still young. And now you're human. So: maybe yes. Why should I know, to tell you?"

"Well, you've done this before! You've been human."

He sighed. "So I have. Very well, then: it is possible for a human and a fox to have a child. Possible for you? Who can tell?"

"If I did, which would it be, fox or human?"

"I don't know. And neither, I expect, would he. He would see whatever it is he expects to see." Grandfather looked at me for a long moment, then said slowly, "I wonder if this is something we can maintain, this magic. There are too many aspects involved in such a spell: his feelings, yours, the wife's, the seasons, the gods. Many things. How long can we do this?"

"Forever," I hissed. "We must."

He was silent for a long moment. The coals in the brazier rasped against its side as he stirred them. "But should we?"

"Are we doing the right thing?" I said slowly. "This is your question?"

"Yes."

"*You* lead this family; why do you ask *me?*"

"I lead, yes: even now, little fox wife. I'm not dead yet. But we did this together, you and I."

"I know why I did it, but why were you willing?"

There was a silence on the other side of the curtain, silence for so long that I thought he had perhaps left. His voice, when it came, was low. "I remembered . . . longing the way you longed for Yoshifuji. And I couldn't watch you grieve as I had. But now I think, this is too far. What if you did have children?"

"What if I do?"

"What will your son be, fox or man?"

"He will be human, like his father." *And like me,* I thought, or perhaps prayed.

"And he will grow up where? Here? In the dust?"

"This is not dust!" I said, but Grandfather continued.

"And when he is older? Whom will *he* wed? Will we steal a human girl for him?"

"It will work out," I said desperately.

Grandfather made a sound of disgust. "You will not listen. Well, at least you are not pregnant yet. Reconsider this life, Daughter."

"He is my husband. I will not give him up."

"Then we continue," Grandfather said. "I hope this is the right thing."

19. SHIKUJO'S PILLOW BOOK
Summoned to court:

*T*he princess responded to my letter by returning my writing brush, its tip colored with ink, laid on the lid of a writing-desk. There was also this note, written on a fine paper once purple, now faded to an alkaline gray:

> *The brush is wet*
> *thrilled to tears to see you again.*

> *Please come visit this one when it is possible.*

And so I have been summoned to court. I am of course no longer a formal attendant of the princess, but perhaps she still feels fondness for me because of my time with her before my marriage. It will be a welcome distraction to return to court, however informally.

20. KITSUNE'S DIARY

*E*veryone was gone, and my women were scenting robes, laying them across frames so that smoke from incense burners beneath them seeped through the silks. I had the screens open, but even so, my house was filled with smoke that coiled in languid tendrils beneath the high eaves.

I sat against a padded armrest, with a scroll in my hand. It was an exciting story, all about a brother and sister who had changed places, so that the brother lived as a noblewoman and his sister as a courtier. I was confused by some of the goings-on, and I had stopped reading to listen to my women trill at one another about the weather. The skies beyond the opened screens were bright with pale clouds. I heard a *uguisu*-nightingale singing somewhere in the garden. There was also a group of graylag geese with harsh braying voices, flapping about in one of the lakes.

I felt very human, doing all this. This was just what a woman would be doing on a day like this — reading and watching her attendants, and commenting to herself on the bird cries. It seemed just a small step to asking for my writing materials and dashing off a poem, and I got as far as calling out Josei's name before the earth started shaking.

The *uguisu*-nightingale abruptly grew silent and the geese flew up as a group, and for a moment, I thought the vibrating of the house was an earthquake; but this made no sense; we had built no such quakes into the magic. A clothing frame fell over, and two of the women screamed, and still the shaking did not stop.

Where was my husband? Picking up my robes, I ran into the garden. I threw off my human form: changing from human to fox hurt a lot, as if my bones had been softened in boiling water until they could be bent and reshaped. When it was over I ran out into the real world, which meant I crouched at the very corner of the gatehouse looking out, terrified that my husband might be lost somewhere outside the magic.

The earthquake was not happening in the real world. The trees shivered in a cold wind, but the ground was solid underfoot. The main activity outside the magic was in Kaya no Yoshifuji's house.

When my brother and I had explored the buildings of Yoshifuji's home, before he had come from the capital, the spaces had been quiet, unused. Even when he had lived there, many of the rooms were dark; and even in those where he and the members of his household lived, the lights were muted and the constant human chattering was no louder than a stream rattling against stones, or crows arguing over a carcass. But now every room of every building was filled with light. Torches ringed the verandas, pouring smoke straight up in the autumn air. Many screens had been pushed back, so that we could see into the rooms, where lanterns hung from the eaves.

In our fox-magic world, things were much better ordered than this. Here, in the real world, people were everywhere, thick as sparrows in the rice fields, a seething constant movement of colors: the indigo and white robes of peasants or low-grade servants; the pale grays and oranges and whites of various priests and monks; and all the gaudy greens and golds and scarlets of the women there. There seemed to be no order to the movements, and for once the women seemed to mingle freely with the other people of the household. I recognized no one. Every attempt to make oneself unique — robes, perfumes, hair — are all just nuances that never conceal the underlying continuity, that all are human.

The noise was incredible. It had been loud before, from the edge of the garden; but now it was nearly deafening. I flicked my ears back, for a moment longing for my human ears, which were less sensitive than fox-ears. The cymbals clashed in the hands of the priests; and one group had set up a high monotonous droning noise. I suppose this was a chant, but even now it is very difficult for me to see the point of such music, if music it is.

Loud and bright and frightening: I crouched enchanted, drugged with the excitement.

A man emerged from a room clogged with clouds of incense. He looked worried, and after a moment, I recognized him as an important servant of Yoshifuji's (in general, humans always looked somewhat similar to me; even now they were hard to identify unless I could hear their voices). I supposed he had summoned these diviners and begun their chanting.

A sudden clash of cymbals made me jump from the bush I had been hiding in. For an instant I was completely exposed, but the attention of the humans on the verandas was absorbed elsewhere.

A diviner had marched from the main house onto the veranda. He was dressed in saffron and white, with a strange tall hood. Acolytes clustered around him, and Yoshifuji's servants clustered around *them*. The acolytes carried cymbals and skin-covered drums and racks hung with brass bells. The chanting had resolved itself into a summoning of the Buddha. They were asking for his help in finding Kaya no Yoshifuji.

A shiver ran down my spine. Why hadn't I thought of this? Of course they would look for him. They would walk around their gardens, and they might find him under the gatehouse, or see him in the half-world where he hunted with my brother. And if they didn't find him, they would keep looking. And they might very well call on a human god to help them, just as the rabbits by the moonrock called for help from the rabbit-god when they wished to escape.

The diviner staggered down the stairs, as if being drawn by a silk cord. His movements seemed so artificial that, had I still been a woman, I might have laughed despite my fear. But I also felt something real happening in the diviner, like the heat waves that rise from coals that otherwise look dead. I didn't know what it might be, but I cowered anyway, afraid for my life, afraid for Yoshifuji.

The diviner took a staggering step toward me, and then another. He knew where I was, or was being led toward me. I slid backward through the bush. The thing moving inside him suddenly flared: the Buddha. There was nothing to see, nothing to smell; but the Buddha was as real as Inari's moon-foxes had been. The humans had summoned him, and he had come. And now the diviner walked awkwardly toward me, pulled by invisible threads.

But why should the Buddha care about us and Yoshifuji? He was a great god (if that was what he was; I was often confused by theology) who taught that concern over things of this world was a waste of time; and I was a single insignificant fox who had happened to fall in love. Surely my family and my husband were beneath his notice. The diviner walked closer, and the Buddha-fire washed across my face: the attention of a god turned in my direction, like a sudden piercing shaft of sunlight direct in the eyes. I could feel the fox-magic house shaking in the magical earthquake. I knew it would not work—I was already burning alive in the focus of his attention—but I crushed my eyes shut and worked magic furiously: I am nothing, little and humble, irrelevant, unimportant, not here not here not here.

And then the glare lost focus and moved past me. The diviner and all his attendants moved away, down a path toward the foot of the garden.

The Buddha had noticed me but didn't care. Perhaps to him we were all — foxes, humans — illusions within the larger reality of the universe. The house still quivered with tremors, aftershocks of the Buddha's attention.

I couldn't hold my shape. My robes trembled around me: silk to fur to skeletal leaves knotted into mats. I fell to my knees, and felt the dirt cold against my four paws, my fingernails scratching the surface. I was on the polished wood of my veranda, which exploded into dust beneath my toes, my hands. I staggered upright.

"Wife?" The voice came in layers, to fox-ears, woman-ears. Yoshifuji was back from wherever he had been. The walls rippled around me and re-formed. "Wife, where are you?"

The voice was closer.

"No," I cried, in a howl like a fox's cry. "Don't come in —"

"You sound ill. Where are you?" He was frightened now. I heard it in his voice, and smelled it through my fox-nostrils. My robes were choking me. I threw back the layers, which fell like shed snakeskins around me. I clawed with hands that trembled between toes and fingers to pull free the sash that held my under-robes.

Light flared and dimmed: my pupils changing their nature. "No," I said again, but it came out as a bark.

A paper door broke open, tearing like a cobweb. *"Kitsune!"*

Kitsune: fox. This was the end, then: he had seen me for what I was. He had never called me this, although I knew the knowledge scratched at the edges of his mind. I watched him blur and sharpen in my changing eyes. He dropped to his knees beside me.

Was it fox-nature or woman-nature? I snarled at him, seeing me like this, bit at the hand he extended. Which was I? "Leave me," I grated out between pointed teeth, past a throat that only inconsistently carried sound.

"Wife —" he breathed. I smelled it on him: wanting. *What can he want?* I thought, but I responded, anyway. I was hot and dizzy with the changes, and the smell of him in my nostrils.

Hands on fur, on flesh. I ran my hand along his cheek, saw blood spring from the scratches that appeared under my claws. The blood smelled cloying, sharp and sweet. I snapped at his neck, the death-bite, and my woman's lips pressed against the soft skin of his throat, felt the pulse run under me, tasted the blood that dripped from his face.

He caught me by the hindquarters. I whirled to kiss, to slash at him. He bared himself, and took me.

I was on my paws, tail curled over my back; I had no tail; I was on hands and knees, he behind me, hands dug into the soft flesh where my legs hinged into my body. I clawed at the dirt in front of me. There were whimpering noises. Was this he or I? Fox-me or woman-me? What was he thrusting into? The hot sheathing of the blood that fell from his scratches made us slick and wet.

I don't know what he was doing, how he saw this. I only know what I felt, which was the shivering of self into shards of fox and woman, all lost in the heat and the flickers of light behind my eyes.

I know we screamed together in the end, like prey under a killer's teeth.

I came back to myself: a naked woman in shredded robes.

Now it was all in control again. We were in my rooms. The floors were clean. My bed robes were soft and warm. A voice outside the sliding doors: Josei directing the fixing of the torn screen, as well as other earthquake damage. Outside the curtains of the bed, a woman moved quietly, gathering our discarded clothes, stirring the brazier. But like a fading shadow, I also saw him as he was: sleeping in the dirt in a tangle of filthy sweat-, sex-, and blood-soaked robes.

When he awakened, he had no memory of the night. He seemed unaware of his wounds. And he never again called me *kitsune,* fox.

21. THE NOTEBOOK OF KAYA NO YOSHIFUJI

Foxes half-seen
     in the darkness I have courted
          knowing less of my lady.

Is this poem my own, or do I merely remember the poem of another?

22. KITSUNE'S DIARY

My brother was gone a lot. As is the nature of foxes, in times of plenty we hide away food in caches that we retrieve a few days later, if things are not so good. We had done this; but it had rained for days, and now the caches were all dug up and eaten, and Brother hunted and brought back food for us (little dumplings filled with sweet stuffing which were really a half-eaten hare; bean paste candies that were really the ragged torso of a dead swallow).

When he was with us, he seemed restless and unhappy. Though he was handsome as a man, he didn't adapt well to the behaviors of humanity, and seemed not to care if he did things properly. I never saw him practice calligraphy, even though I knew he had responsibilities that required writing elegantly. He did practice archery sometimes, and I loved to watch when I could. The preciseness of targeting and release reminded me of pouncing, and I longed to try my hand at it.

But in general he was humorless, my brother. He did what was required of him as the son of an important house, and beyond that he was simply not there.

But there were times. One afternoon after days of rain, my husband was visiting me, and we were talking of everything and nothing, as is the nature of husbands and wives — the roof (which needed repair after a tree branch had fallen on it the night before), and our general discomfort as all the insects of the outdoor world moved into the shelter and warmth of the house, so that we seemed to be inundated with spiders and fleas.

Brother showed up, walking not from the other wings of the house, but straight up from the gardens into my rooms. His trousers had been laced tight against his legs, but even so, the pale violet brocade was wet to his knees, and autumn seeds clung to his *tabi*-socks.

Yoshifuji and my brother and I chatted for a time (the deer that had been down from the mountain lately—we could hear its cries sometimes—would this bring down wolves?). And then the men ended up outside, on the pale sand around my rooms. Yoshifuji taught my brother to play a game called *kemari* in which they used any part of their body except their hands to toss back and forth a small soft ball; Brother was very good at it, and (even though Yoshifuji had explained that the point of the game was the elegance of the passes) they ended up trying to trick each other into dropping the ball. Brother smiled as they played; and when Yoshifuji left to complete some documents for the capital, he came up and dropped onto a mat beside me, for once lighthearted and relaxed.

"That was fun," he said happily.

"It looked like it." I tried to keep the jealousy out of my voice, wanting my brother's rare pleasure to be uncolored by my own ill feelings.

"It was not the same as when we two played, back when we were foxes. But fun nonetheless. Sister—" He stopped, suddenly serious, as if choosing his words. "This life—when you first chose it, I was lonely. You never played with me anymore, and I couldn't see the point of changing ourselves like this. But there *is* something special about humanness, isn't there?"

"Yes," I said, but he wasn't listening to me.

"They see things differently. They *want* things, to win or know or understand." He shook his head. "I can't think of the words."

"I know," I said. And I did: I felt this way as well, had felt it since falling in love with Yoshifuji.

"Poetry—" he said. "Perhaps there is something to it, after all?"

After that, my brother seemed to take his humanity more seriously.

It was about this time that I made a discovery.

Mother shrieked when I told her. "Pregnant?"

"I can feel it, a little male."

"How can you tell?"

I stared at her in silence, for I had no idea: perhaps something about the magic made it possible, but she rattled on:

"A son! Oh, such news! You will bring such honor to the house!"

"How can it? I am a fox. My child will be a fox. He will see, and leave me."

Mother laughed at me. "You have lived all this time with a man, and you have not learned the first thing yet. He will see a son, because that is what he wants. He will be so happy! I am going to go tell your grandfather. A son!"

It was just as she said. Yoshifuji was thrilled.

23. SHIKUJO'S PILLOW BOOK
It was several days:

It was several days before I was ready to attend the princess. There were rituals to purify me before entering the palaces, and I wanted to fast and clarify my mind, so that I would be a worthy companion. The princess expected all this, of course, but she wrote affectionate letters urging me to make such haste as I could.

She sent a purple-walled wickerwork carriage and a cluster of elegantly dressed men to attend us. I kissed my son and mother (my father was at court already, attending to his responsibilities), and then Onaga and I gathered our heavy robes and stepped into the open courtyard. The men—all functionaries

of the fifth or sixth rank — were too tactful to stare openly at us;
but they were, nevertheless, watching, and I found I was no
longer used to the casual glances of courtiers. I blushed furiously
and hurried into the carriage.

The interior was lined with gold and silver papers painted
with fringed grasses soaked with dew; the brushstrokes were so
fine that I could lean forward and see the reflections of sunlight
on individual water drops, and a tiny insect like a gnat standing
on a grass blade. Incredibly, the insect moved, and I pulled back
with an exclamation of distaste: it was not a painting but a living
flea.

Fleas (and their equivalents, all the tiny harassments of life)
are everywhere in this world, an unpleasant reminder that life
is not as perfect as we would prefer. But I was traveling to
attend the princess; such a reminder at such a time was unwel-
come. Onaga saw my distress, and using a soft paper that had
been tucked in her sleeve, she crushed the tiny animal and
dropped it through the window-grille.

The brilliant light that fell through the grille settled sharp-
edged as knives across the reds and greens of our court robes.
The air that came in was cool and smelled of the city. The streets
were thronged as they always are in the capital; I heard vendors'
shouts, the clattering of horse- and ox-hooves and wooden clogs,
men singing as they worked.

After a short time, we paused at a gate to transfer to a smaller
carriage drawn by men. The noise of the city abated somewhat,
until we were able to hear the hushing of leaves moving in the
breeze.

We travel all the time, I suddenly realized. In a handful of
months, I traveled to the Tani valley and back, and here in the
capital from my own house to my parents', and now to the palace; my husband traveled to the coast and back; my mother and
father to Lake Biwa and back. And even when we are settled
in one place, still we all travel. From room to room, and garden
to garden, and house to house and shrine to shrine.

And beyond all that, were we never to leave our beds, still
we would travel. My husband travels along strange roads in his

dreams and his obsessions. My son travels often in his games: to distant Korea or even more distant China, or to places that have never existed, except in his mind. I would say that I have not done so; but then I remember my fever dreams of the fox man.

So much traveling, and it all seems to end wherever we began. Where are we hoping to go, and what do we wish we would find there? I think perhaps my husband asks these and other, similar, questions.

I do not think travel is truly about getting someplace. I wonder if it is instead desired because it is movement, because it helps ease pain, just as rolling an aching shoulder or rocking with stomach pains helps for at least the moment of movement.

And then the carriage stops, and Onaga and I climb out, and I must compose myself for my time with the princess.

24. KITSUNE'S DIARY

I had never been pregnant, either as a woman or a fox, but I knew in my blood and bones that pregnancy was not supposed to be a complicated thing. One got pregnant and continued to hunt and sleep and eat. One prepared several dens, and when the time came one crawled into one of them, and after a small amount of pain, one delivered one or two or three or four kits, tiny dark-furred hungry things. One's mate brought food for a few weeks, until the kits could be left alone for short times. The little foxes lived or died — ideally lived — and in time left to hunt and sleep and eat and mate and carry on their own lives. The fact that my brother and I were both adults and had not left did not change this expectation in my mind.

As a human, pregnancy was yet another thing that seemed more complicated than necessary. Josei made much of me in the early stages and constantly fretted over me, bringing extra robes even on fine days and forcing me to drink various (generally nasty) nostrums. Nervous for my health, I peeked once through the fox magic to see what I was truly drinking: it was no more

than rainwater cupped in a leaf large as a woman's hand, bright
green mottled with cherry-red and gold. After that, I drank what
my maid gave me without complaint.

After her initial excitement, my mother paid no attention to
my pregnancy. My brother said nothing, though I knew he had
been told. But my grandfather came to me often, though we
never again discussed whether my child might not be human.

My brother and Yoshifuji went hawking together one day. It
was a day of silver and gold: the leaves of the zelkova trees
glittered like coins when the breeze tossed them; the sky overhead was a flat pale glowing gray. They were dressed in dark
and leaf greens. I watched them walk across the pale dead
grasses of the fox-magic garden toward the real world. Men
behind them braced great wood perches against their hips;
hawks half as tall as their carriers clung to the bars.

My brother laughed, a clear delighted sound that floated
across the air to me. I hadn't heard him laugh in a long time;
when did it happen that my husband had replaced me as his
companion?

Even after the men were hidden by the soft curve of the hill
that led to the gate, I saw the hawks teetering on their braces.
A few moments later, a fox slipped from the building next to
the one I stood in, and loped after them, for the world. My
mother, freed for the day, hunting for some small animal to eat.

I was wearing a robe ornamented with monkeys peering from
an autumn tree: there were many-colored clouds of leaves, and
the red-orange monkeys clung to the lichen-splashed trunk with
their long black toes. My underrobes were midnight blue and
gold. All this finery, and there was no one to see.

They spent so much time together, my brother and my husband. I never thought I would be envious of them. And who
exactly was I jealous of? Brother, who had Yoshifuji when I
didn't; or Yoshifuji, who stole my brother away from me?

Or was it both, for running in the sun when I sat here in
the darkness, lost in these great piles of clothes, trying to learn

calligraphy and throwing a small ball from one hand to the other?

I was the center of this magic, and so I stayed with the servants in the house.

Waiting. Again.

25. THE NOTEBOOK OF KAYA NO YOSHIFUJI

The day is surprisingly cold. The sky has the sheen of brushed silk. There is almost no breeze: a good day for hawking.

We walk through the forest. The oaks mingled with the pines and cedars clutch leaves the color of dried blood. My wife's brother looks around in pleasure and curiosity.

"What are you looking for?" I ask.

He blushes and smiles at me, his gold eyes alight. "Nothing. I haven't been this way before."

"Nor have I."

"Where are we going then?"

"Well, there *was* a big clearing up in the mountains. I used to climb up there when Shikujo and I were first married, but I haven't been there since we came back from the capital."

"I guess that would be all right, going up there," he says slowly, as if weighing the safety of such a trip.

"Why wouldn't it? There are rabbits, wood pigeons—if it's not too far for the hawks."

"Why would it be?" he asks, genuinely puzzled.

We walk together up the path. The servants behind us march silently, as tireless as a river. Miyoshi no Kiyoyuki's servants are always perfect: I have never caught one behaving with less than complete propriety. Certainly there has been nothing like Onaga's sour cawings, or my old servant Hito's frettings.

"Do you miss her?" My brother-in-law's voice startles me. "Your other wife?"

I am thinking more about her today than I have in—months? years? Time is strange, I think; it has been a long autumn. "Yes.

Shikujo. She seems dreamlike to me. We fought sometimes, and made love. I remember very little of it all. I think I wasn't a good husband."

"You seem a good husband to me," he says, then blushes suddenly. "From what my sister says, I mean. In what way weren't you good then?"

"I was restless, lost somehow inside myself. I think she could only watch and wait." The woods are at last looking familiar; now mostly beech, they glow around us. It is like walking through the heart of a sun.

"I know what that is like," he says softly. "I understand being outside the screens looking in. And my sister?"

"Your sister." I smile even at the thought of her. She has been unhappy for some reason lately, perhaps due to the pregnancy; but I still delight in every moment we spend together. "She is as vivid as these woods, and as natural."

He seems amused by some joke I can't understand. "And yet she seems very unnatural to me. But then, I'm her brother; I've known her longer than you. I remember when nothing stood between her and the woods."

"What is unnatural about her now?"

"Everything." He looks away for a moment, a glimmer of something that might be sadness in his hard-to-read gold eyes. He reminds me very much of his sister when I leave her. "When we were young, we played together. Ran everywhere. Got into trouble together. Now she spends all her time inside in the dark. Is this 'natural' to you? It doesn't seem so to me."

"What else can she do? She's a woman."

"If being a woman is about that, I'm glad I was a male. Is that it?" He points at a lightening in the trees ahead.

"Yes." We step into a large bowl; folds of land draped like fabric between two legs spill down a mountain's side. I have no idea why there are no trees here; but there are none but the small willows that trace a stream's path down the deepest curve of the fold. The grass is dead, turned pale brown. It hisses in the slight breeze, which smells of pine and unknown spices.

My brother-in-law gestures to the man bearing the largest

bird. He kneels and the boy takes the hawk on his arm and frees its eyes. He looks at me: "Ready?"

I nod. He throws the great bird into the air with an ease impossible for a man as slight as he is. The hawk opens its wings and lifts.

We watch it circle. "No one used to determine my fate," he says. His voice is so soft I think at first that I don't hear it, or that he recites some poem to himself. The latter is, of course, impossible. "But now I wonder sometimes if we are all trapped in a net made of the interwoven fates of others. As I am trapped by my sister's."

"As we all are," I say absently. "Watch —"

The hawk pauses, then folds its wings and falls. It drops out of sight into underbrush at the fringe of the trees; there is a scream and the sound of beating wings, and the hawk flutters backward, then down again. A scream from beneath its feet.

A large animal rears up, slashing heavy claws at the hawk. The hawk dances back again, blood gouting from its breast. A *tanuki*-badger. Amazing: any hawk would normally hesitate to drop on such a creature, but my new family's hawks are (like everything else they own) unusual.

"Hurry!" my brother-in-law snarls, and sprints forward, drawing a long knife. This is no way to conduct a proper hawk-hunt.

"Stay," I call to the men. The hawk is certainly injured, the *tanuki*-badger probably so. The last thing I want is large numbers of people thundering through the bushes getting bitten or clawed.

By the time I catch up to his ground-eating run, my brother-in-law is already in the brush where the hawk dropped, and falling to his knees. The *tanuki*-badger seems to be unwilling to move; the hawk still thrashes against the bushes, blinded with pain and killing-rage.

"Yes," my brother-in-law growls at the *tanuki*-badger, and his voice is like the snarl of an animal. The beast half-curls, protecting its belly. He lashes out with a long arm, but the badger snaps and backs slowly. It turns suddenly and dives toward a small gap in the dense underbrush, but my brother-in-law is quicker. He catches its tail and pulls hard; in the instant before it jerks free, he drives down with the knife. Blood pours upward over his hand, splashing across his hunting costume. "Monster," he snarls. He stabs again, and the badger is still.

He looks up at me, catches me staring at him. He flushes: "What? Have I behaved badly?"

I swallow. "Ah. You were very passionate about killing it."

"My kind hates them all." His eyes are still flat and pale with the killing-rage. "They kill our children. They would kill us if they found us weak or sick or alone. Isn't that enough?"

"*Badgers* would kill you?" I have to laugh. "I know they are occasionally difficult, tricky animals; but unless you leave a baby outside unattended or your family has incurred the wrath of some badger-god, this doesn't make much sense." I pause for a moment: could such an animal kill my child, the baby inside my wife?

"Nevertheless." He catches the hawk by one leg; with the other, he pulls free his sash and wraps it tightly. It snaps at his hands, but he appears not to notice. "Here," he says, and hands the swaddled hawk to me, rising easily to his feet.

I take it automatically, like a parcel delivered by a servant, watching the planes of his face smooth as his anger leaves.

It is not until we have handed the injured hawk to a servant and walk back toward Kiyoyuki's house that I notice I was wrong about his robes. I thought they were stained with blood, but I must have misinterpreted what I saw, for they are unmarked.

He is very interesting, my brother-in-law.

26. SHIKUJO'S PILLOW BOOK
The princess was very kind:

The princess was very kind to me. When I entered her rooms, she was in the midst of a game of *hentsugi*-character matching with her women, but she saw us and stopped immediately. "My dear! How welcome you are!"

I felt suddenly dizzy and could barely prevent myself from breaking into tears right there in front of everyone. She was enough older than I that she might almost be my mother, and I had come to serve in her court when I was little more than a girl. She had treated me gently, those first days when I was so shy I thought I might die from the shock of such a public life — she coaxed me to sit next to her and play *sugoroku*-backgammon; she sent me poems on my occasional absences from court. At first I felt myself specially singled out by her; by the time I realized she treated each of us this way, at least some of the time, my heart already belonged to her. I thought I would always attend her, and I wept when I was sent home, when my father began thinking of marriage for me.

The princess knelt among her women. Her hair was half-silver now, though it still stretched past her feet. Her robes were of hammered silk in shades of gray; their austerity made her look as if she had kept the promise (or threat) she had been making since I had first attended her, the promise to leave this world to become a nun and contemplate the next. Compared to the bright parrot-colors of her attendants, she seemed even more beautiful than I had remembered. "Lady," I whispered, and knelt before her.

"I am so glad to see you, girl!" Her voice was as low as the *biwa*-lute's deepest notes, with the rasp of an always-near cough. "Sit beside me."

And everything was as it always had been, as if the years of separation, of my marriage and her aging and ill health, were gone like ground mist in the sunlight. The game of character matching began again, and I played with the rest of them, straining my mind for clever combinations of elements that might create a word no one else had yet thought of. We played and for a time I forgot my confusion and unhappiness, though the princess seemed to watch me with knowing eyes.

After a time, I asked to leave, but she refused to allow this, demanding I stay at least until the moon-viewing party several days later. I wrote to my father and my son, explaining things. In truth, I was not sorry to stay.

27. KITSUNE'S DIARY

My writing instructor sat on the other side of my *kichō*-curtain. I ruined sheet after sheet, and threw them to the floor in disgust. He is a Buddhist, which makes me laugh — our magic constructs have religions? — but he is at least patient. Me, I was never patient, practicing writing; pregnant, I found I had no tolerance for the slow rituals that married mind and hand for such things.

Poetry has forms. The rules are so simple. The *waka* is five lines of five, seven, five, seven and seven syllables. There is a shorter form, as well: five, seven and five. A poem has what is called a pivot word, around which the sense turns; and a pillow word, on which the poem rests. You try to get in something about a season or a natural image appropriate to the emotions you are trying to convey in the poem. Autumn is sad. Geese mate for life. A deer calling in the mountains symbolizes a heart crying for its mate. Falling snow symbolizes the passage of years. The wax tears of a candle symbolize leaving. (I think my instructor is a sentimentalist.) I knew this in the magic way I knew so many human things, but it made no sense. My paintbrush was like a little tail trapped in a bamboo twig. I wet my brush in the slick black ink-pool, and wrote:

> *The deer in the autumn mountains cries for a partner,*
> *and I'm lonely, too.*

I pushed it under the curtain for the instructor to see. "Well?"

"What did you feel when you wrote it?"

I thought. "I wanted you to tell me it was a poem."

His sigh was barely audible. "Poetry is not like dying silk: throw in the right plants and you get red. And it is not poetry just because someone else tells you it is."

"How else am I supposed to know?" I snapped.

"You are closer to understanding poetry when you splash your paints on the wall."

I threw my brush down. "This is mad! A fox learning to write from a vision."

"How else will you learn?" he said softly, and I knew then that not everyone in the fox world was blind. "Come, we will begin again."

I was impatient like this for much of my pregnancy. I could not build a den, not in this vast ringing house of wings and rooms; but I could endlessly worry at the details of it, and this I did.

I decided that it was a good day to clean out every chest and box in our wing, so my women laid out their contents and took the boxes out into the thin sunlight, to better clean them. I could not go with them; inside, I picked my way restlessly through heaped clothing, bolts of silk and hemp and cotton, and endless trinkets laid out like a rook's prizes on the glossy floor. By the time the men returned, my head had started aching.

I heard my brother's light laughter first, then Yoshifuji's, lower. I barely had time to settle behind a curtain with Josei before they burst in.

"Sister!"

"Wife! Look—"

"Is this a peasant's house," Josei said calmly, "that every man here tears in like cows escaping a thunderstorm?"

"Your mistress doesn't care," Yoshifuji retorted.

"But everything is—"

"Josei, _I_ don't care. We have a present for your mistress." Yoshifuji stepped around the screen. Brother stayed on the other side as he should, but I felt sorry for him, alone as he was.

"Something to keep you company when it gets harder to move around," he said, and held out the thing he'd been cuddling.

It was a puppy.

I froze. It was so young that it seemed only half-formed, with eyes that were bare slits. It was mostly black with white on throat and belly and tail. Blunted triangular ears curled around a blunt face; oversized paws paddled the air. I could see from the shape of its bones that it would grow up to be big, a lean rangy dog with a long face and big pointed ears: larger than a fox. The way Yoshifuji held it, I saw its pink belly, the little fur-tipped button of its penis. It was just on the edge of being able to survive without its mother.

Except for its color, it could be a fox kit. It could be the child I was about to bear.

"Get it away from me," I tried to say, but words didn't come out.

"I know having a dog in such a fine house as this is irregular, but perhaps it will be good luck for you." My husband stepped forward and laid the puppy in my lap.

"Take —" I licked my lips and tried again. "Take it away."

The puppy, tired and hungry, burrowed against my robes. I realized with horror that it was looking for a nipple. "No!" I jumped up, and the dog rolled off onto the floor with a squeak.

"Wife?" Yoshifuji's arms were around me. "What is it?"

"I —" I cast about in my mind. "I have a horror of dogs. I'm so sorry, husband, but —"

"You do not," Brother interrupted with something suspiciously like a snort. "The puppy needs a home, and you need company. What could be better?"

"We can't have a dog!"

"Why not?" Yoshifuji asked.

How could I answer this? "It will ruin everything!" I looked helplessly at Yoshifuji. "Don't you see?" And then I realized: of course he wouldn't.

My brother's voice came through the curtain. "Keep him, Sister. The dog will be fine."

"We'll ask our grandfather," I finally said.

• • •

But Grandfather, to my surprise, said the puppy could stay. "Why?" I said, when I got him to myself. "How can we keep it? It must know we're not what we seem!"

"Must he?" Grandfather barked a laugh. "Dogs always accept the myth their owners create. They're all fools, Granddaughter, especially young ones. What does the puppy know? He thinks that this is normal, foxes living like noblemen under a gatehouse."

"Could it change to a human the way we did?" I asked, seeing a sudden horrible vision.

"No," Grandfather said. "Dogs have no magic."

I do not know if this is true, or if it was just my grandfather trying to separate us from the dog —*see, we have magic and they do not. See, we are not animals.*

28. SHIKUJO'S PILLOW BOOK
The moon-viewing party:

The fifteenth day of the eighth month was perfect. The current emperor, who was the princess's nephew, had asked her to attend, which meant all her attendants attended as well. Since coming to visit, I had fallen into my old duties easily, carrying messages and amusing her whenever she seemed to need it. It was as if we had both decided to overlook the intervening years — my marriage, my son.

We are all generally elegant and well-bred women, but on this day we ran about like peasants and chattered like children. Knowing I would need them, my mother had sent to me several trunks filled with my best autumn silk robes: I selected a dark blue-gray robe with an almost invisible dyed pattern of rabbits dancing in court dress, and dark red underrobes. The rabbits made the princess laugh out loud.

We left just after the sun set. The day had been warm, but it grew cool quickly, and I was grateful for the close company of the other women in the carriage. I was not with the princess in her carriage: she did not like traveling, and sat alone with her closest woman, who was burning a special incense to prevent illness. The twilight breeze brought its sharp scent back to us.

We pulled into a graveled courtyard. Curtains were set up to protect the princess from prying eyes, and we were led to a screened-off portion of a pavilion.

We drank wine with the men of the court, waiting through the dusk. They could not see us, of course, for we were hidden behind the *kichō*-curtains, but still they exchanged poems with us.

The sky deepened from pale blue to violet. The moon appeared over the pines to the east: amber-colored and improbably large. The princess was beside me; I heard her breathe:

> *"The moon rises and I set —*
> *How can I leave when there are so many moons*
> *I have not seen?"*

Tears glittered silver on her face.

My cheeks were cold, and I realized I also was crying. This had been my life before my marriage: poems written on the insides of *sake* cups; tears at the sight of the moon.

29. THE NOTEBOOK OF KAYA NO YOSHIFUJI

My wife's brother and I are off to view the maples at the head of the valley, which are beautiful this autumn — but right now he writes something (unusual for him: he does not write much), and I find myself with time to spend. One man moves through the garden setting torches: he is preparing them, I know, so that the garden can be illuminated tonight, when my wife's brother and I return.

Beyond the walls of the garden, peasants have bundled straw from the fields, and laid it against raised logs, so that the racks look like unkempt thatch. The peasants are gone, but an animal must walk there, for suddenly finches fly up, a scattered cloud. With my eyes I follow them into the sky, up and up; my gaze settles on the branches of the white oak towering above me. The dirty gold leaves are unmoving in the calm air, and seem a real, solid wall between me and the sky, like a filigreed carving — until a sudden slight breeze breaks the wall into shifting flakes of color laid over the real and solid sky.

If the right sort of wind came up, would the day sky shiver into blue fragments dancing over an unknown something behind it, something real? The sky seems no more (or less) real than the leaves. The reality of everything seems fragile these days.

I remember my former life, with Shikujo and Tadamaro, but it is like a letter left out in the rain. The ink runs and blurs; when I try to read it later, I do not know if the words I think I see are real, or remembered, or even false memories created by my mind to fill the forgotten gaps. I remember being un-happy, but I remember being happy, as well, and neither seems more (or less) real than the other. I think perhaps reality has always been more fragile than I would want to think.

30. SHIKUJO'S PILLOW BOOK
At court:

Most of her women had retired to their rooms at the court, to intrigue with men (or sometimes other women) or sleep, according to their inclination. I rose to leave with them, but the princess gestured for me to stay. There were only a half-dozen of us left. I helped the princess out of her many robes and into quilted sleeping robes. She stretched out on a thick mat, sighed with relief and tucked her feet in.

"Better," she said. "Much better. I am too old to kneel in cold weather without feeling it."

"I understand," I said, thinking of my own aches.

"I don't think you do, my dear, not yet," she said, but without asperity. "That comes soon enough." She sighed again. "So, tell me how you have been, these last years."

I hesitated, and she understood more than I wished. She spoke kindly: "I know about your husband's doing so poorly back in the appointments at the New Year. I felt bad for you, but such things happen. And then he dragged you out into the country to sulk with him. I was relieved when you returned, and I wondered how you were."

"It was not precisely like that," I murmured, but I realized that it might as well have been.

"No, it never is precisely like that," she said. "But you wish it might be different than it *was*, don't you?

> *"Two things as hard to change as a river in spring —*
> *an untrained dog,*
> *an intractable husband."*

She saw my confusion and laughed. "I can say all this, of course: I am allowed. So tell me. There is more to this unhappiness in you than the really very unimportant lack of appointments."

"I hadn't known I seemed unhappy."

She snorted. "Of course you are."

"I am fine. Really, everything is well," I said.

"Hah," she said. "You are lying to me."

"Certainly not!" I exclaimed.

"Of course you are," she said again. "It is obvious. You are unhappy and confused about your marriage, and you have fled back to your home, to the safety of familiar places."

"No—" A tingling flood ran through my heart. I felt faint. "Please—" I began.

The princess looked up at me, concerned. "Are you all right? Forgive me, girl: I spoke the truth without thinking you might not be ready for it."

"No, it is nothing," I said, and stood quickly. "Just a headache. Please forgive me, but I must leave."

And then I fainted.

· · ·

I awoke. The room in which I lay was very small, unfamiliar. My woman, Onaga, sat in silence with me, her face scarcely visible in the dim red light thrown by a small brazier's coals. I heard soft voices a short distance away, a quick stifled laugh, then a door sliding open and closed. I remembered where I was, and how I had disgraced myself, first by trying to leave the princess without permission, and then by fainting.

Perhaps I moaned, for Onaga leaned to one side and slid a screen aside, and murmured something to whoever was outside. She bent forward and laid a gentle hand against my face, her skin cool as well-water. "My lady?" she whispered. "Are you awake?"

"Yes," I said: she knew already; there was no point in dissembling. Tears leaked from the corners of my eyes.

"We are in an attendant's room; the princess had you brought here to rest. I just sent for a healer to attend you, as she insisted."

I cried harder at this.

"Please, my lady," she said, and a tear gleamed dull red against one of her cheeks. "She has forgiven you already for fainting. Don't be too hard on yourself."

"No," I said: because only I knew what I had been feeling. I had not felt this for many years, and when I finally did it was wildly inappropriate, aimed at my princess, who asked questions and called me a liar only out of love.

What I had felt was raw anger.

The princess would not allow me to leave after this. She snapped at those who said it was unlucky (if not downright dangerous) to permit a sick woman to linger in the court. "She is not ill; she is sad and confused," I overheard her say once, "and if that were enough to get someone sent from the palace, spiders and mice would nest in all our beds."

31. KITSUNE'S DIARY

I had been pregnant for five months when we had the *iwataobi*-belt ceremony. Yoshifuji gave me a maternity belt along with certain ritualized good wishes. Just as for the wedding, there was no one really there but us foxes and Yoshifuji, but still the ritual was comforting: this is what any man acknowledging his child's mother would do.

The sash itself was very beautiful, of silvered brocade patterned with autumn grasses and clouds. The puppy discovered it and chewed it one evening when I was in sleeping robes and distracted by a game of *go*; even though the belt fixed itself in the night, I was distraught. Yoshifuji had given it to me, and I had been so careful not to see it as anything but a silk belt.

I did not like the puppy, but at least it was real and cared for me. I could not bring myself to reject this.

32. SHIKUJO'S PILLOW BOOK
Emotions:

Tranquillity is best, of course. One strives in one's life for calm acceptance of circumstance, whether good or bad.

Happiness is the pleasantest of emotions; because of this, it is also the most dangerous. Having once felt happiness, one will do anything to maintain it, and losing it, one will grieve.

Regret and sadness. One grieves for the dead, but also for friends forgotten, and things lost or mislaid. I lost a writing desk long ago; even now, I remember it on occasion and feel a pang of regret.

Anger is never acceptable. It is a sort of madness pulled from one's soul by the cruelty or carelessness of others. No: this is not true. I have talked with the princess about anger, and I have learned this, that anger comes from a sense of powerlessness. If I cared less, cruelty or carelessness would not matter to me.

But there is no power in this world. We are dandelion chaff

in the autumn wind—blown wherever the wind chooses, until we fall at last on bare rock, or in the salty sea. Does this mean everyone is angry all the time?

Does this mean I am angry? I hate this and fight it with other, simpler thoughts: the delicate smell of spider lilies; the brilliant red of *sanshō*-ash berries; the dense flavor of yams. Tranquillity is easy enough, if one just does not think too much.

33. KITSUNE'S DIARY

I had trouble falling asleep when I was pregnant. I could not get comfortable. My belly was too big to sleep in any position except on my side, and whenever I wanted to shift, I had to fully awaken to carefully rearrange my bulk to the new position. My back ached always; after a time, my breasts hurt as well. My husband was gone (traveling with Brother, who knew where?); my mother changed into her fox shape and slipped out every dusk; my grandfather was nowhere to be found, presumably hunting. I watched my women, who stayed up to keep me company and were sewing robes for the colder weather, but my mind kept fretting about poetry.

When we were foxes, we sometimes dragged home bones as long as our bodies from the abandoned kills of larger animals, knowing there was unclaimed marrow inside. We would chew on them whenever we were idle, hoping that this would be the time that we finally broke the bone and got to its contents. This was like that, but the bone did not crack. I fell asleep still worrying at the poem and the thought of poetry.

I wandered in a forest in my sleep. There were *torii*-arches, as there had been at the shrine of Inari, but these were as tall as the highest cedars, and they flickered like lightning, cold indigo flashes. I stepped beneath the first and heard it crying; when I looked up, I saw great dark blurs against the light. One dropped on a silken cord as I passed beneath its arch. It was a spider as large as a fox. Its eyes were faceted gold; characters flickered across their surfaces, poems I could not read. It settled on my shoulder. A voice spoke. I suppose it must have been the spider saying, "Home is the web between us." I felt nothing when it bit deep into my shoulder and dissolved the flesh there. I ran forward, under the last of the arches.

The moon-foxes were there, which was no surprise. Two bowls stood before them, as they had before the statue of Inari in the shrine so long ago: one held clear water and the other cooked rice.

"So, little fox woman," one (or both) said, in a voice (or voices) like silver bells echoing to a far-off thunderclap. "Which are you? Fox or woman?"

I wanted to say, as I had said to my grandfather, "Woman," but I could not. "Both," I whispered.

Their laughter chimed at me. "Say rather: neither. You will be closer to the truth. You are nothing and no one. You don't even have a name."

"My grandfather is Miyoshi no Kiyoyuki. I am his grand-daughter."

"Is that a name?" one (or both) jeered. "You borrow finery he has himself stolen."

"Please," I said. "I must do this."

"We have a poem for you," the other fox (or both) said. He (or she, or they) bowed and touched noses to the bowls, and the bowls changed to the corpse of a fox curled around a dead kit. I screamed and dropped the moon, which I did not realize I had been holding in my hand. It fell on the dead fox and flared up, a cold white blast that left me queasy.

"Can you reply?" the voice or voices said. "Of course not."

Their laughter was like the wind blowing dust past silver bells: a high hissing noise.

I woke crying and calling for my women. My experience with bad dreams was minimal: as a fox I had dreamt sometimes of running, not sure whether I was predator or prey. This was far more horrible than that.

"My lady?" Josei ducked beneath the blinds that shielded my sleeping area. "Are you all right?"

My face was cold with tears. Josei wrapped my robes close about me, snapping orders at the other women: bring a lantern, hot *sake*, new incense. I curled into a crook of her arm. I could not stop shaking. I told her: "I don't know."

34. SHIKUJO'S PILLOW BOOK
Conversations with the princess:

ike a spider or mouse, I nested for a short time in the small room the princess had assigned to me when first I fainted. The other attendants were very kind, I suppose because the princess had ordered them to be courteous, but also I hoped because some had been friends so many years ago. I received affectionate letters from the princess begging in the most elegant fashion for my company. I always wrote back, thanking her for her kindness in allowing me to stay comparatively close to her shining presence, but feeling too weak to attend. How could I see her? I had been crying and my eyes were unattractively swollen; my face was blotched from tears.

Onaga was always with me, and in the end it was she who goaded me to action. "Do you want them saying you are half-wild from living in the country?" she cawed at me; this moved me as no other plea had, and pride at last forced me upright and into *hagi*-colored robes: purple-red lined with green.

Silence fell when I stepped into the princess's room for the first time; she herself broke it. "My dear! You look lovely, so refined." I assumed this meant "haggard," but I was grateful.

Over the days that followed, she was all solicitous attention. She was old and so did not sleep much, and when nightmares or simple sleeplessness kept me from my bed, I often found her curled up beside a brazier, her closest attendant asleep beside her. Her cough was nearly constant now, a frequent low barking that did not stop even when she swallowed syrup of *kinkan*-oranges.

We talked then.

"I'm dying, you know," she said. "I haven't told my nephew the emperor yet."

I said nothing, but the cough had indicated she was not well, and I had been staying with her and her women for too many days not to have heard this already.

"The diviners came," she said, "and some physicians, and a priest and some North Island barbarian famous as a healer. Some tell me that I will be well soon, but I know this is just wishful thinking—men who know nothing trying to cheer a member of the royal family. Hah."

"Perhaps they are right?"

"No." She pushed a coal in the brazier with the poker in her hand. It broke in half and flared; for a moment I saw her face, wrinkles fine as mulberry threads in paper. "There was a ten-thousand-lights service. My nephew had a Healing Buddha erected. Everything indicates the same problem, something eating at my lungs. The diviner said it was a demon; everyone else thinks it is a sickness. Me, I don't care. I'm glad you were here in the capital, child: I'm leaving for the nunnery at Kasugano very soon. New robes, hey? Soon I'll be in gray and yellow: better for a woman my age than the gaudy things you children love. A nun, and then death will be easy. I look forward to seeing whether there is a Pure Land, after all."

"Please don't leave us," I said.

"I'm leaving whether you want me to or not," she said dryly. "It is just a matter of whether I do so in stages, with a pause at the nunnery; or die directly from here. And that would be bad luck for the emperor. No, I look forward to a little peace before my death." She looked up at me sharply from the corner of her eye. "So what do you say now, my girl?"

"Um." What could I say? "My lady, there are a hundred poems in the *Manyōshū* and elsewhere, all dealing with death. And at this instant, I am too numb to think of a single one."

She snapped out a laugh, which turned to a thick hacking cough. She spat into a soft paper slip she pulled from her sleeve. She dropped it in the fire, which flared up for a moment; her woman shifted and then settled back into sleep. "Believe me, I am grateful. My women have been boring me to tears with all of them." She glanced at me again. "Are you surprised at my attitude toward the poems? I leave for the nunnery as soon as I can get permission from my nephew; I think I can afford to be honest with myself about things now."

"My lady, what are you telling me? Don't you care for these things? —for poems and propriety and courtesy?"

"Of course I do, girl. They're important, just not as important as living well."

"But they *are* living well!"

"No." She coughed for a moment, then: "They're living beautifully. There is a difference."

And another conversation with her, a day later. We watched two of the women playing at archery with short bows. The princess was pale and tired-looking, and retired to rest, asking me to attend her. I led her to her sleeping dais, and took her outer robe. She did not sleep immediately, so I sat beside her, and her attendant carefully did not listen to us.

"Your son. Tell me about him."

I smiled. "He is eight."

"That is no answer. What is he like? Hasty, polite, graceful, funny?"

"All those things, from time to time," I said. "And handsome."

"He must have that from your side of the family." She coughed. "So, tell me all about him."

"I don't know what you wish to hear. He is still very young. He is never clean, and loves to run about outside."

"Mine was like that, too —*and* my daughter, until I straightened her out. They're all like wild animals, aren't they?"

"No," I said, through lips suddenly numb. "Not my son. My son is perfectly human."

"No one is saying he isn't, my girl." She looked at me for a time. "You have nothing to worry about: he will settle down eventually."

That is not what frightens me, I thought, but I did not say it.

"I have wanted to talk with you for a time now," she said. "I have certain rights to do so. First, I am royal, and so free to say what I wish; second, I am old, and thus doubly freed from propriety; third, I have been married for many years, and am experienced with men and their ways. Fourth, you were my handmaiden, and I have no secrets from you, nor you from me. Last, I am dying, and I have a wish to see the people I care about at peace. And you are certainly not at peace."

"I —"

"I don't want to hear it. You still can't face unpleasant truths, can you?"

I remembered the anger, the flare that had filled me as water fills a drowning man's lungs: a stifling pressure. "I face what I must."

She snorted, which turned into a cough. She rested for a moment and began again. "I have known you for a long time, girl. You face only what you cannot avoid."

"Would I be a better person if I faced these things?" I said bitterly. "If I saw life as an aggravation and a disappointment?"

"Is that what you think life truly is, that you hide from it?"

I pushed at a camphor-wood box beside the brazier. "Is it not?"

"Of course not!" she snapped. "Well, no: it is, but it is all the good things as well, and you'll never know how sweet they are if you do not see the others. Be angry, be sad, be glad, Shikujo — at least you will be alive. It is gone soon enough."

Incredibly, I found myself telling her everything about my husband and the coldness between us, the sex that had tied us together with threads as thin and ephemeral as spider silk, his restlessness and obsession with foxes; my loneliness. After a time, I thought from the absence of coughing that she had fallen asleep, and so I told her about the dream of a fox man, and how he had returned to my dreams this past summer.

There was silence when I was done. I sat beside her, emptied by all the words, feeling light, like new-dyed silk blowing in the drying wind.

"So. You are not so perfect, after all." The princess's voice startled a cry out of me.

"I am hardly perfect," I said with a laugh.

"And yet, you seem so to many people. Does he know this, your husband?"

"How could he not?" I asked; but in retrospect, I wonder. Would it have been better for our marriage if I had been more honest, less polite? I do not know; I only know that I would perhaps have felt better.

We also talked of divorce. It would be simple enough. Divorce is never technically that hard; with my husband behaving so strangely, sometimes it doesn't even seem that difficult to me. It might be better for my son, since my father's influence (and even my own) is likely to be of greater use for my son's career than is my husband's.

But divorce would leave certain words unspoken, certain things undone. I cannot do it, not now.

Neither can I return to that house and my husband. But I fret—perhaps I should have stayed after all?—knowing that I couldn't have, that his madness would have destroyed us all. If you had just talked to me, my lord . . . or if I had talked to you. When did it get so hard to speak to you?

In the end, I was forced back to my father's house, after all. My monthly courses began, and I could no longer stay in the royal palaces until I was again clean.

35. KITSUNE'S DIARY

I sent a message to my grandfather, asking him to visit me. Proprieties indicated I could not demand his presence, or even tell him how much I needed him; so I waited impatiently, hoping he would read the characters that were not written, and come quickly.

Mother was with me—unusual these days; she preferred fox-shape and the forest behind Yoshifuji's house, and we did not see her often. She seemed to live less and less comfortably in

the world we had made. Now she was woman-shaped, but her
robes were filthy and covered with cobwebs. She had nothing
to say. She held a gnawed bone in her hands as if it were a
flute; I tried not to notice that no music came out when she bent
her head to it.

"Granddaughter? I can only stay a moment. Why did you
summon me?" Grandfather settled near us.

"I had a dream, a terrible dream." I found myself shaking
again, just at the memory. "About Inari's moon-foxes. They said
terrible things to me. Why did they come to me?"

"What would I know about dreams?" he said.

"Well, was it a message? Did it mean something?"

"They all mean something." It was my mother's voice. Grandfather made an annoyed noise as she put down the bone (or
flute) and turned her face to me, eyes focused on my face.
"Sometimes they mean that the rabbit you ate had strange plants
in its belly. Sometimes they mean you are pregnant, and the kits
you carry are telling one another stories. Sometimes they mean
that you are afraid of something, and that whatever-it-is comes
to hunt you in the night, when you can't run away. Sometimes
it means more."

"But what?" I said. "I have to know."

"Ask the diviner in the woods," Mother said. "He knows such
things."

"What diviner?" I said.

"A dream interpreter," she said. "It's what humans do, when
their dreams disturb them, visit him. He's mad, but he would
have to be, wouldn't he? Dreams are an uncomfortable study."
She abruptly shifted to fox-form.

"Mother!" I exclaimed. "Grandfather, she will ruin everything
if she doesn't stop this."

Mother shifted back as suddenly; this time her robes were
clean, but embroidered with cobwebs, and dyed in patterns like
the staining of mud.

"She can't do that," I said shakily to my grandfather. "It's too
dangerous."

"You've tried to stop her, yes?"

"Yes."

"And she doesn't stop. So."

"So what?" I asked.

"So we will have to accommodate her and trust to Yoshifuji's blindness."

"Is she right," I asked, "about the dream interpreter?"

"Probably. Sometimes she understands more about humanness than any of us."

"Hah," I said.

Grandfather snorted. "Madness is a uniquely human state, little one."

Mother said nothing, preoccupied with licking her hands.

36. SHIKUJO'S PILLOW BOOK
The illest of omens:

*T*he *illest of omens.* Can it be averted?

Life was very difficult. I had been in the capital for over a month, and I had been back at my parents' house for almost a week. I couldn't help wondering about my home, my husband. The weather was hot again with the false summer that sometimes comes in autumn, and the air was so thick with some overbred autumn bloom's perfume that my head throbbed with it. Something moved under my skin: an itching, a restlessness. After my conversations with the princess, I felt wild and irrational, ready to perform any insane act.

So I asked Onaga to arrange for me to walk in the garden. She seemed shocked (indeed, I shocked myself a little, even thinking of this: how could I act so?), but agreed when I pointed out that I would in all likelihood walk in the garden whether she arranged for proper privacy or not. (Would I have done this? What has gotten into one these days? The city is so loud; perhaps one is not sleeping well.)

It would have been so much simpler back at the estate, where the only man of any importance was my husband. Provided he didn't need the garden for something or other, it would have been a small thing to leave orders that no other men were to enter the gardens. Why did I never do this, then, walk along the paths and touch the trunk of the thousand-year oak I had seen myriad times from my wing?

No: I was content to watch from the lattices, then when I could have walked every day.

Mercifully, my father was gone to court, and my brothers were all away, at court or on pilgrimage or visiting one or another wife. In a short time, Onaga returned to me: servants had cleared the garden. It was mine.

Compared to the garden in the country, it was small, hardly more than an acre or two. All cunningly arranged, like the little boxes that nest into a picnic box: no space was wasted. I looked at the pond my son had told me about and found that these fish my father so prized were nothing but oversized, distorted carp. With a shiver, I started hunting for the great porcelain basin that contained my father's pride. Horrible as the regular fish were, what must this monster look like?

Onaga disapproved: why brood on unnecessary unpleasantness such as misshapen fish? But I insisted. Still complaining, she led me at last through a little gate of varied sizes of bamboo to a small courtyard half-roofed with the overhanging branches of pines hung with ivy, floored with huge smooth stones almost hidden in two sorts of moss. The fallen needles had been swept from the moss. The rich textured green made brighter the blue and white of the basin, and the bright gold of the cast-aside bamboo covering and the red of blood.

The fish had been as horrible as I had thought. I could see this from what remained. Now it was worse: half torn away altogether, shreds of brightest orange skin and blood as red as my own. Should I have screamed? I did not.

It was foxes, of course: foxes after all. Onaga tried to tell me that it was one of the cook's thousand cats, but I saw the tuft of fur beside it. Perhaps there are cats that color; I suppose there must be. But it couldn't be: for it to be other than a fox would make no sense. I wasn't free of them.

The illest of omens. I have sent for a priest.

37. KITSUNE'S DIARY

Traveling to the dream-diviner, I felt the shock when we left the fox-magic world for the real world, like stepping through a waterfall of glittering dust. I had been afraid of the shift, but to my relief I was still a woman on the other side. There were a half-dozen women, and a dozen carriers of our litters, and another half-dozen men accompanying us, for our safety. Josei knew where the interpreter was to be found and gave the instructions to the leader.

I'd never been in a litter before. Awkwardly I hunched myself and my huge belly into a small box walled with woven reeds and lined with pale brocaded silk. There was a single window, a panel of black wood carved into cutouts of leaves clustered on water, and the water's ripples. I didn't see much through the window, and braced myself instead against the litter's frame, trying not to be bruised. I think we must have moved at a rate that would have been a slow walk for a fox.

At last we stopped. The men withdrew to a discreet distance and my women made things decent for me.

I stepped out into a little weed-filled clearing, in front of a dirt-floored hut with shedding thatch.

"Hah. You again," said a voice from within the sagging doorway.

"Who—" I stooped to look into the darkness and found myself face-to-face with the man who had refused me his skull so long ago. He cackled.

"Didn't expect to find me still alive, did you?"

"I wasn't looking for you. I was trying to find a diviner."

"Me." He slapped his chest and coughed. "Come in, don't make me squint at you, out in the light."

"Not inside." Josei's voice behind me. I turned to look at her: did she think he would attack me? "One minute, my lady." Josei gestured, and a servant moved forward to lay out a cloth for me to kneel upon at the doorway.

"*You're* the diviner?" I asked as I sank down.

"Of course. Do you think I'd still be alive if I weren't so good at telling what my dreams mean? Now they tell me it's my lungs. Hah. What do dreams know? So, fox, I see you succeeded at what you wanted."

I couldn't help preening a bit. "As you see."

"I bet it was easier for you to get up here the first time, hey. Was it worth it, fox maid?"

"No maid," I said proudly. "I am married and expecting."

"So why are you here? Not for my skull," he said sharply. "It's still not yours, you know."

"I don't need that," I said. "I had a dream, and they tell me that you can read these things."

"Who told you that, hmm? Well, I can. If I wish. If you leave me something."

I nodded. One of the women stepped forward and laid a pretty lacquered picnic box in front of him.

"A dead rabbit?" he said dubiously. "Well, I suppose. Now. What does a fox who is now a maid—no, a *woman*—dream?"

I told him, faltering over my words. When I finished there was a pause before he said, "And that was all? No more?"

"Was there supposed to be more?" I snapped. "You're the diviner; you tell me."

"A spider settles and bites you; dream-foxes speak in poems that are not made of words but of images." He laughed.

I frowned. "Don't play with me! I just want to know what it means."

He sighed and lay down, pulling a grimy sleeping-robe over his knees. "You would not be ready to hear it, even if I had the energy to tell you."

"Tell me," I snarled at him. It was hard to be respectful with this foolish old man.

"Fine," he said, and rolled onto his back, eyes closed. "The spider may mean you have trapped yourself in a bigger web than you expected. Or it may mean a lover will come calling, but who the lover is and who he calls on?—Doesn't say. Doesn't say why the spider bites you, either. Or it may mean something altogether different. The foxes? Hmm. May mean your infant will die young. May mean you really are human, for a human god, even a rice-god, to send his attendants to call on you. Why should the foxes care otherwise? May mean you are a fox, for the same reason. May mean you should give Inari gifts, or maybe not." He opened one eye and peered at me. "How am I doing?"

I wanted to cry from frustration. "You have said nothing!"

"Well, then. Maybe I should ask you. What question do you really want answered, hey?"

He watched me through slit eyes when I said, "The kit. Will he be human or fox? And I—which am I? The foxes said neither. Is this true? Does the dream tell you *that?*"

"Your child will be fine, as will you. One way or another. Despite everything. Now leave me alone."

"You don't know that! You're making it up."

"Clever fox woman, figuring us out like that. We all make up all of it—life, dreams, memories, hopes. Be careful getting home." And with that he was asleep, as easily and irrevocably as the sun setting.

I grew heavier, and my body remained only reluctantly my own. It grew harder to sleep a night through. My feet and back and breasts ached continually. I felt the child inside shift and kick restlessly. With a sort of grim humor I thought my child was almost certainly human, for no fox had suffered like this before bearing her young.

I thought much about the old man's words, but they never made sense to me, not then. It is only *now*, this snowy moment as I wait for the sound of clogs, that I think I might understand.

38. THE NOTEBOOK OF KAYA NO YOSHIFUJI

I have not read the *monogatari*-tales the women of the capital seem to love—they are low literature, not worth the attention of men (they say). But I have listened to women read them aloud from time to time—*Flowering Fortunes, The Princess Who Sought a Corpse, The Tale of Genji,* a peculiar story called *The Bat's Tale*—and I have noticed several things about them.

One is that they are all idealized versions of what might once have been reality. It is a perfect world the tales describe: every noblewoman is uniquely beautiful; every poem is a wonder of clarity and wit; every celebration and ritual is worthy of the courts of the gods.

This always seemed unlikely to me. Back in the capital, we all bemoaned the decadent days we live in, so unlike the golden past; but I could not then imagine that things had really changed so much. Many of our houses are beautiful, but often they are shoddily made and poorly tended. The buildings of the palace itself are always dirty and usually leaky, best seen in the dim light of lanterns. Our robes are hard to clean and thus often dirty; all our fine perfumes only imperfectly conceal the smell of unwashed skin when tabus forbid bathing. There are beautiful women, of course—faces like moons, floor-long hair thick as a horse's tail, perfect pale skin like the petals of *kobushi* flowers—but there are far more women who are not. Their skin is scarred by smallpox; their hair is thin, or extended with hanks bought from peasant women.

But then I came to my pretty wife's house. Here it truly is just like the jeweled little world of the women's tales. It is perfect, the stuff of fantasy and dreams.

I had no idea such things could be real.

39. SHIKUJO'S PILLOW BOOK
The message from Hida province:

*T*he message from Hida province came the day after one found the fish. One had expected such a message since then; but despite this, it was no easier to see the note. A twist of plain white paper, hastily marked:

> *In great haste, this individual has traveled from the estate in the Tani valley and now takes the liberty of writing, begging an audience of the wife of Kaya no Yoshifuji.*

Onaga admits him immediately. Quick footsteps; robes brushing against the floor as he kneels on the opposite side of a screen.

"Well" (Onaga says; one cannot, of course, speak to a servant). "My lady is indisposed and doesn't wish to be disturbed. I am an unimportant servant of hers, but you may tell me your message and it will be passed on." This is all a convention: he knows I listen, as surely as I know he knows.

"I am sorry for her indisposition," he begins.

"Tell us now," Onaga interrupts. "What has happened, back at the estate?"

A half-seen shape through the fine silk curtain; his hands wave helplessly. "I am Tabibito. My lord Kaya no Yoshifuji's major domo, Hito, sent me to you. I left the estate fifteen days ago, traveled at a terrible rate, ignoring directional tabus to get here as quickly as I might. It is of no matter what luck I might bring upon myself; the news I bring is more important. When I left, my lord, your lady's husband, had been missing for ten days."

"Hah," Onaga says, and smiles grimly at me. "It is as well I didn't disturb her. Why would you want to waste my lady's time with this? He has gone on another of his pilgrimages."

"No." The man sounds most certain. "I am so sorry, but Hito is his most trusted servant, and he said nothing to Hito."

"Then," she says with a certain satisfaction, "he has found some low peasant mistress in the neighborhood."

"My lord is not so lost to propriety and what is due to his rank as to stay with such a woman for more than a night. They would have nothing to talk of—it is unthinkable."

"Maybe they didn't talk."

"He has taken nothing, not so much as a comb."

"Might he have joined a monastery?" Onaga asks.

"He would not forget to inform us, if he left this worldly plane for a life with the blessed. Truly, we are all concerned for him. Perhaps something has happened—"

"Or perhaps he is back now, and feeling sorry for himself about the loss of some baseborn lover."

"Or perhaps not," he says with a certain sharpness. "Perhaps he is dead, eaten by wolves."

"What do you expect my lady's presence to do about that— about any of these possibilities?"

"Perhaps he was a little saddened by her leaving so precipitantly. Perhaps her return might tempt him back if he is nearby, in retreat at some local temple. If he is not alive, Kaya no Tadamaro is his son. He will need to return, to set into movement such rites as would allow my lord's soul to rest comfortably before rebirth."

"I will inform her," Onaga says. The servant leaves in silence.

I cannot move, cannot speak. My mind whirls with dread and fear and anger. Onaga steps away, returns immediately with a tiny pot of something warm and sharp-smelling. She pours a little cup and hands it to me, and the spell breaks.

"My lady?" Onaga kneels beside me. The cup contains a medicine of some sort, ginseng and juniper.

"How could he vanish?" I whisper. Meaning: *how could he be so inconsiderate?* He might be dead or injured or lost in the mountains, and there will be no further discussion between us. I will never know what really happened in his heart or my own. And I am enraged that he might not be dead or lost, that he might have frightened us all, frightened *me*, like this out of self-indulgent pity.

Onaga says nothing, not even when my tears start.

The dead fish was as evil an omen as one had feared.

We will go, of course.

40. KITSUNE'S DIARY

My delivery of my child was easy, comparatively painless as these things go, or so I am informed. My water broke, and I was moved to a raised bed wrapped in white. I was hidden behind a maze of curtains and screens and hangings, but I could hear men in my rooms, hustling about with still more curtains. Priests and monks and diviners — every holy man the fox magic could contrive — chanted and sang whatever spells or prayers or sutras they thought were important. Men played *sugoroku*-backgammon for luck; they shouted their bets at one another. I bit my lip during the contractions that ripped at my belly, unwilling to cry out in the presence of so many. A fox bears her young alone in a close-walled dark den, her only noises panting and the occasional scrabbling of her feet in the dust. Surrounded by so many, my body struggled for a time to hold the child in before relaxing at last.

Mother had vanished again, back into her fox-form and the real world. Josei held me, urged me to breathe and push, her voice scarcely audible over the din the men made.

After the child was born, Josei allowed my husband behind the curtains. The stained cloths I had littered in were gone now, replaced with gleaming white silk and hemp.

"My son, let me see him!" he said. "You marvelous wife of mine!"

I gestured for the nurse to show my husband the child. He

peeled away the tight cloths. "What a child! Wife, you are extraordinary. A beautiful healthy boy."

I said nothing, seeing in my exhaustion the shadow of a man in filthy, ragged robes crouching in the dark to kiss a fox kit on its closed eyes.

41. SHIKUJO'S PILLOW BOOK
Some farewells:

Some farewells are comparatively simple, as when one knows that the parting is for the best. Even then it can be painful.

Other farewells are forced on one. A letter comes with bad news, and one leaves with scarcely enough time to pack a few trunks. One's good-byes to one's father and mother are little more than exchanges of bows and quick words. One's parents offer to keep Tadamaro, but I cannot bear to let him stay behind. There are threats everywhere, even in the city; at least if he is with me, I will be able to keep an eye on him.

The hardest farewell has been the letters between the princess and oneself. I was not able to return to her before the message from the country; now I must leave without even the briefest visit. I wrote her a letter, broad strokes of black ink on white paper flecked with crimson, tied with a hank of dead grass, pale gold. It explained things to her, and ended:

> *The nights grow longer than the days —*
> *Already they seem endless,*
> *knowing I will not see you before leaving.*

She wrote back, saffron-colored paper tied with a dried aster:

> *Where I go now the nights are endless*
> *in keeping with my sadness.*
> *We will not meet again in life.*

*We will meet again in the Radiant Land. Be brave and be
alive.*

Her health is failing, she adds. She leaves on a litter for the
nunnery as soon as a certain directional tabu permits her to
travel to the south. I thought of her long hair, to be cut so short,
and I started to cry—as if the hair were the woman, as if it were
her life. I prayed to the eight hundred myriad gods and all the
Buddhas—everyone I could think of.

There have been a lot of farewells lately for me. I think perhaps there should be fewer.

Onaga gives me *sake* and asks how I feel. She is as insistent
as she can be, given our respective positions. I say nothing because I do not know *what* I feel. But at least I try to examine
my emotions, because I know it would please the princess for
me to try; if I find only a sort of numb waiting, then that is
what there is to be found.

I leave in the morning.

42. KITSUNE'S DIARY

*L*ike everything else humans involve themselves with, the time
after childbearing was unnecessarily complicated by ceremony. For a fox it is easy enough: the mother sleeps and nurses,
cleans her cubs, eats the food her mate brings her. For us it was
not so simple: Yoshifuji had no idea how to hunt, and it was my
brother who brought rabbits and grouse to me.

As humans, it was much more complex than this. We wore
white for the first seven days, not a good choice around a new-
born. The whole undertaking was wrapped round in rituals and
ceremonies at a time when all I wanted was the chance to sleep
and nurse. The first nursing; the severing of the umbilical cord;
the first bathing (and many subsequent bathings, two a day with
associated rituals); the readings; the gifts of swaddling clothes;

the attendants' gifts and the priests' gifts and the family gifts —
all of these were done in an approved manner.

We placed certain lucky objects on the infant's head: a pine
branch, a wild orange, a gold coin, a sliver of wood carved to
look like rhinoceros hide, a piece of snake's-beard greenery. Pre-
dictably enough, the child cried, but we could not tell whether
this was auspicious or not.

There were banquets every other day for half a month, but I
was happily excluded from them. Nobles and powerful men
from the capital came to the parties. They toasted Yoshifuji's
son (whom we called Shōnen, "boy," having no facility for nam-
ing) and played still more *sugoroku*-backgammon, and recited
poetry and drank.

The largest banquet was the night that Yoshifuji presented
the sword to his son. I had not known there could be so many
people in the fox world, but my husband was important. The
nobles were without exception handsome and articulate (dozing,
I heard their voices through the screens; I watched as they came
and went), but I never saw or heard them before or after that
time.

I didn't pay as much attention as I might have, since I was
tired and preoccupied with the child, and I left it to my husband
and my women to do things properly.

On the fiftieth day, Yoshifuji came and fed Shōnen from an
assortment of rice cakes, presumably for good luck. Later at the
banquet, Yoshifuji bragged about his baby's new teeth, the first
two already showing.

The whole time had the feeling of a dream.

43. SHIKUJO'S PILLOW BOOK
The trip back:

The trip back had many of the features of a nightmare. The
weather had turned cold, so I and my women were constantly chilled, even crowded as we were into the carriage. We
traveled in such haste that we often drove into the evening,

stopping only when the full darkness of the early nights prevented our going farther.

A handful of days into the trip, while traveling a road so soaked that the dirt had turned to a mud sticky as drying liana syrup, the axle on my cart broke. Two of my women tumbled out into the road, fortunately sustaining no damage worse than the utter ruination of their robes and a certain amount of hysterical weeping. The male attendants helped us out and across the mud, then sent back to the nearest village to see if a smith or wagon builder might be there to help us. As a steady rain began to fall, we took refuge in a clearly abandoned hut, which most regrettably turned out to have no roof, nor much of a floor. Still, I was grateful for the rain: it meant that it was too early for snow, which would have been much worse.

It took three days to have the axle replaced. By this point Tadamaro and his nurse had both caught *kaze*-colds (will there ever be relief from colds?), and we had to find a local healer who would make ginger syrup for them and apply *moxas*. They recovered slowly, and we were obliged to let them rest for several days, though they did not sleep well, because of the sounds of the crow-scarers clattering all day. The first day it would be possible to travel was tabu for movement in the direction we were going; I sopped my conscience and the gods by having the carriage pushed a short distance north into some sort of pasturage, justifying the subsequent travel in the forbidden direction as a mere continuation of a long curve that had at least started acceptably.

In all, it took three weeks to return.

44. KITSUNE'S DIARY

Time is not a constant thing. The shift from season to season — winter to spring to summer and autumn—is constant, but time itself—the sequence of event and thought and dream—is at best inconsistent. I recall certain days with absolute clarity, as if I carried them about with me carved like a sutra in characters of gold on tablets of lapis lazuli, ready to be consulted whenever necessary. Other times — whole years — are vague and jumbled together, as if I overheard a conversation in which someone only mentioned them in passing. And yet I know I passed through those times, one day after the other, like stepping on the stones of a garden path.

I say the shifting of seasons is constant, but this was not true in our fox world. It was always autumn here. I did not worry so much about Yoshifuji noticing this as I used to.

When Shōnen was three, we had the trouser ceremony. Grandfather presented the boy with his first set of *hakama*-trousers and we refitted his room in miniature furnishings that evening, an acknowledgment of sorts that he was growing closer to adulthood.

The boy was growing up healthy, but he was wild and kept doing things that ought to have shocked Yoshifuji. My husband took him to watch dragonflies one day, and Shōnen instead grew interested in the insects that were so thick in the grasses, and caught and ate blue beetles, crunching them between his teeth and laughing at the noise they made and the tickling of their struggling legs. Yoshifuji told me of this that evening. "Didn't you stop him?" I asked, dry-mouthed.

"No," he said, and looked puzzled. "Why would I? It's his nature, after all."

This frightened me. My husband noticed some things, missed others. I did not know how he truly saw the world we had made. There were times I felt he saw it more clearly than any of us, but for some reason did not care.

45. THE NOTEBOOK OF KAYA NO YOSHIFUJI

This I must write about.

My wife's brother and I have taken the dog and gone out to practice our archery, to the large clearing where he killed the badger a few days ago (or is it months? years? No, it cannot be that: it is still autumn). The weather has been beautifully warm, though there was a windstorm last night that knocked over a few potted plants in the garden; even now the wind leaves creamy pearls of foam at the lake's edges.

Our men have taken targets (hulking straw men; my brother-in-law seems to find this very funny, the prospect of shooting arrows at false men) and set them up, and then left us alone with our targets and a vast array of picnic supplies.

We do precisely this: practice shooting at straw for a time. Now half-grown, the dog chases from target to bowman and back, barking hysterically until at last he grows too tired to stand and flops in the shade panting. When we grow bored with that, we start shooting at targets picked out for each other: willow branches, tree boles, a wood pigeon ill advised enough to flutter through the clearing. I hit more often than I miss, but my brother-in-law's aim is flawless.

When we run out of arrows, we stop and pull open the little boxes that nest together, filled with our meal. Everything tastes good (as it always does). The *sake* is excellent and we drink much too much of it.

I point at a half-concealed path. "Have you ever been up there?" I ask.

He looks carefully. "I don't believe so. It's real, isn't it?"

I have no idea what he means by this. "There's a place up there, where the mountain has a cleft and water comes up to make a little pool, steaming hot. Sulfur."

"That explains the smell," he says, and looks wise; but I can't smell anything. We are a long walk from the spring and the wind blows away from it. How can he smell anything?

"There's a shrine up there. Very old, maybe older than all my ancestors, or even the first emperor. I used to walk up there and leave rice and wine, but I haven't done that since I was a boy."

"Was there a priest?"

"No, no one at all. It looked completely deserted, and I never saw a sign that anyone else ever left anything. Only me."

"Why would one build a shrine in the middle of nowhere?" he says idly. He is trying to balance the *sake* jug upside down on a rock, which is proving difficult. I hadn't noticed before this that his sandals are laced in brilliant sky-blue, an outrageous but charming color.

"Well, it's not the middle of nowhere," I say, frowning.

"It is for anyone but deer and *tanuki*-badgers and wolves, isn't it? No one lives up there, no one visits. What's the purpose then?"

This is another one of those questions his family asks that leave me struggling. How can he be ignorant of this? "The mountain lives there. And it may please the mountain to have a shrine like this. If it *is* for the mountain, and not for the springs or a tree or something else up there."

"You don't even know what's being worshipped?" he says incredulously. "And you still left rice?"

I roll onto my back. "Well, I couldn't read the characters on the shrine: they were filled with moss. Whatever it was, it was holy enough that someone thought it was a good idea to build a shrine to it. That makes it worthy of respect." The clouds overhead are purple in their heart, but soaked in brilliant sunlight from the west. There will be a storm soon. I find myself idly looking forward to this: autumn thunderstorms have always been a delight.

He starts laughing, and somehow I feel defensive. "How can you not know this?" I say. "You and your sister! I mean no offense to your grandfather, but sometimes I feel as though you were raised by demons, or wolves."

He frowns. "It is like poetry and so many other things. I feel sometimes as though there must be a point to it. And I hear what you tell my sister, when she asks about poetry or Buddha, or anything else. Nothing you say about any of it ever makes sense."

"I suppose it doesn't, but then, that is what religion and poetry and painting are about, aren't they? Making sense out of nonsense? — And life, too, actually."

I roll to my side to find my wife's brother watching me curiously. For a moment he looks exactly like his sister; they are a good-looking family, the clan of Miyoshi. The ones I've seen, anyway — I still have never viewed my mother-in-law, of course.

He jumps to his feet; the dog follows suit. "Come, let's go to the springs. Perhaps we'll see something to shoot on the way there."

This seems unlikely to me; the woods around us are dense, and the muddy path shows no footprints but our own, and those of a single animal whose tracks I do not recognize. The sky is darkening quickly as the heavy clouds move over us. "Perhaps we should — " I begin, but he has loped on ahead, black-fletched arrow and bow in hand, the dog at his heels. He can hear nothing.

"Was anyone ever this hasty?" I ask the woods aloud, but I already know the answer: *I* am. It is my nature as much as his to think only of here and now. *Hah*, a voice says in my mind; I recognize it as my wife's grandfather, who occasionally speaks to her in this tone. *What do you know of here and now? You're too lost in dreams and memories.*

My brother-in-law is out of sight now, and I can't even hear him as he runs, though occasional barks drift back. I have never known anyone so fast and agile. I lace my trousers close to my leg to get their bulk out of the way as I run, and trot after him. I am panting within minutes, far sooner than I expect. Well: I must be growing older.

The woods are afire with reds. The windstorm knocked many of the leaves down, but a stand of diseased pines have turned to rust and flame on a ridge; the *kuzu*-vine threaded through the nearer trees has flared to crimson.

We are almost to the spring and the shrine. The path has

turned to irregular stone stairs lost in fallen leaves. The sky is growing darker and a cold wind gusts, tearing leaves and needles free of the trees, snapping them at my eyes and face. I think for a moment of *tengu*-demons and stumble forward.

A shout ahead of me: my brother-in-law's voice thick with the jubilation of prey in range, which suddenly chokes into a surprised warning. I dash around a curve into a small clearing with a building. Brother's bow is drawn, arrow nocked, but he is not aiming it. A blur of rust-red arcs across a tiny stream and disappears into the ferns under the trees, followed by the dog.

They've flushed a fox.

I shout, too late. The dog lunges forward. The bushes explode: red fur and black-and-white roll back into sight. Clear even over the dog's savage growls, the fox makes a sound like a sob.

"No!" I shout, and leap across the creek, dashing to the fox. But it is too late. Perhaps she would have survived, but the dog has caught her by the throat and shaken her. Her body flops from side to side, loose and boneless.

We scream at the dog; he lets her go and vanishes into the woods.

The fox is dead, an aged little female lying on her side in the broken grasses. I can't tell: she is old, she might have been one of the foxes I knew from before, when I still lived with Shikujo. No: that was another valley (I think), and besides, it was years (or was it months?) ago. They would all be dead by now.

As is she. No breath lifts her ribs; one gold eye presses without flinching against the ground. Blood seeps from her throat.

My wife's brother stands beside me, the fierce glow of killing fading from his face, being replaced with shock and horror. "No," he says, stunned.

I tilt my head back, trying not to cry. Something terrible has happened here. I just do not know what it is.

A flash of indigo-white light and then thunder, simultaneous. I smell the sharpness of lightning. Even through the ringing in my ears I hear my own shout, and the tearing of wood from a struck tree. Another flash; another peal which leaves me feeling as if the air has been stripped from my lungs. The trees around the clearing suddenly are filled with clamoring, and the first hailstone hits me. A struck *hinoki*-cedar starts its languid fall, each flash of lightning catching it a stage closer to the earth.

"Hail!" one of us shouts, just as the other shouts, "The shrine!" I don't think either of us knows who says what, wet to the skin, bruised and deafened and blinded and maddened by the fury around us. We both know what we mean: we must find cover.

A flash of light as merciless as truth exposes the shrine and jagged shreds of steam rising as hailstones fall into the hot waters of the spring. We dash across the small space and dive into the shelter under the shrine's eaves.

The shrine has no inner chamber, is really only a wall and two cypress pillars holding up a shingled roof. I suppose at some point there must have been something under this roof—a carved rock, a wood tablet, a statue. Now there is only us, shivering in soaked silks. My companion's skin glows in lightning-flash, but I know it is not merely the light that makes his lips appear blue.

And then, amazingly, I am laughing and shouting, mad from the storm. My body is aroused, manhood hard and hot against my clothes. I feel awash in wildness. For an instant I remember the tales of fox spirits possessing humans, and I wonder if the old little female entered me as she died. I do not understand why this seems funny, and I laugh harder.

Because, even though the fox is dead (and despite the laughter, I feel tears of grief hot against my cheeks), I am alive. And in this moment it seems to me as though I had forgotten this for many years.

46. SHIKUJO'S PILLOW BOOK
The female attendants she left behind:

The female attendants she left behind in the country run to her carriage as it pulls up to the veranda of her rooms. The night is full of lightning and rain; the air thunders around us. "Lady!" the women shriek, voices shrill as marsh-birds raised over the howl of the storm. "He's gone! He's lost in the woods, maybe he's dead!"

"Stop it!" Onaga shouts as she climbs from the carriage. "You are upsetting my mistress."

I step down. I am under an awning, but the wind snaps cold rain into my face, making me gasp. Onaga snatches a waxed-paper umbrella from one of the women and holds it over me. Fitful lamplight picks out a pair of mandarin ducks painted across its surface. They seem to eye me.

We ascend the steps to the veranda like a gabbling flock of geese. Everyone has something to say; everyone says it several ways. It is a relief to step inside and slide the screens and panels shut. Lightning still flares coldly, casting the triangular eave-openings in blinding relief. Rain still puffs in, but I can ignore the occasional drop that falls on me.

Perhaps I could have prevented all this if I had remained. I know this is a lie, however: fate determines everything. I am a piece of dyed silk fabric, rinsed in the river, drying in the wind. Everything about me — my color, my pattern, the movements of the air stroking me — is determined by things outside myself.

The rain is very cold. Inside, a spiderweb hangs over my head.

47. KITSUNE'S DIARY

It was a bad night, an unlucky night. The diviner had told my women that I should not sleep that night, but stay up and fast. I didn't know why—the lives of humans seemed ringed 'round with arbitrary rules and tabus—but I was human now, and would do what humans did, even where it made no sense.

I thought of having my son brought to me, but what would be the point of waking him so that I would have a distraction from my fears?

Yoshifuji and my brother had not returned from wherever it was they had gone, though their men had all returned earlier in the day, sent back after escorting them to their picnic site. I knew from what the men told me that my husband and brother had gone out into the real world, away from the fox magic, and this always made me nervous: what if the spell did not hold? What if something somehow happened, and Yoshifuji were hurt and did not come back? I was learning the *Manyōshū* then— many poems by many dead people, all apparently moaning about their lives in nearly identical language—but I could not concentrate, and I jumped and screamed at an unexpected noise.

"What are you yelping about, little bug-eater?" Grandfather had been sitting near me, flirting in a perfunctory way with Josei. "You've heard thunder before."

"I'm so sorry!" My heart beat so loudly that I could scarcely hear the murmuring of my women. "I'm just nervous tonight. With my husband outside—" Outside the magic, I meant.

"He is getting a soaking, he and that brother of yours. And it serves them right. If they stayed inside, they would still be dry like sensible people."

I did not feel very sensible just then. The energy in the air made the tiny hairs on my arms stand up, made me want to run and shout and throw things. But that would not have been right, of course, so I sat and read poems, and imagined taking the shining ball my grandfather had given me and hurling it against a wall as hard as I could.

48. SHIKUJO'S PILLOW BOOK
Terrifying occurrences:

One has just returned to one's home on a stormy night. Lightning illuminates the garden so that it looks as though it belonged to the dead.

A thunderclap immediately overhead.

Hailstones. They rip through the screens, and bounce across the floor in an icy wind. It is as if they are searching for one.

A horse begins screaming. It panicked because of the storm, and thrashed about inside its stall until it broke a leg. The screaming goes on for some time before a decision is made for dealing with the animal.

A dog suddenly barks, very close. What is it barking at?

In a time of great stress, one's son cries in the night and abruptly falls silent. He has fallen asleep in the midst of tears over some childhood fancy, but one does not learn this immediately. There are what seem endless moments when one's own adult fancy imagines the most horrible things. Indeed, it may take much of the night for one's heart to stop pounding and allow one to sleep.

Bearing a child was terrifying, though in a different fashion: one was prey to fancies about the child. Would it be normal? healthy? alive? Even after his birth, one had moments of panic.

One has a horrifying dream, filled with blood and pain. Fierce creatures with many legs and glowing eyes eat one's flesh, eventually tearing one's shoulder altogether away. One wrenches into wakefulness to escape their sharp teeth, only to see gold eyes in one's bedroom, and realize one is still dreaming.

Of course, this is only speculation.

49. THE NOTEBOOK OF KAYA NO YOSHIFUJI

The storm continues for a time. The hailstones stop, to be replaced by sheets of icy rain that the wind hurls at us. We
stand close, watching the rain fall.

As if to prove my mind is as numb as my hands, I can't
stop thinking about the little dead fox. I peer through the
rain-filled night, trying to see the body, but I cannot seem to
find it. Either I can't remember exactly where in the clearing
it happened; or she was not dead, after all, and has run off.
No: I remember the eye against the dirt, the ripped throat.
She was not spared.

The rain seems to have moved off, but even with the clouds
clearing it is nearly dark. The moon is due later: well then, we
will wait until it rises and find our way home by that. But in
the meantime, I can barely stand for shivering, while my wife's
brother seems to be faint from cold. "Come," I say, and my
words chatter out as puffs of fog in the chill air. "Let's warm
ourselves in the springs."

We feel our way toward the little pool. The fallen tree nar-
rowly missed it; but branches trail into the steaming water,
scenting the sulfur air with pine's tang. We peel free of our
soaked robes, silk layers clinging as if reluctant to part, and lay
them carefully over rocks. We will have to get into them later,
and they will still be just as cold and wet as they were before,
but I can't be bothered with that right now: it is enough to know
I am about to be warm, deliciously warm.

To step into the water is like stepping into the depths of a
fiery hell. I lower myself into a small pool that looks as if it is
nothing but steam, but I find myself up to my thighs in nearly
unbearable warmth. I hope the waters have not grown hotter in
the years since last I visited, or we will be boiled alive; but no.
I grow used to the water and ease myself lower, until I am sitting
on a stone, up to my shoulders. Brother has watched me warily,
and steps in after me, flinching a little as he settles. Then he
sighs, abandoning himself to the heat.

For a time we say nothing. The spring's pool is a small one, a bowl shaped of large rocks. At first I try to keep my feet politely out of the way of his feet, but give it up soon enough, allowing them to settle together like sleeping puppies. I lean my head back on one of the fallen pine's branches. Tendrils of steam stroke my face like fingers. Steam settles on my cheeks, collects on my eyelids. I look up through a gap in the tall trees, and see a handful of stars gleaming tentatively. After a time, they are flooded out by the moon, which fills the sky with a silver haze.

I say:

> *"After the storm, the moon shines,*
> *but who remains to see it?"*

"Mmm. Poetry," he says.

"We killed a fox," I said, tasting the words to see how I felt about them.

Splashing noises: I open my eyes to see him sit up taller. "What?"

"The fox. Well, we didn't exactly kill her, but the dog did."

"That wasn't real," he says flatly, frowning.

"Of course it was real!"

"No. It was *not* real. No one died. No one was hurt."

"But I saw it. You don't think she crawled away—" I stop. The flatness in his tone, I suddenly realize, is pain or guilt. "What's wrong?"

"It would be bad luck," he says finally, "to kill a fox."

I recall the stabbing burst of sorrow when I saw the fox was dead. I had no idea he might feel the same way, that anyone but me might care for the life of a fox, tricky and dangerous as so many seem to think they are. But clearly he cares: his gold eyes are so filled with grief that for a second I forget he is not the sister he looks like, and I long to put my arms around him, comfort him.

After a moment, he continues, as if the words are torn from him. "I was caught up in the chase. I forgot everything—who I was, where I was. And the fox jumped out, and for just a moment,

I forgot—I thought she was just a fox, I was going to—" He swallowed.

"Are you afraid the fox might have cursed you?"

"No," he says with a laugh that wrenches into a sob. "Not exactly. I just wish I could remember what is real and what is not."

"And what is real?" I whisper. Strange question: but at this moment, I want his answer to this, want it desperately.

"My sister knows. Sometimes. And the fox was real. But so are you, and so is this." He meets my eyes. His face is wet.

I am hungry and exhausted, as is he, which must be why this conversation makes so little sense. But life is such that things don't have to make sense to cause pain, and his grief is real enough.

The moon has inched to a gap in the trees, and the steam coils around us like smoke from a strange incense. He is as beautiful as his sister, and my body stirs. I lean forward and touch his shoulder, pull him close. He looks soft and smooth, but I feel muscles under his slick skin, as if he does many athletic things. He is crying in earnest now, and I stroke his head.

The kiss seems so natural that I am not sure who initiates it. His mouth is simultaneously soft and hard, narrow lips so very different from his sister's fuller mouth as they move under mine. He tastes of something rich and feral, of sulfur and flesh. First the kiss is gentle, but then his tongue flicks against mine, and I find myself wanting him fiercely. I want to bite, and I do, pulling at his lip with my teeth. When he breaks away, I find myself gasping, or snarling.

"What are we doing?" he says breathlessly even as he reaches for me, hand closing around my manhood, fingers cool compared to the heat of the water. "I am male!"

I slide toward him, wrap my own hand around him. His manhood is like him, long and slender. "Have you never played with friends when you were a boy? Never been with a man?" I stop. Of course he has not, though every boy his age—every one *I* ever knew when *I* was his age—has at least experimented this way.

He groans, "But—" and then speaks no more, as we embrace again, all fire and thrust, mouths fighting.

He is as inexperienced as his sister was when first she and I had sex, but he knows what he wants, perhaps has thought much about sex with men, to have so much enthusiasm. I pull him to me, out of the water and onto the rocks. Entering him is hard, with only the bitter water and my saliva to make it easier, but I gentle him with my hands until he relaxes and allows me in. I move inside him, slower and then faster. He cries aloud, but does not ask me to stop, and instead reaches back and pulls me against him when I pause.

We release: my fluids released deep in him; his a brief cloudy mist in the water. Afterwards, we settle into the water again, my arms around him, his elegant body pressed thigh to shoulder against my chest and belly. By now I have learned enough of his family to know better than to attempt any sort of poetry exchange with him, and so there is a simplicity to the time afterward that I have never known before.

I have had sex with men before. For others I know, it is a great passion, but for me it has always been a thing of little moment. Friends drink too much *sake* together, or admire one another's poetry or wit; or they simply long for the touch of skin against skin and turn to someone they hold in affection or trust, or even whoever is available. This is one of those things, or another: jubilation at being alive after the close call of the lightning and the storm; or sadness at the killing of the fox. Or perhaps it is something altogether different.

50. KITSUNE'S DIARY

A t dawn, two things happened. The first was this: Yoshifuji and Brother returned exhausted, in wet, filthy clothes that reeked of sulfur. They had been caught by the storm and taken shelter at a shrine in the hills. I remembered that shrine from my days as a fox: I had never been there, but on one of our hunting paths we could smell it sometimes, when the wind was right. The smell certainly was no incentive to explore further. There seemed some constraint between the two men, for Yoshifuji went immediately to his rooms with scarcely a word to any of us, and only a smile for me.

The second thing was this: Brother said nothing, just walked straight through my rooms (women scattering before him as poultry used to, back in his fox-days) to our mother's chambers, Grandfather and I trailing behind him. "Mother?" His voice was rough, as if he had shouted or wept much in the night. "Mother!"

"She is sleeping," Josei said, and when Brother slid open the screens around her sleeping dais, my mother seemed to be asleep, half-buried in sleeping robes, her hair cascading across the floor. He jerked aside the top-most robes. Josei and the other servants around us glided away, or perhaps dissolved into the air.

My mother certainly appeared to be sleeping, except for the blood on her torn throat. He turned his face away with a sob. "So it was real. It happened."

I knelt beside my mother. "What happened?" Her robes were askew, dyed nearly black with blood. She was curled into a ball, as if she were again a fox, as if she had been trying to ease the pain, to lick at or bite at her wounds.

"We were hunting, outside," Brother said, "in the real world. She ran across our path as a fox."

"He killed her?" I was horrified. "But you were there to stop him."

"Not him," Brother said in a low hopeless voice. "The dog. But I didn't stop the dog. I was so caught up in being human that I didn't even recognize her until she was dead."

"But the magic! Didn't she seem human to Yoshifuji at least? Couldn't he tell?" I was shivering. I touched her face, which was cold and damp against my fingers. Her eyes were still open, clouded with dirt.

"I don't know what he saw. And then there was a storm, and lightning nearly struck, and—" His voice suspended itself on tears.

Grandfather gave him a sharp look. "So." He knelt heavily beside my mother's body, and pushed tangled hair off her face, smoothing it back from her forehead. "Poor little daughter. You were never very good at humanity, were you?"

"What happens to her now?" I asked.

"Nothing. She's a fox. She's dead."

"But the old man who wouldn't give me his head told me that foxes had souls. Is that gone now? What about rebirth?"

"That old man is a fool. Humans are all fools." Grandfather stood carefully. I saw suddenly that he had grown older since we had taken human shape—there were fine lines drawn from the corners of his eyes almost to his temples. "As are we. No. We die, and that is all there is to it. No ghosts, no Pure Land paradise awaiting us, no reincarnation. Just *now*, and then death."

I lay down on the sleeping robes beside her, curled myself around her as if she were still alive and I were still her kit, sleeping against her in the darkness of our scrape. My eyes hurt as if some poisoned thing melted there. After I time I realized I was crying.

"Why am I sad?" I asked. "I have never grieved for death before. It was just the way things are."

"That is another of the prices humans pay—loss."

"Humans pay a lot of prices," I said bitterly. "I had not realized how many."

"You have not begun to know, Granddaughter," Grandfather said harshly.

Footsteps on the veranda outside. "Wife?"

Brother flinched. We three looked at each other in horrified silence. "Wife? Josei? Anyone?" I heard a screen slide in another room, and footsteps moving toward us. "Where is everyone?"

And then he slid a door aside and was in the room with us and my dead mother. Unlike Brother's robes, his were clean and sweet-smelling: he must have changed before coming to find me. "What?" He stopped, frowned, looked at her. "Isn't this the fox that—?"

My grandfather answered. "Your mother-in-law has left this tearstained world. She is dead."

"No," Yoshifuji said. "That is not her. I see the wounds."

Brother gasped.

"You see nothing," Grandfather said heavily. "There is nothing to see."

"But —" Yoshifuji shook his head as if trying to shake free of spiderwebs.

"You see precisely this: a woman dead, her family mourning. No more. No less."

"I suppose so," Yoshifuji said slowly. "I must have still had the dead fox in my mind. So your mother is dead, too. I am so sorry, pretty wife." He reached down and took my hands, pulling me upright and holding me close, not minding my tears on his silks. "We will summon the priests. And your mother will awaken in the Pure Land."

"I don't think so," I said, and started crying in earnest.

Brother covered his face with his hands and ran from the room.

The dog returned a day later. I could not blame it for the death, for it had no idea of right and wrong. It was only a dog, after all.

51. THE NOTEBOOK OF KAYA NO YOSHIFUJI

The little fox we killed —
curled in a ball, as if sleeping —
reminds me of the sleeping one.

52. KITSUNE'S DIARY

We prepared my mother's body for the funeral. Priests chanted until their voices became a steady background to our thoughts, of no more importance than constant rain, or the hammering of a woodpecker a long way away.

My women and I washed her. A priest painted words on her body—sutras splashed across her skin. We dressed her in her best robes and laid her in a *hinoki*-cedar coffin, tucking certain precious things beside her. It was traditional to place small pottery figures in with the dead, but I was confused. Her understanding of humanness was weak—how could she gain from human figurines any of the benefits that she should? Perhaps fox statues would be better. But there was no precedent, of course: when had a fox ever died and been given a Buddhist funeral? In the end we gave her no statues at all, and worried that their absence might harm her.

The pyre was large, lit by my grandfather. The smoke smelled of sandalwood (as it should), but it also smelled of decay: for in truth there was no fire. There was only my grandfather and brother dragging her body outside the magic's range, to where the crows and rats and beetles would eat her fox body, leaving only scattered bones. After that, when the wind was wrong, we could sometimes smell the rich gaminess of her decaying body, and that scent became the smoke of her pyre.

We did what we could to make her passage into the next world better, offering medicines and clothes and sutras in her name. Would they count toward her well-being, received as they were by phantasms, by fox-magic constructs? Was a Buddhist priest created as part of our magic truly a priest of Buddha, or was he just the shadow of such a man? And the Buddha they prayed to? Was that truly Buddha, or another shadow? I hoped they would somehow count, but I was afraid. If the Buddha, the true Buddha, cared enough about us to hear our prayers, might he be offended that they were somehow not real?

Mother had talked sometimes about gods. I wished there
might be a god who cared for foxes, who might offer more to
her than death. Perhaps another life, something gentler than a
fox without wits?

I had so many questions, but my grandfather was stern, silent
in a way that did not encourage me to ask them of him. He
performed his part in the rituals, but always watching my
brother, who wept steadily without pause.

We took the forms of mourning. For forty-nine days we wore
the browns and charcoals and *usinubi*–blue-grays of sadness.
Even Shōnen wore gray, though it seemed ill suited to his youth.
We wore the proper rough-woven overrobes; ordered the correct services for her. On the fiftieth day, we wore layers of
unrelieved black, and even my son was subdued.

I was in retirement, but my calligraphy instructor sent me a
letter of condolence. He ended with this poem:

> *My grief will not be shown*
> *'til the mountains are bare,*
> *every beech tree gone*

Beech gives us the black dye for our mourning robes; I suppose this is what he meant, but just then poetry did not seem
terribly important to me.

53. SHIKUJO'S PILLOW BOOK
I had my husband's manservant summoned:

First thing the next morning, I had my husband's major domo
summoned. He arrived immediately, as if he had been expecting the call, which I suppose he must have.

"My lady has sent for me?" Hito asked.

"Yes. Tell me about his absence."

"Yes." I didn't see it, of course, but I know he bowed then.
"It has been nearly two months, since the end of the sixth

month. We have performed rituals, and I sent for diviners, but they were unable to find anything."

"And he visited no temple, no friend, no mistress."

A hesitation. "To my knowledge, my lady, no."

"And you would know such a thing."

"He has always honored me with a considerable degree of candor as to his actions before this. I do not think —"

"What did the diviners tell you?"

"Nothing — or rather, strange things, my lady. They say he is not dead, so far as they can tell, though they also say he might be."

"Hito, do you recall, those last few weeks before I left . . ."

"Yes, my lady. He seemed very interested in the natural world." He meant foxes, of course, but he found it as hard to speak of this as I did.

"Did you mention this to the diviners?"

He hesitated. "I took the liberty of doing so. I thought it was important. But they found nothing."

"What of the woods?"

"Naturally we have searched there. We had feared he might have lost himself, perhaps hunting, but . . ." His voice trailed off.

"We must institute further searches. He might have been injured, lost in a storm. Anything." I listened to my calm voice, amazed. It was as if I were speaking of something distant, an abstract religious precept or the death of a distant relative I had never met. "You will send all the male servants, all the peasants. You will ask every savage and every monk living in the mountains. He is here, Hito. I know this. And you will hunt with all the rest of them."

"It has been two months. I am afraid it is too late."

"Then we will find his body," I said harshly. "Now take them all away and leave my husband's house in peace again."

Hito bowed and left. I heard his footsteps out on the walkways and across the gravel of the wisteria courtyard, and then, wonderfully, quiet. My women moved about; but with the sounds of women, soft voices and gentle footsteps.

Despite my words to Hito, I am not sure of anything. I must know whether he is alive or not. Onaga suggests we consult the old man in the woods, but I don't want to see him: he is a fraud!

He must be alive.

54. KITSUNE'S DIARY

B rother never seemed to recover from our mother's death, even after the one-year purification rites were completed and we all went on with our lives. He still went out with Yoshi-ifuji, but he seemed more restrained with him, and I did not hear him laugh again. I worried: perhaps there was more to this emotional sickness of his than loss.

I saw him in one of the pavilions one day, with writing desk and papers. I asked him what he was writing, and he blushed furiously. "Poems," he said.

"You understand poetry?" I exclaimed.

"Yes. No. But I will understand it. I *will* be human, Sister." He started putting away his papers and brushes.

"Let me see!"

"No." I grabbed a sheet away from him. He snatched at it, but I bared my teeth at him as if we had still been foxes and read it.

The paper was gray flecked with scarlet; the calligraphy what my tutor would have in his polite way called "variable."

> *When the last leaf has fallen, what then?*
> *Will you leave, as well?*

"This is a poem?" I asked. "I don't understand."

"It is not for you," he said furiously, and tore the sheet from my hands.

"But what is it about, then?"

"Autumn's end," he said, and left me.

I shook my head. He seemed so strange, my brother: he had

only reluctantly come to humanity. That he embraced it now was as strange to me as anything. Even now, he was as alien to me as the rabbit on the moon.

My brother came to me one day when I was bored.

"She's back, Sister."

"Hmm?"

"Yoshifuji's wife. She has come back."

"Why? It's been years! I would have thought she'd have given up by now."

"No: for them it's been a few months only: barely a season. What did you expect? When he didn't come back from his walk, they searched and found nothing. I'm sure they called his wife back."

"*I* am his wife," I said automatically, but I knew my brother did not refer to me. "But it's been years."

I shook my head, then remembered he couldn't see me; I was behind my *kichō*-curtains. As always. "What's she doing?"

"Crying, I expect. It seems to be the only thing humans do consistently."

I frowned. "He doesn't want to be with her. He wants to be with me."

"She doesn't know that. Sister, what are we going to do?"

"She can't do anything," I said.

"She can do a lot of things. What if she calls on her gods? What if she sees him?" His voice broke.

My brother was always so calm, so resistant to everything we had done to become human. This made no sense, the break in his voice. I knelt and looked around the edge of the curtain. There were tears on his face.

"Brother?" I pushed the curtain aside. "Why is it so important to you?"

"We can't lose him," he said, and looked at me miserably. "We need him too much."

"To stay human, you mean?" He hesitated a moment, then nodded. "Why would we lose him to her?" I continued. "He came to me once already. And his gods did nothing."

"And he can step back, Sister, just like that. It's the real world outside. It's too simple for him to step from one to the other."

I shivered, knowing it. "Where is he?"

"With Grandfather in his rooms. They are reading some papers from the capital. They didn't ask me to attend them."

"All right then. Let's see what's happening."

Brother tipped his head to one side. "You wish to join me?"

I stood. "As a fox, yes. We can sneak closer to her home then, and find out what she plans. If anything." I knew that was a foolish thought. Of course she was planning something. Why else would she be here?

"When were you out last, Sister?"

"I don't know," I said. Years? Months? Since before Shōnen was born, anyway. "I like to be here when my husband is around. But now —"

Now. He knew what I thought, my brother. We needed to be clever and resourceful, and that meant knowing everything we could.

At dusk, we stood at the very edge of the magic (a long walk from the front gates of our fox-magic house, barely a step past the shadow cast by the gatehouse over our scrape): a woman and a man. "Now?" my brother asked.

"Now," I said.

I bit my lip, not wanting to cry out. Brother had always shrugged easily into and out of his human shape, as if it were just another set of robes; this time it seemed harder for him, as well. We hung our heads and gasped for a time, forcing breath through now unfamiliar chests and throats.

Once I was used to the shape of my fox-legs and body again, running was sweet. A fox's body is so perfectly shaped to run and dance and pounce, and my brother and I did all these and more. I missed a mouse I jumped at, and chased it for a few steps, just for the delight of feeling the dead grasses slap past my legs. It had been too long, perhaps, since I had run like this.

The house was filled with noise. Brother grew more nervous as we approached, and finally stopped, legs stiff with fear.

Discussions were had. Priests were going to be called, but this I could ignore: had we not already fooled the Buddha himself? Another search would be made: but we had avoided the humans before this, and now the shorter days and dull skies of late autumn would make the searches shorter and not so effective.

"We have to go," Brother whispered. "We can't stay." Not so changed after all, my brother.

"And miss this? Don't you want to know what is happening here?"

"Yes. No." He mouthed my shoulder, but I shrugged him off. "Yoshifuji will miss us."

"You thought it would be good to see what is happening."

"I know. I just didn't expect to hate being a fox again so much. I want to be back in our world."

"I'm staying. I have to know what she is doing." Meaning: his wife. What plans did she have? What schemes? I said no more, only crawled under the building that contained her rooms. After a time, I ceased to notice my brother. I assumed he slipped away, but for all the attention I paid, he might as well have fallen asleep (or died) there.

It was quieter here: in fact, it was almost silent. I lay belly-down in the dust for a long time, listening to the noises from the main house. Strange, this pond of stillness, surrounded by storm. After a while, I heard rustling in what I had taken to be an empty room, and I realized someone had been there, sitting still, and perhaps doing what I had been doing: watching or listening to all the activity. This of course would be his wife. Who else would wait in stillness, calm as a spider?

Late that night, when all of her women were sleeping (or seeming to sleep), I smelled new salt on the air, and heard the faintest of breaths and recognized these for what they were. She was crying.

It was just dawn when I returned to the fox-magic world. I stood sobbing in unbleached robes, tinted the red of certain maple leaves by the first rays of the sun slanting beneath the gatehouse. Grandfather stood beside me, for once not insisting on a curtain or blind between us. His voice was hushed, with the tones people use when talking at dawn in a house with paper walls.

"Still crying, Granddaughter? You have cried a river you might drown in by now."

I explained about Shikujo and her tears. "I caused this," I whispered. "I had no idea I would be hurting her so."

"No, I suppose you didn't," he said brusquely; then, in a gentler tone: "Poor little human woman. What do you think of your decision to steal him now, Granddaughter?"

"I was—" I stopped, swallowed. "I didn't expect her to suffer. If only I could have him without hurting her!"

"Hah. Nothing in the human world even hopes for the absence of pain. You were a fool to think it might be otherwise."

"I was a fox! How was I supposed to know?"

He sighed. "You weren't, of course. But that makes neither of us less fools."

55. SHIKUJO'S PILLOW BOOK
Difficult imaginary conversations:

Difficult though it would be, one would very much like to find her husband and ask him this: if you loved me, how could you skulk away without telling anyone where you were going? What do you gain by this? Is it selfishness or misery that drives you to be so callous?

One dreads the conversation with her son about his father's absence. *Where is father?* I do not know. *Is he dead?* I do not know. *Doesn't he care for us?* I do not know. I had thought so.

Perhaps most difficult of all is the conversation one might have with the fox man of my dreams of so long ago, the one who left me a poem. He would come to me in the dusk and bow formally. *I did not expect you to return,* he would say.

How could I not? Perhaps I would be somewhat sharp, since I have been very concerned.

I am so sorry for the loss of your husband, he would say.

What do you mean? I would ask: *Do you know something about this?*

He would sigh. *What has happened to your husband is not my story to tell. I know he will be hard to get back.*

I suppose, I would say. *But I will have to try.*

He would say: *I can swear to you that I did not steal him away because I wished to court you again.* Or perhaps he would say: *I did not steal him away so that I could read poems to you again.* It is hard to know precisely.

Well then, I would say, *why are you here? All I can think about is my husband's absence. I do not have time for anything else.*

Are you so sure? His voice would be as sweet as the lowest note of a *koto*. *I did not make him go away, but he is nevertheless a heedless fool. You have been lonely for a long time, lady: I would like very much to begin again our conversation* — or was it "connection"? — *of so long ago.*

Lonely? One supposes this is true, when one's husband is more caught up in his own thoughts and feelings and has no time to spare for one's own. It is not an expected thing, that a husband should care for his wife's feelings so much that he would change his behavior accordingly, and yet it is a common occurrence. Men have loved women to such an extent. Unexpectedly, I might find myself crying. *Yes, lonely*, I would think, but I would not say this. Instead I *would* say: *It is impossible.*

Why? he would ask, his voice impatient now.

Because I love him, I would say finally. *I do not want anyone else. Even if he is a fool, he is the man who taught me to laugh, and the man who stayed up all night with me to watch for shooting stars, and the man who* —

I see, he would say, and he would bow. *I had not realized. Please forgive me for disturbing you like this. I will not do so again.*

Can you at least tell me where my husband is? But he would only shake his head and bow again.

No, he would say. *As I said, it is not my secret to tell.* And he would be gone, as quickly and silently as a dream or an animal.

This would be a difficult conversation to have. Except that perhaps I have had it? I cannot remember.

56. KITSUNE'S DIARY

After that, I tried not to think of Yoshifuji's human wife drifting through her darkened rooms. *Her life hasn't changed at all,* I would think when I could not avoid it, after listening to sad folk songs or reading depressing *monogatari*-tales. *I have taken nothing from her.* But I knew this was a lie, and that I was saying this because I wanted to believe it.

I also knew there was not such a great difference between her life and mine now. A woman's life is shadows and waiting. Even mine.

One rainy night after Yoshifuji was asleep, I dug from a trunk the robe he had been wearing when first he came to me. Tearing a sleeve free, I cut the flesh inside my wrist and dropped blood on the silk, and then I left the sleeve at the edge of the garden, where I knew it would be found and brought to Shikujo. Better for her to mourn and accept and forget.

57. SHIKUJO'S PILLOW BOOK
They have found his sleeve:

They have found his sleeve, torn and covered with blood, at the foot of the garden. The servant who found it; Hito, who brought it to me; Onaga and my other women: everyone wept.

But I did not cry. Numb, I turned the sleeve over in my hands. It is of unbleached silk, from one of his most casual robes, but now it is patterned, marked with grass stains and mud stains and, everywhere, blood.

I press the sleeve against my face. It smells as though some creature had made a den with the robe, but beneath the animal smell, I think I can smell the amber-and-musk scent of him. I do not know if this is my imagination.

It cannot be. He cannot be dead. Why does this appear now, after he has been lost for months? I am only making excuses, hoping it is not so. He cannot be dead—I had too much to tell him!—and yet he must be.

In my shock I have another conversation, this one with myself, as if I were a child talking myself out of a fear of spiders. *How do I feel?* I do not know. *Did I love him?* Yes. *Do I still?* Who can tell? I told the fox man that I did, but honesty is a part of love, and when was I ever honest with Yoshifuji? There is a dishonesty of omission. I was angry, and I never told him. I was sad, and never told him. Fear. Grief. Loneliness. I never told him I felt these things, too involved in propriety to speak the truth.

And the foxes. I spoke the truth when I said I feared the foxes, but I did not tell him why, about my fever-dream of the fox man. And I did not tell him how I felt about that dream, which was the most frightening of all.

But then, he is not the only person to whom I was lying.

I cannot allow his corpse to lie unburned. I will summon the priests of merciful Kannon and ask for their intervention to seek it out.

58. KITSUNE'S DIARY

My son was playing with the dog. I would throw my ball, and he and the dog would chase after it as it rolled across the room. Sometimes my son caught the ball, and he would walk across the room with great stateliness and bow as he presented it to me; sometimes it was the dog, and when I got the ball, the presentation was soggy and much less formal. I still did not like the animal much, but I was used to it, as it was used to me.

Grandfather had been right; the dog believed what we showed it. Or perhaps it simply did not care what the truth was: despite their transparent emotions, what a dog sees as important is still a mystery to me.

Shōnen's nurse sat with us, an open scroll beside her. "Boy! Attend!"

The boy and the dog exchanged glances, speaking in a non-verbal language only they understood. This worried me as a possible sign that my son was less than human, but Grandfather assured me that any number of people were close to dogs and parrots (and, amazingly, cats) in this way; and I didn't know how to separate them without distressing Shōnen. The boy did not quite sigh heavily, and came to kneel docilely beside his nurse.

"The plants that symbolize autumn?" she asked.

Shōnen listed them easily: bush clover; *obana* grass, *kuzu*-vine, fringed pink maidenflower, *fujibakama,* morning glory. But then I had always been able to do this as well, repeat lists I did not remember learning. Was he truly learning anything or merely drawing from the same fox-magic knowledge?

"And spring?" she said.

"Um," Shōnen said.

"You don't know the herbs of spring?"

"It has never been spring, nurse."

Josei burst into the room. "My lady! I was speaking with the major domo, and he tells me that your brother is packing to go somewhere."

I looked up from the boy. "Where? I know of no pilgrimage he plans on making. But he's always leaving for one thing or another."

"No! He is *leaving.*" And I understood suddenly. He was leaving the magic. I stood. The ball fell to the ground and rolled off. "Is he gone already? Without saying good-bye?"

"Not yet," Josei panted. "But — "

"Is he in his rooms?"

"I do not — " But I was gone already, not waiting for her answer. Lifting my robes, I ran along one of the walkways to my brother's wing. He stood in the largest room, stroking his chin as he watched his people fill a small iron-bound trunk with robes and a traveling writing set.

"Brother! What are you doing?"

"I am going away, Sister." His face was hard, as if he were clenching his jaw against words he didn't wish to speak.

"But why?"

"There is no place for me here."

My hair had fallen into a tangle across one eye; I lifted it aside. "Yes, there is! What about your government work? What about your duties? Your family?"

"They are a lie, Sister, an illusion. I think they will all get by without me."

"But we won't. You can't leave us!"

"I can and do." He met my eye for a moment, and I saw his misery. "I can't stay here any longer. Please understand."

"Explain it, if you want me to understand!"

"You don't know? I loved him, too."

"Of course you do. How could you not?"

"No. He was my lover, Sister."

I frowned, puzzled. "Sex?"

"Did you think you were the only one? We are alike, as you always said."

I felt over my thoughts, like sucking on the place where a tooth has just fallen out. I was not jealous: why would I be? Yoshifuji was my husband, the father of my child. He was not less this for having also been with my brother. Jealousy is a little like poetry, incomprehensible to me. "Why are you leaving, then? Has there been a disagreement?" Surely it could be worked out, and we could stay together.

"No!" Brother burst out. "But it was a casual thing for him. He does not love me. I must become human."

"He loves me, and I am a fox," I said slowly.

"Does he? He loves what he thinks you are. No. Being human is a tool to you, something you do because it is the only way you can have him. But it's more than that, Sister. I know that now."

"Do you think I don't?" I said hotly. "I try so hard to understand what humans do, to do it right!"

"You don't want him to catch you acting incorrectly." His lip curled. "You know no more about humanity than a monkey trained to wear robes and eat with sticks."

I gasped, speechless.

"See," he said, and half-laughed, "you are not properly human, but at least you have the compensation of being his wife. I don't have that. And I cannot bear this false world we have built."

"But you are his friend," I exclaimed. "Yoshifuji needs you."

"No, he doesn't. Not as I need him." Brother laughed bitterly. "Humanity is harder than we were warned, Sister. Take care."

I ran to tell my husband, but by the time he came, Brother was gone, escorted by a single servant carrying one small trunk. Yoshifuji ran out to find him, but he had no luck: the rain had washed out his footprints, and there was no way to follow.

59. THE NOTEBOOK OF KAYA NO YOSHIFUJI

I lied to my pretty wife about finding my brother-in-law. His tracks were dissolving into indistinct mud, but there were enough marks to follow. I caught up to him in a small clearing, where the rain poured down our faces as we talked, colder than snow.

He is leaving because of me, because we had sex at the spring so long ago. I remember the experience, though it has been months (or years) since then. I recall the slick feel of his sulfur-wet skin, his taut hunger, my flesh driving into him. But I have thought of that experience, when I thought of it at all, as an interlude brought on by the storm and the old fox's death: affection and isolation combining in passion. I thought our actions were casual; it seems that for him this was not so.

I should have thought of this, but it did not occur to me that he might not see our encounter in the same light. In my life—

my world — sex is often a casual thing. But it is not always so. And my brother-in-law fell in love.

(Aside from my thousand other thoughts, I cannot help but wonder at this. Why me? I am not extraordinary in any way, not a great poet or a brilliant administrator, not famed for my features or my dancing. What does he see in me? — Because perhaps, if I knew what he and his sister think they love in me, I could become that thing.)

And now he and I have hurt my pretty little wife. And he is hurt, and I find I also am hurt, saddened by his loss. Was Shikujo saddened by the women and men I shared pillows with? I never realized she might be, that she also, for reasons I cannot understand, might have loved me.

60. SHIKUJO'S PILLOW BOOK
Dreams can be very unsettling:

Dreams can be very unsettling. I did not sleep well last night, but stayed up watching the autumn sky. There was a storm at dusk, which terrified Tadamaro, so he and his nurse sat with me. He is still too young to wear adult trousers, but I shielded my face from him as if he were a full-grown man because I didn't want him to know I was as terrified as he was, though not at the storm.

After a time, the boy fell asleep with his head in my lap. His nurse offered to take him back to his rooms, but I wanted him there. He will be gone soon enough, grown to manhood and sent to court, if all goes well. One of my women slid open the *fusuma*-panels between us and the veranda. I watched the moon slide out from behind the thinning clouds. I saw fallen leaves like spilled ink, branches blown into the lakes, bushes crumpled by the passing of some animal or the wind. The garden struggles always to return to the wildness we disturbed, back in the spring.

It was cold, and one by one my women retreated back into the house's depths, until only Onaga, the nurse and I remained.

The women fell asleep over a game of *go* played in the moonlight, slumping over the board as if enchanted. And then I also fell asleep.

I dreamt I saw my husband walk across the lower end of the garden, dressed in hunting garb. He seemed to be surrounded by light as he moved.

I called his name and jumped to my feet, rolling my son off my lap onto the floor. The child understandably burst into tears, which woke my women. It was just before dawn, and there was no one in the garden except for a single rabbit, who ran when I cried out.

One needs to accept his loss, and perhaps this means seeing a corpse, however horribly disfigured by animals and the weather. One has summoned the priests of the goddess Kannon. She offers mercy and kindness: she will understand one's plight and return his body to one.

This terrible grief. I miss him so.

61. KITSUNE'S DIARY

*T*ime *was strange in the fox-world.* Years passed for us, and for Yoshifuji; Shōnen grew rapidly, until he hunted birds with *koyumi*-bow and toy arrows and began to ride a fat gold pony with a thick black mane and tail. Years passed for us, caught up in the fox magic, but in the outer world, it was only weeks.

I was not a natural mother — or not a natural human mother, anyway. A fox does her best for her kits and then sends them off to their own dens and mates and kits. Only humans seem to linger over their children, as if hoping to repair any mistakes they might have made. No, I am wrong: our grandfather and mother kept us long after they might have driven us away. But they can hardly be typical.

As a human, I had not thought much about a child, and when it came, I had a hard time understanding it or my feelings about it. I wanted Yoshifuji; there had been nothing in my dream about anyone else. Perhaps it is sometimes like this for human women.

Yoshifuji, however, seemed to love the time he spent with Shōnen. They played with kites, even though it was not spring-time, the correct time for such activity. He helped Shōnen at his lessons as the boy studied the *Thousand-Character Classic* and the *Classic of Filial Piety*. They tossed my ball to each other, and played *kemari*, keeping a bean-filled bag in the air without touching it with their hands. Yoshifuji made straw whistles for the boy and taught him the first simple melodies.

When the child was five, he fell from small stilts, and broke a bone in his leg. I took him away from his father for several days after that, for the child kept trying to lick the injured limb. A healer came and set the bone straight and tied it with silk cords against a stick; and after a while, it mended, and the child ran straight-legged again.

When he was seven, we held the skirt ceremony. His beautiful long baby-hair was cut into a man's style, and he received his first pair of grown man's *hakama*-trousers, so long that he struggled not to trip. He was as beautiful as the seven precious stones, my son; only the gold of his eyes was unsettling.

62. SHIKUJO'S PILLOW BOOK
My son:

adamaro has gone from boy to man, overnight it seems. In grief for his father, he has rejected his toys, and studies his sutras and *Analects* with a sober intensity that does not sit easily on so young a boy. He came to me yesterday and swore he would do something about his father's death; but what can he do? Death is the only thing that cannot be rescinded. Nevertheless, I allowed him to stay with me when I met the priests of Kannon.

There were a half-dozen men sent from her temple several days' walk away—two priests and a number of monks and acolytes. They arrived at dusk on a chilly evening. Clouds high in the sky still flared with the red sunset, but the house was hidden in the mountain's shadow.

Hito brought the priests to the guest house. Their breath puffed around them as they stamped along the walkway. Their robes were dusk-dark but flared red as sunset clouds when the priests stepped past a lantern hung from the eave. Acolytes and servants followed them, bearing warming foods and beverages: I smelled the sharp scent of *sake*, and tea, like summer straw in the rain.

I watched from a darkened veranda, sleeve over my face to keep my tears from chilling my face. I wondered sometimes if my constant tears were eating me away from the inside, like driftwood hollowed in an endless salt sea.

63. THE NOTEBOOK OF KAYA NO YOSHIFUJI

I haven't written much, I see. I've been very busy. Orders from the capital are keeping me busy.

Shōnen is eight now—tall and handsome. I watch him with awe; I was never so graceful when I was young. I think of sending him to the capital to serve as a court page, but I am reluctant to have him so far away.

The autumn has seemed very long. I cannot remember when last I saw cherry blossoms or snow. Perhaps the turning of seasons, spring to summer to autumn to winter, is not as immutable as I thought. If this is the case, then all things can change.

64. KITSUNE'S DIARY

I knelt with my women, listening to a traveling nun read sutras. Shōnen was with us; he was restless, but occasional whispers in his ear from his nurse kept him from disrupting the reading. The nun's voice chimed on and on.

Josei had not been sitting with us, and it was Josei who interrupted the reading. I heard the clatter of clogs and her shouts as she ran along the veranda: she had not even taken time to remove her footwear when she approached. "My lady! My lady!" Her voice was tight with urgency. The nun's voice stammered to a halt; for a moment we all sat immobile, like insects caught in pine resin. Then Josei slammed open the screen.

She stood, disheveled, panting heavily. I thought she had gone mad. "My lady! Something terrible is happening."

I stood, shook loose the folds of my kimono. "What?"

She did not answer, but only caught at my sleeve. "Josei —" I began, but then I looked and saw tears standing in her eyes. I had never seen her weep before, did not even know it was possible.

"Please," she whispered. "There is something — outside."

"Show me," I said. "Madam nun, please forgive me, and continue." I bowed — as Josei did, rapidly, almost as an afterthought — and we hurried back along the veranda. Her tears were falling freely now. She sobbed as she led me to the edge of our garden and pointed out, over a split-bamboo fence and across the empty rice fields. It was nearly winter, and the crops were in. The peasants were already tucked into their little huts for the night. Far away a dog barked.

"Not there," she said. "*There.*"

She pointed again, and this time I realized that by "outside," she meant outside the magic. How could she see this? How could she even be aware? My vision shifted and I saw where we were: Josei still stood, a slim elegant woman on a boxwood walkway (where else could she be? she was wholly magic — she had no existence in the real world, or so I had imagined); but at the same time, I crouched beneath the corner of the gate-house, looking out toward the house Yoshifuji had shared with Shikujo before I had claimed him.

Behind me, Josei spoke slowly, as if forcing the words past some obstruction. "They are searching for him, my lady."

I looked at the house in the gathering evening. The air was

cold, but many of the screens had been pushed aside, and inside the rooms I saw movement and warm lights. I shrugged. "They tried before, Josei, and failed."

"No!" She said. "This is different. I can tell."

"How can you see this?"

She dashed tears from her face with one hand. "I don't know. I watched the dog once, when he left here. After that, I could see—outside, if I tried. I would come here sometimes, to watch them."

"But—"

"Please, my lady! There is something happening—"

Shouts from the house, a cluster of men hauling something up a walkway. I shivered. "All right. I'll look. Go back to my rooms and watch Shōnen."

This time, crawling out of my woman's form was excruciating, as if it were my own flesh I ripped from my bones. I hunched over until the pain and the sense of loss eased. When I felt a little better, I lifted my head and left the space under the gate-house.

It was early evening, and the stars were still washed out with the brightness of the western sky. I loped across the formal garden, moving in the trees' short shadows. When I leapt across the stream beside the half-moon bridge, I caught a glimpse of my reflection in the moving water, and it startled me enough that I stumbled when I landed and rolled into a ball. Despite my fox-shape, I had seen a woman in my reflection.

There were lights in the house: torches set along the verandas, and braziers and lamps in the rooms. Many of the sliding walls were open despite the chill weather: I watched the silhouettes of bats, catching the season's last insects, drawn to the lights.

The north suite of rooms, Shikujo's rooms, were dimly lit. I crept up almost to the veranda and looked in. I couldn't see her, but I smelled her (chrysanthemums and salty tears) and saw her sleeves, the brown of dead leaves, half-exposed under her *kichō*-curtain. A priest knelt in front of the curtain, chanting the su-tras. The night's breeze pushed aside one of the curtains; before one of her women could pull it back in place, I saw Shikujo, listless and sad in the gloom.

The house's main rooms were full of light. My husband's other son—his human son—stood there, dressed in somber robes that seemed too dull for a child. He was half the height of the men with him: Hito and other high-level servants, with a Buddhist priest and his acolytes. The ordinary servants—kitchen- and field-workers and various peasants—crowded in the garden watching the men in the rooms. Everyone was dressed strangely; in mourning, I realized. It surprised me—no one was dead—until I realized it must be my husband they were mourning.

The heavy thing I had seen men carry into the house was a segment of a cypress-tree trunk as tall as a man. It had been laid on wood supports; tools gleamed on a hemp cloth beside it. A priest bent over the trunk and chanted something I could not hear. Incense hung in the cold still air, glinting dull gold from the torches and lanterns. After a time, he picked up a chisel and mallet and handed them to the boy. Solemnly the boy laid chisel to wood and chipped at the cypress trunk, a formal action. Then with a bow the boy passed the tools back to the priest, who began carving.

I inched forward and stared at the wood: close like this, I could see that it had already been hewed into a rough image of some sort, though I could not tell of what. The priest laid down his tools. Two assistants threw more incense on the braziers in the room. Everyone else in the room and the garden lay down on their stomachs and began to pray softly. The priest fell forward and chanted again, this time in a loud voice.

He was praying to the Eleven-Headed Kannon (when I squinted, the crude carving made sense this time: there was the cluster of heads, and the arms and the crossed legs). When he called this god my fur rose on my shoulders until my skin prickled. *I hate this*, I thought, but I could not leave.

The voice went on and on, asking Kannon's help. She was a goddess of mercy, I knew: now the priest prayed for mercy, asking for the rest and peace that would come to Yoshifuji's family if they just knew where his dead body lay and could burn it, as the Buddhist faith dictated.

This surprised me: why should they care what happened to Yoshifuji's body? They thought he was dead: well, then, his body would just be decaying flesh. There was no point to saving it. But they had before. I remembered the body I had seen burned so long ago, the humans' incomprehensible burying of the woman whose skull I stole, my husband's insistence that my mother's body deserved a pyre. I had been so clever, with the sleeve and the blood; it should have ended there. But they kept searching!

There was no reason to worry. I remembered the priest who had called on Buddha and walked past us anyway. How could this one fare better? Once I had realized that the Buddha would not (or could not) involve himself with us, the fear had become a playful thing, like a crow that teases wolves, knowing that they can kill it but that they probably will not.

But this was not like that. The Buddha had been uncaring, but this god cared deeply—I felt a strange muffling warmth, like quilted sleeping robes laid over us all, and I knew this was the Kannon. I did not think I could hide from her.

Incense snaked from the braziers and out onto the still air of the garden. One tendril seemed to move toward us, like a smoke-snake questing. A tiny cold wind lifted its tip, so like a snake's head that my courage broke and I bolted, my heart so hot and heavy with panic that I could hardly see the garden I ran through.

I ran under the gatehouse and rushed back into my woman's shape and stood there, shivering. Josei waited there, hands out, but I ignored her. "Husband?" I called. "Husband? Where are you?"

I ran through the rooms and hallways, careless of being seen by the men of the household, calling my husband's name. I was on one of the verandas when Yoshifuji emerged quickly from a brightly lit room, dropping the blinds behind him.

"Wife?" he said. His face was wrinkled with a frown. "I have emissaries. We could hear you all over—"

"Husband!" I panted. "I am so sorry — I know this is most unseemly — it's just that I was so afraid. . . ."

His face softened, and he moved forward quickly to hold me. "What's happened? Shōnen?"

"No, he's all right, but I — "

"It's all right now, whatever it is, I'm here."

I swallowed, tried to control my breathing. "No, not our son, he's fine." What could I tell him? "A snake of smoke, and it was looking for you. I — must have had a bad dream. I woke up, and I was all alone, and I felt so afraid."

"Alone? Where were your women?"

"They were there. I just meant — lonely for you." I threw myself against him, my arms tight around his neck, and sobbed against his cheek. He held me and made soothing noises. After a while, he loosened my hands and passed me to Josei, who stood waiting in the shadows.

"Better?"

I sniffed.

He took my hands. "I'll take care of this little bit of business, and then I'll come and sit with you, all night if you like."

"Yes," I said. "Hurry."

I waited in my rooms. The dog whining at my feet, I sat in the near-dark, and tossed my ball, and cried with the horror of that snake of smoke, and longing for Yoshifuji. The nun was gone, and Shōnen had fallen asleep and been removed to his rooms, but his nurse carried him in to me so that I could watch him sleep, curled up in a nest of robes. "See, my husband must love me," I said to myself. "Here is the evidence: no god can take this away. No god can threaten his love for me." Then I would think of the snake of smoke and I would jump up and pace and stare out at our pretty fox-gardens again. And Yoshifuji did not come.

But the Eleven-Headed Kannon came. Kannon came as an old man with only one head, and holding a stick; but I knew it was she: the old man was not made of fox magic, in a place where everything and everyone was. He smelled of the priest's incense. Who else could he be? He walked across the gardens, stepping through the carefully placed trees, and our rocks, and the ornamental lake; and he left a path in his wake, like a man raising mud when he fords a stream. The magic tore and shredded where he walked, leaving bare dirt and the shadow of the gatehouse overhead. The magic eddied and sealed the break a few steps behind him; but he carried the gash of reality with him, like a court train.

He walked straight through all our creatings, toward the house.

"No," I screamed, and ran out onto the veranda. "Leave him here!"

The old man walked forward. I ran to the room where my husband was, burst in to where he sat with an emissary from the capital and his secretary. "Husband! Run!"

"Wife—?" he said, but I felt the veranda beside me shiver and dissolve. I fell to my knees. Yoshifuji jumped up, his sword sheath in his hands. I clawed at the Kannon's robe as he passed me, locked my hands in his thick belt, until he was pulling me forward with him. He did not even slow.

"What are you—" my husband bellowed, as the man prodded him with the stick in his hand. Yoshifuji jumped backward, and pulled his sword free.

I screamed. The sword shivered into a handful of dirty straw. My husband looked at it in disgust and threw it on the ground. The man prodded him again, and Yoshifuji moved backward, through the house.

"Leave him, please leave him, they mean nothing to him, I love him—" I begged and prayed as the man dragged me through our house, out into the gardens. My hands bled from the hard edge of the belt. If nothing else around us was real, I knew this was, this hot blood in my palms. Yoshifuji kept turning back, trying to help me; but the man just jabbed at him again, and forced him stumbling away.

The belt was slick with blood; my fingers slipped and I fell behind the old man, in the dirt below the side gatehouse, beside one of the support posts. The Kannon gave my husband one more jab, and he crawled out from our home, and stood upright in his garden—the real one, the nonmagical one. I crawled after him, but I knew it was too late already. I lay by the side gate-house in my robes, blood on my hands, my long hair trailing on the ground.

It was still dusk there; three months since Yoshifuji had come to me; ten years in my fox world. Nearly all the men who had watched the carving ritual huddled in little clumps in the garden, talking among themselves. Yoshifuji staggered toward them. He was two things in my eyes, like something seen and distorted through water: handsome in his dress robes, a little dusty now, still carrying an empty sword sheath; and covered with filth, casual robes stained and torn, holding a little worm-eaten stick: a man who had lived in the dirt with foxes.

Shikujo's child was the first to see my husband looking around him.

"Father!" he shouted, and ran to Yoshifuji. "Is this you?"

"Son?" my husband said hesitantly. "Tadamaro?" I saw memory coming back to him; but the fox magic was strong enough to shape his understanding of things. "How have you not grown more while I was gone?"

Tadamaro threw his arms around the man. "Oh, Father, what has happened to you? You look so old!"

Yoshifuji looked at the boy in his arms. "It doesn't matter. Your mother is back? I was so desperate after she left, and she was gone so long. But I met a wonderful woman, and married her, and we have had a lovely little boy."

"You have *me*," the boy said, almost in tears. "I am your son."

"Yes," Yoshifuji said hesitantly. "But my other son—and my wife—I love them so."

The boy looked up at a darkened room of the house. I saw a form there, robes shifting softly, and I realized it was Shikujo, watching, too aware of the proprieties to come down to greet her husband in front of so many people. The boy straightened. "Where is this son of yours?"

"Why, over there," my husband said, pointing at the side gate-house.

They saw me then. "A fox!" one man shouted, and they all took up the cry: "A fox! A fox!" Men ran toward me and the gatehouse, carrying sticks and torches.

"Husband!" I screamed. "Stop them!"

He hesitated, obviously confused. "Wife?" he asked unsteadily.

"A fox!" the people yelled.

"Please!" I cried, and held out my arms to him. He stepped toward me; the boy threw himself into Yoshifuji's arms, over-balancing him.

I looked up at the house again, in the instant before the men caught up to me, and, for the first time, I saw her face clearly, where she stood on the veranda. I saw tears on her face, and I knew that she, alone of everyone here (save my lord), saw me for a woman.

They chased us, the men. They stuck their torches down so they could see under the gatehouse floor, and poked around with their sticks. My family fled in all directions. I tried to run to my son, but they hurled a torch at me, and then a stick, and my son, who was only half-grown, ran, shielded by his nurse's arm. I saw my grandfather struck in the side with a club; the black-and-white dog stood confused until a man hit it with a stick, and the dog ran off yelping.

The men followed me until I threw off even the seeming of my woman's body in blind panic. The pain drove me out of consciousness, but my fox's body ran anyway, on its bloody pads.

It was days later before I came back to my woman's shape.

BOOK FOUR: WINTER

Did you come here?

Did I go to you?

I don't even know —

Was it a dream? a reality?

Were we sleeping? were we awake?

—ARIWARA NO NARIHIRA (825–880)
TRANSLATED BY BURTON WATSON

1. SHIKUJO'S PILLOW BOOK
Means of healing a sick individual:

Curative fires.
We burn herbs as incense; usually the herbs are not pleasant to smell, and they give off thick smoke that makes one's eyes water. Sometimes they seem so foul as to raise even the dead; one in particular made the major domo retch when he attended my husband.

My husband has aged many years in the brief months he was gone. His hair is thinner and has gone gray. He would still be handsome (for a man a decade older) except that he appears to have starved himself since the end of summer, and his skin is pale and seamed with wrinkles. Even washing has not yet removed the inlaid grime from his hands and feet. I wish I could get him to eat a little watered rice, but he has not awakened since collapsing in the garden.

Steamed plantain leaves laid under one's sleeping mat. This is another unpleasant smell, though it reminds one more of peasants' cooking than dead matter. We tried this for only a short time. The wet leaves soaked his sleeping mat and robes and ruined the boxwood floor beneath. He tossed and sobbed in his sleep just as before, tangled in wet cloth.

Massages and hand-pressure. *Nademono* dolls: we have tried transferring his illness into them and then tossing the dolls into the stream. This required breaking the thin skin of ice that had formed there overnight.

The fever has not broken. I touch his forehead and it is as hot and dry as the charcoal on a brazier. He shivers and sweats. He weeps for his son and his wife and his home, but when Tadamaro or I speak to him, he twists his face away. If I did not have my own guesses about what happened, I would imagine he is mad, that he has spent the days and nights since summer's end eating beetles and dirt, singing to ground squirrels.

Moxas have been burned, pastilles made of dried *yomogi* leaves burned on his skin. I cannot watch this, for as they burn down they scorch his skin and raise blisters that break and weep tears of their own. My husband writhes as the healers apply the *moxas*. Sometimes servants are summoned to hold him down.

Other treatments are more benign: the holy man who tries the Goshin method for protecting the body and soul does no more than chant formulas and burn incense and make finger gestures.

It is cold and the snows visit the peaks these days, crawling each day farther down the mountainsides toward our valley. Despite this, they have all come to treat my husband: the holy men and *genza*-exorcists, the Buddhist priests and the yin-yang diviners, the Shinto priests, a Korean-style physiognomist, various local garden-variety herbalists and healers. They talk (and argue) about what might be ailing my husband. Is it possession? A mental sickness? *Tengu*-demons? A curse? They make various prescriptions, for rituals and pillars to be erected, for sutras to be read and gifts to be given. And still my husband shakes with fever. Hito sits with him most nights; on occasion I do, as well.

He babbles then about a wife who is not me, and a son who is not Tadamaro, and a house that is not this one. I feel a pang when I hear these things. Was I not enough? Was my son in some way inadequate? It all makes a story as strange as a fairy tale from Ise; and it is all a symptom of his madness (or possession, or illness), say the wise men. But I know differently.

I had feared the foxes, for good reasons of my own. And they stole him. And now he is back, but they have changed him. I am not afraid of them returning for him; Kannon has defeated them and they have no power against her. But still I am unsure as to what the end result of all this will be.

2. KITSUNE'S DIARY

I came back to myself suddenly, as if I had been sleeping and someone had thrown water over me. I was not there; suddenly I was, a shivering naked woman weeping and kneeling in a clearing on the ridge that overlooked Kaya no Yoshifuji's house. The sky was filled with heavy clouds.

My woman's skin was scratched in a thousand places, so that my body seemed marked with a calligraphy of blood, the wildly scribbled characters of a child or a master. The palms of my hands and soles of my feet were smeared with blood that had leaked from damaged fox-paws. My hair was tangled, its river of black clotted with snarls and twigs and dead leaves.

I was alone. My grandfather was gone. I thought he must be dead, for I did not see how he could have survived the blow or the heartbreaking pace of the escape from the gatehouse.

Shōnen was also gone. I called his name and looked around the clearing in a panic, but it had been days since I had become a fox, and I had run a long way. He was too young to have kept up with my mindless flight, and too young to have survived alone. The pain from the thought stole my breath, stabbed at me like a knife of stone; knowing it would be hopeless, I shouted his name until my voice grew hoarse. Now I cried in earnest. The tears were cold by the time they fell from my face to my breasts.

I could die, I thought. What would be the cost of this, if I stayed a woman, naked and alone in the mountains, far from warmth and light? It did not pain me to think of this. Kaya no Yoshifuji was gone, summoned to his other life; my child was gone; my grandfather, my brother, my mother — all gone. I could return to the oblivion I had found while I ran as a fox these past few days. The unaware self: humans strove for this, pursued it doggedly. Why should I not embrace it?

Or I could die. Either seemed acceptable. Either seemed too much work to pursue. So I knelt in the cold and cried.

The bushes rustled. I no longer had my fox sense of smell, and the air carried nothing I could recognize. *Wolves*, I thought. I was high enough in the mountains for them. It would simplify my decision; wolves would eat me, and I would be saved even the trouble of dying of exposure.

But it was not wolves. I heard a whine. For an instant I thought it might be my son, still alive somehow in fox-form. The bushes moved again, and the spotted dog crept out, belly close to the ground. He crawled close, tail pounding the earth, ears flat, mouth reaching for mine—the gesture of a dog looking for a pack mate or a master.

I knelt and wrapped my arms around his neck, burying my nose in his fur. His musky smell caught at the back of my throat and tightened my chest. I wondered if I would cry.

We fell asleep like that, in a nest of dead ferns. I curled up around my dog, his warm fur against my belly.

A cold space against my stomach awakened me. The spotted dog had arisen; now he stretched luxuriously, bowing deep. It was night. I had not changed back to a fox. I was still a woman, still naked. My family were still lost to me.

But at some point in my sleep, my body had made the decision for me, the decision to live. I realized suddenly that I was famished and freezing. The dew had been heavy; my skin gleamed with it in the crescent moon's light, seeping through a gap in the clouds. My breath puffed from me in little clouds that flared with moonlight before they dissolved. I couldn't stop shivering, sometimes so hard that my teeth clattered, making my jaw ache on top of everything else. The dog looked sidelong up at me from brown eyes and whined, which I took to express concern. (Dogs may be kin, but they are hardly close; I think perhaps humans understand them better than foxes do.)

Clothes or shelter—warmth, anyway—and then food. I looked around to get my bearings.

I was still in the clearing in which I had first found myself. The pines towered over me, aimed like arrows into the sky's heart. The slender moon drifted behind tree branches, so that in places its light lay hard as lacquer over everything, and in others it was shattered into splinters; in some places, there was no light at all. A gap in the trees showed me patches of the valley below: harvested fields showing a haze that might have been rice stalks or might have been ground fog: huts and houses huddled beneath thatching that dripped with dew; Kaya no Yoshifuji's house. I saw the thousand-year oak in his gardens and the clearing where the rabbit-god's moon-rock would be (though I could not see the rock); but there were no lights visible, for the heavy roofs concealed much of the buildings. Smoke eased upward from eave openings in his rooms. The sullen color of hammered iron, it moved slowly, pressed down by the heavy cold air.

The night was so still I could hear things across the valley. An owl cried a great way off, and some small thing screamed. Beside me, the spotted dog's light breathing was perfectly audible, as was the soft shuffling of his feet when he shifted weight and sat. Down in the valley, a dog barked fiercely, sounding the alarm against some nighttime creature. Where was my son tonight? Dead or dying.

Shivering seized me again; I gasped with the strength of it. Clothing. Where could I go, bare-skinned and alone and starving? Tears of self-pity thick as poison burned in my eyes.

We would go to the old man in the woods, the crazy old diviner. He was human: he would know what to do. And it was not so far from this clearing.

My traveling was different this time. When I had been a fox— cuddled in my pelt, on sturdy footpads—walking a stony path in the cold woods was of no matter. My eyes had been fox's eyes; it was a simple thing to see at night. And as a woman, it had been daylight when I came here before. I traveled in a litter accompanied by attendants. My feet had not actually touched earth, I realized: there had been a mat set down before I climbed from the litter.

But now my bare feet were numb from the icy ground of the path. I was glad of this; otherwise the scratches and bruises on the soles of my feet would have made it hard to walk. Even so, I limped.

The spotted dog paced beside me, tireless, absorbed in his own thoughts, whatever they were. When I stopped for breath, he stopped as well. I crouched beside him and pressed my hands against his belly, looking for warmth. After a bit, the cold drove me forward again.

Above the clouds, the moon set and the night became impenetrably black. I slid my feet along the ground one after the other, trying to follow the path by feel. The dog aided me; he walked ahead, and if I held my breath, I heard his light panting just in front of me. Following him with hands stretched out, I managed not to stumble too much.

I did not see the trees on either side of the path, and there was little enough to hear. But in some fashion I must have sensed their nearness, for I knew when I entered a clearing. I saw the dimmest glow ahead of me—brazier embers seen through the crack of an ill-fitting door cover. I had found him.

"Old man?" I said softly. My voice was hoarse, too loud in the muffled air. I still could not see my feet or the ground in front of me, but the dim light gave me courage to move more quickly. The dog trotted forward.

I was close to the door, which was no more than heavy oiled fabric, nailed to the broken lintel. I tipped it aside just enough to look in. The brazier was no more than embers, dull red light cracking through a darker shell of dead coals. I could see a man lying beneath an untidy heap of cotton robes and rags. I had been right; this was his clearing, his hut. I had found him. He would know what to do, where to go, how to get Yoshifuji back. And right now, he would have clothing and food. I could sleep by his fire and be warm again.

I stepped inside. Heat (or a lessening of the cold) washed over me. The dog hung back for a moment, following only when I ordered him to.

I touched the old man's shoulder and then shook it. He was dead, still warm beneath his covers. A gleam of eye showed beneath a half-closed lid. Age, or a cough, or Buddha: I did not know what would kill an old man.

Warmth and then food. I poked the charcoal in the brazier until it brightened a little; and I pulled the heap of robes from the old man's body and curled up in them (he was dead, he felt no cold); and I gnawed on half a rice ball I found fallen beside his hand. After watching the corpse warily for a time, the dog curled up beside me and dozed. A coal in the brazier split and sparks flickered upward; the dog sat up suddenly, watching the air intently. I followed his gaze, but saw nothing. "Are you there?" I asked the air, hoping the old man's ghost might have lingered. There was no answer, and the dog resettled himself. No one here could help me.

I fell asleep again, with a dead man and a dog for company.

I dreamt of my master, Kaya no Yoshifuji. We stood in a Chinese garden, where it was spring. Josei was in another part of the garden; I heard her voice giving orders for our dinner. Yoshifuji gave me a tiny orange, round as the moon but so small it nestled in my palm. "Every moon contains its own crescents," he said to me, and the orange broke into segments, little half-moons forming a flower in my hand.

Had I known I was dreaming, I would not have awakened.

"My lady."

I startled awake. I had thought I dreamt of Josei's voice, but it was truly her. She knelt before me on the dirt floor of the hut, arms full of silk. The dog sat beside her, grinning as dogs do.

"How did you find me?" I asked, rubbing grit from my eyes. Meaning: *how are you here, outside of the magic?*

She answered the question I asked, not the one I meant. "I have looked everywhere for you, lady. We all have. We've been so worried." Wrinkling her nose, she lifted the old man's robes from me. "I am sure this place is riddled with fleas, even in this cold."

"My son?" I asked her, my heart suddenly pounding. "Have you seen him?"

"I am so sorry. No. I don't see how he could have survived."

"I suppose not," I said dully.

She looked at me for a moment, as if gauging my mood. In silence she wrapped me in the robes she had brought, and slipped clogs on my feet, and twisted my tangled hair into a great unruly knot which she fastened at the back of my neck with a piece of silk tape. "Shall we go home?" she said gently.

I met her eyes. They were gentle, concerned, as they always

had been. But they were also *aware*. Somehow, she knew she was not real without me, and she had come to find me. I do not understand this, even now; but I followed her home.

The fox magic existed still; the house stood in its gardens beneath the gatehouse. Silent servants undressed and bathed me and untangled my hair with a teak comb. They brought me food in pretty little *hinoki*-cedar boxes and dressed me in clean padded silk the gold of chrysanthemums. Josei led me by the hand to my bed-enclosure and laid quilted bed robes over me.

I cried myself to sleep.

3. SHIKUJO'S PILLOW BOOK
There is no hope:

There is no hope of leaving, of course. Five nights ago, the first snow began falling. Leaving my husband's bedside, I stood on the veranda and watched in the torchlight: huge clumps like the tangles of silk pulled from a silkworm's cocoon or the feathers from a goose's breast. After a time, the snow put the torch out, and in the end I watched only with the light from the lamps in my husband's rooms, which touched the flakes into dull gold, like cinders flying on a foggy night. I could hear no noise from the garden or even the other buildings, and Onaga's voice behind me seemed muted. The air itself seemed silenced.

I have never seen such a thing. In the capital, snow is infrequent enough that we revel in its presence, treating it as a movable festival that changes date according to the gods' whim. We make snow mountains and gawk over silver basins of snow carried in from outside. We invite our friends over to watch the moon shine on the snow. We make snow people and assign them names and lineage and histories; when they melt, a handful of days later (if so long), we even mourn them and give mock funerals.

When I returned from the capital in the autumn, I overheard the local servants speaking of winter. They sounded grim, as if bracing themselves for some horrible thing. I laughed with

Onaga about this, the only laughter in this house of sadness and waiting: trust peasants to overreact about a handful of snow!

And then the snow began, and stopped and began again. By the time it ended, two days ago, the eave openings were nearly drifted shut, so that the air in our rooms was foul with the smoke from our fires. Before we could leave, we had to brush the thigh-deep snow off the veranda, to prevent it from falling into the house when we slid aside the wall-panels.

The garden has re-formed itself into unfamiliar shapes. The bushes are small mountains now; the walkways are gone altogether, buried first under pine needles brought to insulate the mosses, and then by the snow. I came out one morning from sitting with my husband and saw the gardeners covering the moss, and it seemed very odd. Why all this fussing to protect moss, when the forest is filled with moss that survives without such ministrations?

Certain trees are covered with wrappings of straw or tied together to protect their branches from gathering too much snow and collapsing; their shapes seem strange. Many trees are barren. Bare branches web the gray sky, and through them I can see things that were never visible from the veranda before: the fence on the mountain side of the garden, the ruined gateway, the base of the thousand-year oak, the moon-rock—or what used to be the moon-rock: now it is only another mound. The lakes are still open, dark stains against the overpowering white, but they are smaller than they used to be. I imagine they will freeze over completely soon enough.

I am told we are well prepared. *Ogi*-leaf snow blinds hang in our buildings. They keep out the blown snow, but since they don't do much to keep us warm, we usually leave them open if the snow allows. The kitchen storehouse and several outbuildings are stuffed full of roots and vegetables from the garden. Fish lie pickled, tightly packed as ladies in an ox-carriage, in barrels sent from the coast.

The servants from the capital are not happy to be here. They do not complain precisely (or rather, none of them complain directly except Onaga and one of the junior ladies, who cries

for the capital late at night when she thinks we are all asleep)
but there are a lot of ways even the best attendant can express
her feelings. Stitches are placed more carelessly than before:
after all (as my women say to one another in just-barely audible
voices), who is here to care? There have been a disproportionate
number of poems about the capital and longing for home, all
recited with failing voices.

The stable yard and the walkways are cleared of snow, but
the road beyond the gate has vanished completely. I am told (by
Onaga, who heard it from one of the women, who heard it from
someone in the kitchens, who heard it from a snowshoed peasant) that the path from the valley is drifted shut. There is little
for any of us to do except worry, and wait, and watch my husband burn in his fever.

When we lived back in the capital, there was a summer when
Onaga brought me a chunk of ice the cook had acquired from
a vendor. The ice was very clear, threaded with tiny lines, but
suspended inside was a small red and green snake, its black eyes
hard and bright as beads. I think perhaps I am that snake: frozen solid, waiting for something, anything, to break the cold
stillness.

Except that when the ice melted, the snake did not revive.

4. KITSUNE'S DIARY

I lived alone with my servants. If nothing else remained, this
did: the routine. Josei continued to boss my women about.
Rice continued to be cooked with fish or pickled *yamadori*-
pheasant and brought to me at regular intervals. The wicks of
the many lamps that illuminated the house periodically became
ragged and were trimmed. My writing instructor attended me
every day, his arms full of exemplary calligraphy.

It was colder than it had been. It had been autumn; now it
was winter. Snow sat heavily on my blue-tiled roofs. A stone-
ware jug broke when the water inside froze one night. My

women wore heavier robes, and sat close to braziers, tucking warmed stones against their feet.

For my part, I behaved as one grieving. I walked through the mountains calling for my son. As the days passed, I called less and instead sought some sign of his passing, a scrap of silk or a huddle of bones. My hope died, but I did not stop searching until Josei spoke with me and forced me to accept his loss.

I slept under Kaya no Yoshifuji's sleeping robes so that I could breathe his scent. My dreams of him were vivid. Waking from them and realizing they were only dreams was not quite as painful as not seeing him at all would have been.

Waking, I stalked through the silent rooms, twisting back and forth between anger and sadness. I bit my fingernails until they were bloody nubs: they grew back when I slept and I bit them again, the pain in my hands a sort of punishment — for what, I did not understand. I cried for my lost family, and screamed with anger, and tore the paper walls when I struck out at them.

I still had the moon-shaped fan I had stolen so long ago, before any of this had happened. I turned it over in my hands again and again. The words mocked me. They were poetry, and I could not understand them. Yoshifuji had written them and he was gone. In the language my calligraphy instructor taught me, a fan meant a reunion, but this one meant nothing. It was only sticks and paper and ink. It was a fragile thing, but I never quite crushed it in my hands, and it did not break when I threw it from me.

Anger and sadness, but when I was tired (which was often: I fed myself now, and the cold weather was draining), there was another feeling deep beneath those two. It said: *I can ask for death. What do I have to live for now?*

There was no Grandfather to give me advice, no son to protect, no Brother or Mother. And no Kaya no Yoshifuji. It was for him, or for him and me, that this magic had been formed. Without him, only the routine itself kept these things happening.

Writing classes continued, but I did not often write. Cold sunlight would slip through a crack in the blinds and fall on my

hands, and I would become entranced by the texture of my
ragged nails, the tiny multicolored flecks that made up their
matrix. I watched my hands rather than the ink drying on the
brush because at that moment, my nails were more important
to me than any poem I might write.

Is this possible? That the "perfect poem" is irrelevant compared to the hands that write it, compared to the process and
means of writing it? If this were so, then being human would
be the easiest thing imaginable, because I already knew that
lesson back when I was a fox—that it was the doing of a thing
that was important, that every goal is relevant only as it relates
to the doing of the thing.

After a time, I noticed that things were not staying the same.
Without my family, without Yoshifuji as the goal, it was hard
to maintain the house and the servants. I had an aloes-wood
table with three celadon bowls on it. Then there were two bowls
and then none, and then the table was gone.

I owned a silvered-bronze Chinese mirror that I had used
when I painted my eyebrows. I thought the perfect reflection
was growing dull and this worried me—Josei once said that a
mirror dims when the owner's soul is unclean—but it was not
the surface. The mirror itself was fading, dissolving like mist in
my hands. Perhaps (I thought, when life seemed particularly
grim) it meant I never had a soul.

The garden vanished under snow and then faded like ground
fog. The house was dissolving room by room; I didn't leave my
wing much, not wanting to know how far it had gone, this melt-
ing of my home. My servants were fewer now, and more silent
than before. Even Josei was quiet as she moved through her
duties.

I thought of leaving, stripping off the humanness one more
time and running in the woods again; but I found I could not,
though I did not know the reason. I could not be a fox, but I
was also not simply a woman.

5. SHIKUJO'S PILLOW BOOK
The fever broke:

The fever broke on the twelfth day after we found him. In truth, it broke a dozen times in those days, but never completely. He would suddenly be drenched in sweat, but a short time later he would grow hot again, and toss and babble.

None of the treatments worked (though many of the healers later claimed some limited credit for the recovery), and at last we were obliged to fall back on the oldest and simplest of treatments, laying cold damp cloths on him to cool his blood. He was gaunt as a peasant in a bad year, and he turned his face away from the water we tried to drip into his mouth.

Hito had gone to pray for his master, so I watched over my husband alone. Perhaps I should have been praying as well. Instead, I watched by a single light. I cried steadily, like snow on a roof in the twelfth month. I would not have thought so many tears could exist, would have thought they would have bleached the floor beneath me white.

From time to time, I heard soft footsteps and a screen sliding behind me; I felt the pressure of eyes and whispers. I did not turn to look, only with shaking hands kept to my task: wet the cloth in a silver basin and wring it out, lay it on his hot neck, take it away and do it all again — the perfect wife keeping vigil in the dangerous hours of the night.

I have a secret. I thought he was dying, and I shook and cried, but in fact I felt nothing. It was not grief or fear that made me cry, but the shock that stuns an injured child; shock that made me shake.

And not even this is the truth. I thought he was dying, and I shook and cried — and I felt much. But it was rage — absolute hot rage. How dare he do this? How dare he hurt us — myself, our child, even his servants who cared for him — for so stupid a reason, to grub in the dirt with foxes? Perhaps he *should* die, perhaps he owed it to all of us, to leave this life and start over again somewhere else, where I and this household would not be hurt by him. But then he would be gone, and I would never even be able to face him, force him to recognize how he had hurt us all.

As if I would. I have never confronted him over anything he has done. Should I have? Would things have been different? Perhaps, but karma is like the patterns of a formal dance or a familiar song. No variation is possible, and the highest ideal is to move through the measures correctly. I thought I moved gracefully through our life together — no unpleasant jarring actions, no ugliness.

But perhaps there is something more correct even than elegance. My father owns a set of *sake* cups, a treasure that has been in his family for a thousand years (or so he says). They are hand-formed of rough pottery randomly splashed with black and green and silver. There is nothing delicate, nothing elegant, about them. But there is something beautiful and strong about their irregular shapes and their coloring, like leaves under moonlight. As a child, I liked them better than the facile perfection of porcelain. "They are honest," my father said then. "They do not break when you drink wine."

Perhaps honesty could be stronger, more beautiful than elegance and correctness.

My husband suddenly sat upright in sweat- and water-soaked robes, and said, "Where are you, wife?"

"I am here," I said, though I was afraid I might not be the one he called for.

He smiled, but his eyes were blind. He said: "The tiles were the color of the sky — but were they tile or sky?"

Perhaps it was a poem. There was no way of telling.

After this, the fever broke.

6. THE NOTEBOOK OF KAYA NO YOSHIFUJI

I am weak, but I find I cannot sleep. I do not have the strength to grind my own ink, but Hito has brushed the dust from my ink stone and mixed some for me. This brush, slim as it is, is almost too heavy to lift.

I was awakened tonight by a scratching noise. For half a month (I am told) I have slept through storms and ritual gongs and shouting and running feet; I have awakened only to eat and drink and relieve myself, and even these required assistance for many days. It is just past the full moon tonight, and the light seeping through the eaves is very bright to my sickness-altered eyes. An immense spiderweb shivers: my spider must still be here, which surprises me until I remember that for me it was ten years; for her, a single season.

Where are the spider's young? Grown and gone, dead or sleeping out the winter. I see no spiders here, but it is a big space, and spiders are small.

The scratching noise comes again, and the web quakes. The vibration seems to radiate from one corner, too massive and violent to be an insect. A tiny shape no bigger than my thumb skitters along one beam. A mouse came down from the thatch and disturbed the web in passing.

The spider does not emerge from whatever hiding place she calls home, which is perhaps as well. Some prey cannot be kept, and is best allowed to leave.

I miss her, my pretty fox wife.

7. KITSUNE'S DIARY

It was dawn, and I was hungry.

I hunted in the woods, but it grew dangerous there as the prey animals grew scarcer with the colder weather, and the predators, the wolves and *tanuki*-badgers, came questing for food. More often I hunted in the garden my husband shared with Shikujo.

I cannot tell you whether I was fox or woman as I hunted. At times it seemed that I pounced and trapped prey between front paws, tearing with fox-teeth; other times, I think I crouched and grabbed with cold hands, and stabbed with a little knife of bone no longer than a finger. Perhaps the world itself did not know which I was, only knew that I killed an animal and therefore delivered the corpse to me.

Many of the trees and shrubs had shed their leaves, and I moved through the skeleton of a garden with little shelter. The cranes and loons that had lived on the lakes were gone. The only animals I saw were two crows on a roof peak, speaking to each other. The screens were all shut tight against the cold. Early as it was, a pair of servants trotted along a walkway, heads low against the wind, sheltering whatever they carried in their hands.

There was not much to eat. The insects were gone, and all the young foolish animals that had fallen to my brother and me in the summer were dead or grown now: beyond my reach in either case. It had been a good year and the mice in the garden were fat, but mostly they slept in their holes, heads filled with the dreams that take a winter to complete.

So: it was dawn, and I was hungry. I walked across a patch of lawn blown nearly free of snow; the crisp dead grass numbed my toes. The air was cold and perfectly still, so that I felt as though I pushed through ice or the heart of a jewel. It was so silent that I heard my breathing, and then wings high overhead and the thick liquid splashes of two geese landing in the nearest pond, late for their migration. Everyone moved in pairs, it seemed, but me. It was too cold to smell much, though cedar and pine seem always to filter through, no matter how cold it is.

There was another noise, a half-familiar wet grinding. The scent came just as I identified the sound: a rabbit eating grass in the dawn.

I moved carefully, willing my heart not to pound too loudly.

She was full-grown, a female with gray and white fur, not a half-dozen paces from me. She had moved from cover to the patch of exposed grass. She was a long way from the moon-rock and safety. I could catch and kill her. I would not be hungry.

Cats hunt by creeping close to a thing and then lunging across at it. Mostly dogs rely on surprise; they yell at their prey, hoping to startle it for the moment it takes their legs to close the distance. With foxes it is different: we stand tall and leap across a distance several times a man's height, an arc calculated to trap our prey between our paws.

A woman has all these options, though she does not leap so far as a fox, or shout so loudly as a dog. Or walk so quietly as a cat, I am afraid. I eased forward: a step. The rabbit's back was turned. It was probably deafening itself with the crunching noise of its eating. Another step. I was so hungry.

The rabbit heard me and lifted its head. I froze as it looked around. One liquid black eye watched for a moment and then the rabbit returned to chewing. I stepped again, and again. Its head came up again. We stared at each other: the killing stare.

I did not blink.

The gasp behind me might as well have been a shout. I cried out and whirled and the rabbit bolted, all at once. Shikujo stood on a walkway leading from my husband's rooms, dressed in padded sleeping robes, a porcelain basin in her hands. She was so close that I saw the individual strands of hair that had fallen across her face, and her eyes, flat with something that might have been fury or fear.

"You have not gone," she said. Her voice was calm, as though she were commenting on a painter's style, but her hands shook.

Humans so often speak the unnecessary: I was free of this, at least. I gathered my robes close and looked at her in silence.

"The servants said you were still here," she said in the same conversational tone. "They're leaving, the ones who have family here in the valley. They say the house is cursed. Are we?"

I said nothing. I knew I had not cursed them, but she was not really asking me, after all.

"Go away," she said, and her voice began to shake. "Haven't you done enough?"

"I have done nothing but love him," I said. "And now you have him, our husband. You've won."

"Did I?" She laughed bitterly. "He is old and broken now; he does no more than sleep and cry."

"He did not seem old to me," I whispered. "I loved him."

"Love?" she hissed. "What do you know of this? You have no soul, you foxes. Love is pain and patience and suffering."

"I thought love was laughter and companionship," I said. "But if it is also pain, then yes, I know of it."

"It is both," she admitted. Tears fell on her face. "Leave us alone. Haven't you hurt us enough, all of you?"

"It's more than me, isn't it?" I said slowly. "You were my grandfather's reason for humanity, all those years ago."

"No!" Shikujo hurled the basin at me. It hit the hard ground and broke into a thousand pieces: flowers and leaves shattered into random shapes of blue and green.

"Did you love him, my grandfather?" I asked.

"No," she whispered, her anger (or was it fear?) evaporated. "There was no one there. It was all a dream, that's all. Like this one."

"This is real," I snarled. "As real as anything can be. I am real. Unless you prefer to lie to yourself."

But she wasn't listening to me. She examined her fingers, breathed carefully, as if she were afraid she might break. "He was gone so much, my husband. And the man who told me the poem—he was no fox! He was polite, charming, quite respect-ful. He can't have been—I didn't know who he was, or what he was, only that he wanted me so."

"As I wanted your husband. I loved him, and bore his child, and now Yoshifuji is gone and my son is dead, and you have both husband and son." I paused, thinking. "Wife of Kaya no Yoshifuji, what color are your son's eyes?"

"He's normal." She ground the words out. "He is my hus-band's son."

It was a lie; I knew this. Her child's eyes would have gold in their depths.

After a moment, she went on: "He had no heart." This was not her son or her husband; I knew this, too.

"How do you know what heart we have?" I said softly. "I am his granddaughter, and I know this: that he loved you."

"He had no soul! None of you do."

"My lady?" Hito walked from the dark doorway behind Shikujo. "Are you speaking to someone out here?" He peered out at me, but saw nothing.

She lifted a sleeve and turned her face away from him, and met my eyes. Fox wife and human wife. "No one," Shikujo said. "My own fears. Do you see the fox in the yard?"

He squinted. "It is beside the potted pine?"

She hesitated, and I closed my eyes, waiting for my sentence. I wanted to live, but at this moment I had no strength to fight for my life. She would order him to kill me, and I could not run this time.

"Please have the servants drive it off," Shikujo said.

8. SHIKUJO'S PILLOW BOOK
Even now:

*E*ven now, after all this, we are haunted by foxes.

This morning while watching my husband, I dropped into sleep and immediately dreamt. It was of foxes, of course — or one fox, anyway. In the dream, we spoke to each other, but when I try to remember our words, they slip away to hover just beyond reach, like dragonflies or someone else's cats. I remember only the feelings the dream caused: fear and anger, sadness and dread.

It was a dream, of course. I awoke from sleep, and found myself walking on my husband's veranda, having dropped the basin I carried.

We will never be free of them. There will always be dreams

and visions and night-fears about the foxes, because even if we never saw a fox again, even if our son grew old in a world that had not seen a fox in a hundred years, the foxes have marked us, stained my family and me and changed us from what we were. This cannot be a good thing.

I want to storm back to my husband's rooms and shake him awake to tell him that he has ruined us all with his self-indulgent dreams. I want to scream and weep and shout and sob. But he is still not well; he is too weak for such honesty. To protect him I spill my anger and my fear here, ink on paper.

But this is not honest, either. If I were to rage and throw things and cry until my nose ran and my eyelashes grew sticky with tears, the stress on him might cause a relapse. The fever could return and he might run naked into the woods and die in the snow, mated to a tree-*kami* or a mouse. But that is unlikely. What seems more likely to me is that he would look at his hurt, angry, flawed wife and he would despise her. And I would despise myself. Crying and throwing things is not how a beautiful or a wise or a strong person behaves, however honest it might be.

The *sake* cups of my father are strong and beautiful and honest, all at once. My husband was honest but not strong, and I was beautiful but not honest. What was the fox woman?

9. KITSUNE'S DIARY

I did not wait for the servants but ran immediately. This was not the mindless fox-footed panic of my escape when my life had come apart. Now I ran consciously, down through the garden, past the thousand-year oak's clearing and the three lakes. The cold air scraped at my throat as I ran, escaped in puffs of breath like steam. I tucked up my robes and climbed over the snow-covered timber of the (still ruined) formal gate at the garden's lower end.

On the other side, I paused for a moment to catch my breath. There were no servants after me. The rice fields were nearly empty—water and rice gone, leaving only snow and stubble. I saw no one but a handful of peasants, indigo-bright in their quilted hemp, cutting bare stalks still standing in one field. They paused to watch me, but they seemed to think there was nothing unusual in the sight of a woman in ragged silk robes climbing over a collapsed gate—if that is what they saw.

She had not ordered me killed. This might have been an act of kindness, or a triumphant gesture—see, she had my husband, she could afford generosity!—or the heartsickness of a woman too tired to kill, even for a reason. I did not know.

I had been living in a haze, as if fevered, as if gossamer hung between me and the world. Perhaps it was the confrontation or the reprieve or the run (though I had run often enough before this, hunting prey); but the veil seemed gone, shredded into threads that blew away and left me bare to the world.

I will steal him back, I thought. I would find Kannon, and tell her she was mistaken to take him from me, that as goddess of mercy, she must know I deserved Yoshifuji's love.

I had no idea where I might find Kannon. In the fox-magic world there had been shrines to Kannon. I had even visited one, with a white-graveled courtyard and a wide staircase that led under the eaves. On each side of the stairs had been a tree in a huge square ceramic pot. The trees, a dogwood and a cherry, were thick with prayer flags, but I had never looked at the slips of mulberry paper tied into the trees, reluctant to see how shallow (or deep) the magic ran. Now I wished I had: perhaps the fox-magic world (which seemed so isolated, the four of us foxes and Yoshifuji) was larger than I had imagined. Perhaps the prayer flags came from others—foxes or ghosts or spirits—who somehow shared the myth that we might be able to convince ourselves that we were in fact human.

But I had never seen them, these hypothetical people. I knew only silent perfect servants and contented peasants, occasional anonymous crowds of nobles arriving for celebrations and funerals. And now my world slipped away. I did not even know if my husband's rooms still existed. There seemed little hope for a fox-magic shrine that had been half a day's journey away. And

I dreaded going back into the magic to look for it, afraid to see
the decaying limits of my world.

A single snowflake fell on my face, stinging for an instant
before it melted. Another fell and dissolved, and another. The
shoulders of my robes were spangled with them, tiny as fleas.
The peasants noticed the snow, as well: with curt cries, they left
their task and ran back to a thatched-roof hut. They did not
look at me. Perhaps they had not seen a noblewoman in silks,
after all. I tried not to think about this, but shivered, perhaps
from the cold.

What about out here, in the world I had *not* made? Kannon
was a goddess; her shrines were everywhere. There was one in
the mountains above Yoshifuji's estate; I had never been there,
but I had heard Shikujo speak of it. Back in the summer, Yoshifuji had traveled to another on the coast many weeks away. But
was Kannon there, at one or the other or both, or at yet another
shrine of which I had never heard?

I had never seen a god, except when the humans summoned
one. The priests called the Buddha, and he (or something that
had answered when he was called) came. I had fooled him, then.
The priests summoned Kannon, and she came as an old man, to
steal Kaya no Yoshifuji away from me and scatter my family.
Perhaps that was the way of gods, that they came when called,
like dogs or servants. It seemed unlikely, but I was cold and
wet and alone, with no idea how else to find her.

"Goddess?" I said aloud to the air. My voice sounded dead
in my ears, muted by the falling snow. I waited a moment, then
spoke louder. "Kannon? Will you speak with me?"

The spotted dog must have been prowling nearby in the tall
grasses by the road; he heard my voice, and barking, galloped
up to dance beside me, leaving wet dirty pawprints on my robes.
Even through my disappointment, I felt myself smile. Perhaps
only dogs truly came when called.

Very well, then, I thought. *I will go to the shrine in the mountains.
In the real world.*

10. THE NOTEBOOK OF KAYA NO YOSHIFUJI

My son Kaya no Tadamaro visits me today. When Hito allows him into my rooms, the boy gallops up to dance beside me, eager as a puppy. His nurse makes the hushing noises universal to such women and he settles down, bowing formally and then kneeling beside my bed.

"I am glad to see you looking well, Father."

I smile weakly. This is obviously something his nurse told him to say, for it's clear from the boy's face that he thinks I look anything but well. Still, it is courteous: the boy is growing into a polite man. "It's good to see you, child. Have you been keeping busy?"

"I watched the peasants cut ice yesterday. They use saws and cut the river-ice into big blocks. They told Nurse that they are going to send the blocks down the river in the spring and make their fortunes. And I followed some rabbit tracks, and I—"

"Have you managed to fit any studying into your busy schedule?"

He makes a face. "Yes, sir. I am supposed to be memorizing the *Analects*."

"Mmmm," I say noncommittally. I remember this task from my own childhood, and I recall liking it as little as he seems to.

The nurse clears her throat (I can read the meanings of her throat-clearings: this one means *Aren't you forgetting something?*) and Tadamaro wriggles a little. "I wrote you a poem, Father." He pulls something from his sleeve and hands it to me. It is a sheet of thick white paper, tied with bright red cotton cord. A tuft of cedar needles is tucked into the ribbon. I unroll the little scroll and read, in careful calligraphy:

> *The rivers and lakes are covered in ice,*
> *I will lend you my sleeve to keep you warm.*

> *I hope you grow well and happy again, esteemed sir.*

I carefully roll the letter and tie it up again, fumbling a bit because of the tears in my eyes. "Thank you, Tadamaro. I will write a response later, and send it to you."

"A letter!" He hops to his feet and hugs his nurse. "A real letter!" She clears her throat again (this one says, *Sit down, young man, right this instant*), but I say, "No, let him poke around a bit. Boys do not sit still for long."

She sniffs (*Very well, but don't blame me if he bothers you*) then moves to be near him, for he has picked up a fire-tong and pokes at the brazier's contents. He tries to stack the coals into a pyramid, but they tumble down with the soft scratchy noise of charcoal rubbing together, releasing a wave of heat.

A strange poem for a child. It is absurd to think of a child lending his sleeve to keep his elder warm. It is the business of children to grow big enough to do this effectively, when their parents are old and feeble, but Tadamaro is still far too young for such responsibility. Still, before I went to my fox wife's house, I did expect certain things of him, things as absurd as warmth from a scrap of fabric. I wanted him to be happy and strong and wise, not for his own sake, but because then I might find peace with the fact that I felt I was none of those things. Life seemed meaningless: one lives, one writes poetry, one learns a series of sad or tedious or painful lessons, and finally one dies, after which one either starts over, goes to a not-terribly-interesting Paradise, waits for attention from one's descendants (who are busy with their own meaningless lives), or is obliterated, depending on which religion is right about death.

Tadamaro might not have to learn those lessons, I think. *Tadamaro might succeed where I have failed.* But the thing I forget is that Tadamaro's life, good or bad, filled with disappointment or joy, is his own to live. A small boy should not have to carry the burden of mine, as well.

Tadamaro has stopped playing with the fire; now he walks along one wall, bent over to look at the floor. He seems to have forgotten my presence, though it may also be that he does not feel he must be on his best behavior here.

My fox wife had a son. We did the same things together that

Tadamaro and I have done. I watched Shōnen and laughed, delighted to see him discover his world. But I never brooded over him as I had Tadamaro, pining for lost joy. My joy seemed to come from inside myself then.

"Father, look." Tadamaro walks carefully toward my bed, his hands cupped around some secret he does not wish to lose. He carefully kneels. I peer into the shadows between his fingers, but I see nothing until he spreads his hands wide.

The cold has finally killed my spider. She lies on his palm, a tangle of legs and a pale husk of a body, so light that the breeze slipping through a crack rocks her back and forth on my son's open hand. We look at her together, my son and I.

I did not allow anyone to harm her and she built a web as soft and bright as silk, with patterns as fine as lacquerwork. She lived and bore young and died. It was a good life, I think.

Later that night, I write my response to my son's poem:

> *With your sleeve you brush away the snow.*
> *The lake still flowed beneath the ice,*
> *But now it can see out again!*

> *I will grow stronger.*

11. KITSUNE'S DIARY

I found Josei writing when I returned to the fox-magic house. She knelt at a low table, her brush moving quickly down milkweed-colored paper bound into a notebook. When she saw me, she dropped the brush and stood, running across the room to me. "My lady, you look disturbed. Are you well?"

"Yes—no," I answered, distracted for a moment. "What are you writing, Josei?"

She blushed. "It is nothing, a poem of no great skill."

"You write *poetry?*"

"That is not important, my lady. You are upset?"

I took her hands in mine. "I am leaving, Josei."

She gasped. "But you have just returned! You should not leave so quickly again: it is too dangerous. You do not know what you will find, or —"

"Josei." I knelt, pulling her down by our linked hands onto the bare floor. There was very little left in this room: the low table, a single large chest and a plain iron brazier. "I know. But even though it was dangerous, you came after me when I was in the woods, didn't you?"

She averted her face. "That was quite different, my lady. You were lost, and I knew I must find you."

"This is not different. We need Kaya no Yoshifuji." Not wanting to disrupt whatever kept her real, I did not say more, that without him our lives dissolved, that I did not know where it would end. "He is my husband. I am going to find Kannon and explain to her why she must give him back to me."

"I do not think the shrine still . . ." Josei's voice trailed off.

"I'm going to the shrine in the mountains," I said. "Outside." I pulled free of her hands and stood, brushing dust from my robes. There had never been dust in my house when the magic had been strong. "I do not know how long it will take, Josei."

"You will need food and clothing. Clogs," she said automatically as she stood. "But, my lady —" and her eyes filled suddenly with tears "— please do not do this. There are too many things — *outside* — that can hurt you. There are animals, or you might slip and fall, or be caught in a snowstorm and freeze, or —"

"I must," I said.

In silence she replaced my silks with quilted robes and an oiled cloak. She pulled my hair into a single long tail and tucked it into my collar, and placed a broad plaited-straw hat on my head, tying its tapes under my chin. These were simpler clothes than I was used to, traveler's clothes.

Josei whispered, "What will happen to me without you? To this?" She gestured at the room.

I touched her face; her tears were cold as rain. "Someone must watch this house while I am gone. Please wait for me." I was afraid the house would fade away if no one remained, but my real fear was that she might dissolve. I could not bear to watch that.

"I do not think I can —" Her lips trembled.

"You *must*." The fox-magic ball was tucked in my sleeve, as it always was. I slipped it free and laid it in her hand, where it glowed like a tiny moon.

"But —"

I laid her other hand over it. "Keep it for me until I return, Josei. *Wait*. Please."

She was silent for a time. "I will try."

My cheeks were also cold with tears when I stepped into my wood clogs and down onto the walkway. Josei clung to a pillar on the veranda. The house and the pillar seemed half-lost in fog; I hoped it was fog, though the air was clear and icy cold. As I left, she called something out after me, but I could not hear it as I slipped from the fox magic to the real world. It might have been a poem.

It was midmorning when I began my journey. Snow still fell as it had since I left Shikujo, but it was very light, made of tiny flakes that stung when they touched my bare skin. I followed the path that led past the ruined gate up into the mountains. It was not wide, since no one used it much in the winter, but peasants had beaten it down with snowshoes until it formed a single narrow track between tall banks of snow. The spotted dog trotted ahead of me, ears pricked to catch sounds under the snow.

I saw only one person, a peasant man wearing a straw hat and cape. For some reason, he led a black bull along the path toward me, tugging at a braided rope tied to its nose ring. I watched them approach. My dog barked twice at them, then dropped to his belly beside me. My feet were very cold, so I inched closer, trying to warm my toes in his fur. The man paused when they were a few steps away. There was no room to pass: one of us would have to leave the path.

"Well?" the peasant said, not unkindly. The bull's black shoulders were spangled with snow like stars. Fog puffed from its nostrils. Even the dog seemed cowed by the animal's size, but the bull seemed uninterested in any of us. It might have been a Buddha centered on nothingness; or it might have been focused on the passing moments of its life: *mate, eat, stand in snow.* Not so different, perhaps: nothing and everything.

I asked the man, "I am told there is a shrine to Kannon along this path. Do you know where it is?"

The man spat. "You've picked a bad time for a pilgrimage. Small snowflakes means a cold night, cold enough to freeze the tears in your eyes. And you won't make it to the shrine before nightfall."

"Do you know how to get there?" I asked.

"Yes. Not that I've ever been. There's a split in the path, by a stone-*kami.* Leave an offering and then take the upper path and listen for the sound of running water. There's a waterfall that never freezes up there."

"Is it far?" I asked.

"Farther than you'll get." He looked more closely at me. "Perhaps you would want to stay the night with my wife and me? It's warm at least, and the weather might be better tomorrow. Though I doubt it."

"You are kind, but I have to go now."

"Huh. Pilgrimages," he said. "Well, I suppose you wouldn't achieve any merit if it were easy. Good luck, then. If you find nowhere to stay tonight, dig a cave under the snow and cuddle up with pine boughs. That might keep you alive."

He stepped aside and heaved on the rope until the bull finally shifted and stepped belly-deep into the snow. "Good luck," he said again as we passed. It wasn't until much later that I realized I had no idea what exactly the peasant had seen when he looked at me.

The path was easier for a while, since the bull had trampled it nicely. It wandered toward the fold between two mountains, with occasional side trails that threaded toward farmhouses. The closer I came to the forest that cloaked the mountains, the fainter the path grew, until it was just a roughened area showing the dim outlines of snowshoes. The dog did not like that very much: he had trouble breaking a path and so he fell in behind me. The quilted robes and the cloak kept me warm for a time, but a wind started up and then the cold drilled though me, chilling my bones. The tiny flakes slashed at my face and hands. My nose ran steadily. When I touched my face, it felt cold and smooth, as if carved of jade. My feet were numb in their wooden clogs, past hurting.

We walked up and up. I held my arms close, hands tucked into my sleeves. The wind caught at my oversized straw hat and pulled it from my head, but I couldn't untangle my numb hands fast enough to catch it before it blew out of reach. The snow was too deep to follow. After that, strands of hair pulled free and blew across my face, stinging my eyes.

Up and up. The forest reached down the mountain flanks with long fingers and the path met them and slipped under the evergreens. The wind abruptly stopped, though the air still felt charged with its energy, and the treetops hissed overhead. The snow was only knee-deep under the trees and the ground was even bare in places, exposing the fallen tree bark and needles under my clogs. It was hard to see a trail, so instead I watched the snow for the slight depression caused by the path. In gaps between the trees I could see the sky. Beneath the holes were chest-high mounds of snow as fine as rice flour.

I carried a rustic basket over one arm, the uncut ends of the reeds making a sort of fringe. Inside were all the possessions I had left: the worn summer fan, and a piece of dried fish, and rice pounded into cakes. The house might well be gone by now: I could not know. I thought of Josei and my eyes filled with tears which froze in my eyelashes.

I was colder than I had ever been. The air bit at my face and lungs, and I longed for the hat, which would at least have captured some tiny bit of the warmth from my breath. I watched the spotted dog trot ahead of me, and envied him his thick fur, his leathery paw pads, his lack of awareness—everything. I could not change to a fox myself, but neither was I truly human. I did not know *what* I was, and changing would not make this clearer.

The trail climbed up and up. The snow was getting deeper, as if by climbing I entered a new land. I had to wade through it, and it piled up against my knees as I kicked through. I cut a branch from a *hinoki*-cedar and stripped the smaller branches. I could lean against it, and help break up the snow ahead of me.

Scrambling around a fallen tree, I slipped and fell to my hands and knees, the great river of my hair falling forward over my shoulder in front of me, a great filthy tangled twist. I was so tired that the hair seemed too heavy to lift, snarled with scraps of twig.

Kaya no Yoshifuji had loved my hair: he used to plunge his hands into it, feel it slide like silk past his fingers. He buried his face in it, tickled my breasts with its ends after sex. But now — I pulled free the little bone knife and hacked until the hank fell free, and my hair hung no lower than my jawline. The spotted dog sniffed the discarded hair and whined.

I stood and we walked on. It was gloomy under the trees. I had seen no shelter since a hut down in the valley, half a day ago. This was the land of trappers and bear hunters and madmen and visionaries: no one truly lived here but animals. Very well, I was an animal, or had been. I would survive.

Things changed as I walked. My quilted silks became cottons without my noticing the change. The robes were shorter, darker: peasant clothes. Why was this happening?

The stone-*kami* was obvious: a fat black rock as tall as a man, solidly in my path. Someone ancient had carved a face into the rock. It stared blankly ahead, with snow drifted about the dead ferns at its base. There were no fresh offerings for this god, only faded ragged scraps of fabric that might once have contained gifts. I bowed. "Spirit?" No one answered, but I left my piece of fish and a rice ball. When I took the higher path, the spotted dog vanished for a moment and returned licking his lips. A *kami* can look after its own things; if it chose to let a dog eat its offerings, there was nothing I could do about it.

Someone had marked the path by writing words in bright red paint on large stones beside it. The calligraphy was bold, great splashings of crimson paint, but the characters were fading, sometimes half-hidden under dead leaves and snow. The stones made no sense, a random assortment of unrelated words. *Wave's crest. Memory. Heart. Turning. Silver.* Were they a poem? Or was each stone a poem, a stone/paint/word that would mean something altogether different if the character had been written on another stone, or with black ink or a finer brush?

Poetry. The dog didn't notice, only lifted his leg against one of the poem stones, which changed that poem (if poem it was) to one of stone/paint/word/urine.

Parsley. Knife. Tears. Moon.

It grew darker.

Correctness.

12. SHIKUJO'S PILLOW BOOK
If we were in the capital:

If we were in the capital, we would all be talking about the Gosechi dancers. There might be snow on the ground there, but it would be the pretty dusting we are used to, and the air would be delightfully cool, instead of this icy cold that keeps me trapped in my rooms, unwilling even to walk to my husband's wing. There would be crowds everywhere in the palace as we all prepared for the *daijōsai* thanksgiving rituals. There would be ceremonies to placate the spirits, and banquets and games and singing and drinking. I look back and there were years when I served the old princess that I do not recall sleeping at all, from the end of the tenth month right through to the final banquet.

It is pleasant to remember this activity at a time when we can never seem to get warm. My women and I huddle together in the innermost of my rooms. We have gathered every lantern and brazier we can find, but the cold air still creeps in through the thin walls and the eaves. Lately we have taken to sitting under quilts. The women tell stories and bicker with the ease of people who have spent too much time together without a rest.

I always loved to watch the Gosechi dancers as they entered

the palace. The girls themselves were so solemn in white, but their attendants were often charming, dressed in matching robes of green-printed white, or blue, or brown and green, or whatever whim their sponsors were indulging that year. But it was when they danced that I truly loved them.

It has been years since I attended the banquet at which they dance, and only now do I realize something. I always thought the goal of the Gosechi dancers was to be correct in all things. It is necessary to perform the steps precisely; necessary to demonstrate the correct restraint in one's movements, the proper flicking of fan or hand: necessary to wear the correct robes and cords and headdresses for a given dance.

But more than this is required. There is passion, and this shines through even the careful movements of the best Gosechi dancers. One cannot point to the difference between this girl and that one, when both have practiced hard and are elegant and graceful. But one is merely pleasant to watch and the other catches the eye and sets fire to the heart. I know when I watch such a girl that, of all the dancers, her prayer will be best heard by the gods.

Correctness and passion. I must remember this. Kaya no Yoshifuji, all passion and no correctness, has perhaps failed. But have I been better? If I were one of the Gosechi dancers, I would not humiliate myself by performing badly in front of the court, but I think that the gods might not listen to me.

13. THE NOTEBOOK OF KAYA NO YOSHIFUJI

My mind wrestles with the contradictions of the past time. Sometimes it gives up in exhaustion. It has been a season: it has been a decade. I am young: I am old. I live here: I live in a house with blue-tiled roofs which is actually the space beneath an outbuilding. I am married to Shikujo; I am wed to my gold-eyed wife, who may be human or may be a fox. I have a son. I have two.

Urushima must have felt like this when he returned from the sea-princess's court and found that many years had passed in what was only a night for him. My mind wrestles and rejects what it cannot understand. I find I forget too much.

I look back and I remember her, in a dress painted with tiny monkeys, her smooth forehead crinkled as she asked me about souls. I see the ball in her hand, the ink splashed on the walls and floor, the stone lantern in the garden that glowed at night without ever being lit. And — what I never saw when I was there and she was my wife — I see the darkness under the gatehouse and smell the filth and my own rank stink trapped in my grimy robes. I remember kissing a fox's mouth.

Fox or woman, her eyes were made of light. I had always thought (if I thought of it at all) that the eyes of foxes would be the same liquid brown as a dog's eyes. But they are not. They are gold, and one can see inside them, to the pattern of lines that hides inside. Foxes don't have souls? This is not true: I have seen it.

I have been listening to a priest read the sutras. He remained here, perhaps understandably preferring our house to his cold monastery. I am sick and weak, and so I listen; but he speaks so quickly and in such a monotone that it becomes mere noise, like wind in trees, or the susurrus of crickets at dusk in summer.

Why was I there, with my fox wife? I know all the reasons: she seemed as free as the fox she was; her lovely house and gardens and perfect servants made every day I spent there an experience out of the tales that women read, too like a fable to be true. (And so it was: the world seemed perfect to me, because I expect it was created for me.)

No, the surroundings were not the interesting part of my life with my fox wife. I wanted to feel alive again, and that had nothing to do with her perfect world, and everything to do with the adventure of being with her. Life is better lived as an adventure than as a work of art, I think.

I felt better about myself when I was with her because for a time I forgot the hopelessness that drove me. She had no ex-pectations of me (except that I be there). I never disappointed her, because she was surprised and delighted by everything, and I never disappointed myself, because I was willing to be what I was. Despite the perfect world we lived in, there was a lot of space for errors in my life there.

Would it have changed things between us if Shikujo had been less perfect, if life with her had remained the adventure it began? I think perhaps she never made such claims of perfection, that I'm the one who thought she was perfect, and resented her for it. She was what was expected of her; perhaps this chafed her as much as my own expectation did me. I did not think to ask her.

I think I wouldn't have seen my fox wife's illusion if I hadn't wanted it so much. That was a world where no one aged. My fox wife was eternally beautiful. Even thinking about her, even seeing her for that instant as what she was—flea-bitten, a fox with wary gold eyes—I still want that fluid woman's body of hers. I still long for her company, her touch, her dreadful poetry.

That was an eternal world. I walked in her garden for ten years. Autumn never ended. Thinking back, I realize how strange this is. Where did all the leaves that drifted around our ankles come from? The trees must have dropped a thousand, ten thousand, more leaves than ever they bore.

I was running from death, from the rotting of the corpse, from the skull beneath the skin. From the tiny wrinkles that showed when Shikujo laughed. The teachings of Buddha tell me this is not something to fear, that it is the unhealthy clinging to pos-sessions—youth, a strong body, happiness among them—that causes grief. Simpler: the Amidists tell me that all I have to do is call on Amida Buddha's name and I will be reborn into the Pure Land.

Reborn. That's the problem. I don't want to go into the dark-ness, even if there is the possibility of rebirth. When my father died, I lit the pyre. As the fire caught and smoke threaded through the timber, the fabric over the coffin lifted, puffed out with caught smoke. I saw the wood catch fire, and I realized: *I'm next. Now I go.* And even my son couldn't help with this.

Someday he will light my pyre, perhaps with tears, perhaps not. This house, these gardens, will become his, and I will be smoke in the sky, torn to nothing by a steady breeze.

I wasn't ready to face that.

And now I'm an old man. I find hairs in my comb each morning. I am always cold: I prop my feet against the brazier as if I were a peasant, and, worse, I don't care so much who sees me. Death is closer than it was.

I have to wonder which I was more afraid of: dying or living.

14. KITSUNE'S DIARY

Passion. Squirrel. Sand. The path climbed up and up. It was growing dark, and I found it harder to read the writing. There was nowhere to stay, and even the path seemed to have vanished, except for these words, this poem/stone trail that led into the darkness. I thought I had gone past shivering, but now a spasm wracked me, and I shook so hard that I was afraid I would bite my tongue. The dog seemed cold as well, and stopped frequently to bite at his paw pads, trying to dislodge the ice balls that grew there.

And then on this primitive path, I came to a gateway leading off to one side. I suppose it was a gateway — it had uprights and a crossbar — but it stood three times my height, and was made of moss-covered cedar logs lashed together with *kizuta*-ivy. The crossbar was so far overhead that the towering trees hid it in places. Characters had been carved into the wood. *Home. Curious. Five. Rain.*

The supporting logs were rotted along their sides, as if they had lain on the ground for a long time before being hoisted upright. I touched one and found the wood was spongy. When I chipped at it with my knife, a sliver as long as my hand broke free, and I found a beetle, dead or asleep, beneath the surface. I thought of eating the insect (I was very hungry), but lowered my arm and let the dog snap it up.

The peasant said nothing about this gateway, but he also said he had not been here. Perhaps it was new. The snow seemed shallower and I saw that the road beneath the gateway was broader than the trail I was on, wide enough for an ox-cart. This was absurd: there was no way to get a cart into these mountains, no way even to get a litter up this trail. People who came this way would have to be strong (and young); they would need to walk single file.

Primitive as it was, the gate looked like the sort that led into the main gardens of a *shōen*-estate, though I saw no fences and no garden beyond, only more of the forest, snow and trees and dead ferns, and beneath them all, the mountain's shoulders. I saw no house, either; but I did see a dim glow, like a paper-screened house seen from a great distance.

No. I would rather sleep in the woods, wet and freezing and hungry, than go up that strange path, under that rotting gate. No.

The dog made his own decision. While I stood thinking, he sniffed the posts carefully, even though they were too cold to hold much smell. He did not urinate on them, which puzzled me: a post anywhere was an open invitation to every marking animal in the neighborhood. He bolted through the gateway, barking loudly.

"Dog!" I ran after him, under the gate and up the road. It was dusk now, but I saw the flashes of his white tail ahead of me. I staggered through snowy heaps of fallen needles and leaves, over fallen branches.

The light did not come from a great house a long way away: it was candlelight through a single tiny window of a collapsing hut scarcely taller than I was. Expecting something very different, I almost slammed into it before I saw it. The dog jumped at its door, still shouting. I pulled back, knife in hand.

The door pushed open and gold light and a wisp of warmth emerged. A slender man ducked out. "What — ?"

"Brother!" I ran forward, threw myself into his arms.

"Sister?" He pushed me away to see, then caught me closer. "Sister, what are you — "

"I thought you were dead! Are you well? You vanished and — "

"How did you — ?"

We embraced again, and he finished his thought first. "I'm fine, but, Sister, how are you here? Why?"

"He's gone," I said, and, cold as I was, my eyes filled with tears. "Kannon came and took him."

"I heard. Grandfather was here."

"He's *alive?*" I thought again of the club and the terrible noise he made when it thudded into his side.

"He was. Now, I don't know. Sister, you're freezing. Let's go inside."

I let him lead me through the low doorway into the hut. It was (slightly) warmer here, lit by two oil lamps with many wicks. The single room was tiny, perhaps three paces in each direction, and crammed with human-things; but what Brother had collected made no sense. A broken wagon wheel was set as if it were a shrine. A rotted scrap of rope hung from the eaves, tied in an unfamiliar knot. Broken pottery shards lay in patterns on the ground beside a gourd filled with the bits of a broken silver hair ornament. Leaves and rags were lined up against one wall, folded into birds that flopped or cracked along their edges. Ragged pelts filled a corner.

Brother bowed deeply and then spoke: *"Veils. The cat's claws remember blood / The fox in the mountain barks fire.* But you're cold, aren't you?" He handed me a tattered wolf skin, too worn for even a poor man's use. "Here, wear this robe and sit closer to the brazier. Where are your women? Shall I order a screen placed between us?"

He was being ironic, of course. The words he had spoken made no sense, and there was no robe, no brazier, no screen — no servant to move it if it did exist. "Tell me about Grandfather. Where is he?"

"Gone," Brother said. "He was hurt when Kaya no Yoshifuji was taken, and he ran away and ended up near here. I found him and brought him home. He told me about the Kannon. He didn't stay long."

"But I remember the club. . . ."

Brother knelt on the dirt floor beside me. "He was struck hard enough to hurt something inside. He coughed and blood came from his mouth. He said it didn't hurt. But then he left, to find a quiet place to die. But he left this for you, in case you came here." Brother felt in the sleeve of his filthy robe and pulled free a rolled piece of bark. When I unrolled it, it cracked. I saw characters scratched on its inner side as if with the tip of a knife, or a claw.

> *Fox or woman? Fox or man?*
> *The forest is very wide,*
> *and paths are very narrow.*

> *Do not forget me, Granddaughter. It may be that we will*
> *meet again.*

I let the bark reroll itself, and the letter fell to pieces. I had already thought Grandfather was dead, and I had wept and mourned for him; why then was this so painful to hear, that he had lived for a time before dying? I mourned all over again. My tears ran, warm on my chilled face. Brother sat in silence, watching me cry.

"Sister, why are you here? Did you run also?"

"No. I have the house still." *Or something like it,* I thought. "There is a temple to Kannon here in the mountains. I am going to her, to make her give him back to me."

"Why do you want him back?" Brother asked. "He's gone."

"I *have* to have him back. He was the heart of the magic." *We will lose everything,* I did not say: he was not acting as I would have expected him to.

"You don't need him anymore," Brother said offhandedly. "None of us do."

"My house is dissolving! I can't make the magic alone. Yoshifuji has to be there."

Brother snorted. "Nonsense. Look at me." He gestured around the room. I swiveled to look, but I saw nothing, only a small hut filled with refuse. "I did this," he said proudly. "Without you, without Yoshifuji. I have managed what you dreamt of. I have become human."

"You did what?"

"This," he said impatiently. "This house. The wings, the garden, the gates. I built it all." He saw my expression. "What's wrong?"

"Brother," I said gently, "I see this hut and I saw the forest. And I see you and me and the dog. But that is all."

He snorted. "You can't see this? Look!" He pulled me upright and dragged me to the hide hung over the door. "See the brocade? The layered patterns? As fine as anything we had in the valley, Sister. Except that *this* is real."

"No," I whispered.

"Here, it's much bigger than the old place." He smiled. "I am delighted with it. It's taken months to get it just so. It took a while to find a craftsman who could make good *shoji*-screens so far from anywhere. I had to request some of the icons from the capital; but I think they look very fine, don't you?"

"Brother—"

"Come see the west wing! You will stay?" He grabbed my hand and dragged me out through the door, and up the slope in the gloom.

"No!" I pulled away. "There is nothing here! What are you showing me?"

"You really can't see it?" He shook his head in disbelief.

"There is nothing to see!"

"The panels, the tiles, the mats—how can you not see it?"

My eyes hurt from crying. I looked again. The moon was very bright in the clear cold air and, under the dusting of snow, the rotted tree bark and fallen branches that covered the ground had been pushed this way and that. I realized they formed lines and squares.

Children do this sometimes: play house by tracing the outlines of a building with long lines of heaped-up leaves and twigs. *These are the mother's rooms; these are the second wife's; these are the father's. This stick is a sliding screen. This pile of leaves is where the father will sleep.* This was like that. Brother played house, but there was nothing there. Or did I not see it? Magic was strange, after all.

I did not resist as he led me through his pointless maze of detritus, pointing out rooms, screens, furnishings that only he could see. Who was confused here, he or I? Kaya no Yoshifuji drank from fallen leaves and kissed a fox kit's closed eyes. What was the difference between that and this? I knew there was a difference. There had to be, because this was madness.

Fighting panic, I tried to see what he saw, but there was nothing here: no magic, only a heap of castoffs, leavings.

"I have a gift for you, Sister," he said, and knelt to pick up something. He bowed. "Something to wear in your hair, come springtime."

Numb, I put out my hand, and he laid an icy object in my palm. It was a frozen mouse, hard as a stone. I screamed and threw it away from me. "Stop it!"

Brother looked hurt. "Don't you like—"

"Stop it, You're making this all up!" I wanted to put my hands over my ears and eyes, wanted to scream until I woke up.

"Making it up," he said slowly. "Don't we always? Don't we all?"

"No! This is—wrong!"

"Because it's not *your* reality?" Brother laughed. "Mine doesn't fade, Sister."

"It's not real, don't you see that? There is nothing there."

" 'Real'? I watched you learn poetry for him, change your body for him. What was 'real' about that?"

"I had to. I loved him! It was part of the magic. It was part of being human."

"Love and magic and humanity. They're not the same things. I can tell the difference—can you?"

"Stop it!" I screamed. "Leave me alone! You're mad!"

"I'm so sorry you can't see it," he said softly.

I turned and ran, as if for my life.

15. SHIKUJO'S PILLOW BOOK
Listening to sutras:

A woman sits, listening to a visiting priest drone out his sutras. She tries to pay proper attention. This is the way to peace of mind and salvation, after all, but her thoughts nevertheless wander.

People leave their lives to take on other lives all the time. I remember when Lady Tsukinomono left the court to become a nun. This despite the fact that one of the princes begged her not to do so! Most other women would have allowed the urgings of a prince to sway them, but Tsukinomono, no.

I saw her some months after. I was on my way to the shrine at Nara to dedicate a sutra in my husband's mother's name (she had died recently, irritable and critical to the last). A little bored by the chants, I pled a headache and left the hall with my women. On our way back to the guest area, we got lost, and ended up near the nuns' residences, on a veranda overlooking a little courtyard paved in black stones. A cluster of women were crossing the courtyard. Most were bald, but several had shoulder-length hair, for they cannot shave a noblewoman, even for investiture; our hair is our glory, our finest feature. I did not recognize her at first, but one was Tsukinomono. Her hair had been thick and even and fallen past her feet; to cut it to shoulder length, the length of any peasant girl's, was divorce enough from the world she had known.

Other women I knew had withdrawn from the world, but had retained this or another thing from their previous lives: they followed their sons' careers in the court, or they retained several servants, or they wore brocaded robes beneath their gray-green nun's garb.

But Tsukinomono! She knelt with the rest of the nuns, her cropped hair brushing her cheeks. If she hadn't been so unique a beauty before (those elongated eyes, and the fact that she never shaved her eyebrows and replaced them with painted ones higher on her face, despite all the conventions), I would have imagined her one of the ordinary nuns. She murmured and ran the bright jade beads through her fingers.

When she was done, I sent Onaga to ask for a moment of her time. She came willingly enough, but frowned slightly as if called back to an unpleasant duty. We spoke for a short while.

She truly gave everything away, Tsukinomono. She was there not to leave the world (as we so coyly put it, we on the outside). She went *to* something, to Buddha and the hope of enlightenment. She sacrificed all for a dream. And by now, my princess has done this—if she is not already smoke.

My husband left everything for a dream. I don't think it was his dream, though.

Even if he recovers, even if he does not choose to throw himself back into the madness that has taken him for all this time, what do I have? A man who slept with foxes, a man who deserted his family to pursue an uncomfortable dream.

This has happened before, in a thousand ways. (Sleeping with foxes is one of the less common; I suppose I can comfort myself with that, at least.) Men leave their families to start new ones, or to join the priesthood, or simply out of restlessness. Other men do not leave their lives, but they move through them as if sleepwalking. It seems the opposite of possession: no one has taken control of their bodies; rather no one dwells in that body, not even the man to whom it rightfully belongs. His mind is far away from his wives and concubines and friends, far from anything real and solid.

Before he ran away to live with a fox, this is what my husband did. He was restless and unhappy and, though I did not realize it, he was already gone. And it is not (or was not, then) possible to remove the restlessness from the man; they were one and the same. Kaya no Yoshifuji rested with me for a time; did I expect him to stay? Well, yes. I did.

So: which was it then? Did he pursue a dream or merely run away from reality? I imagine not even he knows the answer to this.

· · ·

Was I too constrained—by fear, by what I thought you wanted, by what everyone told me I must be? I was brave once and faced my life without flinching. When first my father told me I was to wed you, Kaya no Yoshifuji, I tossed my head. *Perhaps,* I said, knowing what an outrageous statement this was. And then I met you and loved you. Or thought I loved you; it was not until later, when you taught me to laugh, that I knew even a little of who you are, or were.

I did what I was allowed to do: I reached out from the screens and invited you to come to me. You saw the robes, the perfumes and my hair like a river. Dare I say that since coming back here and finding you gone, I have thought of cutting it all off? A nun cuts her hair to show she is leaving behind the world; might I not do the same, saying, I am not a thing of the world, but my own thing? If I did, would you then see me, instead of the robes?

No: you would never understand this. Your restlessness is enough for both of us; when I have expressed my own small whims, you do not see them, too wrapped up in your miseries to look past your clenched fists.

And I no longer have the courage. My hair is what I am. Servants wear their hair short and hopefully neat; a lady's hair is as long as it can be. If her hair breaks off too soon, at knee or waist, she buys extensions, countrywomen's hair. They are woven in, secured with threads fine as spiderwebs.

Cutting my hair would not hurt. There is no pain. I have brushed it and never felt loss of the hairs that showed in my boxwood comb afterward.

And there is another reason. Leaving the world for a convent was Tsukinomono's dream and my princess's. And for once I would choose to find my own dream.

16. THE NOTEBOOK OF KAYA NO YOSHIFUJI

I am reading my diary from before. In the capital it was an endless list of court visits, horse races, cockfighting, *dakyū*-polo — all interspersed with stilted self-observation. Even after we arrived in the country it seems pretentious, full of pompous posturings. I look back from a decade (or three months) — did I truly feel those things?

One thing I found is an old poem:

> *Why does the disorder of a forgotten garden*
> *move me as my tended yards never did?*

I know now that I loved my ordered garden; but I still pined for the disorder. And I left for that, trading one for the other, without looking at why one might be preferable, or whether it was preferable only because it was not mine.

It was easy to see my wife as no more than an ordered garden, careful predictable layouts of plants and hills and stones based on principles brought over from China centuries ago. As if that were all she was.

But this discounts so many things we were with each other. We drank *sake* from a single cup and finished one another's poems between sips. We wrote letters — endless letters! I still have a box shaped like a lotus petal filled with her letters.

She mixed my perfume. I sat with her on an autumn afternoon — years ago now — watching the blood-colored leaves pounded down into the gravel of the garden by a steady rain. She knelt, surrounded by vials of oil, each with a twist of waxed paper around its neck telling what was inside. The names were poetry in themselves: *Dark Winter Incense. Chamberlain's Perfume. Hundred-Pace Scent.* Her hands mixed delicately, dipped bamboo wands into unstoppered bottles, measured oils drop by drop into a small silvered glass vial. I caught her hands as they worked and held them against my cheek; they smelled sweet and spicy.

Her friends brought her the latest *monogatari*-tales and notebooks but sometimes I listened to her read this "women's literature" when I was tired of the elaborate (and often impenetrable) writings acceptable for men; we discussed their tales and poetry.

I sat inside her screens, played with her combs and bracelets and fans. When she turned her face away, I pushed her hair back so that I could see her pretty ear.

This discounts her laughter. I remember now. One winter dawn back in the capital, warm under our sleep robes, we watched through a crack in the screens as a red squirrel dragged a nutcake half its size through snow it found belly-deep; when it dropped the cake into a small drift and dove in after it, she laughed, a sweet trill without affectation or manner.

She teased her brother when she was younger and he visited, before he was sent off to his governorship in Harima province.

She had a sense of humor, my wife. Is it gone now, or did I stop listening for her laughter?

This discounts our sex, and the kissing, and the contented play on summer days so hot that she lay in a single natural-color unlined robe that clung to the sweat on her breasts and thighs, when she could do no more than moan like a kitten from my wet hands on, in, her. Or her mouth on me on a night so cold that my skin crawled, and her saliva cooled on me in the breath between one stroke and the next.

Wasn't this enough? Evidently not. Because I was restless. I wasn't looking for something, I was running away.

All the running I did, and nothing has changed. I return to the place I began. I still must face my wife. I still must face myself.

17. KITSUNE'S DIARY

I ran and ran, the dog panting beside me. I do not know why I ran so hard—nothing pursued, after all, only the horror of my brother's madness, and that was still with me when I finally stopped, gasping, in a clearing.

My lungs ached from the harsh air. I listened to my breath scrape in my throat, my pulse slam like muffled drums in my ears. Steam rose from my skin, as if I were a corpse burning on a pyre. I had left behind the basket; I felt in my sleeves and my sash, looking to see what I still had, but even my little bone knife was gone. I had nothing but the moon-shaped fan I had once stolen, tucked into the back of my sash and forgotten.

No food, no means of getting food. It was still bitterly cold, and I had lost the path. This clearing was small, a saddle between two pine-covered slopes, but there was enough space between the trees for me to see the sky filling with clouds again. The moon was already hidden; the stars slipped away in twos and threes, lost behind the blackness. I did not know if a normal woman could smell the snow in the air, but I could: a sharp cold dusty scent. My only hope was to find the path before the night grew absolutely black and the snow began.

I tried to retrace my steps, but the snow had drifted over my footsteps, and after a time, I could only guess the direction. I had run up the slope; well then, if I walked straight down the mountain, I would eventually find the path again. Where could it go? Paths do not blow away because they are not held down by sufficiently large rocks.

It was almost completely dark under the trees. I walked with my hands in front of me, hoping to find the trees before I walked into them. I missed one and stepped into it, which hurt my frozen toes so much that I fell from the pain. The wind hissed through the trees, a dry noise.

When I came to a gap in the trees, the wind changed notes and became harder, and for the first time I realized that the snow had begun again. I watched my feet inch forward (here, where the trees did not meet overhead, I could just see them, black blurs against scarcely less black snow), feeling snow and pine needles and round stones shift under my clogs. The ground before me dropped off suddenly.

I had found a 'gorge. The bank was steep as a cliff. I had no idea how far away the other bank was. I could not cross, so I turned and walked along the bank. It was slow going, for I moved carefully so close to the edge, but at least I could see a little.

I stumbled against something set across my path. At last I worked out what I found: two logs tied together with vines stretched across the gorge from where I stood. This had to be the path.

I felt my way onto the bridge. The dog whined and paced. He did not follow me until I lifted him bodily and placed him on the fallen trunks. The only way to cross was to balance on the rounded top of one of the logs, which were smoothed by footsteps and slick with snow. I stepped warily, sensing the open space beneath me as I moved from the bank. Blown snow slapped my face and hands; the wind itself pressed me to one side, solid as a wall. I leaned against it and walked. Scrabbling noises behind me told me the dog was following, digging his claws into the gap between the two trees. Far below me was a river or a stream, rough ice drowned in drifts. It could be a man's height below me; it could be a very long way. I could not know, in the wind and the darkness and the snow. I walked.

I think I must have stepped on an icy place, for I felt my foot slip. Every muscle in my body clenched like fingers catching at a railing; knowing I was falling, I threw myself forward and slammed into the crook between the two trunks, where I lay for a while until I stopped shaking. I crawled the rest of the way across the bridge, huddled as close to the wood as I could get. When I got to the end of the bridge I realized I had lost my wood clogs.

What would Inari's moon-foxes think of me—huddled bare-headed and *tabi*-footed in a blizzard in the dark? I could imagine their laughter like temple bells. *A foolish way to die,* they would jeer—if they cared at all. *Neither fox nor woman goes out on a night like this. If you are neither, what are you?*

Dying, I thought. Neither woman nor fox, but dead. The dog whimpered and nosed at me, but I could not move from where I had collapsed, coiled in a tight ball, *a fox-ball*, I thought with a glimmer of humor. The wind hurtling down the gorge slashed at me like steel-headed spears; the snow pierced like arrows. I had not eaten since I gulped down a rice ball as I walked the morning before. I had not been warm since I left Josei and my house. The snow on my face no longer melted; I felt the tiny flakes flutter against my eyelids, tossed by the wind.

I was not done yet. I wanted my husband back. I wanted to find Kannon and yell at her, and this was more important to me even than my misery. Recalling the peasant's words, or perhaps remembering fox lore, I crawled through the drifting snow to the pile that had grown at the roots of a tree. With numb hands, I pushed the snow aside until I had a hole, just big enough for the dog and myself. I pulled him down beside me. I dug further until I came to pine needles and curled up there. It was warmer out of the wind, surrounded by the snow. I pressed my hands and feet against his side; he wriggled in discomfort but let them stay there. I would have envied him his fur and longed for my old pelt, but what was the point? Even foxes died on nights like this.

I fell asleep like that.

I think I might never have awakened, except that the dog beside me suddenly went rigid with listening. He tried to jump to his feet, but the snow had drifted over us as we slept and our warmth (such as it was) had hardened it into a shell in places so that we were encased like an insect trapped in ice or amber. He barked, a deafening noise in the silent space, then tossed his head and cracked the shell. He clawed me as he floundered up, barking all the while. After a moment I heard men's voices and then shouts.

They dug me out, and lifted me blinking into the brilliance of daylight. The dog bounced around us.

"Are you all right?" One man held me in his arms, so that I felt the glossy softness of his furry robe. There were two of them, big shaggy hunters dressed in skins, their snowshoes and packs and long spears leaning against a tree. "What are you doing out here? Everyone has been tucked in tight for the blizzard."

Drowsy as a kit, I looked at the gorge beside us. It was far wider than I had thought, and the tree trunks that made up the bridge were narrower than they had seemed. I could not see to the gorge's bottom from where we stood, but I could see the opposite bank, steep as a wall.

"Look at her feet," the other man said.

The man holding me said, "Mmm. Yes." I was too tired to lift my head and see what they saw, but I felt no pain. "We'll take her to the temple. They'll know what to do. Can you ride on my back, pretty one? Promise not to claw me, hey?"

And so it was that I was carried the last miles to the temple. I remember little of that walk, only the moments when the sun touched my face. Then there was a sun-filled clearing and more voices, steep-roofed buildings and the sound of running water, the smell of sulfur, the man's voice — "Good-bye, little one. Good luck" — and then, amazingly, warmth.

18. SHIKUJO'S PILLOW BOOK
The snow stopped and the sun came out:

The snow stopped and the sun came out. By then I was heartily sick of my rooms, their clutter of chests and treasures. The voices of my women rasped on my nerves. Their words circled the same thoughts again and again, until they were as meaningless and repetitive as the barking of dogs. I was tired of the priest's sutras and counsels, tired of my husband's thoughts (for he was thinking much, I could tell), tired of everything.

Someone outside scratched at a *fusume*-panel. Onaga and I looked at each other over our sewing. The walkways were still drifted over: who would come here? "Mother?" a voice said.

I smiled. He would be a new face, at least. "Tadamaro. Come in." The panel resonated like a drum as he shoved it aside and bustled in, trailing scarves of snow as he approached. His nurse shook her robes clean and followed, saying, "My lady, I apologize for the lack of warning, but he insisted."

"That's fine," I said to her. "So, child, did you watch the snow fall yesterday?"

"Yes," he said. "*And* the day before. Nurse has a *kaze*-cold, so she didn't want to come here." She turned her face away from me, but whether from embarrassment or the sneeze that wracked her, I could not say. My son bowed to me for the first time, as if he had forgotten his manners until then. "I trust you are well, Mother?"

"Yes, I am well," I said. "And you?"

He wriggled. "I want to see if the rabbits by the moon-rock have left any tracks yet."

"Hmmm," I said, then to Onaga: "I am going for a walk with Tadamaro."

"Mother?" he said, his face lighting up. "You'll come with me?"

Onaga put down her sewing. "My lady, there is nowhere to go. The master your husband is undoubtedly still resting, and—"

I looked at my son. "I think we will walk in the garden. Perhaps even beyond its gates."

"What?" she said. "*Outside?*"

I sighed. "Yes, Onaga. Outside."

"But the snow—there are drifts, my lady. You will get quite wet. You might be seen—by peasants, even!"

"Perhaps," I said. "But just this once I am going to do what *I* want to do. Who will care? Not I, and not the peasants." For a moment I sounded just as my husband had before he had gone to live with foxes: casual, almost cavalier about the conventions. It felt surprisingly good. "Please bring me my red wadded-silk robes."

"They'll be ruined!"

"They will not," I said. "They will get wet, but then they will dry and the water spots will vanish and you will put them away and I will wear them another time."

"Yes, but — "

"Onaga," I said, and the sharpness of my voice surprised even me. "The wadded-silk robes, yes?"

She pulled them from an iron-bound chest, muttering to herself: " — though why she would wear these, when no one of any importance will see her, is beyond me."

I knew why I wanted them. I wanted them because the snow was very white and the red robes would be bright and warm as fire. And because for the first time I would walk in the garden with my son. And because *I* would see them, and it would please me to do so. I waited until she wrapped me close, and then held out my hand.

"Come, child." The nurse sneezed again and heaved upright. "No, not you," I told her. "I will watch him." She subsided with a poorly concealed sigh of relief.

Tadamaro took my hand and we stepped outside together.

The snow was deep, and I had to kilt my robes up like a peasant woman to walk; my crimson *hakama*-trousers were thick with clinging snowflakes. Tadamaro plowed ahead, leaving a swath of broken snow through which I picked my way.

I had been so afraid of allowing him out, into the wild; but I had never actually seen him here. And I found he behaved exactly as any child would in a garden filled with new snow. He tossed snowballs for a time. He jumped around, leaving footprints, then found a stick with which he wrote characters in the snow, trying each word several times. *Snow, day, rabbit, mother, me.* He jumped up and ran to the path that led to the moonrock.

I was alone for a moment. There were no words for the sweetness of the air, or the beauty of the garden. The eaves of our many buildings puffed out great silver-white heaps of smoke, as solid-looking as clouds.

"Are you coming?" my son called. I smiled and followed him.

Rabbit tracks threaded across the clearing, looking like a careless needlewoman's stitches in a white robe. Tadamaro squatted in front of the rock, pushing snow away from a hole with his stick, utterly absorbed.

"Lady."

Why was I not surprised to hear his voice? I turned.

The fox man leaned against a tree trunk, dressed in white-tipped russet hunting robes, still tall and slender but with gray in his hair now, and lines that pain had carved in his face. He held himself carefully, still an elegant man. My heart pounded, but I do not know why.

Tadamaro said nothing, didn't even notice the man's presence. For an instant I thought perhaps I dreamed all this; but the bright day, the air sharp with the smell of pine — I knew this was real, just as (I remembered suddenly) his previous visits, and my time with him, had been real.

"Sir." I bowed slightly, numb.

He nodded his head toward the boy. "He is a fine child. You are glad?"

"Yes," I said. Truthfully, I was. Tadamaro is a good boy.

"I did not expect to see you again," he said. "I came here to say farewell to the rabbits. They have been clever enough to outlive me; the least I can do was congratulate them."

I took a step forward. "You are not well?"

"No." He laughed once, a little bark that turned into a cough. "I am not. So, little monkey woman, what have you learned in this life?"

"I am no monkey!" I said indignantly. "Are you dying?"

"It's an embarrassing habit in which we all indulge, like catching fleas or cleaning ears. I will retire to pursue it in decent privacy soon enough. But first I will tell you what *I* have learned. I think we might have been more honest to one another, when first we met."

"Honesty is not a part of what men and women share," I said.

"Don't be a fool," he snapped.

I blinked: when had he ever spoken thus to me? "You read

poems to me. You were kind to me. And we did this thing. What would honesty have added?"

"Who knows? But it would not have hurt," he said. "Also, I think perhaps I should have told my granddaughter how it had been for me, when I saw and loved the wife of Kaya no Yoshifuji. Perhaps she would not have had to learn these hard lessons."

He had loved me. "Perhaps everyone must learn such lessons," I said slowly. "I—did not know."

He smiled slightly. "You did not know that we cannot protect people from the lessons we ourselves have learned? Or you did not know I loved you?"

"Both, I suppose," I said.

"I think you did not choose to know." He coughed out another laugh, and pulled a soft folded paper from his sleeve to press it to his lips. "We always want to save the ones we love from pain. Sometimes that's ourselves."

I looked at Tadamaro, singing to himself and drawing rabbits in the snow. "I tried to protect my son from the wilds. But it wasn't that, was it? I just didn't want him to be hurt—not just by the wilds or his blood, but by anything. And we can't, can we? Fox or human, everyone must learn."

"Yes," he said sadly. "I am sorry to leave just when your life is getting interesting. But I am glad I saw you awaken from your dream."

"I don't understand."

"Don't you? You stand in the sunlight, woman-who-lived-in-shadows. Perhaps you will tell me about it all when you have died, as well. Farewell now." The crystal air between us shivered and he was gone. Instead a fox, no taller than my knee, with matted fur and a worn-looking tail, stretched his legs as if he hurt, and turned to go.

"Wait!" I stepped forward. The hems of my robes spread out on the snow crust around me like a crimson pool.

The fox tipped his head. His eyes were gold and wild. His narrow muzzle was gray, and there was blood there.

"Tadamaro?" I called over my shoulder.

"Mother?" The child came quickly, looked up at me curiously with his gold-flecked eyes.

I took his hand and pointed. "Look, child. There, beside the tree."

"Oh! A fox!" he said in awe.

"Yes."

The fox watched us, and I spoke a poem to the fox. And we knelt in the snow, my son and I, and bowed to him.

The fox bowed his head in return and left. Where he had stood, the snow was bright with blood.

> *Love and memory and thought and dream —*
> *My favorite poems have never been written in words.*

19. KITSUNE'S DIARY

It was summer and I lay in the sun, flicking my tail at a green dragonfly that kept settling on my foot. Finally I snapped at it. "Have a care, child," it warned. "You'll knock off the compress."

The dragonfly's words puzzled me enough that I woke up. A man in moss-colored robes knelt beside me, rearranging a warm sack of something over my feet. He felt me move and rocked back onto his heels. "Ah, you're awake."

I looked around. I was in a small building, not much bigger than a hut, with two plaster walls and two latticework walls. A panel was pushed aside; sunlight on the snow outside was so bright that it lit the room I was in, showing the low eaves. The small heap of my clothes lay beside my head, the stained fan beneath them. A shrine hung from one wall, plainly made, but lined with gold behind a small dark figurine. "I am at Kannon's temple," I said, figuring it out.

He clapped his hands, then twittered at me, exactly like a dull-feathered songbird. "Good! You're doing better, then. Yes, this is the shrine—well, not precisely; this is a guest house we don't use much, just in the summers when people come. No one comes in the winter usually. You are fortunate the bear hunters found you when they did. We thought you might lose a toe or two, but they're looking much better now; the hot salt compresses and the prayers seem to have worked. The Kannon must be watching over you. I expect—"

I interrupted him. "Where is she?"

He tipped his head to one side. "Was someone else with you? Your dog is here and quite well, but it is a male, of course, so no doubt you do not mean it. Should we—"

"The goddess." I sat upright and pushed the compress off my feet. I was dressed in unbleached wadded-cotton robes, clean and warm. I wondered who had dressed me, if it had not been the magic. "Kannon. Is she here?"

He bowed to the little shrine. "She is everywhere, my child. She watches—"

"No. Is she present here? I must speak with her."

"You can pray to her here," he said doubtfully. "And she will answer, in her own way and at her own time. But she does not come when called, you know."

I struggled upright, fighting a wave of dizziness. "She comes when she pleases. I *must* speak with her."

"It's more complicated than that." He stood by the door, hands fluttering in nervousness. "There are purification ceremonies, and you must speak with the head priest. And there's the gift, of course."

"Gift?" I laughed bitterly. "She has left me nothing to give."

"Of course you must give a gift!"

I picked up the fan. "She will accept this. It is all I have. Take me to her."

He frowned slightly. "It's not that simple. You *must* speak with the priest. And the purification ceremonies—"

"I am not impure," I said.

"Well, perhaps not, but you do not wish to show disrespect to the Kannon, do you?"

I left him twittering behind me and stepped out onto the guest

house's tiny veranda. The snow was so bright that it blinded
me. I waited for a moment until the black spots in front of my
eyes vanished. The dog slept curled up on the guest house veranda near me, oblivious in the sun.

A flat courtyard extended to the walls of the temple enclosure;
paths had been stamped down, and off to one side a great mountain of snow was heaped higher than my guest house. A man in
monk's robes came through the gate with a huge basket filled
with snow, which he emptied onto the mountain before returning.

At the other end of the courtyard was the splashing water I
had heard when I first was brought here. A stream rippled
through a series of pools, each no bigger than a washing tub.
The air over the open water was thick with steam. Two old men
soaked chest-deep in one of the pools, eyes closed as they talked
idly, faces cherry-red from heat. All around us were the dark
trees of the forest and the mountains. The snow was sharp white
with purple-blue shadows, like a delicate robe combination.

A pair of wooden clogs rested on a low stone beside the veranda; perhaps they belonged to the monk, but they fit me when
I stepped into them. Ignoring his noises, I walked across the
courtyard, toward the shrine's gate.

The space inside the gate was filled with activity. Monks and
acolytes swept the inner courtyard clean with rice-straw brooms,
scooping the snow in baskets that they carried out through the
gate. A laughing boy no older than my son caught up a handful
and tossed it at the wall. The snow splashed against the timbers,
leaving a white mark. My son had never seen winter; my throat
suddenly hurt as if I had been stabbed.

The temple had to be the large building in the courtyard's
center. No one seemed to see me as I kicked off my clogs and
climbed its stairs.

It was large inside and very dark, with a thousand great pillars reaching into the eaves. There were only two candles: their
gold flames flashed like eyes. Strangely, there was no one inside:
no priests, no monks, no worshippers. And there were no statues. I stood in an empty space.

"Kannon?" I asked, as I had once before. "Where are you?"
Silence.

"Speak with me!" I shouted. Outside, a bell rang.

"Welcome," said a voice (or was it voices?) that echoed like bells in thunder.

The moon-foxes of Inari coalesced from the darkness. What I had thought were candles were the flames that flickered on the tips of their noses, gold to their silver. "So, little fox woman?" one (or perhaps both) said.

"Why are *you* here?" Tears burned my eyes, my disappointment a lump in my throat.

"Perhaps we are visitors, just as you are."

"Where is Kannon?"

They seemed amused. "We are Inari's foxes. Why should we know?"

"I *must* speak with her!" I cried. "I have to make her see what a bad thing she's done."

"How does a goddess of mercy behave badly?"

"She stole him from me! My grandfather is dead, and my brother is mad, and my son is lost, maybe dead, all because of her!"

"Strange," the foxes mocked. "Men have died or gone mad before this; children have died or been lost. There are even women who have stolen the men of others. And no goddess was the source of such tragedies. Unless you are important enough to earn a god's hatred?"

"Do not laugh at me! She *must* be here."

"Why?"

My tears burned my chapped cheeks. "Because he is gone, and the magic slips away. I lost so much because of her cruelty, and now I'm losing everything. I will make her help me."

"How? Will you urinate on her statue? Bite her? Cry until she changes her mind? Difficult to threaten a goddess."

"I know," I said miserably. "But I have to try. I will die if I go back."

"All the best people die, eventually," one or both of the foxes said. "Go back to what?"

"Being a fox," I said, then: "No, that is not it."

"Being human is better?"

"Yes. No. Humanity is sweet, but—so filled with pain." *Shadows and waiting*, I thought suddenly. "And I have to ask her: what am I?"

"Why should she know?" the foxes said. "Why should anyone but you know?"

"She is a goddess. She has power and knowledge I'll never have."

"It is a simple question. No goddess will waste her time answering it. Which are you? Fox or human?"

"Both. Neither. I am myself."

The room filled with the sound of gongs. One of the foxes flared bright as a full moon; its shape ran and shifted, and became a woman.

Kannon.

20. SHIKUJO'S PILLOW BOOK
  The winter:

I went for a walk today, wishing to pray at Inari's shrine. The shrine was really very close: why had I never been to see it before this?

Onaga and the rest of the women who felt they needed to watch over me trailed behind, their skirts dragging like Chinese scarves in the snow. I ignored Onaga's complaints, and tucking my robes into my sash so that they did not trail behind me, walked down the path; even beaten down by snowshoes as it was, I sank past the tops of my wooden clogs in crunchy snow.

The air caught in my lungs like a sweet, wild incense. A few rust-colored needles and fallen leaves in sharp reds and golds had shaken down onto the snow's crust, and patches of gilt sunlight were laid over all: patterns worthy of an emperor's robe, or a fine paper before a perfect poem has been written on it. When I stepped through each patch of sunlight, the warmth was as pleasant as a brazier on a winter's day.

We might have (perhaps should have) been carried in litters to the shrine. But we met no one, all of Onaga's forebodings notwithstanding. And I was not even a little tired when we got there.

The shrine was a small one: a single *torii*-arch twice the height of a man. Beyond it was a clearing and a roofed construction half my height. A flock of winter sparrows flapped away as we approached, and I saw they had been eating, for heaped around the shrine's open front were little sacks of raw rice, and cooked rice on tray-sized leaves, and blue-and-white glazed pots of *sake*. I gestured: one of the women came forward and laid our own offerings to one side. Another laid out a little reed mat for me before the shrine's opening. I knelt carefully, arranging my robes on the trampled snow.

I wanted to thank the god (or goddess) for a good harvest, and for whatever small part she (or he) might have played in returning my husband. There are so many gods; it's a mistake to think they don't get involved in one another's affairs from time to time. I bowed and looked into the shrine.

Two pale wood foxes stared back at me with painted eyes. I watched them for a long moment before I remembered the fox statues that attend Inari shrines. They weren't real.

I had to laugh. Of course they were real: they were real statues of foxes. Everything is really what it is—so long as one is honest about what it is.

The foxes had never been the problem. That lay between me and my husband. If there had been no magical foxes, my husband would have found some other outlet for his loneliness and dissatisfaction, and I would have fretted about whatever the other thing was—gambling, professional women, scheming at court. I do not excuse the fox woman from responsibility for pursuing my husband, but I cannot blame her. My husband chose his life.

As I choose mine.

21. KITSUNE'S DIARY

*H*ow *could you!*" I hurled the fan at the goddess Kannon. It was light and fell at her feet, with all the drama of a moth settling.

She was smaller than I would have expected, fine-boned and soft-fleshed. Her hair was arranged in the Chinese fashion, and she wore a towering crown, filled with hands and eyes. In the palms of her hands were flames that moved as she moved, writing strange characters in fire on the air between us. The remaining moon-fox twined around her ankles like a cat before curling up at her feet. The room had been dark; now it was full of candles and light, and statues and gold ornaments and silk and gifts.

The goddess picked up the fan in her long white fingers. "You have brought me a gift."

"Gift? That is no gift! You have hurt me in ten thousand ways."

"Have I?"

"You have destroyed everything I fought for. There was no mercy, no kindness in what you did."

"Kindness and mercy are not the same. Kindness is a gift. Mercy is the truth."

"Then I wish you had been kind," I whispered.

She turned the fan over in her hands, one eyebrow raised as she looked down at it. "Kind? A man lies to his wife because he does not wish to hurt her. He is being 'kind.' A woman is courteous to her husband, never showing her anger or loneliness; she does not wish to burden him. She is 'kind.' A woman overprotects her child, afraid of what he will grow into. It is for his own good, she thinks, a 'kind' action."

She looked up suddenly and caught me watching her. Her eyes flamed when they met mine, and I was trapped by the killing stare of a goddess. "Someone builds a world where everything is pleasant and perfect, where no one must face the painful truths of the self; she yells at a madman, to shatter his illusions and bring him back to an unhappy reality. And this is 'kind.'

"I, however, am *not* kind."

"I am sorry," I whispered. "I just wanted him, is all."

"I know," she said softly, and amazingly, her eyes filled with tears. "Poor little fox woman. It has been so hard. I have felt so sad for you."

"Then why did you do it?" I said.

"Did you think I have a choice? Unlike a woman or a fox, I act as I am made."

"You're a goddess! How can you say you have no choice?"

She lifted her chin, as if defiant. "I am Kannon. I have many things — power and wisdom, the ability to understand the pain of others, a great and wonderful duty. But I do not have the luxury of choice. Prayed to, I must listen. Summoned, I must come."

"You did not listen when I prayed to you, or come to me when I asked."

She smiled. "Did I not? Truth is a small thing, easy to overlook."

"Then tell me the truth. My son," I said, and bit my lip at the sudden pang the thought of him brought. "Please, did he live?"

"Perhaps." She looked down at the fan again. "Perhaps he is alive, snatched away by his nurse and taken somewhere safe, far away. Perhaps he is dead. Either way, his story is no longer yours."

"But—"

Kannon touched the tears on my face. "I understand your grief, but I cannot tell you how another's story will end."

"You have no 'choice,' " I said bitterly.

"No," she said. Something in the goddess's tone made me look at her face. She met my eyes, but this time there were no flames, only an infinite sadness in her gaze.

"Then I am sorry for you," I whispered. "Choosing is good."

"Yes," she agreed. "So choose."

"But what will happen?"

"Live and find out. Life guarantees nothing, not even itself."
Kannon held my fan to her face and nodded slightly: the bow
of a goddess. "Farewell, fox woman."

When the priests came in, they found me kneeling in the barren
temple. The fan was gone, so she must have accepted the gift.

22. THE NOTEBOOK OF KAYA NO YOSHIFUJI

The air is very still today. There is no wind, and this makes
Shikujo's return from wherever she has been walking
clearly audible. Footsteps on one of the walkways; women's
voices rippling; a woman's laugh, clear and high as a silver bell.
I have not heard that sound since returning to this world: my
wife's women (and the woman-servants; everyone, in fact, except for my major domo, Hito) have been avoiding my presence
and mostly keeping their voices down, no doubt in recognition
of the "difficult" times in which we find ourselves.

And this is infuriating me, though I did not realize it before
this instant. When I see my wife, she treats me with the careful
courtesy of a nurse for a sick man. How dare she accept all this
so easily! I have behaved badly, I know: how dare she discredit
my folly by not confronting it, with tears and anger of her own?

Fired with this emotion, I push myself to my feet and walk
to her rooms. A screen is pushed aside to let light and air in,
and they must hear my heavy footsteps (I do not move so well
as I used to, particularly in cold weather). By the time I tap on
a door and Onaga lets me in, Shikujo's women are hidden
away somewhere else. My wife stands in the wedge of sunlight
that came through the eaves. Her curtains, her screens and
blinds, are gone, and there is nothing but dust and shadow and
sunlight between us. And Onaga: she brings a tray with two
cups and a teapot before vanishing herself, leaving my wife and
me alone.

"Wife."

"Husband." Her voice is perfectly calm. I feel a flash of un-
reality: so many conversations between us have begun this way.
This might be one we held six months ago, everything between
now and then a restless dream. No. My life with my fox wife
was real. My life here and now is real. Everything has been real
except for the words, the screens we spread between us.

"We need to talk," I say.

"Oh, yes," she says. "It is time for the truth."

23. SHIKUJO'S PILLOW BOOK
   And so:

And so I told him—of the fox in the dream and the poem he
spoke, of my sadness and loneliness, of the tedium of waiting, and the sadness of wondering. He listened and said nothing,
not even when in a pang of anger too sharp to bear I hurled a
cup at the floor, and then threw myself against him, to cry until
my hair was matted with tears and my robes were stained with
salt. I do not know whether I cried in his arms because of love
or the shared sorrow of our past. Truth is not unambiguous.

Stories never end this way, not in all the tales I have read.
The abandoned wife weeps and dies of some undiagnosed disease; or she throws herself into a river and floats like ice until
her silks pull her beneath the water, into its clear winter depths.
Or she flees in the most mannerly of ways—cuts her hair and
takes a holy name and retreats into religion, as cool and inac-
cessible and unaware as if she had drowned.

But I am not interested in brooding. My husband brooded. I
also brooded, more quietly.

Onaga would gasp if I said this to her, and so instead I take
my tiny steps toward honesty and whisper the great truth here
in my pillow book, and perhaps someday into my husband's ear
(whether Yoshifuji or another). Perhaps there is a Pure Land
where we go when we die. But perhaps there is not. And either

way, it is wise to live well, here and now. I will not run. I will be alive.

The fox woman, my husband, and I. Of us all, she understood this best.

24. KITSUNE'S DIARY

I returned to the house, footsore and hungry, the dog alongside. I did not stop on the way, though I passed my brother's great gateway and the poem/rocks: I knew I needed to talk to him, to apologize or explain, but not yet. There were other things that must be done first.

The house was quiet. Perhaps because it was dawn, the mist that had hidden the walls and concealed the fading of my home was not there. For the first time since my husband had been taken from me, I saw the house in its entirety: two small wings linked by walkways to each other and to a handful of little outbuildings. The garden was smaller than it had been, and simpler. There were no lights anywhere, and the house seemed abandoned, lifeless as a drawing.

I burst into the larger of the wings, to my rooms—smaller, simpler than they had been. By the dim dawn light that crept through the eaves, a lone woman folded silk robes and tucked them away into a trunk, as if preparing for a long trip. She turned to me as I ran in: Josei. "Mistress!" Her face lit up, then fell as she saw me more clearly. "Your hair! Oh, my lady, your beautiful hair."

I shook my head impatiently. "It will grow. But, Josei—" I stepped back from our embrace, looked at her from arm's length.

"You're still here! You waited."

She bit her lip. "It was hard. The others—I am so sorry, my lady, but most could not stay. But there are a few." She raised her voice: "The lady has returned!" Sleepy shouts; a handful of people stumbled onto the verandas of my wing, rubbing their eyes. The dog began barking, dancing among them. The calligraphy instructor, my cook, the man who kept the falcons, a maid, a gardener—eyes averted but faces alight, they bowed.

I bowed in return. "But do not hide your faces. I am so glad you remained!"

"We stayed," Josei said. "We kept hoping you would return, that you would bring our master back and everything would be as it was before."

"I have not brought him back," I said.

"But we *need* him, don't we?" She looked up at me, and I knew she meant: *to survive, to stay in the fox magic.*

I smiled. "I do not think so."

"Without him, what are we?" *What are you? Fox or woman?*

"Whatever we want to be."

25. THE NOTEBOOK OF KAYA NO YOSHIFUJI

The sky has been overcast all day, with the heavy clouds that will eventually either drop silent flakes large as dragonflies on us all—or perhaps move on to another place, where it will do this.

The house is hectic with activity. Everyone—from Shikujo to the least of the peasants, from Hito to my son—has something they must complete before tomorrow's New Year's celebrations. I walk through the color-filled rooms, seeing ribbons waiting for the balls of herbs that will be hung tomorrow. I am rooms away from Shikujo, but through the paper walls I hear her laughter, a low delighted ripple, as if she has heard an amusing poem or a funny story.

This laughter is not for me. We are not comfortable together, she and I. We speak with some of the awkward courtesy of children who have brawled, but at least we speak. There is nothing slick and perfect about this new conversation between us. Often we stumble into silence, tripped by the meanings of our words, now that we listen to that instead of their sounds.

And there are times when I wish for the flawless Shikujo. This one, this real Shikujo, has a temper; her hurt over my time with my pretty fox wife lingers. It was easier to desire the woman who seemed as perfect as the doomed mistress of some hero in a woman's tale. Dim lighting and elegant language conceal much. It should not surprise me if some of the flaws they hid were not mine.

But it is preferable, this new way of speaking, this new language we are discovering. We do not know yet if we will divorce. The thought is painful; my chest feels the pang my feet sometimes do, when I slip and my toes grab desperately at nothing. I love her. But sometimes love is not enough. It is more important that our lives be good; whether that means alone or together, I cannot say.

We do not know yet whether, after the New Year, Shikujo will return to the capital with our son. *Her* son, I remind myself, and feel again the flare of mingled pain and anger; I had no part of it. Back in the capital, it is not uncommon for a woman to bear the child of a man not her husband, but I am hurt and jealous. I raised this child; I *loved* him, and he was not even mine. Then, suddenly: *but he is*. I taught him to hunt; I gave him his first sword; I held him when he had toothache and his mother and nurse could not keep him still until the medicines were administered. He is mine, by choice. I will always have that.

My life with Shikujo, my life with my fox wife — they were both illusions. This does not surprise me. Of course this was so: everything is an illusion, even humanity. I still love my fox wife, our life together, our son, but, as I have said, sometimes love is not enough.

The priests say I am healed of the madness that drove me to a fox's den. I don't know; I did not feel ill. This is not true: I was sick, but the sickness came first, a blind self-pitying misery. I have run away twice now: once from Shikujo into my fox wife's world, and once away from her, back to Shikujo. I have injured them both with my running. The least I can do is stop running from myself.

I have already given the orders to Hito for the gate to my house to be rebuilt. It is time.

I see a flake of snow, and another; and the sky is suddenly full of snow. It will feel good to write a poem again — this time no neat set of images, but something as bright and true as sunlight.

26. SHIKUJO'S PILLOW BOOK
New Year's preparations:

I need to make sure the rice cakes have arrived from Omi for Tadamaro's New Year's wishes. Tomorrow we will place nine of them on his head, and his father will pronounce the auspicious words for the next year.

Tomorrow we replace calendars: this year's for next year's. I look forward to unscrolling the days.

Onaga is finishing my robes. They are red-plum in color with a floating white overrobe. I love the red color: it is filled with light. It makes me smile, and will be a delight to wear.

In the capital things would be more complicated. There would be social calls, and carolers, and the New Year's archery meet, various ceremonies celebrating the Emperor's honor — ten thousand things. We are busy enough here.

The Obeisances to the Four Directions. The Buddhist Names Service.

The demon-scaring. Tadamaro is especially excited about this: he loves the chaos of noise and running and hurled rice and beans.

The cook assures me that the proper foods will be ready — the spiced wines and herbal drinks, the mirror cakes and radishes and melons and salted *ayu*-trout.

The snow will make things especially pleasant tomorrow. Onaga and the other women are talking about making snowmen: more, whole snow mountains! I have to laugh, but in truth I look forward to this as much as they. I have never built a snow mountain before.

Tomorrow.

THE NEW YEAR

Since I no longer think
of reality
as reality,
what reason would I have
to think of dreams as dreams?

—*SAIGYŌ (1118–1190)*
TRANSLATED BY BURTON WATSON

KITSUNE'S DIARY

I *wait in kaya no Yoshifuji's garden,* as I have so many times before. But this is the last time I wait; even now I wait only for one thing.

It was autumn we spent together, Kaya no Yoshifuji and I. Now it is winter. Snow has fallen, a cold cloud deeper than my wooden clogs. The spotted dog waits beside me, patient, belly in the cold snow. Tomorrow is the first day of the first month: the New Year. Tomorrow there will be running and laughter and herb balls hung from the doorways and games. *Now,* this instant, time hangs, an eternal *now* without past or future, strung like a bead with all the other *nows* I have known and will know.

I have a plan, if a simple one. I know Yoshifuji so well. He was sick for many months, but he seems better now, healthy enough to return to certain old practices. He will come out into the garden tonight, to write about the snow and the New Year and his life. And I will roll my white ball across his path. If he sees it for what it is, he will find me, and we will be happy — or at least we will talk of what has gone between us. And if he is content here, with Shikujo and the child, it will only seem another piece of the snow.

I have thought of something:

> *Priests, you can cure him of anything*
> *but love.*

I think this is a poem.

I have thought of another thing: well as I know him, I know myself better. I love him, my master Kaya no Yoshifuji, and I say this and it is as short and sharp as a bark. But I do not need him—no more than Josei needs me to live long and write her own poems and dream her own dreams. He sees the ball or he does not: there will still be laughter and rice cakes and the remembering of ghosts in my house this New Year.

We make our own worlds. My brother had fashioned his world: it seemed madness to me, but it was not mine to judge. I have fashioned and refashioned my own reality. It was the fox world, and then it was magic, and a human world of sorts: robes and poetry and, at its heart, Yoshifuji. If he sees the ball rolled across the snow, I will be so happy, but it does not matter: I will still build a world of the best of all these things.

Human legends are full of fox men and fox women. Most fail and fall back into foxness. Or become human, lost in pain. But some humans learn joy and some foxes grow souls. Thieves, princes, dancers, charcoal-burners—they are connected in that they have discovered this path for themselves.

This is the gift of humanity: that it is claimed by the self. None of us—Shikujo or Yoshifuji or my grandfather or myself or my brother or my woman, Josei—are human unless and until we claim it for ourselves. But nothing can stop that claiming—not the eight million gods nor the spirits nor ghosts. Nothing but ourselves, anyway.

And our lives become the poems we were born to tell.

I hear his footsteps.

AUTHOR'S NOTE

Kaya no Yoshifuji's tale is a traditional fairy tale set in Bitchū province in the late ninth century. An excellent translation of the original can be found in *Japanese Tales*, edited and translated by Royall Tyler for the Pantheon Fairy Tale and Folklore Library. I have moved the tale's date and location, and drawn from Heian story collections the names of some individuals and places; others are generic.

In the course of researching this book, I read many contemporary tales, histories, poetry collections, and secondary sources. Among these, certain works were particularly informative or entertaining. The *Pillow Book* of Sei Shonagon in Ivan Morris' translation is one of the most enjoyable books I have ever read: elegant, witty, by turns frivolous and thoughtful. Also of interest: *The Tale of Genji* and the *Diary* of Murasaki Shikibu, translated by Edward G. Seidensticker and Richard Bowring, respectively; William H. and Helen Craig Mc-Cullough's translation of *Eiga monogatari*, called *A Tale of Flowering Fortunes*; *As I Crossed a Bridge of Dreams*, in part the diary of Lady Sarashina's journey to the capital, also translated by Morris. . . . It's hard to know where to stop such a list, as there are so many books worth reading from this period. Far and away, the best secondary source for Heian-era Japan I found was Morris' *The World of the Shining Prince*.

My favorite translations of Heian poetry come in *From the Country of Eight Islands: An Anthology of Japanese Poetry*, translated and edited by Hiraoki Sato and Burton Watson; *String of Beads: Complete Poems of Princess Shikishi*, translated by Hiraoki Sato; Laurel Rasplica Rodd's translation of *Kokinshū*; and *The Ink-Dark Moon*, poems by Ono no Komachi and Izumi Shikibu translated by Jane Hirshfield with Mariko Aratani.

Kitsune and her family do not always behave as typical foxes might: among other things, the females' breeding cycle is off-season, and Brother remains with the family even after Kitsune has mated with another. But then they are not typical foxes, and their exceptions to the norm are based on instances observed by researchers. While I read too many books and articles to willingly list them all, two works I found useful and informative were *Wolves, Dogs and Related Canids*, by Michael Fox, and *The World of the Fox*, by Rebecca Grambo (which had charming pictures).

I wish to thank the following individuals for their assistance: editors Gardner Dozois, Claire Eddy and Bob Gleason; Ron Foster, who supplied Japanese field guides; artist and calligrapher Shih-Ming Chang; Canids Bertie and the Efficient Baxter; Allena Gabosch, Marybeth O'Halloran, Madeleine E. Robins, and the Thousand Monkeys—Wolfgang Baur, Mike McGinnis, Bridget McKenna, Chris McKitterick, and Lorelei Shannon—for moral and critical support; and Peg Kerr, for everything.

Mistakes in this book are, of course, wholly my own. Mercifully, this is fiction.

> *On the leaf-bright pond*
> *the geese stayed a night but left*
> *at dawn. So, too, words.*

—KIJ JOHNSON
SEATTLE, DECEMBER 1998